Sing As We Go

Born in Gainsborough, Lincolnshire, Margaret Dickinson moved to the coast at the age of seven and so began her love for the sea and the Lincolnshire landscape.

Her ambition to be a writer began early and she had her first novel published at the age of twenty-five. This was followed by twenty-one further titles including *Plough the Furrow*, *Sow the Seed* and *Reap the Harvest*, which make up her Fleethaven trilogy. Many of her novels are set in the heart of her home county, but in *Tangled Threads* and *Twisted Strands* the stories included not only Lincolnshire but also the framework knitting and lace industries of Nottingham. The Workhouse Museum at Southwell in Nottinghamshire inspired *Without Sin*, and the beautiful countryside of Derbyshire and the fascinating town of Macclesfield in Cheshire formed the backdrop for the story of *Pauper's Gold*. *Wish Me Luck* returned to Lincolnshire once more and the county is also the setting for *Sing As We Go*.

www.margaret-dickinson.co.uk

Margaret Dickinson

Sing As We Go

PAN BOOKS

First published 2008 by Pan Books
an imprint of Pan Macmillan Ltd
Pan Macmillan, 20 New Wharf Road, London N1 9RR
Basingstoke and Oxford
Associated companies throughout the world
www.panmacmillan.com

ISBN 978-0-330-45262-5

A CIP catalogue record for this book is available from
the British Library.

Typeset by SetSystems Ltd, Saffron Walden, Essex
Printed and bound in Great Britain by
Mackays of Chatham plc, Chatham, Kent

Visit www.panmacmillan.com to read more about all our books
and to buy them. You will also find features, author interviews and
news of any author events, and you can sign up for e-newsletters
so that you're always first to hear about our new releases.

For my grandson, Zachary John

'When I saw thee, I gave my heart away.'
Longfellow

Acknowledgements

My grateful thanks to the staff of Lincoln Central Library and of Skegness Library for helping so much with all my research, and to Brian and Jean Gabbitass for the photo of Brian's father, James, who served with ENSA during the Second World War.

As always, my love and thanks to Robena and Fred Hill, David and Una Dickinson and Pauline Griggs for reading and commenting on the script, and to all my family and friends for their constant support and encouragement in so many ways.

Thank you to Darley Anderson and everyone at the Agency, and to Imogen Taylor, Trisha Jackson, Liz Cowen and all at Pan Macmillan, for always being there.

One

Kathy pulled on her wellington boots and tied a head-scarf over her blonde hair and under her chin with a quick, angry movement. She pulled open the back door of the farmhouse and, walking through it, slammed it behind her so that it shuddered on its hinges, the wood creaking in protest. Immediately, she regretted her action. Her mother deserved an extra few minutes in bed if anyone did. Especially after last night.

Pale fingers of a frosty dawn crept across the yard as she marched, hands thrust into her pockets, across the cobbles towards the cowshed. The cows had already been fetched from the field and her father's only greeting was, 'You're late.'

'You call half past six on a winter's morning "late"?' Kathy snapped, her blue eyes bright with resentment.

She banged the lower half of the byre door, making the cows move restlessly. Ben, their collie, ran to her, tail wagging, tongue lolling. She bent and gave him a friendly pat. She wouldn't vent her ill temper on him.

'Ya'd be able to get up in a morning if ya went to bed the same time as decent folk.'

'I was home before midnight. And you'd no right to

1

lock me out so that Mam had to come down and let me in.'

'I lock up every night at ten. If you're later than that, then I want to know. And I want to know why, an' all.'

'I went to the St Valentine's dance in the village hall. You know that. I did – ' her tone took on a sarcastic note – 'ask permission.'

'Aye, ya asked your mam because ya knew ya could wheedle your way around her. And don't use that tone of voice with me, my girl, else—'

'Else what?' Her eyes sparked rebellion and her small, neat chin jutted with determination. Two pink spots that had nothing to do with the cold morning burned in her cheeks. 'You'll take your belt to me? I'm a bit old at nineteen.'

Her father, shoulders permanently hunched, carried a bucket full of fresh, warm milk to the end of the cowshed. Pausing as he passed her, he thrust his gaunt, lined face close to hers. 'You're not of age until you're one and twenty, and until then ya'll do as I say or else . . .'

She faced him squarely, but her voice was quiet as she said, 'What, Dad? Just tell me what the "or else" is?'

'Ya can pack ya bags and go,' he growled. 'I'll not have a chit of a girl back-answering me in me own house.'

'Very well, then,' Kathy nodded calmly. 'I'll go. I'll go this very day – if that's what you want.'

For a moment Jim Burton stared at his daughter. Then he gave a sarcastic, humourless laugh. 'Oh aye. And where would ya go, eh?'

'Lincoln,' Kathy said promptly.

'And what d'ya plan to do there, eh? Ain't no cows in Lincoln. And that's all you're good for, girl.'

Kathy nodded slowly. 'Yes – yes, I have to admit you're right there. But that's down to you, isn't it? Making me leave school the minute I was old enough. Setting me to work on the farm for no pay—'

'Pay? What d'ya need paying for? Ya've everything you need.'

'Need, maybe. Want – no.'

'Who's been putting fancy ideas in your head, girl?' He eyed her keenly, his dark eyes narrowing. 'Is it your mother?'

Now Kathy laughed aloud. 'Mam? Put ideas like that into my head? Don't make me laugh. As if she'd dare, for a start.'

Jim grunted. He was thoughtful for a moment, dismissing his idea as nonsense. The girl was right. His wife wouldn't dare make any such suggestion. 'Then it's that chit of a Robinson girl. Flighty piece, she is.'

Kathy hid a smile. Amy Robinson was the only real friend she had. And Jim wasn't done yet. 'No better than she should be, that girl.' He'd seen Amy only the day before with a boy in the copse between his land and the Robinsons' farm. 'Up to no good they were, I'll be bound.' And after evening milking he'd marched across the fields to warn his neighbour that his daughter was going the right way to 'get 'ersen into trouble, if you ask me'.

For once, the mild Ted Robinson had been stung to retort, 'Well, no one's asking you, Jim Burton, and I'll thank you to keep your opinions to ya'sen. I trust my daughter. She'll come to no harm. What's a kiss and a cuddle in the woods, eh? We've all been young once, haven't we?' Ted had paused then and eyed his irate neighbour. 'Mind you, I have me doubts if you was ever young, Jim. Born old, I reckon you were.'

'Oh, so that's what you think, is it? Just because I've worked hard all me life and done me duty. Where'd me family's farm have been by now, eh, if I hadn't worked from the minute I was old enough?'

Ted's anger had died as swiftly as it had come. 'Aye, I know, Jim, I know. You've not had it easy with your dad dying when he was fifty and you having to take on the farm so young. And then losing your poor mam only a few years later in that dreadful flu epidemic of 'eighteen, but—' Ted Robinson had put his hand on the other man's shoulder. 'Look, Jim, I don't want to fall out with you. We've known each other a long time, but if you'll take my advice, you'll ease up a bit on that lass of yourn. If you don't allow the youngsters to have a bit of fun now and again, then they'll take it anyway, whether you like it or not.'

Jim had shaken off Ted's friendly gesture. 'And I'll thank *you* not to interfere with the way I bring *my* daughter up. She'll do as she's told else she'll feel the back o' me hand. And sharpish.' With that he had tramped back across the fields, his anger still simmering and bursting into rage when he found that Kathy had already gone out to a village dance.

'What d'you let her go for?' he'd thundered at his wife. 'Did I say she could go? Did I?'

'Well, no, Jim, but I th-thought it wouldn't matter. Just this once. They always have a d-dance in the village hall the Friday night after Valentine's Day . . .' Edith Burton had stammered, her faded eyes fearful, her thin face creased into lines of perpetual anxiety. Although still only in her late thirties, the harsh life she was forced to lead had taken its toll. Her shoulders were rounded in a permanent state of submission and her hair was prematurely grey. Kathy was the only brightness in Edith's cold and cheerless life. As a naïve nineteen-year-old girl, the youngest of five daughters of a hardworking farm labourer, marriage to Jim Burton, who'd inherited Thorpe Farm at the age of twenty, had seemed too good to be true. It was – as poor Edith had soon found out. She'd long ago realized she did not love her husband and she doubted now that he'd ever really loved her. She wondered if he'd ever known the real meaning of the word 'love'. All he'd wanted, after the death of his mother, was a housekeeper and some-one to give him an heir. He'd picked Edith, thirteen years his junior, thinking that she would be sufficiently strong for farm work and healthy enough to bear him a son. But after the birth of their daughter, Edith had been told she should have no more children. Jim Burton's interest in her had ceased totally. Since that time, he'd treated her no better than he would a servant and while they still slept in the same room, in the same double bed for the sake of convention, all intimacy between them had ceased years ago.

'Valentine's! Sentimental rubbish! Don't you let her out again without my permission, d'you hear?'

'Yes, Jim,' Edith had said meekly.

Now, as Jim argued with his daughter in the cow-shed, all his frustration and resentment surfaced again. Deep down, he envied his neighbour. Why couldn't he have found himself a wife like Ted's? Betty Robinson was, in Jim Burton's eyes, the perfect farmer's wife. She was a superb cook and a helpmate about the farm, while his own wife hardly lifted a finger to help him with the outside work. And it wasn't as if she was even a good housewife. Edith was a poor cook. Some of the meals she had placed before him in the early days of their marriage had been scarcely edible. And she barely kept the house clean. Edith was not a bit like his dear, house-proud mother. Sarah Burton must be turning in her grave. Oh, he'd made a bad mistake in marrying Edith. He'd not realized she'd been spoiled and cosseted by her parents and older siblings. She'd never been taught how to keep house or to cook. And that wasn't her only fault. She'd failed to give him a son like Betty Robinson had given her man. He remembered the surprise the whole village had felt at Maurice's birth. No one had even known that Ted's new wife had been expecting, until, all of a sudden, there was Betty proudly wheeling the little chap around the village in a huge black perambulator. It wasn't until five years later that Amy Robinson had been born, only two months after Jim's own daughter. And then, when the doctor told him the devastating news that it would be dangerous for Edith to have more children, the resentment had begun. Not bearing him a son had been Edith's greatest failing in her husband's eyes.

Jim's envy of the Robinsons made him critical. While part of him wanted to ally his daughter to that family by her marriage to Maurice, another devious and embittered part of him half hoped that one day Ted's perfect life would be shattered. And now he knew how that might happen.

'That lass – ' he jabbed his forefinger towards Kathy as he spoke of her friend again now – 'would do well to knuckle down and help her father on his farm, instead of acting like a whore with all and sundry. He's too soft with her, but then, of course – ' Kathy held her breath, knowing exactly what was coming next – 'Ted Robinson's got a son to help him.' Jim turned away

6

with a swift, angry movement, slopping milk over the edge of the bucket.

Kathy's gaze followed her father for a moment, feeling a mixture of emotions. Just now and again she could find it in her heart to feel sorry for him. His disappointment in being blessed – or in his eyes cursed – with only one child, and a daughter to boot, was understandable, she supposed. It was a frustration he'd never tried to conceal, and Kathy had been aware of it for as long as she could remember. It never occurred to her father that Thorpe Farm, which had been in his family for four generations, could pass to a woman.

But Kathy's feelings of compassion lasted only a moment and her own resentment surfaced again. Adopting the same sarcastic tone he'd used, she said with deceptive mildness, 'I thought you liked the Robinson family. You're always trying to marry me off to Morry to give you a grandson.'

'Ya could do a lot worse,' Jim growled.

Yes, Kathy thought, I could. Morry Robinson was a nice lad but he had no ambition, no dreams to fulfil. He was perfectly content to work on his family's farm for the rest of his life. He didn't care if he never saw the world outside the farm gate. He even avoided trips to the local market town if he could. And as for visiting a city or – heaven forbid – London, well, he'd likely die of fright at the mere thought. Kathy smiled at the thought of Morry. She liked him. Of course she did. You couldn't help but like Morry. Everyone did. He was plump and cuddly like a teddy bear, with big, soft brown eyes, reddish brown hair and a round face liberally covered with freckles. She'd danced with him last night, feeling his hand hot on her waist and returning his shy, lopsided smile with kindness. He was the

7

sort of chap you couldn't *dis*like, couldn't be cruel to, but as for marriage, well now, that was something very different. She could see her life mapped out so clearly if she were to marry Morry. Years and years of working on a farm from dawn to dusk. Oh, she liked the Robinson family – loved them, really. Amy was her best friend – had been since school. Ted Robinson was a darling of a man and his plump and homely wife, Betty, always had a smile of welcome for anyone who called. A cup of tea and a sample of her latest batch of baking were always readily on offer. There were constant laughter and playful teasing in Betty's kitchen and her energy was boundless. Just watching her made Kathy feel tired. The whole Robinson family, even Amy, was contented with their lot.

But it was not the sort of life Kathy wanted for the next fifty or sixty years. Not what she dreamed of. And her father had got it wrong. It was not Amy who was the flighty one, it was her. It was Kathy who yearned for the bright lights, for excitement and to see a bit of the world. But now, for once, she wisely held her tongue. She said no more and went to the end of the byre to milk the cow in the end stall.

'Now then, Buttercup,' she greeted the animal cheerfully. 'Let's hope you're in a good mood this morning.' She patted the cow's rump and then bent to her task.

'Have you been putting ideas into her head? I wouldn't put it past you,' Jim growled as he sat down at the supper table, while his wife hovered at his side ready to place the plate of cold ham and pickles in front of him.

Edith cast a frightened glance at her daughter and

8

then looked back at her husband. 'I – I don't know what you mean, Jim.'

' "I don't know what you mean, Jim," ' he mimicked in a high-pitched, whining tone.

Kathy sat down on the far side of the table and picked up her knife and fork as she said calmly, 'Dad threatened to turn me out, so I told him I'm going anyway.'

Edith's eyes widened in terror and she dropped the plate she was holding. It fell to the floor and broke into four pieces.

Jim rose slowly to his feet and raised his hand as if to strike her. 'Now look what you've done, you stupid, stupid woman.'

Kathy was on her feet at once and launched herself between them. 'Don't you dare lay a finger on her,' she blazed. 'It's only because of her that I've stayed this long.'

Father and daughter glared at each other, but then, for once, Jim's gaze was the first to fall away. Maybe he'd seen something – a new strength of resolve – in his daughter's eyes. Perhaps he realized that if he pushed her just that little bit too far, she would carry out her threat. She would leave.

What Jim did not realize – could never have believed it – was that Kathy had already made up her mind. Maybe not today, or tomorrow, but one day very soon, she really would go.

Two

'You coming to church this morning?'

Amy Robinson's merry face peered over the bottom half of the cowshed door. She leaned on the top of it and rested her chin on her arms to watch her friend finishing off the morning milking with Cowslip in the nearest stall. Amy's dark brown eyes danced with mischief. The light dusting of freckles across her nose only accentuated her natural prettiness, but her light brown hair was as wild as ever. No matter what Amy did to try to tame her locks into a smooth, sleek style, the unruly curls escaped. Kathy glanced up, smiling. 'Of course. Would I *ever* miss singing with the choir?'

Amy threw back her head and laughed aloud. 'Choir? You call that a choir? Old Mrs Pennyfeather warbling off key. Mr Jenkins growling at the back and three cheeky little brats trying to look angelic but actually dreaming up their next prank to play on poor old Miss Tong.'

Miss Tong was the organist who was also the unofficial choirmaster – or 'mistress', Kathy supposed – until someone more proficient should apply for the post. But no one seemed to want the job and St Cuthbert's motley choir struggled on to lead an ever-diminishing congregation at the Sunday services.

'My darling girl – ' Amy teased and adopted a lilting tone – 'you'd have to go to Wales to hear a proper choir, look you, isn't it?' She mimicked the accent perfectly, for her maternal grandmother had been Welsh and Amy had spent a week's holiday every summer on her granny's farm in the heart of the Welsh countryside. Even now her face sobered and took on a dreamy, faraway look as if she were reliving those happy days.

Pulling her friend back to the present, Kathy asked quietly, 'And how do you think the choir would manage without me?'

The question sounded arrogant and for a moment Amy blinked. It was so unlike her dearest friend to show even the faintest trace of conceit.

'Oh, 'ark at 'er!' she mocked. 'God's gift to St Cuthbert's choir, a' you?'

Pink embarrassment tinged Kathy's cheeks. 'I'm sorry,' she said swiftly. 'I – I didn't mean it to sound the way it came out . . .'

Amy laughed. 'I know you didn't, you daft 'aporth.' She pulled a comical face and gave an exaggerated sigh. 'It pains me to admit it, but you have got the best voice of anyone, apart perhaps from little Charlie Oates. You wouldn't think a little tyke like him could sing like an angel. Mind you, his voice'll break. Yours won't. You've got it for life. You're a lucky devil, you know. Dad says my singing sounds like a frog croaking – and an injured one at that!'

For a moment, Kathy's mouth was a hard line. 'Lucky, am I? Well, I'll tell you something, Amy. I'd swap places with you any day of the week, voice or no voice.'

Amy's face sobered at once. 'Aw, ducky, is your dad giving you a hard time about the other night?'

Kathy bit down hard on her lower lip to still its

11

sudden trembling. She didn't normally give way to self-pitying tears, but the concern in her friend's tone touched her. 'It's not only that. It's – it's – Oh, *everything*! The way he treats me. I'm nothing more to him than a servant. An unpaid one, an' all. I've a good mind to up sticks and go!"

'But – but if you go away – ne'er mind the choir – what would your poor mam do without you?'

Kathy sighed. 'I know. I've only stayed this long because of her. Because he'll take it out on her if I do leave.'

'Does – does he – hit her?'

Kathy bit her lip. 'He did once. She dared to answer him back about something. I don't know what. I was only ten and I wasn't actually in the room when it happened. I – I heard it though. Through the bedroom wall. She had a black eye for weeks.'

'Has he ever hit you?'

Kathy laughed wryly. 'Oh yes. With his belt. The last time was two years ago.' Kathy smiled at the memory, but it was a bitter smile. 'He hadn't realized how strong I'd grown with working on the farm. And I snatched the belt from his hand and told him that if he ever tried it again, I'd go. I meant it. And he knew I did.'

'But *can* you leave home? You're not twenty-one for another two years.'

'Well, he'd have a job to carry me back physically, wouldn't he? And first,' she added pointedly, 'he'd have to find me.'

No more was said, but Amy went home without the usual cheery smile on her face. 'What's up with you?' her brother, Morry, greeted her. 'Lost a shilling and found a farthing?'

Tears started in Amy's eyes.

At once, Morry put his arm about her. 'Hey, Sis, what's the matter?'

'Oh, Morry, it's Kathy,' Amy blurted out as the tears now trickled down her cheeks. 'She – she's talking about leaving home.'

Morry's round, gentle face was grim. 'Well, I can't say I blame her. Living with that ol' devil. But where would she go?'

Amy shook her head. 'She didn't say. I – I expect she doesn't trust me. And – to be honest – I can't blame her. You know what a blabbermouth I am. And if she does go, she doesn't want *him* to be able to find her.'

'Mm.' For a moment, Morry was thoughtful. 'I'll have a word with her. See if there's anything I – we can do.'

Amy scrubbed away her tears and glanced up at her brother. 'You could ask her to marry you.'

Morry didn't answer. He just smiled quietly.

'Maurice, lad. Nice to see you. Come away in. I'll get the missis to mek a cuppa. Or would you prefer a beer? And a piece of 'er currant cake.' Jim Burton's laugh was humourless, with more than a hint of cruelty in it. 'Or mebbe you'd prefer to give that last one a miss, lad. My missis's baking's not a patch on your mam's.'

Morry gave a weak smile, not sure how to respond. Jim's attitude towards his wife always made the young man feel uncomfortable. 'No thanks, Mr Burton. I – er – just wondered if Kathy was about, that's all. I – er – thought we could walk to church together.'

He felt the older man's eyes searching his face keenly. 'Ah, yes, well now . . .' Jim Burton's mouth was stretched into an unaccustomed smile. 'She's getting ready. I'll call her down.'

'No need, Mr Burton. I'll just wait. She'll not be long. She's never late for church.' He stood awkwardly in the middle of the yard, twirling his cap through nervous, slightly sweaty hands.

'Well, at least come into the kitchen, lad. It's cold to be standing out here.'

Reluctantly, Morry followed the man into the farmhouse kitchen. He'd much preferred to have waited out in the yard, however cold it was.

'Maurice is here, Edith. Mek the lad a cuppa.'

The thin, worried little woman hurried forward. She smiled at Morry, but the young man could see that though her smile for him was genuine, it did not touch her sad eyes. The thought sprang immediately to his mind: what would this nice little woman do if her daughter – her only child – left home? Maybe that was the way to touch Kathy's heart if . . .

'Hello, Maurice,' Edith Burton was saying. 'Come in. Sit down while I—'

But at that moment there were footsteps on the stairs and Kathy burst into the kitchen. 'I'll have to go, Mam, I'm late—' She stopped short. 'Oh, hello, Morry. What are you doing here?'

'He's come to walk you to church,' Jim Burton cut in and there was a warning note in his voice that said: Now, you be nice to this lad. He's the one I want as my son-in-law.

Kathy managed to quell the involuntary shudder that ran through her. She didn't want Morry to sense her revulsion. He was a lovely lad, but – not for her. She loved him dearly, but only as she would have loved a brother. She could never – would never – see him as a husband. As a lover! But, smiling brightly, she crossed the red tiled floor and linked her arm through his. 'Come on then, Morry. Best foot forward. You know the choir can't start without me. Bye, Mam . . .'

When they were a good distance down the lane from the farm, walking briskly both to keep warm and to arrive at the church on time – already the church bell was tolling through the frosty morning air – Morry could contain himself no longer.

'Amy says you're leaving.'

Kathy sucked her tongue against her front teeth to make a tutting sound of exasperation. But it was a good-natured expression. She rolled her eyes heavenwards as she said, 'Oh, that sister of yours! Can't keep a secret for love nor money, can she?'

'She was upset, Kathy. She was in tears.'

At once, Kathy was contrite. 'I'm sorry. I didn't mean to upset her. It's just – it's just – oh, Morry, I've got to go. I can't stand it any more.'

The young man was silent, his dark eyes full of sorrow. 'We don't want you to go, Kathy. *I* don't want you to go.' He stopped suddenly and stepped in front of her, bringing her to an abrupt halt. He caught hold of her arms. 'Kathy – please – don't go. Stay. Stay and – and marry me.'

Kathy's mouth dropped open in a silent gasp. She stared at him with wide blue eyes. When, after a few seconds, she found her voice, the words came out all wrong.

'What's he said to you? What's he promised you?'

For a brief moment, puzzlement clouded Morry's eyes, to be replaced, as understanding dawned, by hurt.

15

'Oh, Kathy – how can you think that of me? Don't you know how much I love you? Don't you know I've always loved you? For as long as I can remember.'

Now there were tears in Kathy's eyes as she reached up and cupped his round face between her hands. 'I'm sorry. I wouldn't hurt you for the world. You're a lovely, lovely man and I love you dearly – as a friend. But – but – Morry, I'm not in love with you. Not in that way. Not to *marry* you. I – I'm sorry, but I never could be.'

His kind face was creased with disappointment, but, strangely, there was no surprise, no shock or disbelief in his expression. Instead he sighed heavily and nodded, 'I – I thought as much, if I'm honest.'

'And we're always honest with each other, Morry, aren't we?' Kathy said softly. 'We're still friends, aren't we?'

Morry managed a weak, but genuine, smile. 'Oh, yes, Kathy, I'll always be your friend, no matter what.' Catching hold of her hands and gripping them tightly, he held them close to his broad chest. 'Whatever happens, Kathy, whatever you do, always remember that I'm your friend.'

Kathy's voice was husky as she whispered, 'I will, Morry. I will.'

It was not the 'I will' that Morry longed to hear her say, but it would have to do.

With a sudden, old-fashioned gesture of courtesy that was way out of character, Morry raised her cold, chapped fingers to his lips and kissed them. 'Good. And now we'd best start running. The bell's stopped.'

*

'So – did he ask you then?'

'Ask me what?' Kathy kept her voice calm but avoided meeting her father's eyes as she ladled potatoes onto his plate.

'To wed him, of course?'

The spoon trembled a little in her hand as she felt her mother's timorous glance. Kathy pulled in a deep breath and let it out slowly as she carried on serving both her mother and herself with vegetables.

'Well?' Jim Burton snapped. 'Are you going to answer me, girl?'

'He did ask me, yes.'

'And?'

'I – I refused.'

'You – did – what?'

A sudden calm settled over Kathy. Whatever her father might say – or do – no matter however much he ranted and raved, she knew her answer had been the right one. 'I refused him,' she repeated, but bit her lip as, out the corner of her eye, she saw her mother tremble and the colour drain from her face.

'You refused him? Have you gone mad, girl?' Jim Burton rose slowly to his feet, his dinner forgotten.

Without warning, he raised his right arm and struck her on the left side of her face. Kathy dropped the dish she was holding. It smashed to the floor, spilling hot potatoes across the tiles. She stumbled and almost fell, but managed to regain her balance by clutching the edge of the table.

'Jim—' Edith pleaded, but he waved his hand in dismissal and the cowed woman shrank back into her chair and shrivelled into terrified silence.

'Now you listen to me, girl—' Jim wagged his forefinger into Kathy's face. 'You get yourself over to the Robinson place this minute and you go down on your knees if necessary and you beg him to forgive you and you ask him to take you back.'

Kathy stared into her father's eyes, seeing him – really seeing him – for the first time. Not any longer as her father, the man who, though strict and dominating, must be honoured and obeyed, but as the man he really was: cruel and self-centred, without an ounce of love or compassion in his embittered soul. Though the side of her face was stinging, she gritted her teeth and determined not to put her hand up to it. She wouldn't give him the satisfaction of seeing that he had hurt her. But the physical hurt was nothing compared to the ache in her heart.

'You hear me. You'll do as I say.' It was a demand, not a request, and in that moment, Kathy's heart hardened irrevocably as he added, 'You'll go to the Robinsons' this very minute.'

Briefly, she glanced down at her mother. 'I'm sorry, Mam,' Kathy said softly. 'So sorry . . .'

For a long moment, mother and daughter gazed at each other and then the girl saw the brief flicker of a smile on the older woman's mouth. Edith gave an almost imperceptible little nod that told her daughter all she needed to know.

'And so you should be,' Jim growled. He sat down and picked up his knife and fork, confident that the matter was at an end, that now he would be obeyed.

Kathy moved round the table and knelt beside her mother's chair. Edith clasped her hand and leant forward to kiss the girl's forehead. 'God bless you,' she whispered so low that Kathy only just caught the words that released her, words that sprang the trap wide open.

She was free. Free to go, free to leave – and with her mother's blessing.

'You – you'll be all right?' Kathy whispered.

They both knew she wouldn't be – not really – but Edith patted her hand, managed to raise a smile and say, louder now, 'Off you go, love. You go to the Robinsons'.'

For a moment, Kathy leant her face against her mother's bony shoulder and whispered, 'I love you, Mam.'

'I know, my darling, I know,' the poor woman whispered back, 'but off you go. It's – it's for the best.'

With a final squeeze of her hand, Kathy rose and moved towards the door into the hall and the stairs. She glanced back just once. Her father was eating as if nothing had happened, his whole attention on the food in front of him, but her mother's gaze followed her.

Then Kathy turned and ran lightly upstairs to pack her battered suitcase.

Three

'Hello, lass.' Ted Robinson greeted her with a wave and began to cross the yard towards her. He was a big man, tall with strong, broad shoulders and a weather-beaten face that crinkled with laughter lines. 'Going on your holidays?'

Kathy set the heavy suitcase down, straightened up and smiled at him as he neared her. 'I've a favour to ask.'

'Owt, lass, you know that.'

'Could Morry take me to the station, please?'

The Robinsons had a dilapidated old truck that carried anything from pigs bound for market to the huge Christmas tree that Ted brought home every year.

'Of course he can. But – but where are you going?'

Suddenly, the euphoria at her sudden freedom that had carried her this far faltered. 'I – I don't really know.'

'Don't know?' For a moment Ted was puzzled. He moved closer, his gaze intent upon her face. 'What's been happening, lass? You've got a right old shiner coming up there.' He frowned, already half guessing what had been going on in the Burtons' unhappy household. He sighed and then said softly, 'You leaving home?'

Kathy bit her lip and nodded. Then she blurted out, 'Morry asked me to marry him and – and I said no.

I'm sorry, Mr Robinson, truly I am. He'll make some-one a wonderful husband, but – but . . .'

'But not you, eh, lass?'

She nodded.

The big man sighed. 'I'm sorry too. Me an' the missis would've loved you as a daughter-in-law, but if you don't love the lad . . .' He searched her face for a glimmer of hope that she might – just might – change her mind. Not seeing it, he murmured, 'Aye, well, mar-riage is tough enough at times when you are in love, ne'er mind when you're not.' He glanced at her again, an unspoken question in his eyes.

She nodded slowly. 'I know. I've seen the conse-quences at first hand. I don't intend to make the same mistake. Not that I think Morry would be like that – like – like *him*, but . . .'

Ted put his huge, work-callused hand on her shoulder and gave it a gentle, understanding squeeze. 'Come along in,' he said firmly, in a tone that brooked no argument. 'And we'll see what's to do.' He picked up her suitcase and walked towards the back door of the sprawling farmhouse, leaving Kathy to follow in his wake.

'Mother,' he shouted to his wife as he opened the back door. 'We've got another for dinner. Set a place at the table, love.'

Betty Robinson bustled forward tutting with disap-proval as she saw the red mark on the side of Kathy's face and the swelling already beginning around her eye. 'Now, what's that old devil been doing? You're wel-come to stay here as long as you want, cariad.' Though Betty had been away from the valleys for many years, there was still a trace of the Celtic lilt in her voice. 'Amy – Amy, come here.'

It wasn't Amy who came into the kitchen, but Morry, his smile of welcome fading when he saw the telltale mark on Kathy's face. For a moment, his benign, kindly face creased into anger. 'Dad – we should go over there. We can't let him get away with this.'

Before Ted Robinson could answer, Amy bounced into the room. 'Kathy . . .' she began and then halted, staring open-mouthed at her friend. 'Wha. . .?'

'You might well ask,' Morry said grimly. 'Been hitting her, that's what he's been doing.'

'Now, now, let's sit down and we'll all have a bit of dinner together,' Ted said. 'You haven't eaten, lass, have you?'

Kathy shook her head. 'No—' She smiled faintly. 'It ended up on the kitchen floor.'

There was an awkward silence. No one knew quite what to say for a moment. Then Betty, ever motherly and sensible, said, 'Amy, come and help me dish up. We'll talk about it over dinner and decide what's to be done.'

They ate in silence for several moments, even though not one of them had much appetite. Each was busy with their own thoughts, working out in their own minds what to suggest. Ted and Betty Robinson were ready to offer the girl a home. Amy was planning much the same, eager to have her very best friend as a sister, and Morry was determined to repeat his proposal. But Kathy had made her mind up and when she laid her knife and fork side by side on the plate, she cleared her throat and forestalled all their schemes by saying, 'I've made up my mind. I'm leaving.'

The other four stared at her and then all seemed to speak at once.

'Oh now, cariad, don't be hasty . . .'

'You can't leave, Kathy. What'll I do without you?' Amy's eyes filled with ready tears.

'I meant what I said, Kathy . . .'

'You stay here, lass. Stay with us for a bit. That'll make the old bugger come to his senses.'

'It's very kind of you and I love you all for it, but I have to go. I – I've been thinking about it for some time anyway. The – the only thing that has kept me here this long is – is Mam.' Her voice broke then and she covered her face with her hands. The Robinsons glanced at each other uncomfortably, lost for words now.

Kathy pulled in a deep, steadying breath and raised her face, even managing to force a tremulous smile. 'But now Mam's sort of – sort of given me her blessing. But it – it doesn't make it any easier. I can't bear to think what might happen to her left alone with him.'

Betty touched Kathy's arm with her plump, comforting hand. 'She'll want what's best for you, cariad.' For a moment, her fond glance rested on her own son and daughter. 'Mothers always do. She'll cope and – if not – then she's always welcome to come here. We'd look after her.'

'You're very kind,' Kathy murmured and her eyes filled with tears. 'I – I don't deserve it.' She glanced apologetically at Morry.

'We know all about Morry's proposal,' Betty said cheerfully. 'And we're sorry it's not to be. But there it is. I wouldn't want you saying "yes" to him just because you want to get away from home. I wouldn't want you using him . . .'

'Mother, please.' Morry's face reddened as he protested.

'You know me, Morry. I always speak my mind. And Kathy should know that by now.'

'I wouldn't ever do that, Mrs Robinson. Not to anyone, and certainly not to Morry.'

Betty nodded, her chins wobbling as she patted Kathy's hand again. 'I know, I know. Morry will find the right girl one day. We all wish it could be you, but like I say, if it's not to be, then it's not to be.'

Now it was Morry who, still red-faced, cast a look of apology towards Kathy.

Ted, tired of all the romantic nonsense, changed the subject to one of practicalities. 'Where do you plan to go, lass?'

'Lincoln.'

They all stared at her for a moment and then, almost as if given a cue, they all laughed and relaxed.

'Lincoln. Why, that's nowt. Only a stone's throw away, lass. Ya not really leaving us at all. I thought you meant you were off to Lunnan or somewhere. Oh, that's all right then.'

Amy clapped her hands. 'I'll be able to come and stay with you and we can go out on the town . . .'

'Now, now, steady on, Amy. You hold your horses a bit,' Betty said. She turned to Kathy. 'Have you got somewhere to go to in Lincoln?'

Kathy shook her head. 'No. But I've got a little money saved up. Though how I've done it I don't know myself, since Dad never paid me a proper wage.' The unfairness of her life was a bitter taste in her mouth and, despite her anxiety over her mother, hardened her resolve.

She was doing the right thing. She was sure she was.

Betty glanced at her husband and voiced her thoughts

aloud. 'D'you think your sister would put her up for a bit? Just till she finds her feet?'

Ted blinked. 'Jemima? Ah, well now, I don't know about that. Not the sort of place you'd want a young lass staying.'

'Oh, I don't know,' Betty was smiling mischievously. 'Might do your Jemima the world of good to have a bright young thing like Kathy about the place. Might liven her up a bit.'

Amy was giggling uncontrollably and even Morry was smiling. Only Ted looked unsure as he glanced at Kathy. He cleared his throat. 'My sister is a spinster and lives alone in a little terraced house with just her cat for company. She does work, though. In one of the big stores in Lincoln. She – er – never married. She – er . . .'

'Such a shame,' Betty murmured as husband and wife exchanged a glance and Betty gave a tiny shake of her head. Ted fell silent, but Kathy had the distinct feeling that there was more to Aunt Jemima's story than either of them were telling.

'You can't send her there,' Amy spluttered. 'She'll have to be in bed by half past nine every night and she won't be allowed any "followers". How's Kathy ever to meet anyone? Make friends?'

'Well, like I say, it's only till she finds her feet,' Betty answered. 'Till she gets a job and can afford a place of her own. Then she can find a nice little bed-sit somewhere.'

Amy clapped her hands again. 'And I can go and stay. What fun we'll have, Kathy.'

'Now, take your things upstairs. Amy'll show you the spare room,' Betty said, rising from the table.

'You stay here the night and Morry can drive you into Lincoln in the morning. I'll come with you and talk to Jemima. All right?'

Kathy nodded. 'You're – you're very kind.'

'Think nothing of it, cariad. That's what friends are for.'

Ted stood up too and, as Kathy rose to follow Amy, she heard him say softly to his wife. 'I've a mind to slip across to Jim's and see how things are.'

'Leave it for tonight, Jim,' Betty whispered back. 'You might make things worse. Let's get her safely out the way and then you can go and see how poor Edith is.'

Kathy picked up her suitcase. The overheard conversation had eased her conscience and lightened her concern. The Robinsons would keep an eye on her mother, and now that she was to move in with a relative of theirs, Kathy would be able to hear if things were all right. The knowledge comforted her and assuaged her guilt – if only a little.

Kathy lay awake half the night, going over and over in her mind the events that had led up to the drastic action she'd taken. She lay in the Robinsons' spare bed, tense and anxious, expecting at any moment to hear a loud banging on their back door. She couldn't imagine that her father would let her go easily. For one thing, he would have to pay someone to do the work on the farm she did for nothing. And that was the last thing he would do. At any moment she expected him to arrive at the Robinsons' to drag her back, by her hair if necessary.

Then another thought struck her. Perhaps he hadn't

realized she'd gone. She'd crept quietly out of the house while he was asleep in the battered armchair near the range.

Only Kathy's mother had seen her go, had held her close for a few brief moments and then given her a gentle push towards the door. 'Go now. Quickly – before he wakes up,' Edith had whispered urgently.

But nothing disturbed the stillness of the frosty night; the only sound was Ted Robinson's noisy snoring in the next room. If her father did know, it was obvious now that he wasn't going to chase after her. No doubt he thought she would come back of her own accord like a whipped dog, contrite and begging forgiveness.

'Fat chance,' Kathy murmured aloud in the darkness. She turned over and, at last, fell asleep.

Four

'Good heavens! Whatever brings you to my door this early on a Monday morning? Is something wrong, Betty? Is it Edward?'

Kathy hid her smile at hearing the use of Ted Robinson's full and formal Christian name.

'No, no, Jemima cariad. We're fine. But we're early because we wanted to catch you before you went to work.'

'Come in, do. You're welcome any time of the day, Betty. It's good to see you.' As the tall, thin woman ushered them into the tiny terraced house, she was still firing questions. 'How *is* Edward? And Amy? Is my goddaughter behaving herself? Hello, Maurice, my dear boy, how nice to see you.' She proffered her gaunt cheek for Morry's dutiful kiss.

Then she turned her sharp grey eyes on Kathy. 'And who is this?'

'Kathy. Kathy Burton.'

Strangely, the grey eyes showed no surprise, not even when they glanced down briefly and took in the suitcase. 'Jim Burton's girl?'

When Betty nodded, Jemima's only reply was a swift nod and a soft, 'Ah.'

It seemed the woman understood without another word of explanation, for she led the way from the back door through the scullery and into the living kitchen.

Remains of her half-eaten breakfast lay on the table set against the wall, but she made no effort to return to it, saying instead, 'Would you like a cup of tea?'

'We mustn't keep you, Jemima. You'll be wanting to get to work.'

Jemima glanced at the clock on the mantelpiece above the range that took up the centre of one wall. 'I've never been late in all the twenty years I've worked there,' she said. 'I don't think they're going to dismiss me for being a few minutes late this morning. Besides, Mr Kendall is a very understanding young man.' She paused, sniffed, and seemed lost for a brief moment in her own thoughts. 'Poor young feller has to be,' she murmured. Then she shook herself and was brisk and businesslike once more. 'Sit down, sit down all of you. Maurice, my dear, fetch another chair from the front room. And then you can tell me what this is about – though I think I can guess.'

When they were all seated, Jemima sat down too, crossing her ankles neatly and folding her hands in her lap. She was dressed ready for work in a smart, navy blue two-piece costume that accentuated her slim figure. Her hair, once a bright auburn but now showing signs of grey here and there, was swept back from her face into a plaited coil at the nape of her neck, the plain style emphasizing the thinness of her face. Kathy guessed the woman must be in her late forties – like her brother and sister-in-law – but she looked older. There were tiny lines around her eyes and her mouth, but when she turned her clear, green eyes on Kathy and smiled, the severity left her face and Kathy could glimpse the pretty girl this woman must once have been.

'Now, my dear,' Jemima's tone was surprisingly kind. 'Leaving home, are you?'

29

Kathy could not prevent a little gasp of surprise and she glanced at Betty, who nodded encouragingly. 'Tell Aunt Jemima – I mean, Miss Robinson—'

Jemima waved her hand and said, 'Oh, "Aunt Jemima" will do fine. I'm sure we can make room for an adopted niece.' Her smile widened and her eyes actually twinkled for a brief moment. 'I'm sure the names the girls at work call me are far less polite.'

Kathy cleared her throat, suddenly nervous. Miss Robinson – Aunt Jemima – seemed kindly enough. There had been no note of disapproval in her tone, yet there was none of approval either. It had been a statement of fact that gave Kathy no real encouragement.

'Yes, I – er – um – I want to come and live in the city. Find a job. Stand on my own feet.'

Jemima's disconcerting gaze eyed her steadily. 'Why?'

Kathy swallowed and gnawed at her lower lip. Then the words came in a rush, as if she could contain herself no longer. 'Because – because I can't stand it at home any more. My father treats me like a servant. I get my keep, as he calls it, but no wage . . .' Now she met Jemima's gaze steadily. 'I want to stand on my own two feet. I want to see a bit of life.'

'I see,' Jemima said quietly. Slowly, the older woman turned her head towards her sister-in-law as she said softly, 'It could be me thirty years ago, Betty, couldn't it?'

Betty nodded. 'Yes, but things are worse for Kathy, Jemima. Your dad was strict, yes, but he was never cruel.' She nodded towards Kathy. 'See that black eye she's getting? He did that to her. Now your dad never hit you. Not that I know of, anyway.'

Jemima closed her eyes for a moment, as if lost in the past. When she opened them she sighed and murmured, 'Only the once, Betty, only the once, but maybe he had good reason, eh?'

Betty stared at her sister-in-law, but said nothing. Kathy looked at Morry, but he was studiously avoiding her glance. She guessed he knew what the two women were talking about, but no one was going to reveal a long-held family secret to her. Not even Morry.

Briskly now, Jemima turned back to Kathy. 'I know your father of old, my dear. Being neighbours, Edward and I, and your father, were all young together. I always thought him a cold fish even then and pitied any woman who was foolish enough to marry him. He came a-courting me once, but I sent him packing, I can tell you.' Her eyes sparkled suddenly with mischief but then, almost as suddenly as it had appeared, the twinkle was gone. 'But your poor mother.' Jemima sighed. 'I expect she was taken in by the thought of a young man owning his own farm.' She gave a quick nod. 'And, yes, it could have been a good life for any girl. Look at Betty here – I don't think she'd change her life with the Queen of England . . .'

Betty nodded and smiled her agreement.

'And your father can be very charming,' Jemima went on. 'When he wants to be!'

Kathy was on the point of arguing. She had never seen any 'charm' in her father, but then she stopped as she remembered how Jim always greeted Morry when he came to the farm. Oh yes, Jim Burton's attitude could be very different when he wanted something from someone.

'But I expect your poor mother rues the day she met Jim Burton,' Jemima added grimly.

For a moment – a very brief moment – Kathy almost felt moved to defend her father. Jemima's bluntness was almost rude. But the words she might have spoken died on her lips. What Jemima Robinson was saying was absolutely true. Harsh though her words were, there was no denying the truth in them.

'So, you want somewhere to stay in Lincoln, I take it?'

'Only temporary, Jemima, just till she finds a job and can afford a place of her own. A little bed-sit or – or something,' Betty finished lamely. She knew nothing of city life and couldn't imagine anything worse than being cooped up in a tiny room in a little house in a row of houses with street after street just the same. Give her the wide open spaces of the countryside any day. Sandy Furze Farm and the tiny village of Abbey-toft were all Betty needed or wanted. But, though she couldn't understand it herself, she could see that the lure of the busy streets and the bright lights were perhaps what the lonely Kathy Burton needed. She just hoped her Amy wouldn't want to follow her friend.

'You're very welcome to stay – for a short while,' Jemima said bluntly. 'But you'll have to try to fit in with me and my funny little ways. Taffy – that's my cat – and I like our routine.'

'Of course,' Kathy said at once. 'Just tell me what you want me to do and . . .'

'Oh, I will, make no mistake about that.' Jemima's gaze scrutinized the girl once more. 'And I might be able to help you find a job. There's a vacancy at the department store where I work. I'll talk to Miss Curtis – the head of the department – and to Mr Kendall.'

'Oh, thank you. That's – that's very kind of you.'

'Kindness has nothing to do with it,' Jemima said,

standing up as if giving a signal that it was time for Betty and Morry to leave and for her to go to work. 'The sooner you have a job and can earn your own living, the sooner Taffy and I will have our house back to ourselves.'

Kathy wasn't sure but she thought she saw – just briefly – the fleeting sparkle of mischief in Jemima's eyes.

Her first encounter with the other occupant of the terraced house was more frightening than meeting Aunt Jemima.

Taffy was a long-haired ginger tom, who padded silently about the house on huge white-tipped paws and glared balefully at the newcomer invading his territory. Their first confrontation happened in the scullery.

Aunt Jemima, having shown her to the tiny spare bedroom and given her a key for the back door, had left for work. Betty and Morry had gone and now Kathy was alone in the house and wondering what she should do. After being used to working from dawn to dusk – and sometimes beyond – she didn't know how to handle the hours that stretched emptily before her.

Perhaps I should go into the city myself and see if I can find work, she mused. But she didn't want to offend Aunt Jemima, who had promised to enquire about the vacancy at the large department store where she worked. So Kathy looked around the neat house to see if there was anything that needed doing. Then she spotted the breakfast things still left on the table. She carried the used crockery into the scullery to wash it. Standing at the deep white sink, she heard a snuffling and turned towards the round basket in the corner. The cat was stretching and yawning, showing sharp, white teeth and even sharper claws.

'Hello, boy. You must be Taffy. My, you're a beauty, aren't you?' Kathy squatted and held out her hand towards the cat, but he arched his back, his fur bristling, and spat at her. As his paw flicked out towards her, Kathy quickly pulled back her hand, narrowly missing receiving a deep scratch. 'That's not a very nice welcome, I must say. Mind you, I am a stranger in your home, so you've every right.'

His green eyes sparked anger and he hissed at her again.

'I'm not going to hurt you,' she carried on, talking in a soft soothing tone, but she made no attempt to touch the animal again. 'I've just come to stay here for a while.' She stood up and turned back to the sink, half expecting that at any moment she might feel those vicious claws raking the back of her leg.

After a moment, she risked a glance over her shoulder. The cat's bright green gaze was weighing her up, it seemed. Kathy tried again. 'I wonder how you get in and out while your mistress is out all day.' She looked around. At the bottom of the back door there was a hole cut in the woodwork and covering it was a metal-hinged flap that swung backwards and forwards. 'Oh, how clever,' she murmured.

Then she saw that the cat's bowls – one for milk and one for food – were filled. 'Seems you don't need my help,' she said as she dried the last plate and stowed it away in the cupboard.

She turned and went back into the kitchen and sat down in an easy chair near the range. Beside the chair and set in the alcove near the range was a shelf of books. Kathy leaned forward and perused the titles, smiling as she saw one of her favourite books there. *Pride and Prejudice.* In her last year at school the class had begun to read it, but she'd been forced by her father to leave school as soon as she was old enough. She'd never had the chance to finish the story. There were few books around at Thorpe Farm. Her father considered them a waste of time.

'Filling your head with such nonsense,' had been his view if he ever caught her reading. 'You'd be better doing something useful.' And by the time she climbed the stairs at night to her bedroom – the only place where she had any privacy – she was usually so dog-tired that her eyelids drooped before she'd read even half a page.

But now she'd time to spare. Carefully, she pulled the book from the shelf and opened it, her heart beating with a sudden excitement. She could read to her heart's content. There was no one to stop her. From this moment on, she could do exactly what she pleased with her life.

As she turned to the first page, the door into the scullery was pushed wider open and Taffy walked into the room. Kathy glanced up, watching him. He stood a moment, his green eyes staring at her. Then, with the easy grace of a big cat in the wild, he padded towards her, his gaze still holding hers. He sat down before her, still looking up at her, still assessing her. She could no longer read his expression; he was no longer spitting but neither did friendliness shine in his green eyes.

'Ah,' Kathy said aloud. 'Am I sitting in your mistress's chair? Is that it?' She smiled. Did she imagine it or did the green eyes soften just a little? Without warning, the cat lifted his front paw, balanced himself for a moment on his hind legs and then launched himself towards her, landing on her lap and sending the book slithering to the floor. His face close to hers for a moment, her stared at her again. Kathy, pressing herself back into the chair, stared back. Then Taffy broke the gaze and turned three times in a tight circle, kneading her lap with his white-tipped paws. Kathy held her breath, waiting. At last he lay down with the curve of his spine towards her and began to wash his foreleg. To her amazement, Kathy heard the deep-throated rumble of a contented purr. Tentatively she touched the cat's head and was rewarded by him pressing against her stroking fingers and purring even louder.

Carefully Kathy reached down to retrieve her book and they settled down together. The cat yawned, stretched his front paw, then curled his head round and closed his eyes. Strangely comforted by the warm little body on her lap, Kathy turned back to her book.

It wasn't until she heard the rattle of the back door opening that Kathy realized just how the morning had flown by. Lost in the wonderful story of Mr and Mrs Bennett and their five daughters, she had not once moved from the chair. And Taffy still slumbered on her lap.

Jemima stepped into the room and stopped, staring in surprise.

'Well, I never,' she exclaimed. 'Now that's something I never expected to see. Taffy's usually most unfriendly with visitors.' Jemima seemed impressed to see her pet sitting on Kathy's knee.

'He wasn't at first. He spat at me and tried to scratch

me, but I just ignored him and then he came and jumped up on to my knee of his own accord.'

Jemima laughed. 'That's the best way to treat him. One thing Taffy can't bear is to be ignored.'

Kathy set her book down and put her hands beneath the cat's hefty body to lift him off her knee. He woke with a start and leapt down, walking angrily towards the door, his ears flattened. The two women watched him as he stalked out and they heard the rattle of the flap in the back door.

Kathy got up quickly. 'I'm sorry,' she said again. 'I'd've done some housework for you, but I didn't like to presume . . .'

'No need,' Jemima said crisply. 'I don't expect you to do that – at least not on your first day. Obviously, I shall expect you to keep your room clean . . .'

'Of course,' Kathy said swiftly. 'And I'll help elsewhere – that is, if you want me to.'

'We'll see,' Jemima smiled.

'I could have got you some lunch ready if I'd known you came home.' Kathy was still apologetic.

'I don't normally, but I have some news for you. Mr Kendall, the manager, is willing to see you at three o'clock this afternoon. The vacant post is in the millinery department. Do you know anything about hats?'

Kathy laughed wryly. 'Not really. The only hat I possess is the one I always wear for church. And that's an old one of my mother's. Nineteen-twenties style!'

Jemima grimaced. 'Oh well, as long as you're a willing learner.' She glanced at the skirt and blouse that Kathy was wearing. Bluntly she said, 'Have you anything better to wear than that?'

Biting her lip, Kathy shook her head.

'Mm.' For a moment, Jemima was thoughtful.

'You're a little bit plumper than me . . .' She chuckled suddenly, her thin face lighting up. For a brief moment it made her look so much younger. 'But in all the right places, I must say. I have a costume that might just fit you.' She glanced at her wristwatch. 'You make us some sandwiches, Kathy, and I'll run upstairs and sort one or two things out. You can try them all on when I've gone back to work.'

While Kathy went into the scullery and found bread, butter, a joint of cooked ham and some cheese, Jemima ran lightly up the narrow staircase to her bedroom. As she prepared the snack, Kathy heard wardrobe doors opening and closing in the room above. Just as she placed a plate of the sandwiches on the table in the kitchen, she heard Jemima's steps on the stairs.

'I've laid out three suits for you and two blouses.' She glanced down at Kathy's feet. 'Your shoes will have to do, but there's polish under the sink in the scullery. Ah,' she said, seeing the sandwiches. 'This looks nice. Why is it,' she added, sitting down, 'that food always tastes so much nicer when someone else has prepared it? Even a few sandwiches.'

'I'd offer to cook for you,' Kathy said, sitting down too. 'But I've never had much chance to learn. Father always wanted me to work outside. Poor Mam had to . . .' Suddenly her throat was tight and she felt the prickle of tears behind her eyelids. But she pulled in a deep breath and steadied her voice. 'Had to manage in the kitchen all by herself.'

Pretending not to notice, Jemima said, 'Your poor mother wasn't cut out to be a farmer's wife. It's a hard life. A good life, mind you, but a hard one nevertheless.'

'Do you know,' Kathy said, surprised to hear herself

saying it and almost ashamed to admit it, 'I know very little about my parents' life. They hardly ever talk about the past and if they do, well, it's only my father grumbling how unfair life has been to him. The – the fact that he's never had a son. He – he's very jealous of your brother for having Morry to carry on the family farm.'

There was a long pause before Jemima asked, 'Is there anything between you and Maurice?'

'No . . . I mean – my father would like there to be and I – er – Morry would too, but . . .' Kathy felt her cheeks redden with embarrassment. Perhaps she had now offended Aunt Jemima by not being able to love her nephew, but the older woman's only answer was her soft, understanding, 'Ah.'

Five

Mr Kendall, the manager of the large department store on the High Street, was much younger than Kathy had expected. As she was ushered into his office by his secretary, Kathy almost gasped aloud in surprise. He looked to be in his late twenties. Young to hold such a position of authority, she thought.

Jemima had explained a little as they'd eaten their lunch. 'The Hammond family owns the store. Old Mr Hammond rarely comes in these days. He suffers cruelly with arthritis, so I understand. Mr James Hammond, his son and heir, comes in most days, but it's Mr Kendall we see about the store the most. He's – er – very actively involved,' she added, sounding amused about something, though Kathy could not understand what.

Now, as she stood before him, he rose, smiled at her and indicated a chair set in front of his desk for her to sit down. She noticed that he was very smartly dressed in a dark, pinstriped suit, gleaming white shirt and neat, sober tie. His short, black hair was sleek and shone in the pale winter sunlight from the window behind him. Though his face was in shadow, she could see the outline of a straight nose and a strong jawline. She couldn't, at this moment, see the colour of his eyes or the shape of his mouth . . .

'Please sit down, Miss Burton.' His voice was deep, but friendly.

Kathy perched nervously on the edge of the chair, gripping her handbag in front of her.

He looked at her for a moment and now she could see that his eyes were a gentle brown. 'Don't be nervous,' he said softly. 'I'm not such an ogre.'

Kathy smiled and relaxed a little. It wasn't really him she was nervous about. It was just that this interview was so important to her. She badly wanted – needed – this job. And having to borrow clothes from a woman more than twice her age wasn't exactly boosting her confidence!

'Now,' he rested his arms on the desk and leaned towards her. 'I understand from Miss Robinson that you would very much like to work for us, but that you have no experience at all.'

There was nothing else she could do except be absolutely frank. 'No, I'm sorry. I haven't. The only work I know is on a farm. My – my father's farm. But – but I so want to do something else.'

'I see,' he said slowly. 'And I presume you cannot furnish us with references?'

Kathy shook her head and her heart began to sink, but hope surged again as he continued, 'Well, in some ways your inexperience might be an advantage. We can train you from the start to our ways. You won't come with any preconceived ideas. Ideas that we might not like.' His smile broadened. 'And because of Miss Robinson's recommendation, I'm willing to give you a month's trial and see how we go.'

Kathy felt the colour rush into her face. 'Oh, thank you. Thank you very much. I won't let you down.'

'No,' Tony Kendall said softly. 'No, I don't think you will.' He stared at her for a long time, taking in the long, blonde hair swept back from her face over her ears and falling in a shining cascade of curls to her shoulders. Her clear complexion was tanned from her time spent working out of doors in all weathers but her blue eyes were direct and honest. She was not the sort of girl they usually employed, and he'd only agreed to interview her as a favour to Miss Robinson, who'd worked for the store for more than twenty years. Jemima Robinson was a revered member of staff who had worked her way up over the years to be head of the ladies' department. More recently, she'd been promoted to the position of supervisor of the whole of the first floor and was responsible for several departments, including mantles, outfitting – and hats! Under her keen eye were the heads of each department who, in turn, had several assistants and juniors below them. Miss Robinson was known to be strict with those under her, but fair. For her alone, Tony Kendall had been willing to give this girl a trial. But now that he saw Kathy Burton for himself, well, reason didn't come into it!

'I'll hand you over to my secretary. She'll fill out all the necessary paperwork and take you down to introduce you to the other girls in millinery.' He rose and moved around the desk, opened the door and called to the woman sitting before a typewriter in the outer office. 'Miss Foster, would you step in for a moment, please?'

'Certainly, Mr Kendall . . .'

'This is Miss Curtis.' Half an hour later, Miss Foster was introducing her to the head of the millinery department and to the other girl who worked there, Stella Matthews.

Miss Curtis was in her early thirties, Kathy surmised, slim with a flawless complexion, dark hair styled in the very latest fashion, and immaculately dressed. But her grey eyes were hard and cold as she looked Kathy up and down, a sneer turning down the corners of her mouth. 'It's unusual for Mr Kendall to employ someone without consulting his head of department.' She gave a small sniff of disapproval both for his action and for the girl standing nervously before her. 'Still, he's the boss.'

'Miss Burton is here on trial for a month,' Miss Foster, an older, more kindly woman, put in. 'She has no experience, but Mr Kendall sees that as an advantage. You can train her to your ways, Miss Curtis.'

Muriel Curtis's eyes widened and she turned towards the secretary. 'No experience? None at all?' She tutted with disapproval and murmured, 'Whatever is he thinking of?' As her glance flickered back towards Kathy, there was a shrewd, knowing look in her eyes. 'Ah,' she said softly. 'Another of his fancy pieces, is she?'

'Really, Miss Curtis,' Emily Foster hissed angrily and, taking hold of the woman's arm, she pulled Muriel a short distance away. But Kathy's sharp ears still heard the rest of their conversation. 'That is a most inappropriate remark. And, for your information, he had not seen the girl before today.'

Muriel's smile was humourless. 'Oh really!' Kathy felt the woman's resentful gaze rest on her again. Grudgingly, she added, 'But with a pretty face like hers, one look would be enough.'

'Jealousy will get you nowhere, Muriel.' Emily's tone had softened and Kathy could detect a note of pity in it. Though her voice dropped even lower, she still heard enough of their conversation to understand. 'Forget about him ... He's not worth it ... not the first ... won't be the last.'

Muriel's whispered reply was even softer. 'It wasn't his fault ... it was *her*.'

Kathy tried to glance away, to make out she could not hear what was being said, but her gaze was held by the sight of Muriel's sudden and obvious distress. For a brief moment, the young woman's face crumpled and she seemed about to burst into tears. But then, with a supreme effort, Muriel pulled in a deep breath, straightened her back and lifted her head. 'You're quite right, Miss Foster,' she said raising her voice deliberately. Obviously, she now intended Kathy to hear. 'Any girl who gets involved with him had better watch out.'

Emily Foster patted Muriel's arm and then turned back to Kathy. 'I'll leave you with Miss Curtis. Perhaps she can begin your instruction today, if she has time. We shall expect you here by eight forty-five in the morning to start work. Good afternoon.' She nodded and began to walk away.

'G-good afternoon, Miss Foster, and – thank you,' Kathy said, her nervousness making her stammer and blush like a gawky schoolgirl.

As the woman walked away, Muriel Curtis said frostily, 'I really haven't time to show you around today. Just mind you're here on time in the morning.' Her tone implied she thought it a waste of her time anyway with a young girl of absolutely no experience.

Kathy forced a polite smile. 'I will, Miss Curtis. Thank you.'

She turned and left the millinery department, walked down the wide staircase, passed through the ground floor and out into the street, straight into the blustery cold wind. Kathy shivered. Jemima's costume might be very smart, but it didn't keep her warm. For a moment, she thought longingly of the heavy raincoat and boots she wore about the farm. But the moment was brief and banished with a laugh as she revelled, yet again, in her newfound freedom.

Briskly, she walked from the city centre to the terraced house that would be her home for the next few weeks.

The following morning passed in a mesmerizing whirl, so that by lunchtime Kathy felt as if her head was spinning.

'We stagger the lunchtime period,' Muriel told her. All morning, her sharp voice had issued orders, explained the work expected crisply and watched Kathy's every move with her disapproving grey eyes. If Kathy had not seen for herself the woman's brief lapse, she would have believed that Muriel Curtis had a heart of stone. But the picture in her mind's eye of the crumpled face, close to tears, prevented the younger girl from disliking the woman on sight. 'Are you listening to me, Miss Burton?' Muriel's voice penetrated Kathy's wandering thoughts.

Kathy jumped. 'Oh – I – I'm sorry, Miss Curtis.'

'As I was saying—' Muriel's voice was frosty. 'We stagger the lunchtime period so that there are always two in the department. As there are only three of us, we can only take three-quarters of an hour each.' She looked at her watch and then glanced around her. 'It's only eleven forty-five, but we're quiet at the moment, so if you'd like to take your lunch now, I'll hold the fort while Miss Matthews shows you where the staff restroom is. And then later, when it goes quiet about four o'clock, she can take you on a tour of the store. It's important you know your way around and to be able to direct customers too.'

'Thank you, Miss Curtis,' Kathy said with unaccustomed meekness.

Away from the head of department's eagle eye, Stella chattered incessantly. 'I'm so glad you've come . . .' She was small, with mousy straight hair and hazel eyes. But her round face was continually wreathed in smiles – even when Miss Curtis found reason to reprimand her, which seemed often. 'There's only been the two of us for four weeks now. The other girl left and though Miss Curtis isn't a bad old stick really, it's been so hard not to have someone of my own age to gossip with.' She giggled – a delicious, infectious sound. 'Not that we're supposed to, of course, but you know how it is.'

Kathy smiled and nodded, but she didn't know. She'd never had anyone to chatter to, only Amy. And she'd only been able to do that once or twice a week. Her father had seen to that!

'How old are you? I'm seventeen. Just. I've been here ever since I left school . . .' The young girl prattled on, scarcely giving Kathy chance to reply. But she didn't mind. Stella was sociable and Kathy soaked up her friendliness like a flower devoid of rain. 'This is the restroom where we eat our lunch. Have you brought anything to eat?'

'Yes, some sandwiches.'

'I expect Miss Robinson told you we all bring our own food, did she?'

Kathy nodded. She wasn't quite sure how much Jemima wanted her connection to Kathy to be known among the rest of the staff. It seemed, however, that the store grapevine had already been busy.

'You're lucky to have been recommended by Miss Robinson, you know. I don't think Mr Kendall would dare *not* take you on.'

Kathy didn't know whether to feel grateful or mortified that she had got the job more because of Jemima Robinson's say-so than because of her own merit. She sighed. This was a whole new world. Things were very different from what she had been used to. But it was the sort of world she had craved and she'd better get used to it.

One thing she knew for sure, there was no turning back. She couldn't bear to think how her father would crow if she failed. Oh no, no matter whatever happened there was no going back.

The afternoon flew by and, before Kathy realized it, it was four o'clock.

'Now, Miss Matthews may take you on a tour of the store . . .' Muriel Curtis began, but at that moment a deep voice spoke behind her.

'That won't be necessary, Miss Curtis, thank you.'

They turned to see Tony Kendall striding towards them. He glanced briefly at Muriel but then turned towards Kathy with a beaming smile that crinkled his eyes and showed perfectly white, even teeth. 'And how is she shaping up, Miss Curtis?' As he spoke, his glance ran up and down Kathy as if implying: She shapes up very well in my eyes.

There was the slightest of pauses before Muriel replied stiffly, 'Reasonably well, Mr Kendall, considering . . .'

'Good, good,' he said, rubbing his hands together. 'I thought I'd come and show you around the store

47

myself.' At last he turned towards the head of the millinery department. 'If you have no objection, of course, Miss Curtis.' The words were courteous, but even to Kathy's naïve ears his statement left the woman with no alternative but to say through tight lips, 'Of course not, Mr Kendall.'

He smiled again as he put out his arm as if to usher Kathy forward. The girl bit her lip and glanced anxiously at Miss Curtis, an unspoken question in her eyes. She didn't want to upset this woman. She would have to work with her – *under* her. Miss Curtis had it in her power to make life very uncomfortable for the younger girls in her charge. Even Stella looked down in the mouth. Obviously she'd looked forward to showing Kathy around the store.

'Come along, Miss Burton,' Tony Kendall ordered, and Kathy was relieved to see Miss Curtis give her a slight nod.

For the next half an hour Kathy followed the manager around the large store, through ladies' apparel, haberdashery, footwear, men's and boys' wear and then up the elegant staircase to carpets, household furnishings, linens and fabrics . . . The store seemed to sell anything and everything. On and on it went, until Kathy's head ached trying to remember where each department was situated.

'And now,' he beamed down at her as they arrived back at his office on the top floor, 'we'll end the day with a cup of tea in my office. I like to make all the newcomers feel welcome and that they can turn to me with any problem at any time. Please, come in.'

He opened the door into the outer office where Miss Foster was still typing, her nimble fingers flying over the keys.

'Would you get us tea, Miss Foster, please?' he asked.

The woman stopped her work at once and glanced up. For a moment, she stared at Kathy and then glanced at her boss. 'Of course, Mr Kendall,' she murmured and rose to her feet, frowning slightly.

Tony Kendall had moved towards his own office and opened the door, holding it for Kathy to enter.

With a strange feeling of trepidation that she could not understand, Kathy stepped ahead of him into his room.

'Did you enjoy being shown round by "sir"?' Stella's greeting when Kathy returned to the millinery department was distinctly cold. Gone was the easy chatter there had been before Mr Kendall had arrived on the scene.

Carefully, Kathy said, 'It was all right. But I'd much sooner you'd've shown me round. My head's aching with trying to remember where everywhere is. I'd've felt more comfortable with you. I could've asked you when I wasn't sure, but – but I daren't refuse to go with him. I'm sorry.'

Stella stared at her for a moment and then the merry smile was back on her face. She touched Kathy's arm. 'No – no, of course you couldn't. It's just that I was really looking forward to showing you round.'

Kathy nodded. 'Me too.'

Stella leaned closer. 'Miss Curtis isn't too pleased, either. She gets all huffy when he interferes with the running of her department. She's been here longer than him *and* she's older. Not much, of course. Mind you, when he first came here I think she fancied her chances with him. There were rumours . . .' Stella was chattering happily again, her brief moment of umbrage completely forgotten. She nudged Kathy and winked. 'Know what I mean?'

Kathy smiled, but said nothing.

The girl seemed about to confide more but instead she muttered suddenly, 'Look out! The dragon's here.'

Kathy glanced over her shoulder to see Jemima walking towards them, pausing every few moments as her glance ran over a display. Her sharp eyes missed nothing, from the tidiness of the counter to a thin film of dust on a shelf.

From nowhere, it seemed to Kathy, Miss Curtis appeared silently and fell into step beside her superior. A short distance from the girls, the two women stopped and turned to face each other. 'Has Miss Burton had a tour of the store yet?'

'Oh yes.' Miss Curtis's mouth tightened. 'She certainly has.' As Jemima's eyebrows rose in a question, Muriel added sarcastically, 'Mr Kendall showed her around himself.'

'Did he indeed?' There was no mistaking the disapproval in Jemima's tone and she added softly, 'Mm. Well, we'll have to see about that, won't we, Muriel?'

The other woman shrugged. 'But what can we do? You know what he's like.'

'I do,' Jemima sniffed. 'But this particular girl is staying with me for a while. Just until she gets on her feet. Maybe I can . . .' Now her voice dropped so low that even Kathy's acute hearing could not catch the rest of the conversation.

*

'So,' Jemima began as they walked home together after the store had closed. 'Do you think you'll like working with us?'

'Oh yes, yes I do. But – but there's a lot to learn.'

Jemima chuckled. 'I suppose there is. I've worked there so long, I suppose I don't see how it must be for someone just starting. Especially someone who's lived out in the sticks.'

Kathy smiled to herself. Jemima certainly didn't mince her words.

'I just hope I will suit. Miss Curtis seems a bit fearsome.'

'Oh, we all are,' Jemima said cheerfully. 'We don't tolerate slackness or slovenliness or idleness in any way, shape or form.'

Kathy was silent.

'But,' the older woman went on, her tone softening just a little, 'the main thing to remember is that the customer always – *always* – comes first and foremost. I know there's the saying "the customer's always right". Well, of course they're not, but you have to act as if they are. In short, my dear – it sounds a funny thing to say – but you have to let the customer walk all over you and still come up smiling.'

'Well, I should be good at that then,' Kathy remarked dryly. 'I've had plenty of practice at doing what I'm told.'

'Mm,' Jemima said as they arrived at the passageway between her home and the next-door house. They walked down it in single file. As they came to the door at the end of the passage leading into Jemima's back yard, she put her hand on the latch and turned to glance back at Kathy. 'Maybe so, but you've

51

kicked over the traces now, haven't you? Well and truly.'

Without waiting for any reply, Jemima opened the door and, in a soft and tender tone, began to call, 'Taffy, where are you? Come to Mummy, Taffy.'

Six

With her first week's wages, Kathy bought herself a smart suit to wear for work. At least, she paid for part of it. Staff were allowed to have an account and, although she was only very newly appointed and still on trial, because she was Miss Robinson's' protégée, the rules had been relaxed.

'I'll need your help, Stella,' she said. 'You'll have to tell me what's suitable.'

As the doors closed on the Saturday evening, both girls approached Miss Curtis to ask if Kathy might be allowed to try on the two or three suits that Stella had picked out for her during quiet moments in the department.

Kathy felt Muriel's scrutiny. The woman's face was expressionless and Kathy couldn't guess what her superior was thinking. She would have been amazed – and dismayed – to know that the overriding emotion that Muriel was feeling at that moment was one of jealousy.

Kathy was quite unaware of her own natural beauty. With her lightly tanned, smooth complexion and well-proportioned features she was more than just 'pretty'. Perhaps the only thing that spoiled the classic beauty was the rather square, firm chin. Her blonde hair had now been styled into the fashion of the day – swept back from her face in pincurls and falling in a shining

53

cascade of waves and curls to her shoulders. With the addition of a smart new suit and a few lessons in the art of applying subtle make-up, Kathy would be more than eye-catching. She would outshine all the other women and girls on the whole of the first floor. Muriel struggled with her feelings, quashing the natural instinct of the envy that one woman feels towards another, younger, prettier girl, and tried to decide whether the girl's looks would be an asset to the department or otherwise. Would her customers, striving for beauty themselves, be encouraged or disheartened by the loveliness of the sales assistant?

It was a question Muriel could not answer, and only time would tell.

Now, she plastered a smile on her face and tried to make her tone friendly. 'Of course. And though you wouldn't ordinarily be allowed staff discount yet, I'll see what I can do for you. Ask Miss Jenkins if you can look at the items in the stockroom. We had a big sale in January because of stock reduction and obviously there are always some items that don't sell even then. Not that I'm suggesting you should take anything you don't like,' Muriel added hastily, 'but it might be worth a look.'

'Thank you, Miss Curtis,' Kathy murmured, touched by the woman's sudden understanding and kindness.

Muriel was looking down at Kathy's feet.

'Er . . .' she began hesitantly, but Kathy, making it easier for her, said quickly, 'Yes, and I'll be needing some new shoes too, though I don't know if I can afford them this week. I must pay my way at Aunt . . . at Miss Robinson's.'

'Of course,' Muriel said swiftly. 'I'll have a word with my colleague in footwear. I'm sure something can be arranged.'

'I'm sure if you asked Mr Kendall, he'd let you have a pair on tick for a week,' Stella put in. Her face was innocent, but Kathy was sure she caught a wicked gleam in the young girl's eyes.

The smile disappeared from Muriel's face as she said tartly now, 'You'd better be quick trying on those suits. The store will be locked up in thirty minutes. Unless, of course, you want to spend the night here.' And with that last sarcastic barb, she turned away.

Kathy stared after her. 'Why did she say that?'

Stella was giggling. 'I think she was insinuating that you might want to get locked in on purpose. Mr Kendall is the only one who can get back into the store once it's been locked up for the night and the night-watchman's on duty.'

Kathy blinked. 'But why—?'

'I expect she thinks you're after him.'

Colour suffused Kathy's face. 'After him? Mr Kendall? Oh, surely she doesn't think that. She can't!'

'Why ever not? You're pretty and Mr Kendall likes a pretty face.'

Kathy was horrified. This job was going to be difficult enough to learn without her superior thinking she was setting her cap at the store's manager. 'But I'm not, I mean, I . . .' Then she groaned and closed her eyes. 'How can she even think such a thing?'

'Jealousy's a funny thing,' Stella said. Though she was younger than Kathy, Stella had a streetwise knowledge that the country girl had yet to acquire. 'And he's not helped. He's never even noticed me. He didn't take *me* round the store when I started here, so you'd better watch it, because I think – even if you're not interested in him – that he's got his eye on you.'

'Oh, crumbs!' Kathy muttered and her blush deepened.

Stella laughed. 'Don't look so woebegone. Just keep out of his way and do your best to butter up Miss Curtis. Now, come on, we'd better get these suits tried on else we really will get locked in.'

'Very nice, dear. Very suitable. You've got good taste. It must come naturally because I'm sure you've never had the chance to buy any smart clothes for yourself before.' Jemima, as ever, was blunt, and at her mention of the girl's former life Kathy wondered what on earth her father would say if he could see her now, dressed in the tailored black suit with a crisp, white blouse beneath it. And he would be outraged at the elegant court shoes in place of her muddy wellingtons. But Amy . . .

Jemima interrupted her wandering thoughts. 'But it will certainly be an asset if you choose to continue working at the store.'

Kathy smiled weakly. Did she really have any choice? Certainly not at the moment. She was honest enough to acknowledge that she had only been given a trial because of Jemima Robinson. Without her support and recommendation, there would have been no job. But she felt impelled to say, 'Stella picked the suits out as being right to wear for work, Miss Robinson, not me. I – I'm sorry.'

Jemima smiled. 'No matter. I like your truthfulness.

56

That goes a long way with me, my girl. I don't like being lied to. Now, we should think about supper . . .'

Over the meal, Kathy tried to broach the subject of Mr Kendall. 'He seems nice,' she began tentatively, but was shocked by Jemima's swift glance and the pursing of her lips. 'Oh, he is,' the older woman remarked dryly. 'Very nice.' Then she murmured, 'Too nice, sometimes.'

Kathy's sharp hearing had heard her words. 'What do you mean? "Too nice"? How can anyone be "too nice"?'

'He should remember his position. It doesn't do for a store manager to be too familiar with his staff. Especially with the young women. It puts ideas into their silly heads. It doesn't do at all.' She sighed. 'But I suppose he's only young himself. He's certainly very young to be in such a high position, but then I understand his mother . . .' For some strange reason Kathy was sure that Jemima's voice hardened as she mentioned Mr Kendall's mother. 'Pulled a few strings. She's well connected.'

'Oh? Is Mr Kendall from a wealthy family then?'

Jemima gave a wry laugh. 'Not really, his mother . . .' Jemima stopped abruptly. 'Dear me! What am I thinking of? Gossiping about my employers like this. I *never* do that. You're a witch, young Kathy, to loosen my tongue so. Dear me. This will never do,' she tutted primly.

Kathy was disappointed. She'd hoped to learn quite a lot about the people she was to work with, but Jemima was pursing her lips as if to stop any further indiscretions escaping them. She tried one last time. 'I just wondered if there was anything between him and Miss Curtis. She—'

'Whatever gave you that idea? Oh, I see . . .' Jemima added, answering her own question before giving Kathy time to say a word. 'Stella.'

'No,' Kathy burst out, anxious that she should not get the young girl into trouble. 'No, it wasn't Stella. It was – well, I saw Miss Foster and Miss Curtis talking and – and she seemed, well – upset.'

Jemima eyed her. 'Kathy, my dear, let me give you a word of advice and you'd do well to heed it. You young girls should learn to keep your eyes and ears open, but your mouths very firmly closed. Whatever you hear in the course of your work either about other members of staff or about customers, you should keep to yourself. It doesn't do to gossip, it really doesn't.'

With that Jemima stood up and began to clear the table, crashing the plates together with swift angry movements.

Kathy bowed her head, dismayed that she had angered the woman who was being so kind to her. She said no more, silently vowing never to raise such a topic of conversation with Jemima again. But in truth the older woman's very reticence had awoken a curiosity in Kathy.

There was some mystery about the handsome Mr Kendall and Miss Curtis, and Kathy was determined to find out what it was.

Seven

Almost three weeks after Kathy's arrival in Lincoln, Amy came to stay for the weekend, arriving on Friday evening when Kathy and Jemima got home from work. Taffy, ears flattened, fled the kitchen with a loud rattle of his cat-flap and retired to the washhouse at the bottom of the yard in a huff. All of a sudden there were too many people invading his domain!

'What fun we'll have!' Amy trilled, hugging her friend.

'That's as may be,' Jemima put in tartly. 'You may be on holiday, but Kathy has a job of work to do. And I don't want her appearing in the department bleary-eyed and looking like something the cat's dragged in.' She paused and looked about her. 'And talking of cats, where's Taffy?'

The two girls glanced at each other and stifled their laughter.

'I – I think he went out,' Kathy said, keeping her face straight with a supreme effort and vowing at the same time to make a big fuss of the animal the moment Amy left.

'Too many people about for his liking,' Jemima murmured, and the two girls were left in no doubt that she shared her pet's opinion.

'We'll go to the pictures tomorrow night,' Amy said. 'I'll have a look what's on when I go into town in the morning while you're at work.'

'It'll be in the *Echo*,' Jemima remarked. She reached down at the side of her chair and held out the local evening paper.

'What time do you finish work, Kathy?' Amy asked, scanning the pages for the advertisement or a review of the city's weekend entertainment.

'Seven on a Friday and Saturday.'

Amy pulled a face but forbore to make any comment in front of her aunt.

'Ah, here we are.' There was a slight pause, then she smiled. 'We're all right. The performance at the Regal is continuous from two o'clock until eleven, so we can just go in when you're ready and see the programme round.'

'What's on?'

'*The Texans* with Randolph Scott and *Trouble in Panama*.'

'That first one sounds like a cowboy picture,' Jemima murmured.

'Oh, I say!' Amy squeaked with delight. 'Tyrone Power's at the Central. He's dishy! Oh, do let's go and see him, Kathy. Please?'

Kathy smiled at her friend's girlish excitement. 'Whatever you want. I've only ever been to the pictures once before, so I really don't mind what I see. What film is it?'

'*Marie Antoinette* with Norma Shearer. It says it's a "spectacular drama of a scandal that rocked the world".'

'She gets her head chopped off in the end, doesn't she? Very cheerful, I must say.'

'But Kathy – Tyrone Power!'

'All right, all right,' Kathy laughed and held out her

hands in submission. 'We'll go. Is it a continuous performance like the other one?'

'Er – not sure, but I expect they'll all be the same, won't they?'

'Well, we'll give it a try.'

'And if we go tomorrow night, we can have a lie in on Sunday morning . . .'

'Oh no, you can't,' her aunt said. 'You'll be up to come to morning service in the cathedral with me.'

Amy's jaw dropped. 'The cathedral? You go to church at the *cathedral*?'

'Of course. Why ever not?' Jemima said.

Amy turned wide eyes on Kathy. 'Have you been?'

She nodded. 'Yes. Last week.'

'I go every week,' Jemima put in primly. 'If not to the cathedral, then to St Mary's. Anyone who stays with me is expected to accompany me. And tomorrow it's the cathedral.'

'And did they hear you sing?' Amy asked.

'Well . . .' Kathy hesitated, the colour rising in her face. 'I just sang along with the rest of the congregation.'

'You mean they didn't ask you to be in the choir?' Now Amy was teasing, but Jemima took her words seriously.

'Oh, you can't get into the cathedral choir as easily as that . . .'

Amy laughed. 'I know, Aunt Jemima. I was teasing Kathy. But she's got an amazing voice. Haven't you heard her?'

'Well, she was standing next to me and I heard her singing – of course I did – but it was nothing special.'

They were talking about Kathy as if she was not sitting there getting more embarrassed by the minute.

'Then she was obviously singing softly deliberately. You should hear her when she really lets rip.'

The corner of Jemima's mouth twitched with barely suppressed amusement. 'Then, my dear, this week,' she said, her eyes twinkling mischievously at Kathy, 'you'd better let it rip.'

As soon as they were alone in the bedroom, Kathy asked, 'Have you heard anything about my mother? Do you know if – if she's all right?'

'Dad went to Thorpe Farm the day you left and saw them both.'

Kathy pulled in a deep breath and held it, fearing what Amy might say next. But her friend was smiling. 'Your mam's fine. Dad said that your dad was furious when he realized what you'd done. He ranted and raved and carried on alarming, but all your mam did was smile and nod. As far as she's concerned, Kathy, you've done the right thing. There was no mistake about that. My dad said.'

Little by little, Kathy let out her breath, but her anxiety was not yet gone completely. 'And since? Has your dad been over since then?'

Amy nodded. 'Oh yes. He goes every other day or so. I heard him telling Mam that he's going to keep an eye on your mam. And your dad too, if it comes to that. He knows what he's like all right and he can't forgive him for the way he's treated your mam and you but, like he says, they've been neighbours all their lives and he'll not see him stuck. He'll let Morry go and help out if he sees your dad struggling with the work.'

Now Kathy let out the last of her breath in relief. She hugged Amy. 'Tell him "thanks", won't you? And ask him to give my love to my mam and tell her I'm fine.'

'Course I will.'

'I've never seen you clock-watching before,' Stella said at ten minutes to seven when she had seen Kathy glancing at the clock on the wall for the umpteenth time. 'Got a date, have you?'

Kathy laughed. 'Not really. My friend's come to stay for the weekend and we're going to the pictures tonight. She's meeting me outside when the store closes.'

Stella sighed. 'Lucky you! My dad's very strict. He won't let me go to the pictures on my own. Says it isn't "seemly".'

'Don't you have any friends to go with?'

The girl shrugged. 'How can I make friends with anyone if I don't go out? The only people I ever meet are at work.'

'Well, come with us tonight.'

Stella stared at her for a moment. 'Do you mean it?'

'Of course I mean it.'

'But – but you're going with your friend . . .'

'Amy won't mind.'

For a brief second the young girl's eyes lit up with pleasure at the anticipation of the unexpected treat. Then the joy in her face died. 'I can't. I'd have to ask my dad first.'

'Yes, I see,' Kathy said sympathetically. She knew, if anyone did, about a strict home life.

'Perhaps we could go another time. Just you and

me – when you've had a chance to ask your dad first, eh?'

Stella nodded and smiled again. 'Ooh yes, that'd be lovely. Thanks, Kathy, I'd really like that.'

As all the staff trooped out of the store, Mr Kendall was waiting by the main exit.

'Good night, ladies. Miss Robinson, good night. Ah, Miss Burton . . .' He put out his hand to draw her to one side. 'Could you spare me a moment?'

Kathy bit her lip. Amy would be waiting outside in the cold for her, but she smiled and stepped to one side. She saw Jemima glance back and raise her eyebrows but then she turned and walked on and out through the door.

'Good *night*, Mr Kendall,' Miss Curtis said pointedly a moment later as she passed by.

'Miss Curtis,' Mr Kendall murmured without looking at her, but he waited until Kathy's superior had got through the door and out into the street. Kathy watched her go and saw her glance back as the door closed behind her. The look on the other woman's face shocked the girl. It was hatred.

She was so shocked that it took her a few moments to gather her wits and to concentrate on what Mr Kendall was saying to her.

'I just wanted to tell you, Miss Burton, how very pleased I am with your progress. Better than I could possibly have hoped, and rather than keep you wondering for a further two weeks, I'd like you to know that I'm happy to confirm you appointment as permanent.'

'Oh!' Kathy blushed. 'Thank you very much, Mr Kendall.'

'Good night, Mr Kendall.' Another member of staff

passed by and the store manager smiled briefly and nodded 'good night'.

'And now that you're a permanent member of the staff here,' he went on. 'I was wondering if you would have dinner with me one evening.'

Kathy's eyes widened. 'Dinner? With – with you?'

He smiled and tiny lines around his dark brown eyes crinkled and then he adopted a hangdog look. 'You don't want to?'

'Oh yes, I mean, I don't know if I should. I mean – is it – well – allowed?' she stammered, completely at a loss to know what to say.

Of course she'd love to go out with this handsome, debonair man, but for some reason she could not explain, she had the uncomfortable feeling that Jemima Robinson would not approve.

Now he threw back his head and laughed aloud, and the last few stragglers leaving the store glanced at him in surprise. To her discomfort, Kathy saw two of the women from the ground floor, their heads close together, whispering to each other as they went out.

'That's one advantage of being the boss,' Tony Kendall said. 'There are only the store owners who might object and I don't think either of them will.' When she still said nothing, he added, 'So – would you like to go out with me?'

Suddenly there was something endearing about the little-boy hesitancy in his tone, as if he really feared she might refuse. Now Kathy felt shy too. It was the first time, the very first time that any man – apart from Morry, and he didn't count – had asked her out.

'I'd love to,' she said softly. 'If you're sure it would be all right.'

'Of course I'm sure, but perhaps – ' he touched her arm – 'it would be better to keep this our secret, eh?'

'Yes – er – yes, all right.'

'Then how about next Saturday night?'

'Yes, thank you,' she stammered. 'That – that would be lovely.'

'I'll book a table and let you know where to meet me. I'd offer to pick you up in my car, but you're still lodging with Miss Robinson, aren't you?'

Kathy nodded.

'Then I think it best we meet in town. All right?'

Again, she nodded and then found herself being ushered from the store, her head in a whirl.

As she stepped out on to the wet pavement, Amy hurried forward out of the shadows. 'There you are! I thought you'd got lost. Or had to stay behind in detention. Been a naughty girl, have you?' She linked her arm through Kathy's, not noticing how quiet her friend seemed. 'Come on, we'll have to hurry if we don't want to miss some of the programme. And I want to see every second of the gorgeous Tyrone . . .'

Kathy walked along the dark street. Her thoughts in a dream world, she scarcely heard Amy's ceaseless chatter.

Mr Kendall – Tony – had asked her to go out with him.

Eight

'So, did you enjoy the cinema last night?' Jemima enquired as they trudged up Steep Hill towards the cathedral the following morning.

'It was great,' Amy enthused, 'but Kathy seemed lost in a little world of her own.' She laughed. 'I think she must have fallen in love with Tyrone. Mind you,' she sighed ecstatically, 'can't say I blame her.'

Kathy smiled but said nothing. The truth was that the handsome and dashing Tyrone Power had reminded her very much of Tony Kendall. He had the same dark hair and eyes, the same handsome face and that smile! Oh, his heartbreaking smile was just the same . . .

'Dear me, I'll have to stop for a moment.' Jemima interrupted Kathy's daydreams and brought her back down to earth. 'I'm sure this hill gets steeper every week.'

All three of them paused for Jemima to catch her breath and Kathy looked about her. On either side of the steep, uneven road, quaint old buildings huddled together: dusty second-hand bookshops, crowded antique shops and artists' galleries. There were little tea-rooms too, enticing the weary walker struggling up the hill to step inside the old-world interior and seek refreshment. There was even a grocer and a greengrocer to serve the people living nearby. What a blessing, Kathy mused, not to have to go up and down the hill every time you ran out of sugar! Even though the establishments were all closed, Kathy peeked into every window until Jemima said, 'Do come along, Kathy. We shall be late.'

At the top of the hill they came to a square with the cathedral to the right and the castle to the left. Kathy cast a longing glance towards the round tower of the castle.

'Another time, Kathy,' Jemima said, reading her thoughts.

As they stepped through the huge doors and into the cathedral, Kathy caught her breath. Although it was the second time she had attended a service, she was struck afresh by the magnificence. She walked to her place in the congregation in a trance, drinking in the sight of the huge pillars supporting the vast ceiling. In front of her she saw the intricately carved dark wood of the choir.

'It's so beautiful,' she breathed and even Amy, seeing it all for the first time, was bereft of words, quite lost in wonder.

As the opening hymn began, Kathy let her pure, clear voice soar into the vastness.

For a few moments, caught up in the joy of singing, she even forgot about Tony Kendall.

As they emerged into the pale March sunlight after the service, Jemima said, 'Well, Amy, you were right about one thing. Kathy certainly has a beautiful voice.'

'She ought to be on the stage.'

'Oh now, I don't think that would be very suitable. Dear me, no, but I think there is a choral society in the city that she might be able to join. Would you like that, Kathy?' There was a pause before she prompted, 'Kathy?'

'I'm sorry. I was miles away. What did you say?'

'See?' Amy said. 'I told you. She's in a dream world. It must be love.'

Kathy felt Jemima's shrewd eyes upon her. 'Dear me, I do hope not,' she murmured, and Kathy felt a shudder of fear. What would Miss Robinson say if she knew that in only six days' time she, Kathy, would be having dinner with the manager of the department store?

'I said,' Jemima repeated, 'that I believe there's a choral society you might be able to join if you enjoy singing. I believe Mr Spencer next door is a member. I could ask him, if you like.'

Kathy thought quickly. If she joined some reputable society, maybe Jemima wouldn't question where she was going at nights. And if Tony Kendall were to ask her out again . . .

'Thank you, that would be lovely. I hadn't realized until today how much I missed singing.'

'Miss Burton, this is the third time today that I've had to reprimand you. Your mind really isn't on your work. Remember you are still on a month's trial. You must try harder or I shall be forced to recommend to Mr Kendall that you are not suitable for the position here.'

Kathy opened her mouth to retort that she'd already been told her appointment had been made permanent, but then she bit her tongue and instead said contritely, 'I'm so sorry, Miss Curtis.'

For the rest of the day Kathy tried hard to banish all thoughts of the handsome young manager. She didn't want to risk losing this job, for several reasons. But top of her list was now one that she was sure would not have pleased either Miss Curtis – or Miss Robinson.

The week seemed to drag, but at last Saturday arrived. As the store closed, Kathy was eager to get home to wash and to brush her hair, then hurry back to the hotel restaurant on the High Street to meet Tony. But Jemima walked her usual, steady pace and Kathy was forced to match her step.

'And with whom are you going to the cinema tonight?' asked Miss Robinson. Her grammar and her diction were always perfect. No trace of the Lincolnshire dialect that must once have been strong in her speech – like her brother's still was – remained. Kathy wondered fleetingly if she had ever taken elocution lessons.

'With – with a friend.'

'A friend? And who might that be? I didn't know you had any friends in the city.'

Kathy ran her tongue around dry lips. This was getting to be like home. Questions, questions, questions! But she answered Jemima politely. She needed to stay here just a little while longer, although she vowed silently to start looking for a place of her own the very next week. As soon as she could afford it, she'd be out of here, she promised herself.

'Stella.'

'Stella Matthews?'

Kathy nodded, regretting the deliberate lie immediately. She was normally a truthful girl. Chin high, she would stand up straight and tell the truth whatever that might be and however it might rebound on her. But this was different. She just couldn't take the risk. Miss Robinson had the power not only to make her homeless but also to get her dismissed instantly from her employment. Mr Kendall might say he had made her position permanent, but he was not the only one with the power to dismiss her and – even if he overrode such a decision – life could, and would, be made very uncomfortable for her by those with whom she worked. Miss Curtis, for one.

No, for once in her life, Kathy could not be truthful. But lying did not sit well with her. And now she would have to involve Stella in covering up for her too. She wondered if she could rely on the younger girl. Kathy swallowed and then opened her mouth to retract her statement and tell the truth. But the words remained frozen on her lips. Just this one time, she thought. I'll see how it goes. If this is just a one off, then it won't matter. But if he should ask me again, then . . . At this moment she didn't know exactly what she would do if Mr Kendall should ask her to go out with him again. Her heart lurched with excitement at the mere thought.

He was waiting outside the restaurant as they had arranged.

'You look lovely,' he smiled, tactfully making no remark that she was still wearing the suit that she wore every day for work.

As they entered the restaurant, Kathy felt awkward and out of place among all the diners dressed in evening clothes, the men in black suits and the women in silks and satins. Heads turned as they were ushered to their table by the head waiter and Kathy blushed in embarrassment.

When they were handed a menu each, Kathy was appalled to find that it was all written in French.

Tony leaned across the small table. 'Would you like me to order for you?'

'Yes, please,' she breathed thankfully.

'Is there anything you don't like?'

Kathy giggled nervously and shook her head. She'd never been asked such a question in the whole of her life. Choice had never been an option at home. She'd always had to eat whatever was put in front of her.

When the waiter had taken their order and moved away, she blurted out, 'I had to tell Miss Robinson a lie. I said I was going to the cinema with Stella.'

Tony leaned his elbows on the table and steepled his fingers. He smiled at her. 'Well, don't worry about a little white lie. Besides, is Miss Robinson your jailer? Do you have to tell her everywhere you go?'

'She – she's been very good to me. Taking me in and getting me the job . . .'

'You got the job on your own account. I admit I interviewed you initially on her recommendation, but once I saw you – ' his smile broadened – 'I couldn't resist you.' He reached across the table and took her hand. 'Now, tell me about yourself. I want to know all about you.'

'There's nothing much to tell. I'm just a country mouse come to town and it – it's all very strange in the city.'

'Are you enjoying your job?'

'Oh yes,' she said at once. 'I still make mistakes and Miss Curtis is very strict . . .'

Tony released her hand suddenly and sat back in his chair.

Thinking she had made a serious mistake in criticizing her senior, she said hurriedly. 'She's very good at her job, isn't she? I wish I could be like her one day. She's very smart and beautifully – oh, what's the word – groomed. That's it.'

When he still said nothing, she fell silent. She was babbling, but instead of covering her nervousness it only made her feel more foolish. She should have had the strength – and the sense – to refuse his invitation. She was out of her depth in such surroundings, ignorant of even the simplest rules of etiquette.

Tony cleared his throat and said stiffly, 'Miss Curtis is an excellent employee. She has been with us since leaving school.' His tone was expressionless and he was using words that he might have done in a letter of reference. There was no warmth, no . . .

He leant forward again and smiled, 'But let's not talk about work. I want to talk about you.'

The starter arrived and Kathy waited until she saw which knife, fork or spoon he picked up before she started to eat. And then she suddenly found she wasn't hungry. Butterflies in her stomach made eating impossible, and though she managed a few mouthfuls, her plate was removed with half the food left on it. She felt embarrassed. What would her father have said if he had seen such waste?

The main course arrived and Kathy's heart sank as she saw what seemed to her like a mountain of food placed before her.

'Are you looking for a place of your own?' Tony asked.

'Well, yes, but only looking. I really need to save

some money first . . .' She stopped, unsure whether she should be saying such things to him. She really would have to curb her tongue. She was far too outspoken for her own good sometimes.

'I might be able to help you there. I know one or two people who might have a bed-sitting room, or even a flat. It'd be tiny though, but at least you'd be able to come and go as you pleased and not be subjected to the third degree every time you wanted to go out. Leave it with me. I'll ask around and—'

The head waiter approached the table. 'Excuse me, Mr Kendall.'

So, Kathy thought at once, Tony was well known. The thought crossed her mind – I wonder how many other young women he's brought here? But the waiter was continuing, 'There is a telephone message for you, sir. Would you like to follow me?'

Tony sighed, threw his napkin on to the table and, without a word, rose and followed the man.

Kathy wasn't sure what she should do and besides, she was still having difficulty forcing the food down her throat. So, thankful for the respite, she laid her knife and fork down and waited until he came back.

After a few moments, Tony hurried towards her, a worried frown on his face. He did not sit down again but stood by the table. 'Kathy – I'm dreadfully sorry but I've had bad news. My mother has been taken ill. I'll have to go home at once.'

Kathy half-rose from her chair. 'I'm so sorry. Is there anything I can do?'

His answer was swift. 'No – no, but I must go. Look, you stay and finish your meal. I'll pay as I leave. Can you get home all right?'

'Of course, but I—'

He held out his hand, palm outwards as if to prevent her from making any more offers of help. Again he said, 'I'm really sorry. This is not how I wanted it to be.'

Kathy sank back down into her chair as she saw him approach the head waiter, speak to him briefly and slip something into his hand. The man looked across at her and nodded. As Tony hurried from the restaurant, the waiter approached her table.

'Mr Kendall has asked me to look after you, madam. I'm sorry your evening has been spoilt, but please enjoy the rest of your meal and let me know if there is anything else I can do for you.' He bowed obsequiously.

'Thank you,' Kathy murmured and picked up her knife and fork, pretending to eat. As he moved away, his sharp glance roaming round the rest of the room to check that no one needed him, Kathy glanced down at the food on her plate. She had scarcely touched it, but now, curiously, she found she was ravenously hungry. She tucked into the food as if she hadn't eaten for a week!

When she'd eaten pudding and the waiter had poured her a cup of coffee, she sat back and let her glance roam around the huge room. Elegant ladies and gentleman sat at the other tables. Her envious gaze lingered on the luxurious fabric of the ladies' gowns, their sparkling jewellery and their beautifully coiffured hairstyles. Kathy felt suddenly very much the little country mouse in her dark suit and sensible shoes.

She became aware that a woman at one of the tables on the far side of the room was staring at her and

Kathy dropped her gaze in embarrassment. Nervously, she raised her coffee cup to her lips to finish the drink and leave.

A shadow fell across the table and Kathy looked up to see the woman who had been watching her standing above her. Without being invited, she sat down in the chair opposite. At once the head waiter was at her side.

'Madam—?' he began, but she waved him away.

'I just need a word with my – friend here.'

'Very good, madam.' He bowed his head and then moved away.

Now it was Kathy who was staring. She didn't know her from Adam – or rather, Eve. She bit her lip. Oh dear, was it some customer that she should remember? Had she served her and—?

'My dear, please forgive this intrusion. Perhaps you won't thank me when you hear what I have to say, but I mean it with the very best of intentions.'

Kathy didn't know what to say, so she remained silent.

The woman leaned her elbows on the table and clasped her hands together. 'Tony Kendall. Have you known him long?'

Kathy shook her head saying with careful deliberation, 'No, not long.' Then she could not stop herself asking, 'Why?' She would liked to have added, 'What business is it of yours?' But she still couldn't place the woman, couldn't think if she should recognize her. But for once she held her tongue and let the woman continue.

'You look a nice girl, but – forgive me – rather an innocent one.'

Kathy felt the woman's glance take in her plain

serviceable suit, her home-styled hair, and her face, devoid of any cosmetic enhancement. In stark contrast, the woman sitting opposite her was beautifully made-up, her black hair smooth and shining like a raven's wing. She wore a blue and silver dinner gown and diamonds clustered at her throat. On the fourth finger of her left hand was the biggest sapphire ring that Kathy had ever seen. Not that she had seen many, she thought wryly. But the stranger's beauty and poise left Kathy feeling frumpish and plain.

'What do you know about Tony Kendall?'

Kathy stared at her. She couldn't believe this was happening. All sorts of ridiculous thoughts flitted through Kathy's mind, but nothing made any sense. She glanced across at the table where the woman had been sitting. A man sat alone there now, watching them with an amused smile. Was he the woman's fiancé?

Kathy took a deep breath. Be hanged if she was going to sit here and take this, even if it cost her her new job. A job she really was beginning to enjoy. Her natural feistiness reasserted itself and fleetingly she wondered how she'd become the meek, subservient being she'd been during the last few weeks. Of course, she'd been trying to please Aunt Jemima, trying to hold down a new job and adjust to the strange environment. She'd been trying to please everyone else. Well, it was high time she pleased herself. High time she stopped feeling guilty for keeping her meeting with Tony a secret, as if it were something to be ashamed of. Because it wasn't. She was attracted to Tony Kendall – yes, she had to admit it, she found him irresistible. Contrary to what she knew would be Jemima's advice, indeed everyone's advice at the department store – even against her own better instincts – she'd agreed to come out with him.

And now here was a complete stranger asking questions she'd no right to ask. Kathy had been in danger of cowering before the stranger, subsiding under the woman's scrutiny.

Suddenly, the old Kathy – the Kathy who'd walked out of her home, had come to the big city, determined to start a new life and to stand on her own two feet – was back. She quelled the sudden tremor of apprehension, and now, instead of shrinking, she met the woman's gaze squarely. Slowly she let out the breath she'd been holding and said quietly, keeping her tone respectful, 'What gives you the right to ask me?'

For a moment the woman blinked and then smiled. 'Nothing, my dear, except that I don't want to see a nice young girl taken in by him and hurt like so many others before you.'

Kathy gasped. 'So many others . . . ?' she began.

The woman's wry smile had a tinge of sadness too. 'I'm afraid so. And I should know, because I was one of them.'

Kathy glanced swiftly at the man across the room. He was still watching them.

'But I've been lucky,' the woman went on. 'I've met a wonderful man – a lovely man – who adores me and whom I love very much. But I have to tell you, my dear, that three years ago Tony Kendall broke my heart – and I wasn't the only one. I saw you come in with him and – forgive me – I've been watching you.' She smiled sadly, knowingly. 'The moment I saw the head waiter approach your table, I knew.'

'Knew?' Kathy snapped. 'Knew what?'

'That it was the same old routine.'

'Routine?' Kathy repeated stupidly. 'What d'you mean?'

The woman sighed. 'I think he must have some arrangement with the head waiter. He must give him some sort of signal that he wants to escape. It's his way of ending an affair—'

'Affair? This isn't an affair,' Kathy said impulsively. 'It's only the first time he's asked me out. How can he want to end it now? So soon?'

The stranger's smile was sympathetic. 'My dear, you have a lot to learn about men, I can see. And about Tony Kendall's sort in particular.'

'His – *sort*?'

'He's a philanderer. A heartbreaker. He'll pick you up and drop you just as quickly if he decides you don't – ' she paused and added pointedly – 'suit.'

'You're wrong,' Kathy was stung to retort. 'I know you're wrong. His mother was taken ill. He had to go . . .' Her voice trailed away as the woman's knowing expression didn't change. She sighed as she rose and, looking down at Kathy with what seemed like genuine concern, said softly, 'Like I say – the same old routine.'

Nine

Kathy walked home through the cold, dark streets, her head in a whirl, though not now with the euphoria of falling in love.

But it's too late, she thought. I like him – I really do – and he likes me. I know he does. She's just jealous. That's what it is. She lost him and she can't bear to see him with someone else. And as for all that rubbish about there being countless others – well, Kathy just didn't believe it. And the nonsense about the 'routine' to rid himself of an unwanted girlfriend? She didn't believe that either.

But a niggling thought burrowed its way into her mind. For some unaccountable reason, Miss Curtis's distressed face was before her and the whispered words with Emily Foster were replayed in her mind.

Kathy reached the tiled passageway leading between the two terraced houses and then the gate into the back yard. Before entering the house she visited the privy across the yard. As she came out, she saw Taffy sitting in the centre of the yard, his green eyes catching the pale moonlight and shining through the darkness.

'Hello, boy.' Glad to have a distraction, Kathy bent and stroked the cat's fine head. She knew he slept in the washhouse, where another hole cut in the door allowed him entry and exit whenever he wanted. How wonderful, she thought to have such freedom, and her heart quailed at the questioning she was about to face.

She braced herself mentally as she let herself into the house to find Jemima sitting in her chair by the range, a book in her lap, the wireless on the small table at one side of her playing softly.

Jemima looked up and smiled. 'Hello. Enjoy your evening?'

Evenly, Kathy replied, 'Yes, thank you.' She waited, expecting more questions, but Jemima's eyes went back to her book.

Kathy glanced at the clock and was surprised to see that it was half past ten. Now she understood Jemima's lack of questions. If she'd indeed gone to the cinema with Stella, this was about the time she would have arrived home.

Jemima believed her. She'd no reason to doubt Kathy's word, but instead of being relieved, she felt even guiltier for having lied to the woman who'd been so kind to her.

'Can I get you anything, Aunt Jemima?' she asked, trying to make amends, even though the woman was ignorant of the need for it.

'No, thank you, my dear,' Jemima murmured without raising her head.

'Then – then I'll say goodnight.' As she reached the door leading to the foot of the stairs, Jemima said, 'Oh – I almost forgot. I spoke to my neighbour, Mr Spencer.'

Kathy blinked and racked her brain. Then she remembered. 'Oh, yes. The man who belongs to the choral society.'

'That's right. He said if you sing as prettily as you look, they'd be glad to welcome you to their group.

You're to go along to their meeting on Thursday evening in the school on Monks Road, just beyond the Arboretum.'

'Yes, yes, I know it.' Kathy's was thinking quickly. 'Do they meet every week?'

'No, once a fortnight.'

Kathy smiled and nodded. She hoped that Tony Kendall would ask her out again and if he did, maybe she could suggest a Thursday evening.

Now all she said was, 'Thank you, Aunt Jemima. I'll certainly go along.'

As she climbed the stairs, Kathy hummed softly to herself. Not only would she be able to sing again – something she really enjoyed – but she would also have a cover story when she wanted to meet Tony in secret.

Now all she had to do, she realized, was to get Stella to back up her story about their supposed visit to the cinema together.

'You're a dark horse and no mistake,' Stella teased, her hazel eyes alight with pleasure at the intrigue. 'Hasn't taken you long to find yourself a beau.' She eyed Kathy speculatively. 'Or was it someone you knew before? Is he the reason you came to the city?'

Kathy shook her head. 'No – no. I – I've only met him since I've been here.'

Stella giggled. 'You're a fast worker and no mistake. Is it someone I might know?' She gripped Kathy's arm. 'I bet it's that spotty-faced lad in hardware.'

'No, no. It's no one you know.' More lies. Kathy sighed. But they were necessary ones.

She didn't see Tony Kendall at all until the Wednesday, and by this time she was feeling hurt and humiliated and almost ready to believe what the woman in the restaurant had said about him. He'd not bothered to give her one word of explanation for his hurried departure from the restaurant, leaving her feeling foolish. She so desperately wanted to ask him about the woman who'd spoken to her. Who was she? And were the things she'd said about him true?

Yet how could she ask him such personal questions on the strength of one date? And only half a one at that. Common sense told her to bide her time and wait until he made the first move.

But what had common sense ever had to do with falling in love?

For three days she worried. She tried hard to concentrate on her job and not incur Miss Curtis's wrath. She was very afraid that, at any moment, the well-dressed woman from the restaurant would walk into the department. Whatever would she say to her if she did?

And then there was Aunt Jemima. Every evening she was on tenterhooks in case the woman asked her about the film she'd supposedly seen. But at least Stella had agreed to cover for her. The young girl, who had little social life herself, had been only too pleased to help.

'Tell you what, though,' she'd said. 'We really should go to the pictures now and again. Then it won't be a real lie, will it?'

Kathy had smiled. 'You're on.'

'What about Saturday?'

'Well . . .' Kathy had hesitated.

'Oh, I get it. Lover boy might ask you out again.' Kathy's heart had melted at the sight of Stella's obvious disappointment.

'No, we'll go. Really,' she'd said impulsively, even though she was regretting it immediately. But the pleasure on the young girl's face was her reward. Like Kathy's own home life had been, Stella still lived under the strict rule of her parents and only the assurance that she was out with a girlfriend from work would make them relent and allow her to visit the cinema.

On the Wednesday afternoon, just as they were laying the covers over the counters and the displays, Miss Foster came into the millinery department. 'Excuse me, Miss Curtis. Mr Kendall has asked to see you in his office.'

Kathy glanced up and then looked away quickly, feeling the colour suffuse her face as she saw Miss Curtis follow the manager's secretary. The minutes passed and the time for closing came and went.

'We can't leave till she comes back and says we can go. I hope she's not going to be long. I'll miss my bus.' Stella groaned. 'Oh, I do hope *that's* not all starting up again.'

'What? What do you mean?'

'Her – and him.'

'I don't understand.'

'Miss Curtis and him. Mr Kendall. They used to go out together. I told you before, didn't I?'

Kathy felt as if the breath had been knocked from her body. 'Used to – go – out together?'

'Oh, yes,' Stella said airily, not realizing how her gossip was a devastating blow to her new-found friend.

Kathy swallowed uncomfortably. Perhaps what the woman in the restaurant had said had been the truth. Perhaps, after all, it was not just jealousy that had made her approach Kathy. Perhaps her concern had been genuine. Kathy opened her mouth to probe further, but at that moment Stella's face brightened and Kathy glanced over her shoulder to see Miss Curtis returning. As she walked towards them she glanced around her, checking the counters and the displays. 'Is everything done?'

'Yes, Miss Curtis,' Stella said.

'Then you may go, Miss Matthews, but as for you, Miss Burton . . . Mr Kendall wishes to see you.'

Kathy's heart skipped a beat, but she managed to say calmly, 'Thank you, Miss Curtis. Goodnight.'

'I shan't be leaving until you come back.' The woman's face was expressionless as Kathy turned away and made her way to the manager's office. As she entered the outer office, Miss Foster was covering her black typewriter.

'Go straight in, dear. He's waiting for you.'

Kathy tapped lightly on the door leading into the inner office and went in.

At once Tony rose from behind his desk. 'Ah Miss Burton, do come in.'

As soon as the door was closed behind her, he whispered, 'Has she gone?'

'Who?'

'Miss Foster?'

'I think she's just about to leave. She's tidying her desk.'

He came round the desk and took her hands in his. 'Kathy, I'm so, so sorry about the other night.'

'It's all right,' she said breathlessly, gazing up into his dark brown eyes and feeling as if her legs were going to give way beneath her. 'How – how is your mother?'

He gave a wry smile. 'She's all right. She's an invalid and this sort of thing often happens, I'm sorry to say.

And I'm sorry that I haven't had a chance to explain before today. I've been racking my brains to think of an excuse to send for you.' His smile broadened. 'And then I remembered, I hadn't officially confirmed your appointment. So now I have. I had to send for Miss Curtis to go through the procedure correctly. She says you're proving satisfactory, though she says you seem a little dreamy at times.' He chuckled. 'I couldn't very well tell her that that was probably my fault.' He squeezed her hands and added softly, 'At least, I hope you were thinking of me.'

Guilelessly, Kathy nodded. 'I was.'

They stood gazing at each other before she said, 'I'll have to go. She's waiting for me to get back before she leaves.'

'Oh, damn!' he muttered. 'I thought we might snatch a few moments alone. Look, what about Saturday night? Will you meet me again? We'll go to the cinema. My mother won't be able to get hold of me there.'

'Well, yes, but if she's ill and needs you . . .'

'My father will be at home this week. He works shifts and last week he was working nights. Mother was on her own, but she won't be this weekend. So, what do you say? Please say yes,' he added with that sudden boyish charm that bowled her over.

Forgetting the warning words of the stranger and without a thought of the promise she'd made to Stella, Kathy heard herself saying, 'Yes, of course I will.'

Kathy steeled her heart against the hurt look on Stella's face. 'We'll go next Wednesday instead,' she promised, trying to lessen the disappointment.

Stella shook her head. 'I can't. My dad won't let me go out in the week. Saturday's the only night he might have let me. Says I need my sleep to be fit for work. No gallivanting in the week, as he calls it.' She gave a wry smile. 'Still there's always another week. Unless, of course, lover boy's going to take you out every Saturday night.'

'Well—' Kathy hesitated. She'd been about to promise rashly that she would refuse one week and the two girls would go together, but her romance with Tony was so new and vulnerable. She didn't know how serious he was and she didn't want to give him the impression she wasn't interested in him. Far from it!

Lamely she said, 'If he doesn't ask me every week, we'll certainly go out together.'

'And I suppose I'm still expected to keep all this a secret and cover for you?'

'Do – do you mind?' Kathy pleaded.

Stella regarded her for a moment and then she smiled. 'Only if you promise me one thing. If I ever get a boyfriend, you'll do the same for me.'

Now Kathy could say willingly, 'Of course.'

On Thursday evening, Kathy went to the meeting of the choral society as Jemima had arranged for her. Mr Spencer, who was also the conductor, welcomed her warmly, but she was dismayed to see that most of the members were more Jemima's generation. There was no one of her own age at all.

'We could do with some younger blood,' Mr Spencer confided. 'Now, my dear, if you'd just like to sit there while we get started. We have a break for a cup of tea about half past eight and I'll give you a trial then.' Mr Spencer was short and bald, with tufts of springy hair growing just above his ears. He was very bow-legged and walked with a rolling gait, but his pale blue eyes twinkled merrily from behind the thick lenses of his spectacles. 'It doesn't do to take a family member's recommendation on trust, I'm afraid,' he went on apologetically. 'We once had a young man come. His mother had told me he'd the most marvellous baritone voice. But, oh dear me, the poor lad couldn't sing a note in tune. Not a single note. So you do see, my dear, don't you, why I must try you out?'

'Of course, Mr Spencer,' Kathy murmured. Briefly, she wondered if finding himself among the geriatric membership the young man had sung off key on purpose. For a moment, she was very tempted to follow his example, whether it had been deliberate or not. But as she sat and listened to the choir, she became entranced. Until now, she'd only been able to sing hymns in church and songs from her school days. Now, a whole new repertoire could open up for her. Giving herself up utterly to the soaring music and the beautiful voices, she even forgot about Tony Kendall.

When the group broke up to help themselves to a cup of tea and a biscuit at the far end of the school hall, Mr Spencer approached her. 'Now, my dear, if you'd like to come to the piano . . . ?' He led the way and sat down at the instrument. 'What would you like to sing for me?'

'Er – I only know hymns, Mr Spencer. How about "The day Thou gavest . . ."? It's one of my favourites.'

'Of course, my dear. Now let me see . . .' He picked up a hymn book that contained not only the words but the music too, propped it up on the music stand above the keyboard and began to play.

Kathy's pure, clear voice filled the hall and the tea-drinkers stopped their chatter and began to move down the hall towards the piano. Now it was they who sat and listened. As the hymn came to an end and the music died away, behind Kathy there was a spontaneous round of applause and she blushed.

'Wherever did you find her, Ron?'

Mr Spencer was smiling up at Kathy. 'Can't take the credit, I'm afraid. It was Miss Robinson who recommended her.'

There was a chorus of, 'You will join us, dear, won't you?'

'I'd love to,' Kathy said. At that moment, she could think of nothing she'd like better than to be able to sing to her heart's content every other week. And there were still the church services on Sunday mornings too.

When she arrived home, Jemima wanted to hear all about it and Kathy's enthusiasm was genuine.

'I'm pleased,' Jemima said. 'I'd wondered if you'd find them a little old for you. Still, it's the singing you're going for and you'll still be able to have your nights out with Stella, won't you?'

At once, the shiver of guilt that ran through her spoiled Kathy's delight in the evening.

Tony had asked Kathy to meet him after work on the Saturday evening. She waited in the shelter of the Stonebow's arches, just across the street from the department store, and watched all the staff leave one by one. At last, when everyone else had gone, she saw him come out of the door, locking it carefully behind him. Then, as he crossed the road towards her, she stepped out into the light.

'*There* you are,' Tony said and took her arm. 'Are you all right? You look a little tired. Are they working you too hard?'

Kathy smiled up at him. If she was tired, it was because her nights were disturbed by thoughts of him. 'I'm fine,' she assured him. 'Where are we going?'

'I thought we'd go for a drive in the country instead of going to the cinema.'

'In the dark?'

'We'll call at a nice little pub where no one will know us.'

'Can you be sure of that? There was a woman in the restaurant last week who knew you. She came and spoke to me after you left.'

'Was there?' he said casually. 'Well, an awful lot of people know me. It's the job, you know. Ah, here we are. This is my car.'

At the kerbside stood a dark green open-top car.

'This is very smart,' Kathy said and was rewarded by the beam of delight that spread across his face.

'It's an Alvis Roadster,' he said proudly as he opened the door for her. 'Hop in.'

Kathy wasn't quite sure how to 'hop in' and ended up scrambling into the vehicle in a most undignified and unladylike manner. She giggled as she imagined what Aunt Jemima would say if she could have seen her.

Tony went round the other side and vaulted neatly over the low door and slid down into the seat.

'Now why didn't I think of doing that?' Kathy said and they both laughed.

'Are you going to be warm enough? March is a little early to have the hood down, but I never put it up unless it's raining.'

'I'll be fine,' Kathy assured him, tucking her scarf around her neck. 'I'm used to outdoor life, remember.'

As he drove out of the city, the wind blew in her hair and she felt exhilarated by the speed and the freedom.

'Now I know how Mr Toad felt,' she shouted to him above the noise of the engine.

'Who?'

'Oh, never mind,' she laughed.

The country pub was cosy and informal and they both relaxed. Though there were no other women in the pub, no one seemed to give her a disapproving glance and, even if they had, she wouldn't have cared. For the first time in Tony's company, Kathy felt she could be herself. This was more her kind of scene. She felt more at home in a country pub than in the formal surroundings of a fancy city restaurant. For the first time she could forget that he was the boss and she just a lowly employee. Here, she could feel she was his equal. Tony too seemed more at ease. He laughed and joked and teased her gently.

'You know, you really are a very pretty girl. So fresh and unspoilt.'

'Unsophisticated and ignorant, you mean,' she laughed. 'A real country mouse lost in the big city.'

'No, I don't mean that,' he said gently and his dark brown eyes looked deeply into hers. 'But you do seem more at home here than in the city, I must say.'

Kathy shrugged. 'Well, I've lived all my life in the country. This pub is very like the one we've got in Abbeytoft.'

'And who used to take you to this pub? Have I got a rival for your affections?'

Kathy laughed as she felt herself blush. 'No, it was

only Morry.' Then she felt guilty at dismissing him as 'only Morry'. Swiftly she said, 'Morry is my best friend's brother. He – he's a good friend to me too. And he's Miss Robinson's nephew.'

'Ah! Do I detect a bit of matchmaking?'

'They can try,' she answered pertly. 'But it won't work.' She forbore to tell him that it never would have done in a million years. That would have sounded very cruel to Morry.

He moved closer to her along the bench seat, picked up her left hand and touched her fourth finger. A shiver of delight coursed through her. 'So,' he murmured, his voice low and deep, 'You're not "spoken for"?'

Kathy's heart felt as if it were turning somersaults in her chest. 'No,' she whispered. 'I'm not spoken for.'

'Good,' he said with an air of authority. Then he raised her hand to his lips and kissed it, while his brown eyes caressed her.

On the way back towards the city, he pulled to a halt down a country lane and stopped the engine. Then he turned and took her in his arms, kissing her gently on the mouth.

'But now, my darling girl, you can consider yourself "spoken for".'

Ten

'Amy's coming for Easter,' Jemima informed her during the first week in April, as she opened a letter at the breakfast table. 'I can't imagine why the interest in visiting her maiden aunt all of a sudden,' she said airily, but her eyes were twinkling with merriment.

Kathy stared at her for a moment and then forced a smile. She had to appear delighted that her best friend was visiting, but in truth her heart was sinking at the thought that she wouldn't be able to meet Tony if he should ask her.

'Do you mind?' she asked, hoping that Jemima would express irritation at yet another intrusion on her quiet, well-ordered life.

'Of course not,' Jemima replied spiritedly. 'She's my god-daughter as well as my niece.' For a moment her eyes took on a faraway, dreamy expression. 'You know, that was one of the nicest things anyone's ever done for me. Asking me to be godmother to their precious daughter. Especially . . .' Her voice faded away and she shook herself and came back to the present with a jolt. Briskly, she added, 'It's nice to see the child, even if it is you she's coming to see.'

'I'm sure—' Kathy began.

'Now, now, no little white lies to make me feel better. I can't abide being lied to, whatever the reason.' There was a pause before she went on. 'I thought I

93

might treat the three of us to a day at the seaside on Monday. There's an excursion with the local bus company to Saltershaven. Would you like that?'

'The seaside?' Kathy's eyes shone. 'Oh, I would. I've never been.'

Jemima stared at her. 'You mean to tell me you've never seen the sea?'

Kathy bit her lip as she shook her head. It did sound ridiculous that a girl of nineteen had never seen the sea.

Jemima shook her head slowly. 'Your father—' she began but then stopped and altered whatever it was she'd been going to say. 'Then we'd better rectify that omission, my dear.' She rose from the table. 'But for now, we'd better get ready for work, else we'll both be late and that would never do.'

Kathy rose to clear away the breakfast things feeling yet another stab of guilt at the deceit she was practising on this good, kind woman.

Maybe I should tell her the truth, she pondered, but although the romance with Tony was progressing, he'd left her in no doubt that he wanted it kept secret. As the days passed she had the niggling doubt that his reasons were more than just the impropriety of the manager going out with a lowly junior assistant. And to add to her worries, he'd made no mention of plans for the coming weekend.

Very well then, Kathy tossed her head as she marched into work, I'll make other arrangements.

'Stella,' she said when there was a break in the morning routine. 'My friend Amy's coming to stay this weekend. And I know she loves the pictures. Would you like to come with us on Saturday night?'

'Why?' Stella asked bluntly. 'Lover boy not coming up to scratch? Not asked you out this week, then?'

Kathy sighed, but forced a smile to her face. 'No,' she said carefully. 'It's time I kept my promise to you and I'd like you to meet Amy. You'll like her. She's bubbly and fun.'

Stella's prickliness dissolved and she said, 'I'd love to. I'll ask my dad tonight.'

'Blimey!' Stella greeted Kathy the following morning. 'Talk about the third degree. My dad wanted to know where I was going, who with and what time I'd be home. Then he said what picture were we going to and was it "suitable" . . .' She rolled her eyes. 'And *then* he said "Are there any boys going, because I don't want you consorting" – consorting if you please, that's what he actually said – "with boys?"' She spread her hands helplessly. 'How am I ever going to get married if I'm not allowed to "consort" with boys? I ask you!'

Kathy laughed wryly. 'Tell me about it. Why do you think I left home?'

'Was that why? Because your dad wouldn't let you go out?'

'Partly,' Kathy said, realizing she'd said too much. It had been Morry's proposal and her father's anger at her refusal that had precipitated Kathy's flight, but she didn't want to confide that much to Stella. The chatterbox might let something slip in front of Amy and Kathy had no wish to hurt her friend's feelings and certainly not dear old Morry's. Sometimes she regretted that she couldn't feel for him what everyone wanted her to. Life would have been so much simpler. But now that she'd met Tony Kendall, she knew she'd been right.

'Anyway, can you come with us?'

'After all that – yes, I can.'

Kathy squeezed Stella's arm. 'Great! We'll have a lovely time.'

Kathy and Amy waited outside the cinema for half an hour.

'Isn't Stella coming? I thought she'd've left work with you,' Amy said, hopping from one foot to the other. 'Oh, do let's go inside. I'm freezing!'

'I don't know what can have happened to her. Miss Foster came for her about ten minutes before closing time. Said there was a message for her in the office and I haven't seen her since. I do hope nothing's wrong, but, you're right, we'd better go inside. She knows where we are.'

The two girls sat in the back row of the cinema among the courting couples feeling as if they were playing gooseberry. 'But we'll be able to see if Stella comes in late,' Amy suggested as they chose their seats.

Later, as they walked home through the dark streets, Amy said, 'I wonder what happened to your friend from work?'

Kathy gave a very unladylike snort of wry laughter. 'Her father. I'd bet my last penny that somehow he stopped her coming at the very last minute. I wouldn't put it past him to drive into the city on his tractor and carry her off home.'

'Poor thing.' Amy tucked her arm through Kathy's. 'She'll end up doing what you've done. Leaving home.'

'Maybe,' Kathy said, abstractedly.

96

They walked another few yards.

'What's up, Kathy? There's something on your mind. I can tell. Is it Aunt Jemima? Getting on your nerves, is she? 'Cos I can't say I blame you if she is. She's a dear, but I don't think I could live with her for long. Her pernickety ways would drive me potty.'

'No, no,' Kathy said at once. 'She's been very kind to me and I like living there, but . . .' Her voice trailed away.

'But?' Amy prompted.

Kathy took a deep breath. She hated not confiding in Amy – her best friend in all the world. She felt a stab of guilt that already Tony had become more important to her than Amy and, even worse, more important than being totally honest at all times. It was something she'd prided herself on always being. She might have many faults, but being untruthful was not one of them. Until now. Until Tony. She didn't enjoy deceiving Aunt Jemima and, even more, she hated not telling Amy. But she just daren't confide in her. If you told just one person – and particularly Amy – then a secret was no longer a secret. Although Amy was lovable in every way, she'd never been able to keep a confidence. The only thing that assuaged Kathy's guilt was that she knew Amy herself would cheerfully acknowledge her own failing and had been heard to remark many times, 'If it's a secret, then please don't tell me.'

'But I think I'm intruding on her peace and quiet. I – I ought to look for a place of my own as soon as I can afford it.'

Amy chuckled. 'Well, we could do just what we liked then, when I come to stay. Stay out all night, if we wanted to. We wouldn't have to trot home like obedient children as soon as the pictures finished. I bet she's watching the clock this very minute and calculating just how long it takes for us to walk home from town. Ooh, wouldn't I love to be an hour late home. Just once.'

Kathy laughed. 'But we won't be, will we?'

Amy gave an exaggerated sigh. 'No, we won't. Because she'd tell my dad and he wouldn't let me come any more.' There was a slight pause before, with a note of surprise in her tone, Amy added, 'But to be truthful, I wouldn't want to worry the old dear.'

Kathy said nothing. There was nothing she could say, but a fresh wave of guilt swept through her at the deception she was practising.

As the three of them boarded the bus on the Easter Monday morning, even Jemima seemed excited. The day was warm and sunny and she wore a flowery dress, broad-brimmed white hat and carried a parasol. It took over two hours to reach the seaside resort of Saltershaven on the east coast and everyone was thankful to climb down.

'Come along, let's complete your education,' Amy teased, linking her arm through Kathy's. 'It's high time a girl of your age saw the sea.'

From the clock tower set near the sea front, they walked until they could see the sea and the beach.

Kathy gasped. 'Oh my! Isn't it big! I had no idea.' She stood and gazed at the expanse of water before her, fascinated by the gentle waves rolling languidly on to the shore. Already bare-footed children were playing on the warm sand, building sandcastles and digging a moat around them, then running to the sea's edge to fill buckets to pour into it.

'I should have brought my bucket and spade.' Kathy laughed. 'I've a whole childhood to catch up on.' There was a distinct note of sadness in her tone. She felt a sense of loss for all the fun she'd missed. A time she would never be able to recapture, at least not until she'd children of her own. Her heart gave a little leap as she thought about Tony. Perhaps one day . . .

'Come along, girls,' Jemima interrupted her. 'I don't know about you, but I need a cup of tea. I think there's a little café at the pier entrance.'

They walked along the sea front until they came to the pier. 'Do let's go on it, Aunt Jemima. Look – it goes right out into the sea. Let's go and stand right at the end of it.'

'When we've had a cup of tea,' Jemima said firmly, but there was a smile on her face.

The day was a huge success. The girls had a donkey ride, giggling as they bounced up and down and ignoring the jibes of the group of children who stood watching the grown-ups acting like children. They weren't to know that, for one of the girls, it was her first taste of seaside fun. They rode on the big dipper, squealing with terrified delight and clutching each other. Aunt Jemima watched from the ground, smiling gently and congratulating herself on having suggested the day trip. As the time approached for them to board the bus again, they walked back to the pick-up point along the sea front eating ice cream and admiring the well-kept gardens and the smooth bowling greens on the foreshore.

All three were tired, but contented. Though she loved Amy dearly and was becoming very fond of Jemima, Kathy's only disappointment was that Tony had not been there to share the day.

If Kathy had placed her bet, she would have won.

'My dad stopped me coming,' Stella greeted her mournfully on the Tuesday morning. 'At the very last minute. He actually rang up Mr Kendall on Saturday afternoon and told him – told him, mind you – to send me straight home after work. And I was so looking forward to it. I even came to work in my Sunday best coat and all. I cried all night, but that man's got a heart of stone. Even my mam couldn't persuade him. Mind you, I don't think she tried very hard. She's almost as bad as him.'

Kathy bit back the remark, I thought as much. Instead, she adopted a sympathetic expression. 'I'm so sorry. We wondered where you'd got to. We waited outside for you for about half an hour.'

'Was the picture good?' Stella asked eagerly. 'Oh, I do wish I'd been strong enough to defy him, but – ' she sighed heavily – 'until I can get a place of my own in the city I daren't cross him.'

'Miss Matthews . . . Miss Burton . . .' They both jumped as they heard Muriel's sharp tone. 'Were you thinking of doing any work today?'

'Of course, Miss Curtis. Sorry, Miss Curtis,' Stella said meekly, and hurried away to greet a customer who had just entered the department. Kathy said nothing but tilted the hat she was arranging on a display to a slightly jauntier angle. As she did so, she glanced thoughtfully after Stella. I wonder . . .

Kathy thought about her idea for several days. Could she and Stella find a flat somewhere near the city centre to share? But as the days passed, the idea became less appealing. Although she liked the girl well enough, she doubted she could live with her. Stella was a moody girl. One moment she was friendly, laughing and chattering and sharing confidences. The next she'd taken offence at some simple remark or action and had retreated into sulky silence. While this might be because of her home life under the harsh regime of her strict father, Kathy felt she daren't take the risk. She very much doubted that Stella, once she knew who 'lover boy' really was, would be able to keep it secret. And, if they lived together, Stella was bound to find out.

Besides, Kathy told herself, things were settling down into a very nice routine in the little terraced house. Jemima had made no hints that she wanted her lodger to move out and Kathy's outings with Tony were covered by Stella's willingness to enter into the intrigue and by Kathy's membership of the choral society.

Throughout the summer, Kathy lived in a little world of her own. While Jemima read the newspapers avidly and listened more and more to the news on her little battery-operated wireless, Kathy was blithely ignorant of the gloom that was pervading the country. Her only thoughts were of the next meeting with Tony, whenever that might be. She ignored the times he arranged an outing and then cancelled it at the last minute, always giving the same excuse. 'My mother's not well . . .'

The first time they planned to go to the pictures on a Thursday evening, Kathy waited for over an hour outside the cinema, earning herself one or two very strange looks from passers-by. She blushed to realize what they must be thinking. Deciding at last that Tony was not coming, Kathy walked towards home, tears of disappointment stinging her throat. Was he tiring of her? Was this his way of ending it?

As she neared the end of the street where she lived, Kathy realized that it was far too early to go home yet. Aunt Jemima believed her to be at the choral society meeting, so that's exactly where she'd go. Instead of turning into the street, Kathy walked on to the school just beyond the Arboretum. She let herself into the main door and tiptoed into the hall, taking her place at the end of the second row, near the other two sopranos. Mrs Sims smiled at her and shared her songbook. After a few moments, miraculously Kathy had forgotten all about Tony as her voice soared to the rafters and the members of the choir smiled at each other, delighted that their little songbird had come after all.

'I'm so sorry I was late,' Kathy apologized swiftly to Ron Spencer as they broke for tea and biscuits halfway through their allotted three-hour meeting.

'We missed you, my dear,' was all the kindly man said. But he asked no probing questions. It wasn't in his nature and for that, Kathy was grateful. But she mentally crossed her fingers, hoping that neither Ron nor his wife Mabel would mention to Jemima that Kathy had arrived late that evening.

The following morning, Tony whispered a hurried apology as he passed through the millinery department, adding, 'Saturday? Are you all right for Saturday?'

Kathy's heart leapt. He still wanted her. 'Of course,' she breathed, her anguish of the previous night swept away.

'Meet me at the restaurant we went to that first evening. Remember?'

She nodded, glancing around to make sure that neither Miss Curtis nor Stella was watching.

'Till Saturday, darling,' he murmured as he moved away. 'Eight thirty.'

For the rest of the day, Kathy hummed happily to herself.

'You're in a good mood,' Stella muttered. 'Got a date with lover boy, have we?'

'Might have,' Kathy said airily.

The younger girl glared at her balefully. 'I really think you might let me in on the big secret. Specially as I'm covering for you. Don't you trust me?'

'Of course I do,' Kathy said a little too swiftly and Stella eyed her suspiciously. 'Look, you've been a brick – a real pal – and . . . and I will tell you. Very soon. Just – just give me a few more weeks. Please, Stella.'

'All right,' the girl agreed reluctantly. 'But I don't know what all the mystery is about. Are you ashamed of him, or something?'

'No, no, of course I'm not,' Kathy declared hotly. 'It's just – just that . . . well, to tell you the truth, I'm not sure of him. I mean – if he really likes me. If – if he's serious.'

'Oh.' Stella was thoughtful for a moment. In her ignorance, she was struggling to understand how it must feel to fall in love. The only experience she had was from the books she'd read or the films she'd seen on the very rare occasions she'd been allowed to go to the cinema. 'You mean, you sort of feel . . . that if you tell anyone it might – well – it might ruin it.'

'Something like that,' Kathy agreed carefully. More lies, she thought sadly. She'd heard it said that if you told one lie you ended up telling a lot more to cover the first one. She was finding out that the saying was true.

Stella was nodding now and smiling, pleased with her philosophy. 'I do understand. But you can tell me, you know. I wouldn't say a word. Not to anyone.'

Kathy doubted it, but she smiled in return, promising, 'You'll be the first to know.'

Placated, Stella was in a better mood for the rest of the day.

Kathy was at the restaurant on the Saturday evening by eight fifteen, hovering uncertainly on the pavement outside. Tony was never early, and rather than run the gauntlet of disapproving glances, she took a deep breath and pushed open the door of the restaurant. Menu in hand, the head waiter approached her. He smiled obsequiously and gave a little bow. 'Good evening, madam? Have you booked?'

'I – er – no. I mean, I'm not sure. I – I'm meeting someone.'

'I see, madam.' He raised his eyebrows in a question. 'Perhaps your dinner partner has placed a reservation with us?'

'Er – yes. Perhaps he has. It's – it's Mr Kendall.'

'Ah yes, madam. Of course. I should have remembered you. I do apologize.' He bowed again and ushered her towards a secluded table at the far side of the restaurant. He held out the chair for her to be seated. As she took her place, Kathy had the feeling that he'd remembered her very well, but that he was far too discreet to mention it. Perhaps he feared that Mr

Kendall might well, by now, have transferred his affections elsewhere and that, for a man in his position, the head waiter would have been committing an unforgivable *faux pas*.

'Would madam care to order a drink?' he asked, shaking out the white napkin and laying it across her lap.

'No – no, thank you. I'll wait.'

'Very good, madam.' He bowed again and moved away, his sharp eyes raking the room, checking that everything in his domain was in order.

Holding her breath, Kathy now risked a glance around. She was so afraid there might be someone there who knew her. And even worse, the woman who'd been there before and had said such awful things about Tony. Slowly, Kathy let out her breath. There was no one she recognized, but then, that didn't mean that there was no one there who knew her. Customers had an unfortunate habit of recognizing shop staff, whereas Kathy found it difficult to remember each and every woman who came in to the millinery department.

The minutes ticked by. Eight thirty came and went and the hand on the clock on the wall crept towards nine o'clock.

'Are you sure I can't get you something, madam?' The head waiter was at her elbow once more.

'No, really, I . . .' She glanced up and breathed a sigh of relief to see Tony threading his way between the tables towards her.

'Darling, I'm so sorry . . .' He slid into the seat opposite her and took the menu the head waiter was holding out to him. 'Thank you, Gregson. Have you ordered, darling?'

'No. I was waiting for you.'

Swiftly, without deferring to her, Tony ordered for them both, but Kathy was quite happy for him to do so. She was just so thankful that he was here.

Eleven

They'd almost finished their meal and had been chatting amiably before the telephone call that Kathy had been half expecting all evening came. Gregson approached their table with an apologetic look on his face.

'There's a telephone call for you, sir.'

For a brief moment, Tony looked genuinely angry. Then he sighed, shrugged his shoulders and rose. 'I won't be a moment, darling.'

As he hurried away, Gregson leaned forward and refilled Kathy's glass.

'Thank you,' she murmured as he moved away, wondering for the second time if there'd been a pre-arranged signal between them.

Kathy kept her eyes downcast and twirled the slender-stemmed wineglass between nervous fingers. She felt as if everyone in the restaurant knew what was going on but her. It was a foolish notion, of course, but it was how she felt.

'I'm sorry,' he said as soon as he sat down again. 'It's mother. She's alone in the house and she's frightened.'

'Frightened?' Kathy snapped, her patience beginning to wear thin. 'What of?'

'Of being alone.'

'I see,' she said shortly. 'Then you'd better go.'

'No, no. We'll finish first. She'll be all right for a little while. I've tried to reassure her and promised I won't be late.'

They finished the pudding in complete silence and when their coffee had been served, Tony reached across the table and took her hand. 'Darling, you're so understanding about all this. No one else has ever – I mean – no one else would be so good. My mother is a sick woman and it's very hard for her and for my father too. I – I feel I have to help as much as I can.'

Kathy was suddenly overwhelmed with guilt. Not this time, on account of her deceit, but because she was criticizing a loyal and loving son. She was reminded too that she'd walked away from her own mother's difficult life and had selfishly followed her own desires. Shame swept through her and made her squeeze his hand and say huskily, 'It's all right. She can't help being ill.'

Tony raised her hand to his lips and kissed it. 'Sweetheart, you're so kind and generous. I do love you. There's so much I want to say to you – was going to say to you tonight – but now . . .'

It was all she needed to hear. He'd said those three little words that meant so much to any girl and especially to her. She would never doubt him again, she vowed silently. She'd be kind and understanding and forgiving whenever their evenings were interrupted or their arrangements cancelled.

'Never mind,' she heard herself saying. 'You go and I'll find my own way home. It's such a nice evening, I don't mind the walk.'

'If you're sure, darling . . . ?' And he was gone.

*

The summer rolled on. Towards the end of August, Amy came again.

'Dad says I've worked so hard with the harvest, I deserve a bit of fun.'

Kathy said nothing, but she wondered just how her father was coping at such a busy time of year without her. She hoped he hadn't forced her mother to take her place. As if reading her friend's thoughts, Amy said, 'And before you ask, your mam's fine and Morry's been helping your dad with his harvest. Just in case he had it in mind to get your poor mam driving the tractor or lugging bales. Now,' she went on briskly, 'What's on at the pictures this weekend?'

Half way through the programme the Pathé News came on and by the time it had finished, the cinema-goers had little heart to sit and watch the next film.

'Let's go, Kathy,' Amy whispered. 'I can't sit here any longer after what we've just seen.'

As they walked home, arm in arm, clutching each other for comfort, Amy whispered, 'I'm scared. All that talk of emergency powers and the sight of those students building great walls of sandbags outside that London hospital. It – it can only mean one thing, can't it? There's going to be a war, isn't there?'

'It was the sound of those sirens that got me. I know they weren't for real this time but . . .' Kathy shuddered as she added, 'I'd no idea things had got so bad. I – I haven't been taking much notice of the news lately.' She bit her lip, longing to confide in her dearest friend, but she still daren't say a word.

'Neither have I,' Amy answered in an unusually subdued voice. 'We've been so busy just lately, I don't think even Dad realizes just how serious things are now. But don't let's say anything to Aunt Jemima. We don't want to worry the old dear.'

Kathy agreed, but when they arrived home, Jemima was listening to the nine o'clock news on the wireless, leaning towards it, not wanting to miss a word. The book she had been reading had fallen, discarded, to the floor.

'Hello, Auntie,' Amy began breezily.

'Shush! I'm listening.'

The two girls exchanged a glance and shrugged.

'Oh well,' Kathy murmured. 'She'll hear soon enough at work on Monday. They'll be talking of nothing else. And come to think of it, she's been devouring the newspapers for weeks. Maybe she's far more aware of what's going on than we are.'

The news bulletin ended and Jemima switched off the wireless. She sat motionless, staring pensively at nothing in particular.

'I'll make the cocoa,' Amy said gently and went into the scullery, while Kathy sat down in the chair on the opposite side of the range. She didn't know what to say, so she said nothing but waited until Jemima should speak.

At last Jemima gave a huge sigh and then said flatly, 'So – it's all going to start again, is it? You'd really think, wouldn't you, that we'd all have learned our lesson the last time? Enough to know not to let it all happen again. The war to end all wars, they called it. Huh!'

The last sound was uttered with an ironic despair.

Though Kathy had no memory of the Great War and little knowledge, she knew it was only twenty-one years since it had ended. Her own parents – and Amy's too – had lived through it and the woman sitting opposite her now must have been about Kathy's age at the start of it. Kathy watched her now and saw the raw suffering in Jemima's eyes. There was a hurt, a wound in them that would never heal. She wanted to ask what had happened back then but she couldn't. But later, when they were on their own, she would quiz Amy. She might know what had happened to her aunt all those years ago.

Amy came in with three mugs of cocoa. 'There now, this will make us all feel better.' She handed them round and then sat down on a chair near the table. 'Perhaps it won't happen,' she said, trying to be cheerful.

Jemima sipped her cocoa but said nothing. She was older and a lot wiser than the two young girls and she was very much afraid that it would.

As they came out of the cathedral the following morning, Jemima stopped to speak to an acquaintance. Kathy took the opportunity to whisper to Amy, 'Your aunt seems very upset by all this talk of war. I mean, more than normal. I know we're all worried, but it's really seemed to affect her badly. And usually she's so – she's so . . .'

'Strong? Resilient?' Amy suggested with a fond smile.

'Exactly. So why?'

Amy glanced back at her aunt, who was still deep in serious conversation, a worried frown creasing her forehead. The girl bit her lip and, for a moment, there was a look of uncertainty in her eyes. She seemed to be struggling to find the right words – or to decide if she should even say them.

Then she gave a little sigh and shrugged. 'I think she – she lost someone in the last war. Dad's always very protective of her and Mum, well, I've heard her say "poor Jemima" more than once. And yet, to me, she's anything but "poor". She's smart. She has a good job, a nice home and she lives in the city. She can do anything she likes. She's not "poor" in any way. I rather envy her. But – I think – there was . . . something . . .' Her voice trailed away and she avoided meeting Kathy's direct, enquiring gaze.

'I bet your mum thinks Aunt Jemima's lonely. Family means everything to your mum. Perhaps she feels sorry for Aunt Jemima because she has no husband or family,' Kathy suggested, trying to prise more out of the usually loquacious Amy. There was a pause as they walked slowly to the top of Steep Hill and then stopped, waiting for Jemima to catch them up. Kathy glanced at Amy, but the girl had her lips pressed firmly together as if to stop them saying any more.

'Well,' Kathy said quietly, 'if you're right and she did lose someone she loved in the war, then that's why she's so upset to think there might be another one. It's going to bring the nightmare all back.'

Still Amy said nothing as they turned to watch Jemima come towards them. She walked straight-backed, her head held high.

'She's still a good-looking woman, you know,' Kathy said. 'She must have been a stunner in her younger days.'

'She was,' Amy said. 'There's a photo of her on the sideboard in our front room. You must have seen it.'

Kathy turned to gape at her friend. '*That's* Jemima? But – but she was beautiful.'

'I know.'

And they both turned to stare at the older woman again.

'Well, well, well,' Kathy murmured.

'Now you two, I've decided we're going out for lunch today. My treat. I need cheering up a little.'

The two girls stepped on either side of her and linked their arms through hers.

'That's what I call a good idea. Where are you taking us?'

'There's a nice little café just down here. It's sometimes open for Sunday lunch in the summer.'

'I need to speak to you,' Tony whispered to Kathy as he passed through the department just after opening the following morning, ostensibly on his rounds to check that all was in order throughout the store. 'My office. After work.'

'I can't . . .' she began, but he'd moved on, smiling and nodding to other members of staff.

Kathy bit her lip anxiously. She and Jemima always walked home together unless Kathy had planned to stay in town. But Jemima didn't like surprises being sprung upon her. She planned their meals meticulously, shopping only for what they needed. She didn't like having her routine altered at short notice.

'What's up?' Stella asked. 'Has the war started?'

Kathy smiled weakly. If Jemima were to find out about her and Tony, there would certainly be a war of words if nothing worse.

The talk at work this last week had been of little

else but the uncertainty about the war. Everyone was worried.

'Is it lover boy? Has he packed you in?'

'No – it's just that – look, I've got to meet him tonight urgently . . .'

Stella's eyes widened. 'You're not in trouble, are you?'

Kathy gasped. 'Good Heavens, no! He's – he's sent word that he wants to speak to me. That's all.'

Stella's eyes narrowed as she searched Kathy's embarrassed face. The girl was thinking, calculating. She glanced round the department. 'I didn't see anyone bring you a message and we've had no customers in yet. The only person I've seen speak to you this morning is . . . Oh my God! It's *him*, isn't it?'

Kathy tried hard to stop the colour flooding into her face, but failed. She grasped Stella's arm. 'Stella – please. Don't say anything. Please don't tell anyone.'

'Oh, don't you worry, I won't. But you're an idiot. A fool.'

'What – what do you mean?'

'He'll break your heart. That's what I mean. Just like he's broken a whole string of 'em before you. Miss Curtis for one and God only knows how many more. But I know there's been a few because when it was all going off with our dear Muriel I overheard snippets. Oh, he's a real lady-killer and no mistake. I wouldn't touch him if he was the last man on earth. And that's a fact.'

Kathy's heart felt like lead in her chest. 'I don't believe you,' she said, but her protest was feeble. And she knew it.

Twelve

'You go on ahead,' Kathy said as closing time approached. 'I've just got something to finish off. I won't be long.'

'Very well then,' Jemima murmured. Her mind on other things, she didn't think to ask questions and Kathy heaved a sigh of relief. She'd worried all day as to how she could snatch just a few moments with Tony after work and then it had been so easy. All she had to do was to pretend she had to stay behind to finish something. That excuse wouldn't work more than once or twice, she realized. But tonight, Jemima seemed distracted. All day the talk among customers as well as the staff had been of the impending war. The merry lunch Jemima and the two girls had enjoyed the previous day had faded already. Once again, Jemima seemed lost in her own thoughts and memories.

When the store had emptied, Kathy made her way to the manager's office. He was hovering in the outer office, waiting for her. At once, he took her hands in his, drew her into his office and closed the door.

'Darling, we can't talk long. I have to get home, but can you meet me on Thursday night?'

'Thursday? Yes, yes, of course I can, but, Tony, I have to ask you . . .'

'Good. I'll pick you up near the main gate of the Arboretum at about seven?' He pulled her to him and kissed her hard on the mouth. 'I must go, but we'll have time to chat on Thursday.' He smiled. 'All the time in the world, my darling. Whatever it is you want to ask me will just have to wait until then.' Before she could say another word, he'd hustled her out of his office and down the stairs. Without realizing quite how it had happened, she found herself outside on the street with the door firmly closed behind her. She stood a moment, looking back, but Tony had disappeared.

Oh well, she thought, shrugging her shoulders. I'll find out on Thursday.

She was only ten minutes later arriving home than normal and to her relief Jemima asked no questions. Kathy hugged her secret to herself. Luckily, this Thursday was her night for the choral society meeting. It would be easy for her to meet Tony instead, without Jemima suspecting a thing.

All she had to do was to be sure she wasn't any later home than usual.

The next three days passed by so slowly. Stella ignored her. Gone in an instant was all the friendliness. At last, Kathy couldn't stand the uncomfortable silence from the girl whom she had thought was her friend any longer.

As they left the store on Wednesday night, she caught hold of Stella's arm. 'Look, Stella . . .'

'I'll miss my bus,' the girl said shortly. 'Then my dad'll want to know what I've been up to. I don't want to be in trouble. You're going to be in enough for both of us as it is. When everyone finds out.'

'But you promised—'

Stella whirled around to face her. 'And I keep my promises,' she said and added pointedly, 'even if others don't.' Kathy felt guilt sweep through her afresh as Stella went on. 'But how long do you think you can keep it secret, eh?'

'We've managed it up to now. Why should anyone find out?'

Stella sighed and shook her head. 'I guessed, didn't I? Oh, I know everyone sees me as a naïve kid. A plain girl who's never had a boyfriend – nor likely too the way my dad keeps me locked up – but even I'm not daft enough to think you can get away with something like this. He's poison, that man. Keep away from him, Kathy, if you've any sense left in that pretty head of yours. I can see why he likes you but he'll not stay with you, you mark my words.' Then she twisted herself free of Kathy's grasp and hurried away towards her bus stop.

Kathy watched her go, suddenly feeling very lonely.

On the Thursday evening, Kathy dressed with extra care. Over the last few weeks she had been able to buy herself a pretty dress and a pair of dainty shoes. She knew she should be saving to be able to afford her own bed-sit or flat, but she couldn't always go out with Tony in the suit she wore every day for work. And the few clothes she had brought from home, well, they were fit only for the ragbag.

'You look nice,' Jemima smiled, looking up from her book as Kathy headed for the back door. Curled on his mistress's lap, Taffy raised his ginger head and regarded her with his green gaze. Kathy hesitated, then crossed the room to stroke the cat's head. If she missed anything from home, apart from her mother of course, it was the animals.

And the Robinsons. She missed the Robinson family. All of them. But the one person she pushed from her mind and determined not to think about was her father.

'I'll be home the usual time,' she called back as she closed the back door behind her. Outside in the back yard, she breathed a sigh of relief and hurried along the passage and out into the street, hoping that Ron Spencer wouldn't emerge from his house and walk along with her to the choral society meeting. She held her breath until she was safely at the top of the street and well beyond his house. Then she walked briskly across the road to the city's park.

Tony's car was nowhere to be seen when she arrived at the main gate. She had waited a few moments when she saw a member of the choral society cycling along the road towards her. Quickly she ran into the park and waited behind a tree until he had passed by.

Still there was no sign of Tony's car and she began to wonder if he was about to stand her up again when she heard the familiar roar of the car's engine. With a squeal of tyres, he pulled up in front of her, leapt out and ran around the car to open the passenger's door for her.

'Sorry, I'm a little late, darling. Mother had one of her turns and I couldn't get away until Father came home. What a pretty dress you're wearing. Blue's certainly your colour. It matches your eyes.' He smiled down at her as he carefully tucked her dress into the car and closed the door. His compliment gave her a warm glow and made her feel special.

'I'm sorry to hear about your mother. Shouldn't you go home? I quite understand if . . .'

'Maybe I'd better not be too long . . .' He turned the car around and drove back across the High Street, then turned up the hill, twisting and turning among streets Kathy didn't know.

'So, where are we going?'

'You'll see,' he said mysteriously. 'It's a surprise.'

Within minutes he was drawing to a halt outside a large house on the corner of Mill Road.

Kathy gasped and her eyes widened. 'Are you taking me to meet your parents? Oh, you might have warned me. I . . .'

'No, no, darling, it's something much better than that. I've found a little flat for you.'

'For me, but . . .'

'She's a very nice old lady. She's been widowed for about five years and after her family had left home and her husband died, she found the house too big for just her. But – she didn't want to leave the home she'd had all her married life, so she turned the upstairs into a nice little flat.'

Kathy looked around her with renewed interest. It was a nice area and the house was certainly big enough to have been converted into two flats.

'I – I don't think I would be able to afford it,' she said quietly. 'It's very kind of you, but . . .'

He patted her hand. 'Now you're not to worry about that. I want you to be independent of Miss Robinson. It's little better than living at home, as far as I can see.'

Kathy almost laughed aloud. If only he knew! But she said nothing as he went on, 'Whenever we're out, you're always clock-watching. And it must be difficult for you working with her too. I can understand that. So – if you have your own place, you'll be able to come and go as you please. Mrs Sutton won't be keeping tabs on you, I promise.'

'Do – do you know her?'

'I've known her years.' He paused. 'She's – er – a good customer of ours. So – shall we go and have a look? It's a lovely flat. I'm sure you're going to be happy here.'

The flat was just as he'd said – lovely. It was self-contained, with a sitting room, bedroom and tiny kitchen that had obviously been converted from a small bedroom. It even had its own bathroom, complete with water closet. A luxury that Kathy had never known. Even Miss Robinson's lavatory was across the back yard. And Mrs Sutton was a dear. She greeted Tony like an old friend, kissing him on the cheek.

'I shan't come up with you. It's my legs, dear. I can't climb the stairs like I used to. You show your young lady round, Mr Kendall, while I make a nice cup of tea. Then we can have a nice chat and see if we'll suit each other.' She smiled at Kathy.

'So do you like it?' Tony asked, when they had seen all the rooms. 'It's not much further to walk to work than you do now, but just in the opposite direction. What do you think?'

'What rent does she want?'

'I told you not to worry about that. I'll help you with the first few months and I'll see about giving you a raise at work so that you'll be able to afford it yourself. What do you say?' He put his head on one side and smiled at her, the lines around his eyes crinkling. Her heart melted. She knew now that she was helplessly in love with him. He was so kind and thought-

ful. She really couldn't believe that he was the philanderer that Stella made out. Maybe he just hadn't
found the right girl – until now. She loved him and she
was sure he loved her. He'd told her so often. Tony
Kendall made her feel special, made her feel really
loved . . .

'Yes, all right,' she agreed. 'But as soon as I can
afford it for myself—'

He laughed and patted her hand. 'Yes, yes, Miss
Independent. So, we'll go down and tell Mrs Sutton
yes. The old dear will be setting out tea and scones on
paper doilies. Come along, we won't keep her waiting
any longer.'

As she walked home, Kathy felt she was walking on
air. She skipped down the dark passage, in through the
gate and then the back door leading into the scullery.
She took a deep breath before she opened the door into
the kitchen.

Jemima was sitting where Kathy had left her, in her
chair near the range.

'Sorry I'm a little late. The practice went on a little
longer than normal . . .' Kathy stopped. Jemima was
looking at her with a strange expression on her face.

'Did it indeed?' Her voice was hard and cold, and
her sharp eyes held Kathy's gaze. Taffy jumped down
from her knee and, ears flattened, headed for the door.
He miaowed to be let through to the scullery and Kathy
opened it. He scuttled through and they both heard the
rattle as he pushed his way out of his own little door.

'Close the door, Kathy, and come and sit down.'

'Shall I – make the cocoa?'

'Not just now.' Jemima nodded towards the chair
opposite her. 'Sit down.'

For a moment there was silence in the room. At last

Jemima asked quietly. 'Where have you been tonight, Kathy? And I want the truth.'

Kathy thought quickly. Somehow, Jemima knew that she had not attended choir practice.

'I – I've been out with a – a friend.'

'You haven't been to the choral society meeting?'

Kathy bit her lip and shook her head. Then she looked up defiantly and met the older woman's gaze calmly. After all, she was not answerable to Miss Robinson. As long as she respected the woman's home, which she did, and came in at a reasonable hour, which she did also, what right had Jemima to question her?

But it seemed as if Jemima felt she had every right to question her. 'And this – er – friend. Would it be a male friend, by any chance?'

Kathy's chin rose higher. 'And what if it is?'

Jemima sighed. 'Kathy, I'm not trying to play the heavy father here. You've had enough of that, I know. But – but it's who this friend is that I'm concerned about.'

'It's no one you know.'

'No more lies, Kathy, if you please,' Jemima snapped, her patience at an end. She closed her eyes for a moment and sighed heavily. 'You disappoint me, Kathy. I thought you were an honest girl. Betty vouched for you. Amy thinks the world of you, and Maurice – well – as for poor Maurice, I expect you've quite broken his gentle heart.'

There was a stillness, as if the whole room was holding its breath.

'I've had two visitors tonight, Kathy. One – Mr Spencer – has only just left a few minutes ago. He came round as soon as he got home to enquire if you were all right, as you hadn't been to the meeting.' She paused and then went on. 'The other was a little earlier. Miss Curtis called to see me and what she had to tell me has disturbed me greatly.'

'Is she not satisfied with my work? Is that it? Does she want me to leave?'

'No, no, not at all. As it happens she's very pleased with your work. She says you're doing very well, particularly bearing in mind that you've had no previous experience.'

Kathy frowned. 'Then – what?'

'She happened to be walking down High Street earlier this evening when she saw Mr Kendall's car. A car, I might add, that she is very familiar with.' Jemima paused to let her words sink in.

So, Kathy thought, the secret was out and Miss Curtis had wasted no time in telling tales to the woman who was not only her landlady but also had the power to have her dismissed immediately and without a reference.

'Is there a company rule against a friendship between employees?' Kathy asked stiffly.

'No,' Jemima said carefully, 'although it is unwise between two people of such differing ranks, shall we say. It can lead to resentment among the other staff if they were to perceive any favouritism.'

'But we – he – has certainly not shown any favouritism towards me at all. He hardly ever comes into the department, let alone . . .'

'I know. I realize that. If he had, I might well have smelt a rat before now.'

'A rat!' Kathy's anger flared. 'Is that how you view – our – our friendship?'

Jemima pursed her mouth and nodded, but there was a hint of sadness in her eyes. 'My dear, you might not believe me, but I really do have your best interests at heart.'

Kathy's expression was sceptical and Jemima, catching sight of it, closed her eyes and shook her head in a gesture of helplessness.

After a long pause, Jemima opened her eyes and looked directly at Kathy. 'There are a few things you should know about Mr Kendall, my dear—' she began, but Kathy jumped to her feet.

'I don't want to hear them and anyway, I'm moving out. I won't be a trouble to you any more. Tony's found me a flat and—'

'Ah, the flat. The famous flat. He's setting you up in the flat, is he? This is worse than I thought.'

'No, he's not setting me up in it, as you put it. You make me sound like a – a mistress!'

'And aren't you?' Jemima asked bluntly.

Kathy felt an embarrassed flush flood into her face. 'No, I am not,' she answered heatedly. 'How dare you imply any such thing?'

'Well, that's one good thing, I suppose,' Jemima murmured, unperturbed by the girl's outburst. 'But once he gets you into that flat where he can visit you any time he likes—' She paused and then added, 'It's the flat on Mill Road, I suppose?'

Kathy's mouth dropped open as she stared at Jemima. Her voice was husky as she faltered, 'What – what do you mean? *The* flat on Mill Road?'

'Kathy – please – sit down. At least listen to what I've got to tell you.'

Slowly, Kathy sank back into the chair. She sat forward, tense and fearful, her hands so tightly clasped together in her lap that her knuckles were white. Against her will, she waited to hear what Jemima had to say.

Thirteen

'Tony Kendall is a very nice young man, I won't deny that—'

'Then why—?' Kathy began, but Jemima held up her hand to silence her.

'He comes from a good background – ' she hesitated briefly before adding, 'but it's his family that's the problem.' She paused. 'He's related to the Hammond family.'

Kathy gasped. 'The – the owners of the store?'

Jemima nodded. 'It isn't talked about because the obvious would be said.'

'What d'you mean? The obvious?'

'That he's very young to be in such an important position. It could be seen as nepotism.' She smiled wryly. 'James Hammond is his mother's cousin and many would say Tony's only the manager because of his relationship to the Hammond family.'

'So his mother was a Hammond?

Jemima nodded. 'It was *her* mother, to be precise, who was the Hammond. She was sister to the old man, as we call him, Mr Anthony Hammond.'

'Tony did say we should keep our – our meetings secret,' Kathy said slowly. 'I expect he thinks Mr James wouldn't approve.'

'Actually, Mr James is a very nice man, down to earth and not in any way snobbish. No, I'm afraid the problem is Tony's own mother.'

'His mother? Has she got something to do with the store?'

'Oh no. But Tony – whom she always calls Anthony, by the way – is her only son. Her only child and she – is a very possessive woman.' Jemima met Kathy's puzzled gaze. 'You haven't met her yet, I take it?'

Kathy shook her head. Suddenly she was feeling very cold inside. This wasn't at all what she had expected Jemima to say and for some inexplicable reason she feared what was coming next.

'How many times have you been out with Tony?'

'Well – several times over the weeks.'

'And how many times has he left suddenly, not turned up at all or cancelled at the last minute?'

Kathy's mouth dropped open as she stared, horrified, at Jemima. 'How – how did you know?'

'Because it's happened before. It's what always happens to his girlfriends.'

Remembering what Stella had told her, Kathy whispered, 'Miss Curtis? It happened to her?'

'You know about Muriel?'

'Yes – someone told me.'

'Stella, I expect,' Jemima murmured.

'Oh, please, I don't want to get her into trouble . . .'

'It's all right. Actually, I'm pleased she has. Perhaps it will help you to believe what I'm telling you now.'

For a moment, Kathy covered her face with her hands and gave a little sob. Then with a supreme effort, she raised her head and said quietly, 'I do believe you. I know you wouldn't lie to me. And – and I'm sorry that I ever lied to you. I hated doing it. I really am a very truthful person – usually. But somehow, I knew you'd try to stop me seeing him if you found out.'

'I most certainly would have done,' Jemima said briskly. 'Make no mistake about that.'

There was silence between them for a moment until Kathy said, 'But his mother's – well – some sort of invalid, isn't she? I mean, if she needed him when his father was working, I didn't mind.'

'Personally, I think she's a hypochondriac who uses her so-called ill-health to manipulate both her husband and her son.' Jemima's expression softened as she added, 'George – Tony's dad – is, by all accounts, a lovely fellow. He's too good, if you know what I mean.' Not having met Tony's parents, Kathy didn't really know. Though she was starting to understand a little more. And she didn't like what she was hearing. 'Beatrice Kendall is a selfish, devious woman who will stop at nothing to keep her son living at home with her.'

'What happened to Muriel – Miss Curtis?'

Jemima shook her head, as if she was still unable to believe herself what she was about to confide in Kathy. 'Poor Muriel. I think she was very fond of Tony and we all thought he was fond of her too. We were pleased for them. Oh, we'd heard rumours about other girl-friends he'd had, but we thought this time it was the real thing – for both of them.' She sighed. 'But then he took her home to meet his parents. Beatrice was very unpleasant towards Muriel. But worse than that, she made it her business to find out about the girl's family. Years ago, there was a scandal about Muriel's father embezzling money from the firm he worked for. Not Muriel's fault, of course. She was only a child at the time. It was nothing to do with her. But Beatrice latched on to it. She tried to persuade Tony that Muriel was not right for him. That his involvement with her would damage his career and his reputation.'

'And he believed her and ended the – the friendship?'

'No – no, credit due to him, he didn't. It was Muriel who ended it.'

'*Muriel*? Why?'

Jemima held her gaze for a moment. 'You do realize that I am trusting you not to say a word about all this to anyone. Not *anyone*, Kathy. I only know about it because poor Muriel was so distressed at work – well, let's just say she confided in me. I shouldn't really be telling you. I never betray confidences.' Despite the gravity of their conversation she allowed herself a small smile. 'Just like you never lie. We both seem to be breaking our own rules, don't we?'

Kathy smiled guiltily.

'Anyway,' Jemima went on. 'It seems that Beatrice sent for Muriel to go to their house – *without* Tony being present. She told her that Tony was too loyal to end the relationship himself, but that if she, Muriel, had any true feelings for him, she would end it to save his career and his good name.' Jemima sighed. 'I suppose Muriel felt she had no choice. There would never have been any kind of friendliness with her in-laws, Beatrice would've made sure of that. And Tony would have been in the middle of what would probably have become a battleground.' She was silent for a few moments, allowing Kathy time to digest it all.

'So Muriel loved him enough to sacrifice her own happiness.'

'That's how Beatrice made her see it, yes.' Jemima sniffed. 'But in my opinion she would have been better to have fought for her man.' Then she sighed. 'Muriel is an excellent head of department, but I'm afraid she lacked the courage to stand up to the woman.'

'And you think I do too?'

For a moment Jemima regarded her solemnly, then slowly, she smiled. 'No,' she said quietly. 'No, I think you're made of sterner stuff. But I can still see you losing in the end. Beatrice is a formidable woman and her methods are clever. No one dares to call her bluff. Certainly, poor George and Tony dare not. She might, indeed, be genuinely ill.' She sighed. 'I expect nothing I say can dissuade you, but at least I wanted you to know exactly what you are getting yourself into.'

Kathy nodded.

'And as for moving into this flat, well, there's no need for that. If you want to stay here, you can.'

'Even if I go on seeing him?'

Jemima nodded and now her smile was pensive. 'Oh Kathy, you might not think it to look at me now, but once upon a time I was young and in love and – I have to admit – very, very foolish.'

'And – you think I am?'

Again Jemima regarded her solemnly, searching the pretty face before her, seeing the determined set of Kathy's chin, the spark of defiance in her eyes. 'I think,' she said slowly, 'that you could be letting yourself in for a lot of heartache. Falling in love should be a happy time, the most joyous time . . .' For a moment Jemima's eyes were alight with joy at her own memories but then they were suddenly clouded with sorrow. Kathy, who had been on the point of asking what had happened to Jemima in her youth, now dared not ask the question. If even thinking about it in her own mind brought back such a sad and haunted look, then asking Jemima to talk about it would be cruel. Though Kathy longed to know. Perhaps she could ask Amy, though she doubted her friend knew any more than she did. It seemed to be a closely guarded family secret.

Instead, she said, 'Thank you for telling me and, yes, I would like to stay here. I can't really afford the flat and I don't want to be – well – I don't want Tony to be paying for it. That wouldn't be right. But – ' she paused and her tone took on a determined edge – 'I do intend to go on seeing him.'

Jemima sighed but said, 'Very well. As long as you understand you will be the subject of some unpleasant gossip and possibly even ridicule for a while. Until they find someone else to tear to shreds,' she added tartly. 'You'll have all sorts of people telling you tales about all the girlfriends he's had and how he's left a trail of broken hearts behind him.'

'I've already had a couple. The first time he took me out, he left halfway through the meal – just like you said – because a message came that his mother had been taken ill. After he'd gone, a woman from another table came and spoke to me. Evidently, she was one of his former girlfriends. At the time, I thought she was just being spiteful. Now I see that perhaps she was genuinely trying to warn me.'

'It'd be a lot easier if he was really a cad,' Jemima sighed. 'But he isn't. He's a nice young man, just weak where his mother is concerned. And whether that can be classed as a fault, even I'm not sure. And usually,' she smiled mischievously, 'I have no problem in making my mind up about folks and saying so too, if I think fit.'

'I've noticed,' Kathy teased and the two women exchanged a glance. In it there was a new understanding, even a fondness for each other that had grown over the weeks that Kathy had been there and had been even more strengthened by tonight's conversation.

'So,' Kathy went on. 'You and Taffy don't want your house to yourselves again then?'

Jemima laughed out loud. 'I like having you around, but I have to admit it's mainly because of Taffy that I'm asking you to stay. If he has taken to you – and he certainly has – then you must be all right.'

The two women laughed together and, getting up, Kathy said, 'I'll make the cocoa and call him in to give him an extra saucer of milk to say thank you.'

Fourteen

The first few days back at work were difficult. The gossip had spread, and Kathy tried to ignore the glances, the whispered conversations that halted as soon as she came near. Hardest to bear was Stella's attitude. One moment she was friendly enough, the next cold and distant.

But it was Miss Curtis who caused Kathy the most discomfort. It must have been her who had told work colleagues. She didn't think Stella would have broken her word and yet now she couldn't be sure. Once or twice she saw her whispering to the young assistant from lingerie, their conversation ceasing as soon as Kathy drew near. She knew that Jemima would say nothing to anyone. So – that left Muriel. Kathy longed to talk to her superior about it, but she couldn't. That would be betraying Jemima's confidence and, now that they had arrived at a mutual understanding and respect, she had no intention of doing so.

As if he too realized that 'the word was out', Tony started coming to the millinery department and speaking to her, making no attempt now to hide the fact that they were walking out together.

'Actually,' he whispered. 'I'm glad it's out. I don't like all this cloak-and-dagger stuff. It's exciting at first, but then it gets a bit wearing.'

Kathy smiled weakly, biting back the retort: Well, you should know about that!

'Have you made up your mind about the flat?'

'Yes, I have. I'm staying where I am for the moment. Now there's no need for secrecy, I'm happy with Miss Robinson. She's been very kind to me.'

Tony looked disappointed. 'Well, if you're sure. It won't be so easy to be together, though, will it? She'll still be keeping her beady eye on you.'

'We can go out to the pictures, to restaurants, for drives in the country.'

'Yes, but I want to be alone with you. I want to – well, you know . . .'

Though a faint blush rose in her cheeks, Kathy faced him squarely. 'I'm not that sort of girl, Tony. Maybe your past girlfriends – and oh yes, I do know there have been a few – have let you have your way with them, but not this one.' With that she had flounced away, leaving him staring after her in confusion.

That night when he took her out to dinner, Tony said, 'You misunderstood me earlier today. I can guess what the gossip is about me, but I want you to believe me that it's not true. Yes, I've had a few girlfriends – ' he sighed – 'but there was only ever one other before you that I was serious about. And she – she was the one who finished our friendship. Not me.'

Before Kathy thought to stop herself, she blurted out, 'Muriel Curtis?'

Tony's eyes widened. 'How d'you know?'

Kathy could have bitten her tongue off. 'I – I guessed,' she lied. 'I saw she was very upset when you'd been into the department one day and I – I overheard a conversation I shouldn't have done.'

'I see.' He was quiet for a moment, though he

seemed to accept her explanation and Kathy inwardly breathed a sigh of relief.

After a few moments, when she had gathered her wits, she asked carefully, 'You had the flat then?'

'Yes, but not for the reasons that I'm sure you and everyone else is thinking.' There was a bitter edge to his tone. Then he sighed. 'I – I have problems at home. Because of my mother's ill-health. I'm sorry, Kathy.' He spread his hands helplessly and looked at her with such a 'little boy lost' look that quite melted her heart. 'I took the flat in the first place because I intended to live there myself. Move out from home, but – well – it became impossible. I was still spending more time at home than I was in the flat. Anyway, I kept it on just so there was somewhere for us to go, just – just to talk and be together.'

Kathy couldn't quite believe what he was implying – that there had never been anything more than a kiss and a cuddle with his previous girlfriends. And what about Muriel Curtis? Surely that had led to 'something more'? But it was none of her business. It was what happened from now on that mattered to Kathy. Whatever had happened in the past was just that. In the past.

'You see,' he went on, as if it explained everything – and in a way, it did. 'You see, I can't take anyone home. Mother doesn't like it.'

On the Saturday evening Kathy was hurrying to leave work on time. Tony was calling for her at eight o'clock. Now there was no need for secrecy, he came openly to the little terraced house and was welcomed by Jemima. Though Taffy made it very clear that he did not welcome yet another stranger. Whenever Tony appeared, the cat stalked out of the room, his ears flattened and his tail thrashing angrily.

'Miss Matthews, you may go,' Muriel said as the last customer left the department and the sheets were placed over the displays. 'But, Miss Burton, could you spare me a moment? I'd like a word.'

Kathy's heart began to beat rapidly and she cast a glance at Stella. But the younger girl studiously avoided meeting her gaze.

'Of course, Miss Curtis,' Kathy replied evenly, though she was dreading what the woman had to say to her. Had Miss Curtis engineered her dismissal to try to separate her from Tony? As other staff called their 'good nights', Muriel drew Kathy to one side.

'I don't want you to think I'm interfering and I want you to know that this is said out of a genuine concern for you . . .'

Kathy was not sure she believed her, but she said nothing.

'You – you must know that Mr Kendall and I were once—' Muriel's lip trembled and Kathy felt sorry for her. But, not trusting herself to speak and afraid that she would say things she shouldn't, Kathy just nodded. 'He – he asked me to marry him.' Kathy stared at her. She hadn't known that. Maybe no one else knew that much. 'But – but his mother intervened. She – she didn't like me. I don't think she would like any girl – that her son got close to.' Muriel ran her tongue round her dry lips. 'He – he took me home to meet her, but she hated me. And no, that's not too strong a word for it. It was hatred – pure and simple. Of course, we could have gone away and got married. But I couldn't do that to him. I couldn't let him be estranged from his family. I couldn't let him carry the guilt of making his mother ill, maybe even of causing her death. How could anyone live with that? I couldn't and I wouldn't want him to either.'

Still, Kathy said nothing.

'You haven't met her yet?' Muriel asked.

Kathy shook her head.

'If and when you do, just be aware that she will hate you on sight and do everything she can to break your relationship up.'

'Well, I can't speak for Tony, but I know one thing. There's nothing she can do to make me end it. Nothing.'

Tears trembled in Muriel's eyes as she smiled sadly and said softly, 'Are you sure about that, Kathy?'

Kathy nodded. 'Oh yes, I'm very sure.'

'Then, I wish you well, my dear. Truly I do. The only thing I have ever wanted was to see him happy. And if you can do it, then I wish you all the luck in the world. Make him happy, Kathy. That's all I ask.'

It was a strange conversation to have taken place between a former girlfriend and the current one. Now she had very mixed feelings about Muriel. On the one hand, Kathy admired her for her selfless love for Tony, on the other she rather despised her for not being strong enough to fight her man. She told no one about their talk. She didn't even confide in Jemima and certainly not in Stella. She was unsure now just how much she could trust Stella. She had the uncomfortable feeling that the gossip that had spread like wildfire through the store had come not from Muriel but from the younger girl. With her new understanding, she couldn't believe that Muriel would be the instigator of tales that would include her own broken romance.

No, in future, Kathy would be careful just how much she confided in Stella Matthews.

The gossip ran on for another few days, but then something happened that drove all thoughts of Tony Kendall and his latest girlfriend from everybody's mind.

On the morning of Sunday, 3 September, Kathy woke with a strange feeling of foreboding. She lay a moment in her bed as if to hold on to the warmth and the security. She had the strangest feeling that once she got out of bed, nothing would ever be quite the same again. There was a soft knock at the door and Jemima appeared carrying a cup of tea.

'I couldn't sleep. The Prime Minister's going to speak at about quarter past eleven on the wireless, so I'm not going to morning service. Maybe I'll go along to St Mary's later.' She placed the tea on the bedside table and moved across the room to open the curtains. She stood a moment, looking above the rooftops to the blue sky. She gave a soft sigh and murmured, 'It's far too nice a day to be declaring war.'

Kathy sat up. 'Is – is that what he's going to do?'

'I'm very much afraid so.' There was another pause before Jemima shook herself, turned away from the window and said briskly, 'Now, my dear, drink your tea and get dressed. Breakfast will be all ready by the time you come down.'

'I should've—' Kathy began, but Jemima smiled and held up her hand.

'It's quite all right. I couldn't sleep. I've been up ages.'

*

They sat down, one either side of the wireless set, at eleven o'clock. It seemed an age before they heard the sound of the Prime Minister's voice and listened to his solemn words. At the end of his statement, they waited in silence until the notes of the national anthem died away.

'So,' Jemima murmured, stroking Taffy absently, 'it's all going to happen again.'

In a small voice, Kathy asked, 'What exactly is going to happen?'

'I really don't know, my dear. Of course they'll use the regular army first, but no doubt they'll expect volunteers and, after a while, they'll bring in conscription.'

'What – what's conscription?' Kathy felt very ignorant. She'd never heard her father, or anyone else in their small village, speak about the last war. She knew very little about it.

'Call-up. They set an age range and then all young men between those ages have to go for a medical. If they're passed fit for service, then – they have to go.'

'Will – will Tony have to go?' Swiftly, conscious of sounding selfish, Kathy added, 'And Morry?'

'They may be able to apply for deferment for Maurice because he works on a farm. But as for Tony – how old is he?'

'Twenty-six, I think.'

'Then he may not have to go yet, but eventually . . .' Her voice trailed away and Kathy shuddered.

At the store the next morning, there was a buzz of excitement running among all the staff. Stella, red-faced and breathless, came running into the department at five minutes past nine. Muriel opened her mouth to reprimand the girl, but before she could speak, Stella burst out.

'They're going to close the store for an hour and we've all got to go to the manager's office at ten o'clock. Mr James is coming in to speak to us all. I'm to go round all the store, Mr Kendall said, and tell everyone,' Stella went on importantly. Then, without even asking for permission from her superior, she marched off to carry out her mission.

Muriel turned slowly to look at Kathy, her expression bleak. 'I wonder how this will affect us all?'

Kathy's hands were trembling, but she tried to speak calmly and hopefully. 'Perhaps – perhaps it won't last very long. When this man, Hitler, realizes that there are people prepared to stand up to him, then – then . . .'

'Germany's a very strong nation, very – committed. My father fought in the last one. He was wounded. He's got medals, you know.' Muriel's voice took on a bitter note, 'But no one remembers the good people do, they only remember their mistakes.'

Kathy said nothing, but she knew Muriel was referring to the scandal surrounding her father that Tony's mother had used against her.

At last Muriel whispered what was really on her mind. 'He might go. Tony might have to go.'

Kathy stared at her, miserably. 'I know,' she whispered, her voice breaking. No longer could she hide her worst fear.

Muriel was the first to speak again. 'Come, we'd better do as we've been told. We'd better tell all the customers in the department that the store will be closed for an hour between ten and eleven.'

*

At ten minutes past ten all the staff made their way to the manager's office. Miss Robinson stood beside Tony, and the supervisors from each department squeezed into his office. The rest of the staff crowded into Miss Foster's office. Kathy was careful to stand at the back along with Muriel and Stella. She and Muriel were quiet and subdued, but Stella's eyes were shining with an excitement that seemed to rub off on the younger members of staff.

'I shall volunteer,' a young boy from the warehouse declared.

'You're not old enough. You're only fifteen.'

The spotty-faced youth flushed, but he still vowed, 'Well, as soon as I am then.'

'Sh,' someone hissed. 'Mr Hammond's coming.'

Kathy looked round to see the tall silver-haired man, smartly dressed in a dark suit and blue tie, weaving his way through the crowded office. He paused now and again to nod and smile at the members of his staff.

'He's a nice man, isn't he?' Stella whispered. 'Always has a word for us. Not stuck up and hoity-toity like some owners'd be.'

Now it was Kathy who, afraid that Mr Hammond might overhear, said, 'Sh.'

He stood in the doorway of Tony's office so that all the staff could hear him. 'This is an anxious day for all of us,' he said, his voice soft and deep and full of concern. 'But we must all pull together and do what we can to face whatever is coming. I want you to know that whatever problems this war brings, you can always come to either Mr Kendall or to me and we'll do our very best to help you. The Hammonds like to feel that the members of their staff are one big family and, in troubled times, that's what families do. Help each other. And for those of you who volunteer – ' the grin on the face of the young boy from the warehouse seemed to reach his ears – 'or are called up, then as long as Hammonds is still here, your job will be waiting for you when you come back.'

Though the kindly man used the word 'when' and not 'if', the thought was in everyone's mind. How many of those who went to fight would ever come back?

But Mr Hammond remained positive. He smiled and nodded at the staff in the outer office and then turned to speak to Tony and the heads of department. Knowing they were dismissed, the rest of the staff drifted back to their departments ready for the store to reopen, but Kathy lingered at the end of the corridor, hoping for a brief word with Tony. But it was Jemima who emerged from the office first, white-faced and stiff-backed. She walked towards Kathy, but didn't seem to see her. She just walked straight ahead as if lost in a trance. Kathy stepped forward, 'Aunt Jemima – I mean, Miss Robinson,' she added swiftly, forgetting in the tension of the moment how she always addressed her when at work. But Jemima didn't notice, didn't even realize she was being spoken to. She was walking in a trance. Kathy touched her arm and Jemima jumped, startled out of her reverie.

'Are you all right?' Kathy asked.

'I—' Jemima hesitated. Her eyes were dark, anguished pools. 'No, I'm not.' For a moment she sagged against Kathy and the younger girl supported her weight. Then she felt and heard Jemima let out a long, deep sigh.

'Let me take you to the staff restroom and make you a cup of tea. You've had a shock.'

With a supreme effort, Jemima straightened up. 'Thank you. I think I need one. Pity we're not allowed a little medicinal brandy. I could certainly do with—'

Suddenly, Mr Hammond was at the other side of her, taking her arm and helping Kathy to support her. 'I think that's an excellent idea. We'll go back to Mr Kendall's office.' He smiled at Kathy above Jemima's head. 'But don't tell the rest of the staff.'

Together, one either side of her, they helped Jemima back into Tony's office.

'Miss Foster, would you be so kind as to get us some tea? Miss Robinson is feeling a little – well, like the rest of us – shocked.'

'Of course. At once, Mr James.' And the fussy little spinster hurried off to do his bidding.

Inside the office, Tony placed a chair for Jemima and Mr Hammond and Kathy helped her into it.

'Tony, my boy, I hope you still keep a bottle of medicinal brandy in the bottom drawer like I always did.'

'Of course,' Tony smiled as he reached for it, but his concerned glance was on Jemima.

Miss Foster returned with the tea and James Hammond poured a generous measure of brandy into it. 'We're all in a turmoil, not quite knowing what it's all going to mean for us.' Standing by her chair, he looked down at her with a serious expression. 'But we do, don't we, Miss Robinson?' he added gently. 'We know exactly what we're all in for.'

Jemima looked up at him sadly as she murmured, 'I'm afraid we do, Mr James. I'm very much afraid we do.'

Fifteen

As soon as they arrived home that evening, Jemima said, 'Go and light the fire in the front room while I get the tea ready.'

'The – the front room?' Kathy gaped at her. 'But – but you – we – never sit in there.'

'Well, we will tonight. Go and light the fire and then make yourself pretty.' Jemima had fully recovered from her brief moment of doubt and uncertainly. Now she was her old self once more, full of determination and fortitude. Her eyes were full of mischief as she added, 'Not that you're not already, but you know what I mean. Tony's coming round later, isn't he?'

'Yes, but—'

'I'll explain when Tony gets here, but first let's have our tea,' was all Jemima would say, but Kathy was thankful that she seemed almost back to her old self. And yet there was something strange about her, something resolute and determined. She's up to something, Kathy thought, as she laid sticks and paper and pieces of coal in the grate. Although it was only early September and not exactly cold, she understood Jemima's desire for a comforting fire this evening of all evenings.

Once the fire was well alight, Kathy ran upstairs to change into her dress and brush her hair. As they sat down at the table together in the kitchen, Jemima picked up the heavy teapot and poured out two cups of tea, passing one to Kathy.

'Help yourself to sugar,' she murmured. 'And make the most of it. I expect it will be on ration soon enough.'

'Ration?' Kathy stared at her. 'What do you mean?'

Jemima set the teapot down carefully. 'Towards the end of the last war, certain foods were put on ration. I expect they'll do it even sooner this time. Of course,' she went on, musing aloud, 'they'll be all right out on the farm, but in the city we'll all have to start queuing for whatever we can get.' A little smile twitched the corner of her mouth. 'You might want to go home.'

'Never,' Kathy declared as she buttered a piece of bread, spreading it thickly. 'I'd sooner starve.'

'Bravely said, my dear,' Jemima said, sipping her tea and looking as if she was relishing every drop. As perhaps she was. 'But not so easy to do.'

'This war changes everything,' Jemima said as, a little later, the three of them sat in her front parlour before the blazing fire. Kathy and Tony sat side by side on the battered sofa, Jemima in the armchair to one side of the hearthrug. The room was cosy, the fire casting a warm, flickering light around the room, illuminating briefly Jemima's heavy old-fashioned furniture. 'I'm guessing that there won't be conscription for a while. They'll depend on the regular army and volunteers. And I expect there will be plenty of them – just like last time.' For a moment she was pensive. Kathy could only guess at her painful memories and her fears for the immediate future too.

Jemima pulled herself out of her brief reverie. 'But if

it goes on for some time, then they will bring it in. I'm sure of it.' Her glance now rested on Tony. 'And if they do, you'll undoubtedly be called up.'

He nodded, not in the least surprised, though Kathy could not help a startled gasp. She hadn't thought it would happen so soon.

She clutched at Tony's hand and held onto it tightly, as if by her willpower she would physically stop him from going to war.

'You must make the most of the time you have together,' Jemima went on. 'And you can meet here. This room can be your haven from the world.' She looked hard at Tony. 'But I'm going to be very blunt. I'm trusting you not to bring shame upon Kathy.'

The young man blushed, seeming for a moment nothing like the competent manager of the big city store, but a rather boyish and shy young man. 'Of course I won't. I – I do care about Kathy. Truly, Miss Robinson, despite what you might think because of my – well – because of my past.'

Jemima waved her hand dismissively. 'I'm not one of the gossips. I do know a little more than you might think and I am aware that it is not all your fault. However, that said, I am *not* in agreement with this flat you have in town. If you set Kathy up there, it would be announcing to the world that she's your mistress—'

'But I'm not,' Kathy declared hotly.

'I know that,' Jemima answered patiently. 'But I'm afraid the gossips wouldn't believe it. They would have a field day and – to be honest – who could blame them? But it'll be very different if you meet here, under my roof.'

Tony and Kathy exchanged an amused glance, realizing that no one would dare to question their conduct if it had Miss Robinson's blessing.

'That's very kind of you and, yes, I do see what you mean about the flat—' Tony pulled a wry face. 'But it was all I could think of. You see – ' now he turned to Kathy as if this concerned her more than Jemima, yet he spoke freely in front of the older woman, wanting her to understand too – 'you see, I can't – I daren't—'

Kathy touched his hand in a tender gesture. 'I know,' she said sympathetically. 'It must be so difficult for you with your mother being an invalid.'

Tony squeezed her hand and murmured, 'You're sweet to be so understanding. Not – not everyone is.'

Though Jemima said nothing, Kathy heard her give a disbelieving sniff.

Now Kathy too began to scour the daily papers for news of the progress of the war. Poland had been overcome, but the expected onslaught on Britain did not happen. Instead, every home was bombarded with public information leaflets and lists of regulations.

'But it's better than bombs,' Kathy remarked, trying to sort out which list of dos and don'ts applied to them.

'They'll come soon enough,' Jemima replied tartly, sifting through the leaflets. 'Identity cards. We've got to carry identity cards and gasmasks at all times. Even children.'

'Did you know that a lot of children from Leeds have been evacuated to the Lincoln area already? They arrived with luggage labels attached to their coats. Poor little mites.'

Jemima frowned. 'Yes, I had heard. I'd like to help, but with us both out all day, it's hardly suitable for us to have a young child, is it? I expect Betty will be the first in the queue to take a little one though.' Her face softened. 'A real mother is Betty,' she whispered. 'Bless her.'

Kathy stared at her. It was the first time she'd seen Jemima sentimental, but the next moment the older woman had shaken herself out of her daydreaming and was briskly asking Kathy to hold the tape while she measured the windows for blackout curtains.

'Mr Hammond has instructed that all the staff can have their curtains made up for free and they can buy the material at cost price. The workroom's going to be busy, but he's certainly setting a good example. I think he's already looking for more staff for the dressmaking department.'

'Mm,' Kathy murmured, holding the end of the tape measure. 'I wish I'd leant to sew. It's going to be useful.'

'I have to admit, it's not one of my skills,' Jemima said, stepping down from the stool and writing figures on a piece of paper. She straightened up. 'Your turn to climb up. But we're lucky, you know,' she went on as Kathy reached up to the top of the curtain rail. 'At least we can get any sewing work done at the store.'

'Stella was saying that the fabric department has been so busy the last few days, some of the shelves are empty. Mind you, we've been quiet. I expect buying a new hat is the last thing on people's minds at the moment.'

'They'll drift back. Things will settle down into a routine soon enough and folks will start to act normally again.'

147

'You think so?' Kathy was doubtful. 'I don't think things will ever feel "normal" again.'

Now Jemima did not answer.

'Will you have to go?' It was the question Kathy was asking continually.

'Not yet,' Tony tried to reassure her. He smiled and pulled a wry face. 'And if my mother has anything to do with it, I shan't be going at all.'

'Why? What can she do?'

'Nothing. At least, I don't think so, but she's quite determined that her precious boy won't have to go and fight.'

Kathy smiled and linked her arm through his as they walked down High Street towards their favourite hotel restaurant, where Tony had booked a table. Whatever the tales were about his mother, if she could pull strings to keep Tony safely out of the war, then she had Kathy's whole-hearted approval.

Surprisingly, the place was full.

'It's a good job I booked or we wouldn't have got in, by the look of it. Ah, good evening, Gregson,' he added as the head waiter hurried forward to hold out Kathy's chair for her and then to hand them each a menu. 'You seem busy tonight.'

'We certainly are, sir.' He leaned forward as if imparting a confidence. 'I think everyone's determined to make the most of the time they have together.'

Kathy glanced round. Many of the diners were young couples like themselves, who at any moment might be caught up in the conflict and parted for goodness knew how long. Perhaps forever. Kathy shuddered and sent up a silent prayer that Tony's mother would start pulling strings right now!

They were halfway through their main course when Gregson approached the table, an expression of apology on his face.

'There's a telephone call for you, sir.'

Tony sighed, but got up at once. 'Sorry, darling. I won't be a minute . . .'

Kathy, now knowing what to expect, carried on with her meal. She had finished eating by the time Tony returned to the table, her arms folded, determination on her face.

He didn't sit down, but hovered near her. 'I'm sorry, darling, but—'

'Tony, sit down and finish your dinner. At least this course,' she added, softening just a little.

'I really can't—' he began.

'Yes, you can,' Kathy said firmly. 'Five minutes isn't going to make any difference.'

'It might. Mother thinks she's having a heart attack and Father's at work. I have to go, Kathy, really I do.'

Kathy rose. 'Then I'm coming with you.'

Tony stared at her, consternation on his face. 'Oh – well now – I don't think—'

'I'm coming.' And for once, Kathy would not take 'no' for an answer.

They reached the house where Tony lived with his parents in less than fifteen minutes.

'Please, Kathy, stay in the car. It's – it's not the right moment for you to meet her. It – it'll upset her even more.'

'Why?' Kathy asked, feigning innocence.

'She might be really bad. I might have to call the

doctor – or – or even an ambulance. Please, Kathy – please stay in the car at least until I see how bad she is.'

Kathy sighed. If the woman really was ill, she didn't want to be guilty of making her worse. And Tony had his 'little boy look' on his face. 'All right then, but if there's anything I can do to help . . .'

'Yes, yes, of course,' Tony said quickly and hurried away into the house.

He was gone a long time. So long in fact that it began to get dark. And still Kathy waited, but now she was growing impatient. Surely Tony hadn't forgotten that she was sitting out here?

A car drew up in front of Tony's. A well-built man with broad shoulders, a bald head and glasses eased his way out from behind the driving seat and reached into the back seat for his medical bag. Kathy watched as he went up the garden path of the Kendalls' home and rang the bell. Almost immediately, the door opened and she saw Tony usher him into the house. As he was about to close the door again, Tony glanced down the path and saw her. For a brief moment he hesitated, seeming unsure, but then, leaving the door half-open, he loped down the path and came to the passenger's window.

'Darling, I'm so sorry. You're still here. I thought you might have gone by now. Let me call you a taxi. Mother's in a dreadful state. I've had to call the doctor . . .'

'I saw,' Kathy replied shortly, trying to keep the impatience out of her tone, but failing. She bit her lip, feeling suddenly guilty at being so selfish. 'I'm so sorry your mother is ill. Is there anything I can do?'

Tony shook his head. The worried look never left

his face and Kathy could see that he was anxious to get back into the house. 'Let me call you a taxi,' he said again.

'It's all right,' Kathy said, climbing out of the car. 'I'll walk home. It's a nice evening.'

'But it's right the other side of the city. It's almost dark and now we've got these blackout regulations, I don't like you walking all that way on your own.'

'It's a clear night. I'll see enough by the moonlight. We're used to black nights in the country. It won't bother me.'

He smiled wryly as he closed the car door. 'A beautiful romantic evening and I can't even walk my girl home. I truly am sorry, darling.'

She touched his face gently. 'Don't worry,' she said softly and kissed his cheek. 'Go back to your mother. I do hope she'll be better soon.'

'I know what's caused it,' Tony blurted out.

You being out with your girlfriend, Kathy thought, but aloud she said, 'Oh?'

'The young man next door's been called up. His mother's in a dreadful state. She came round to see Mother. I do wish she hadn't. She should know how delicate Mother is.'

Kathy almost snapped: And what about the poor woman whose son has gone to war? Are none of you sparing a thought for her? Automatically, Kathy's glance went to the next-door house. It was all in darkness. In mourning already, it seemed, though she knew it was really because the occupants were following blackout regulations.

She pulled in a deep breath and once again tried to see it from Mrs Kendall's view. Although she didn't know the woman – yet – she could imagine a gentle, delicate, doll-like creature for whom life in general and this dreadful war in particular was just too much for her to bear.

She pictured her as an ageing Dora out of *David Copperfield*, a sweet-natured woman on whom all her family doted. With this picture in her mind, Kathy could find it in her heart to forgive the woman who appeared so selfish. Perhaps it wasn't all her fault. Perhaps . . .

'I must go in,' Tony said, kissing Kathy's cheek swiftly and squeezing her hand. 'Do take care, darling.'

The haunted look on his face was genuine. He was torn between the two women in his life. Anxious not to add to his worries, Kathy smiled and reassured him. 'I'll be fine.'

With that they parted, she to walk through the dark streets of the blacked-out city, he to rush indoors to care for his mother. For a moment she lingered, watching until the door closed behind him. Then she sighed and turned away. As she did so, she cannoned into a man walking up the street.

'Oh, I'm so sorry, I didn't see you,' she cried.

The man reached out and caught hold of her steadying her. 'That's all right, miss. No harm done.'

Peering at him through the poor light, she could see that he was dressed in workman's clothes and heavy boots, but his voice was deep and gentle. He nodded to her as he released his hold on her and stepped back. Touching his cap he moved away, but to her surprise, instead of walking on further up the street, he turned into the gate of the Kendalls' house.

Kathy couldn't move. Her curiosity held her there as she saw him go in at the side gate leading round to the back of the house. The gate closed behind him and his shadowy figure in the moonlight was lost to her. For a few moments longer, Kathy stood staring at the house before turning away and walking slowly down the street, her thoughts in a whirl.

Could the man she had bumped into have been Tony's father?

Sixteen

'You're home early,' Jemima greeted her as she stepped into the comparatively bright light of the kitchen. 'Oh, don't tell me! His mother's been taken ill. Again!'

Kathy sighed as she slumped into the easy chair opposite Jemima.

'Got it in one!' she murmured, still half lost in thought. After a moment she asked, 'Aunt Jemima, do you know Tony's parents?'

'No, not really. I know a bit *about* them. And I do remember seeing his mother in the store years ago when she was a young woman and I was a junior. And I do believe – ' she pondered a moment – 'Tony's father has been in the store a few times. But his mother never comes in any more. Not now. She rarely goes out anywhere – so I believe.'

'What's his father like?'

Jemima wrinkled her forehead. 'An older version of Tony. Dark hair – going grey now.' She snorted in an unladylike manner that was so out of character for Miss Jemima Robinson that Kathy almost laughed aloud. 'But you can't wonder at it with that wife of his,' Jemima went on. 'But he strikes me as being a nice sort of chap. Quiet. Ordinary, just like you and me, really. Not at all the sort of chap you'd have thought Beatrice Charlesworth would have married. Oh dear me no. Far too ordinary for her.'

'She must have fallen in love with him.'

'Maybe.' Jemima sounded doubtful.

'Are you trying to say she married beneath her?'

Jemima frowned. 'It's all a bit of a mystery really. Mr Anthony Hammond took over the store from the people who started it. He continued to build it up and obviously he's become quite well to do. Deservedly so, for he's a hard worker and a clever businessman. He's Beatrice Kendall's uncle – her mother's brother. The Charlesworths were actually quite ordinary, but rumour had it that Beatrice was spoiled rotten by her doting uncle. Mr Anthony only had one son – Mr James. No daughter, you see. And he lavished attention and gifts on his niece instead. I believe he even paid for her to go to a private girls' school.'

How ironic, Kathy thought. My father longed for a son and Mr Anthony Hammond craved a daughter. Aloud, she said, 'So how come she didn't marry someone – well – more top drawer?'

'*That's* the mystery.'

'Then she must have loved George Kendall.' Kathy, so in love herself, was adamant. But Jemima merely smiled and conceded softly, 'Perhaps. She wouldn't be the first to fall for someone totally unsuitable.'

Kathy said nothing, but she was left wondering if Jemima still felt that her romance with Tony Kendall was doomed for one reason – or another.

'I think I might have bumped into his father.' Swiftly she explained how she had come to be outside the Kendalls' house and she described the man she had seen.

'That certainly sounds like him. He'd've been coming home from his shift. He works at an engineering firm. Poor George.' Jemima sighed and murmured again, 'Poor, poor George.'

The following day, Kathy heard nothing from Tony all morning. At her lunch break, she headed for his office without waiting for his summons. She knocked, then entered the outer office.

'Good morning, Miss Foster. Is Mr Kendall in today?'

'Oh – er – yes, good morning, Miss Burton. Yes, yes. I believe he is. Er – please would you sit down a moment while I—'

Kathy smiled. She had been about to go straight into Tony's office. Why shouldn't she? Everyone knew they were practically engaged now. But she was amused by his secretary's guardianship and she didn't want to offend the kindly little woman. So she sat down meekly and folded her hands in her lap to wait.

Miss Foster returned. 'He's engaged on the telephone at the moment. If you wouldn't mind waiting a moment, then you may go in.'

'Thank you, Miss Foster.'

Miss Foster returned to her desk and continued to tot up a long line of figures. It was so quiet in the outer office, the only noise the plopping of the gas fire, that they both heard the 'ting' of the telephone receiver being replaced in the inner room.

Miss Foster quickly scribbled a figure and then looked up. 'You may go in now, Miss Burton.'

'How is she? How is your mother?' Kathy asked as soon as she'd entered his office and closed the door behind her.

Tony stood up and came around the desk to take

her in his arms. 'Not too bad. She's resting. Dad's stayed off work today to look after her and I'm taking tomorrow off. Darling, I'm so sorry our date was spoilt and, the way things are at the moment, I don't know when I'll be able to see you again.'

Kathy swallowed her disappointment and smiled bravely. 'That's all right. I understand. I just hope she'll soon feel better.'

'You're very sweet. Not many girls would be as understanding as you are.'

'It's not your fault.' She put the palms of her hands flat on his chest and smiled up into his face. 'But just promise me one thing.'

'I will if I can. You know that.'

'When she's well again, you'll take me home to meet both your parents.'

A look of horror flitted across Tony's face. 'Oh, I don't know about that. She – she doesn't like visitors.'

Kathy put her head on one side and regarded him steadily. 'What you mean is – ' she spoke softly, but now there was a note of firmness in her tone – 'that she won't want to meet *me*. Your girlfriend.'

Tony closed his eyes and groaned. 'You've heard the gossip about Muriel and me, I suppose? You shouldn't believe everything you hear.'

Determined not to tell any more outright lies, instead Kathy said carefully, 'Then tell me what happened with Muriel.'

'I hate talking about this. It – it doesn't seem right.'

'I promise I won't say anything to her. I wouldn't be so cruel. I – I think she still has feelings for you.'

His mouth hardened. 'I doubt it. And I certainly don't feel anything for her now. She ended our – our friendship suddenly and without any explanation. All she would say was that "it would be for the best". I didn't understand it. I still don't.'

So, Kathy thought, with a pang of sympathy for the other girl, Muriel had acted so very nobly that Tony was still unaware that his own mother had been instrumental in bringing about the end of the affair. Muriel had loved him so much that she had spared his feelings. She had even protected his mother, who certainly didn't deserve such thoughtfulness. Yet, Kathy supposed, Muriel had realized that in telling the whole truth she would hurt Tony too.

'Tony – please be honest with me. It's important. If Muriel were to explain everything and – and wanted you back, would you—?'

He didn't even let her finish. 'No,' he cried vehemently. 'No. It's you I love, Kathy. Really I do and – I don't suppose you'll believe me – ' he gave a wry, lopsided grin that melted her heart – 'but I've never felt this way about anyone before. Not the way I feel about you.'

'I bet you say that to all the girls.' Kathy laughed flippantly.

But Tony's face was utterly serious. 'No, I swear I haven't ever said that before. Not to anyone.'

'Not even to Muriel?' Now Kathy's question was serious. She needed to know.

He looked directly into her eyes and she knew he was speaking the truth when he said soberly, 'Not even to Muriel.'

Kathy gave a huge sigh that came from deep within her being. She believed him and vowed she would never again mention his relationship with Muriel, though she spared a sympathetic thought for the other girl and hoped that she too might one day find the kind of happiness that Kathy herself now felt.

But there was still one problem – apart from the obvious one of the war – that overshadowed their happiness. Tony's mother.

'He doesn't want to take me home to meet his mother.'

'Are you surprised?' Jemima retorted tartly. 'He's afraid the same thing will happen again.'

'He doesn't seem to know the full story about what happened between his mother and Muriel,' Kathy said and related what Tony had told her.

Jemima pulled a sceptical expression. 'You surprise me. But then, if I think about it, Muriel was so besotted with him that I expect she sacrificed her own feelings for the sake of his. How very noble!'

'You don't sound as if you admire her for that.'

'I don't. She should have stood up to his mother. Fought for him.' She glanced at Kathy over the top of the steel-rimmed spectacles she wore for reading or knitting and sewing. Her busy hands were already knitting socks for the troops. She had joined the local branch of the WVS and, two or three evenings a week, she was disappearing to meetings involved with war work. 'I don't expect you'll give in to that dreadful woman quite so easily, will you?'

Kathy grinned. 'You bet your life I won't.'

'Good.'

'Only thing is – I can't get him to take me home to meet his parents.'

'Then go and see them yourself. Nothing to stop you.'

Kathy gasped. 'You mean – on my own? Without him being there? Without him even *knowing*?'

Jemima pondered for a moment. 'No . . .' she said slowly. 'No, I wouldn't do that. But what I *would* do is to tell him that if he is serious about you, then you would like to meet his parents and that if he doesn't take you, you will go on your own.'

Kathy stared at her. 'You're absolutely right. That's exactly what I'll do.' Then she laughed ruefully. 'Only thing is, I'm a bit stuck if he turns the tables on me and demands to meet *my* parents too.'

Jemima smiled. 'Ah, well now, that's another story.'

'Are we having a Morrison shelter in the front room or an Anderson shelter in the back yard?'

'Neither,' Jemima answered promptly. 'There's a big cupboard under the stairs. You can get into it from the front room. I'm going to clear that out and make it so we can both get in it. It'll be as safe as any shelter. More so, probably.'

'Right you are. Can I help?'

'I tell you what you can do. Pack up my mother's best tea service out of the china cabinet into boxes and we'll push them to the narrow end of the cupboard.' She was thoughtful for a moment, then murmured. 'I'm sure there's other things I ought to put in there for safety, but I can't think what at the moment.'

Kathy smiled. Jemima had so much on her mind now, she often seemed to go off into a little world of her own. The girl rather suspected she was reliving the events of the last war and that her memories were far from pleasant. But she dared not ask. Jemima Robinson was not the kind of person one asked personal questions. Instead, Kathy said brightly, 'Where can I get some suitable boxes?'

'Mm? Oh yes. Boxes. Er – ' Jemima wrinkled her forehead – 'you could try the shop on Monks Road. They might have something.'

A little later Kathy returned triumphantly with two sturdy boxes and something wrapped up in newspaper. 'Guess what I've got? Four sausages and two lovely pieces of fish.'

'Well done,' Jemima smiled. 'We'd better make the most of them. I'm sure there are going to be shortages very soon. I hear they're cutting the bus services already because of a shortage of fuel, and men to drive them, if it comes to that.'

'They'll have to take on women bus drivers then, won't they?' Kathy laughed jokingly, but Jemima's answer was quite serious. 'Yes, they will.'

'Kathy, please don't do that,' Tony begged.

'Then take me to meet them yourself.'

Already it was almost the end of October. It had snowed during the day, but they were cosy, sitting close together on the old sofa in Jemima's front room, the only light coming from the flickering fire.

Tony ran his hand distractedly through his hair. 'I can't. I really can't.'

'Why?'

'Because – because – ' he took a deep breath – 'Mother won't like you. Oh, that sounds awful,' he added swiftly, gripping her hand tightly in apology. 'It's not you personally she won't like. She doesn't like anyone I take home. Anyone who I might marry and leave home for.'

161

'She wants to keep you at home, tied to her apron strings forever, does she?'

He smiled ruefully. 'I suppose that's about the size of it, but put like that, so bluntly – it – it makes me sound very weak.'

Kathy did not contradict him outright. Instead she said slowly, 'I can see that it's very difficult for you. If she's ill and depends on both you and your father, it would be rather brutal of you just to leave. I do see that.' She bit her lip, longing to ask if his mother really was as ill as she made out. Instead, she toned down the bluntness a little by asking, 'How ill is she?'

Tony shrugged. 'Who's to say? When she has one of her attacks, she certainly seems genuinely poorly. And the doctor's never once hinted that she's not really ill. Mind you, he gets paid for every visit and her stays in the private nursing home – marvellous though it is – cost us quite a lot.'

'When you say "us", I take it you mean that you contribute?'

He nodded. 'Dad works very hard. Does a lot of overtime whenever he can get it, but even then he couldn't afford the fees on his wage.'

He returned her steady gaze. 'You're wondering if she's putting it on just to make me stay at home. To keep me tied to her.'

'No,' Kathy said carefully. 'I didn't say that. I wouldn't accuse her of that. At least,' she added, trying to lighten their conversation a little, 'not yet.'

But Tony could not see anything funny in his situation. He was caught between his ailing mother and the girl he loved. 'Kathy, I know this must sound like a trite line, but I swear it isn't. I've truly never felt this way about any other girl. And oh yes, I know there've been a few, but I've never – ever – asked anyone else to marry me.' He squeezed her hands. 'Marry me, Kathy. Please – say you'll be my wife.'

Tears sprang to her eyes. Tough as she could be, Kathy was always moved by a romantic gesture. There had been so few of them in her life and certainly from no one that she cared deeply about. Even in that moment – the happiest moment in her life – she spared a fleeting thought for poor Morry. How happy she would have made him if she had been able to have given him the answer she was about to give Tony. And how much simpler life would have been. She would have pleased everyone. Her father, her mother – especially her poor, dear mother – and even the Robinsons would have been delighted. But she didn't love Morry, not in the way she loved Tony.

She put her arms around his neck and gently kissed his lips, murmuring. 'Yes, oh yes, please.'

He held her close and they kissed long and hard.

'Let's go and tell Aunt Jemima,' Kathy said at last. 'Oh, I can't wait to tell the whole world.'

'Hey, hey, wait a minute. Slow down,' he protested, but he was laughing as he said it. 'Let's not say anything. Not until I've bought you a ring and we can announce it officially.'

Kathy was disappointed. 'But surely we can tell Aunt Jemima?'

'I'd rather you didn't. I – I must tell my parents first.'

Kathy felt her heart sink. Still, he was afraid of his mother's reaction.

'I see,' she said flatly.

'Darling,' he caught hold of her hand. 'Don't look like that. Just a day or two. That's all I ask. Please?'

She forced a smile and nodded. 'All right. A week. I'll give you a week.' She tapped him playfully on the end of his nose. 'But no longer. That gives you plenty of time to pick out an engagement ring for me and also to tell your mother and father. Then next Sunday afternoon, we'll go to see them.'

Tony pulled in a deep breath and now it was his turn to force a smile. 'All right,' he agreed and Kathy tried hard to ignore the reluctance in his tone.

Seventeen

Beatrice Kendall was nothing like Kathy had imagined. True, she lay languidly on a couch in front of a roaring fire in the front room of the semi-detached house. The room was cluttered with heavy mahogany furniture and ornaments on every available flat surface. But there, any resemblance to Kathy's romantic picture of a pretty, but delicate, woman ended.

Tony's mother was sharp-featured and beady-eyed. Her face was pale and thin, her grey hair straight and cut in a twenties-style bob.

'And who might this be?' was her greeting as Tony ushered Kathy, rather nervously she thought, into the room. The woman spoke with an upper-class accent that Kathy was sure was put on.

'This is Kathy, Mother.'

'Kathy who?'

'Kathy Burton. She – she's a friend of Miss Robinson.'

'Miss Robinson? You mean Miss Robinson at the store?'

'That's right.'

The woman's thin lips curled with obvious disapproval. 'And why have you brought her here, pray?'

'I – she wanted to meet you.'

'To meet me? Whatever for?'

Kathy stepped forward, plastered a smile on her face and held out her hand.

'Tony and I have been going out together now for over seven months so I thought it was high time I met you. And Mr Kendall too, of course.'

There was a brief, fleeting glimpse of fury in Beatrice's eyes and a tightening – if that were possible – of her thin lips. But only Kathy saw all this, for the next moment, Beatrice covered her face with her bony, wrinkled hands and let out a pathetic cry. 'Oh, Anthony, how could you?'

'Please don't upset yourself, Mother. Kathy and I are just friends. We—'

'We're getting engaged,' Kathy interrupted.

Now the woman let out a high-pitched wail and let her head fall back against the pillows. Tony hurried forward, almost pushing Kathy aside in his haste.

'You'd better go,' he muttered to Kathy as he bent over his mother. 'She's having one of her turns.'

'I'm going nowhere,' Kathy said firmly. 'Are you calling the doctor?'

'No, no,' Beatrice protested weakly. 'There's no need. I just need rest and quiet. You've given me such a shock, Anthony. How could you do it?' Her face crumpled and she dissolved into tears, dabbing at her cheeks with her lace handkerchief. 'How could you become engaged without even telling me?'

Kathy noticed the word 'me' rather than 'us' and she was even more shocked and hurt when Tony cast an accusing look at her and said harshly, 'I really think you'd better go, Kathy.'

Her only answer was to sit down in the armchair near the fire. 'I said, "I'm going nowhere," and I meant it.'

'Please, Kathy . . .'

'Anthony, my pills . . . They're on my bedside table. I forgot to bring them down with me this morning.'

'I'll get them,' he said at once and hurried out of the room.

The second the door closed and they were alone, Beatrice sat up and said in a strong, clear voice, 'I don't know what you think you're playing at. My Anthony will never marry the likes of you.'

'Really?' Kathy replied keeping her voice pleasant. 'And how do you know what "the likes of me" is exactly, since you haven't taken the trouble to find out anything about me? I could be anyone.'

'Exactly!' Her glance scanned Kathy from head to toe and her lips curled again. 'Just look at you. Cheap shoes and handbag and a cotton dress. Home-made, I shouldn't wonder.'

'The dress was bought at the store,' Kathy replied calmly.

'A "sale" item, I've no doubt.'

Now the woman had hit the nail on the head, so Kathy remained silent, while Beatrice gave a smirk of satisfaction.

'You're a nobody,' she hissed as they both heard footsteps on the stairs. 'And the best thing you can do for Tony is to disappear out of his life. He'll never marry you. I'll make sure of that . . .'

As the door opened, she lay back against the pillows again and closed her eyes and gave a weak gasp.

'Here we are, Mother.' He was carrying a small brown bottle and a glass of water. He hurried across the room and knelt on the floor beside her chair, holding out the glass. She opened her eyes and raised herself a little, wincing as she did so. She took the water with a trembling hand and held out her other hand for him to shake a pill out of the bottle into her palm.

'Thank you, darling,' she murmured and lay back again, adding bravely, 'I'll be all right now. It was just such a shock. Such a terrible shock. You know I can't do with visitors and for her to tell me such news . . .'

'I'm sorry, Mother—'

What more penitent noises he might have made were cut short by the sound of the back door of the house banging.

'That'll be Dad,' Tony said and got to his feet. 'I'll go and tell him what's happened. Kathy – ' his voice was firmer now – 'you'd better come with me. We'll leave Mother to rest.'

As Kathy rose reluctantly, Tony took hold of her elbow and propelled her towards the door. She glanced over her shoulder and smiled brightly. 'I'll see you again, Mrs Kendall.'

Again, there was a fleeting vicious look in Beatrice's cold eyes. 'I don't think so,' she murmured so that only Kathy might hear.

In the kitchen, Kathy came face to face with the man she had encountered briefly in the street. He was sitting at the table, reading his newspaper. He had not changed from his working clothes and lines of weariness were etched deeply into his face.

He looked up as Tony and Kathy entered. He nodded briefly at his son but his glance rested on Kathy. He smiled at her and some of the tiredness disappeared from his face. His eyes were dark, like his son's, and kindly.

'Hello, love. You're the lass I saw out in the street a while back, aren't you?'

Kathy nodded.

'Never forget a pretty face,' George Kendall chuckled. 'I'd shek yar 'and, love. But ah'm a bit mucky.'

Kathy stared at him in amazement. He spoke with a broad Lincolnshire dialect. She warmed to him at once. Stepping forward, she held out her hand and her smile was wide and genuine as she said, 'I'm used to good honest muck, Mr Kendall. Born and bred on a farm. Please, don't get up,' she added swiftly as he made to rise. 'You look as if you've had a hard day.'

'Aye well, I have to tek the overtime when I can, lass. Needs must.'

'Can I make you a cup of tea or a meal even?'

'Aw no, lass, I couldn't possibly impose on you like that. You'm a guest . . .'

Kathy laughed. 'I'm hoping to become family . . .'

'Kathy, please . . .' Tony began warningly, but she ignored him. Somehow she knew instinctively that she would not get the same reaction from Mr Kendall that she had had from his wife. She was right. A beam spread across his face. 'Well, I nivver.' He glanced at his son. 'Ya've got yasen a good 'un here, lad.'

Tony smiled thinly, still uncomfortable.

Kathy glanced around the neat kitchen. Whoever kept it so clean and tidy, she wondered. Perhaps they had a daily help.

'What can I do? Tell me what you'd planned for your evening meal and I'll get it ready.'

'Ah well, I haven't got much in, lass. Haven't had time to stand in the queues. I'm not hungry when I get in from work. The Mrs eats like a bird and I thought Tony'd be out again. If I'd known he was bringing you home, though, I'd have got something nice in.'

'Then I'll just see what I can rustle up for us,' Kathy said and began opening cupboard doors.

A little later, she set the three plates of food – an omelette with potatoes and vegetables – on the table and called Tony and his father to sit down, saying, 'I'll just take a tray into Mrs Kendall.'

Tony leapt up and almost snatched the tray from her hands. 'I'll take it.'

She stared at him for a moment and then capitulated prettily. 'All right. I hope she likes it.'

Tony disappeared and as she sat down, George Kendall said, 'Thanks for this, lass. It's a rare treat for me to sit down to a meal someone else has made.'

Kathy picked up her knife and fork and smiled at him archly. 'Well, it could become a regular habit if you'll allow me to visit often.'

The man sighed and wrinkled his forehead. 'Truth be told, I'd like nowt better, but the missis . . .'

'Ah. Yes. Of course,' Kathy said gently, but then added briskly, 'Come on, eat up before it goes cold.'

They ate in companionable silence, but Tony did not return to the table and the meal Kathy had prepared with such love and care went cold upon the plate.

'It doesn't surprise me,' Jemima said tartly when Kathy told her about Beatrice Kendall's hostile attitude. 'Not one bit. I did warn you.'

'What's supposed to be the matter with her?'

An amused smile played on Jemima's lips. 'You're quick on the uptake, Kathy. No one knows. She's an invalid. That's all we know. Heart, probably. But how much of it is real and how much is put on, your guess is as good as mine.'

Kathy giggled. 'You mean she enjoys ill-health.'

'Exactly.' Jemima laughed but then her expression sobered. 'But it's George and Tony I feel sorry for. They're in such a difficult position.'

'Why? Why don't they just call her bluff?'

Jemima smiled at her. She was becoming very fond of this rather outspoken but straightforward young woman. She had quite forgiven her for the deception over her blossoming friendship with the store's young manager. Jemima was honest enough to admit that, in Kathy's position, she would have done just the same. 'Think about it for a moment, my dear. How can they? If she really *is* ill, such an action might precipitate a heart attack and how would they feel then, eh?'

Kathy was thoughtful for a moment. 'Yes,' she said slowly. 'I do see.' Then she added vehemently, 'How – how horrible of her to behave like that.'

'Oh yes,' Jemima said calmly. 'She's horrible all right. I'd even go as far as to say evil. The silly, spiteful woman is not only ruining her own life but George's and her son's too. And how – how any mother can – can do that to her own son, I don't know.'

To Kathy's surprise she heard a quaver in Jemima's voice and the older woman turned her head away quickly and struggled to find her handkerchief. Shocked and at a loss to know what to do or say, Kathy sat silently, but Jemima had recovered in a second and turned back with a bright smile on her face. 'Tread carefully, Kathy, where Beatrice Kendall is concerned. That's the only advice I can give you. I can't tell you not to fall for her son. It's too late for that, I know. But I'll tell you now, I just don't know how much Tony is prepared to stand up to his mother. Not even, my dear, for you.'

'You shouldn't have done it, Kathy. You could have made her really ill.'

Kathy stared at him. Was he really so naïve?

They were standing in Jemima's front room. He had arrived a few moments earlier and, as he stepped in through the back door, both women had seen the agitation on his face.

'Good evening, Tony,' Jemima had said calmly, rising from her chair. 'You two go through to the front. I'll make some tea.'

And now they were standing facing each other, Tony with an angry frown on his face, Kathy with shock and disbelief.

She sighed and put her hand on his arm. 'Tony, listen to me. She's not as ill as she's making out. When you went out of the room, she—'

'How can you say such a thing?' Tony said harshly, his voice rising in anger. 'How *dare* you?'

'I dare because I love you and I can't bear to see you taken in like this—'

'Taken in? What on earth do you mean, Kathy? And what gives you the right to say such things about my mother. For heaven's sake, you've only just met her. You don't know her at all. You don't know the years of suffering she's borne. How could you?'

'When you went out of the room, Tony, she was perfectly all right. She sat up and told me that you would never marry the likes of me. She'd see to that, she said.'

Tony stared at her. 'I don't believe you. You're making it up. You—'

'I don't tell lies,' Kathy shouted, incensed that he refused to hear a word said against his mother. Was he so blind that he couldn't see through her devious ways?

The door swung open and Jemima came into the room carrying a tray with three cups of tea on it.

'Now, you two, just stop this arguing. Sit down and drink your tea and talk about the situation calmly.' She set the tray down on a low table and sat down. 'Come along,' she added briskly as the two younger ones remained where they were, glaring at each other. Woodenly, they moved to sit in chairs either side of the fireplace.

'Now,' Jemima began as she handed them each a cup of tea. 'As I've told you before, you're very welcome to meet here if you don't want Kathy to come to your home, Tony.'

'But I could do so much to help with the housework and the cooking. His poor father looks worn out. He'll be the one having the heart attack, if they don't watch out. Not her.'

'She's no right to say that Mother is malingering. No right at all. She's only just met her. How can she possibly know?'

Now they were not talking directly to each other but were using Jemima as a go-between.

'I could tell. When he went out the room, she sat up and spoke normally. The moment she heard him coming, she flopped back on the pillows and acted all weak and faint. And he – ' she jabbed her forefinger towards Tony – 'won't believe me.'

'That's how her illness is. She can be fine one day. She even does a bit of cooking if she feels up to it . . .'

Kathy snorted and muttered. 'I bet that's not often.'

Tony glared at her resentfully, but went on, 'Of course the housework, cleaning and that, is too much for her, but she gets a meal ready for us now and again.'

'Really?' Kathy murmured, sceptically.

Jemima sipped her tea thoughtfully. 'So, Tony, are you really saying that you don't want Kathy to come to your house any more?'

'Not if she's going to treat my mother like that, no.'

'And how – exactly – did she treat her? I mean, I realize she's said things since that you don't agree with, but surely she didn't say them to your mother.' She swivelled to look at Kathy. 'Did you?'

'Of course not,' Kathy denied hotly.

'I don't know what was said when I was out of the room fetching Mother's pills.'

'I've told you –' now Kathy was speaking directly to Tony again – 'she said she'd make sure you never married me.'

'Do you want to know what I think?' Jemima set her empty cup and saucer back on the tray. 'Well, I'm going to tell you whether you want me to or not,' she added. 'I think that Kathy should continue to visit your home, that she should help with the cooking and perhaps a little cleaning too. Make herself useful. She should treat your mother with respect and make no reference whatsoever –' here her tone became even firmer – 'to your mother's – er – condition. She should accept it just as you and your father do.'

'You sound as if you don't believe it either,' Tony said.

Jemima shrugged. 'How can I possibly tell? I haven't

seen your mother for years. Nor am I likely to, except perhaps,' she added impishly, 'at your wedding.'

'I don't think that will be happening for a while yet,' Tony began, while Kathy looked crestfallen at his words.

'You're likely to get called up before long,' Jemima reminded him gently. 'Wouldn't you want to get married before you go?'

'I don't expect to be going. Mother says she'll be able to organize a deferment.'

'Really?' Jemima said dryly. 'The only way I could see that happening is if you got yourself a job on Kathy's father's farm.'

'And *that* won't happen,' Kathy murmured. 'Not in a million years.'

'Mother will ask her cousin to apply for a deferment for me. I'm needed at the store.'

'If the store remains open, your job could be done by a woman,' Jemima remarked.

'A woman? A woman as manager?' Tony laughed.

But Jemima's face remained stonily straight. 'And why not, pray? Women did extraordinary jobs in the last war, so why not in this one? Kathy's age group might well be called up too, but I won't be. And for your information, young man, I could do your job standing on my head.' She got up and picked up the tray.

'Miss Robinson – I'm sorry. I didn't mean to offend you.'

'You haven't. I can't blame you for thinking all women and weak and ineffectual, now can I?'

It was an oblique reference to his mother and they were all aware of it, but it had been said in such a way that Tony could not accuse her of it. Instead, he rose with a sigh and opened the door for her. As she passed by him, she paused and said, 'Now the two of you talk this through – sensibly. You have a problem and you must both deal with it.'

He closed the door behind her, leant against it for a moment and looked across at Kathy. Then he moved towards her and opened his arms wide. With a little sob, she rose and flew across the space between them.

'I'm sorry. I'm so sorry. I didn't mean to be horrid about your mother. But I couldn't bear it if she came between us.'

'I know, I know,' Tony whispered and stroked her hair. 'And we won't let her. I promise. But – but you have to believe me, Kathy. She really is ill. I know she is.'

Against his shoulder, she screwed up her face and bit down hard upon her lower lip. And there and then she made her decision. She would put on the greatest act of her life. She would pretend to believe him. She would pander to the woman just like Tony and his father did. Perhaps the way forward was not by confrontation, but by little acts of kindness that would slowly break down the barriers. It was worth a try. Anything was worth a try if she wanted to keep Tony's love.

And about that, there was no question.

Kathy lifted her head and kissed him gently. His arms tightened around her and he returned her kiss with passion.

For just a little while all thoughts of Beatrice Kendall were driven from both their minds.

Eighteen

Without any warning, Amy arrived to stay the weekend at the beginning of December.

'I've brought you some butter and a few eggs and a chicken. Dad only killed it this morning so it's quite fresh.'

Jemima pounced on them as if they were gold dust. 'How thoughtful of you. Kathy had to queue last week, just to get a couple of ounces of butter.'

'Now, I don't want to put you out, Aunt Jemima,' Amy went on. 'I can sleep with Kathy.' The two girls hugged each other as Jemima answered, 'You won't put me out, my dear. I'm delighted to see you. How's that brother of yours?'

'Oh, Morry's fine. You know Morry.'

'Yes,' Jemima murmured and suddenly her tone was wistful. 'Yes, I know Maurice. He's not going to do anything silly, is he? Like volunteering?'

'Don't think so,' Amy grinned. 'But I am.'

'What d'you mean?' Kathy and Jemima spoke together.

'I'm going to join the Wrens. That's why I'm here. I'm going to find the nearest recruiting office. There is one in Lincoln, isn't there?'

'I haven't the faintest idea, but we can find out, I've no doubt.' Jemima regarded her seriously. 'But Amy, are you sure about this? I mean, wouldn't you be better helping your father on the farm?'

Amy laughed. 'Dad doesn't need me. He's got Morry and he can apply for a deferment for him. Besides, all the old boys in the village are coming forward to help out. What about you, Kathy? Are you going to join up? You'd look cracking in uniform.'

'I might if – if Tony's called up. But I don't want to before he has to leave.'

'But I thought you told me that his mother will get him out of it?'

Before Kathy could reply, Jemima put in, 'She can try, but I doubt she'll manage it. Being a manager in a store selling fripperies is hardly likely to be viewed as valuable war work.'

Kathy leant forward to say in a loud whisper that was intended for Jemima to hear, 'He made the unforgivable mistake of saying that a woman couldn't do his job.'

The two girls giggled and looked at Jemima, who wriggled her shoulders and declared, 'Well, like I told him, I could do his job standing on my head.'

The smile faded from Amy's face as she murmured, 'You might very well have to. Oh, not standing on your head, Auntie, but if this war goes on, you might very well have to step into his shoes.'

At this and all that her remark implied, the three women fell silent.

Despite the cloud hanging over everyone and the restrictions of the blackout, the two girls enjoyed a merry weekend together. Kathy was given Saturday off and they treated themselves to afternoon tea in Boots' café and then to the cinema.

'Aren't you seeing Tony?' Amy asked. 'I don't want to play gooseberry.'

Kathy shook her head. 'No. We thought it best for him to stay at home this weekend.' She had told Amy all about her visit to the Kendalls' house and the quarrel she'd had with Tony afterwards. It felt good to have a friend she could confide in. She hadn't realized just how much she was missing Amy and their girlie chats. Impulsively, she reached out across the table and clutched Amy's hand. 'Oh, I do miss you so much. How is everyone at home? Your mum and dad and – and Morry?'

'They're fine.' She squeezed Kathy's hand as she added, 'And Morry's fine. Don't you worry about him. He's friendly with a girl in the village. Eve Jackson. Do you remember her?'

'A pretty blonde girl.'

'That's the one.'

'I'm so glad,' Kathy heaved a sigh of relief. Somehow, she still felt responsible for Morry's happiness – or rather for having made him unhappy by her refusal to marry him. If he was seeing someone else, then . . . But at Amy's next words her hopes were dashed. 'Of course, it's not serious. Not on Morry's part. There's only one girl for him.'

Kathy groaned. 'Don't, Amy. You make me feel awful.'

Amy laughed. 'Well, don't, you silly goose. No one's blaming you. Not even Morry. We all know – and Morry too if he's honest – that it's no good marrying him if you don't love him.'

There was silence between them until Kathy asked hesitantly, 'Have you – have you heard how my mam is?'

'She's all right,' Amy said gently. 'Mum's been across to see her and Dad keeps in touch with your father. I won't say she's "fine" but she is all right. He's not hitting her, if that's what's worrying you. Mum asked her straight out and told her to come to our house if that happened.'

'Thanks.' Kathy's gratitude was heartfelt. 'And please thank your mum and dad for me. They're the best. They really are. You're so lucky, you and Morry.'

'I know,' Amy said simply. They were silent for a few moments before Amy said with a briskness that was very like Aunt Jemima's. 'Now, let's go and find out where the nearest recruiting office is.'

The days leading up to Christmas were the busiest Kathy had known since she had come to work at Hammonds.

'You wouldn't think they'd be wanting to buy hats, would you?' she remarked to Stella as the two scuttled about the department, with scarcely a minute's breather between serving customers.

'Defiance, that's what it is,' the younger girl said with an astute flash of insight. 'We're showing that Hitler feller he can't get us down. Oh, Kathy, just look at this hat! Isn't it the prettiest you've ever seen?' She sighed. 'I do wish I could afford it.'

'Put it on your Christmas list.'

'Huh!' Stella's mouth tightened in disgust. 'And what good d'you think that'd be? Do you know what I'm getting for Christmas?'

Kathy stared at her and shook her head.

'War Bonds. That's what my father's present to me is.'

Kathy found it hard to hide a wry smile. It was just the sort of thing her own father would have done. But she was saved from having to answer the girl, as three more customers arrived in the store at once.

'What are you doing for Christmas, Kathy?' Jemima asked a week before the day. 'We're lucky this year. With Christmas Day falling on a Monday, we'll get three days off work. I shall go to Sandy Furze Farm as usual and Betty has invited you too. If you want to go, that is.'

Kathy was torn. Once, she'd have liked nothing better than to spend Christmas enveloped in the warmth of the Robinson family. For years she'd lived out the cheerless austerity at home, longing to escape across the fields to her friend's house. Some years she'd managed a visit on Boxing Day and the stark contrast between the homes had left her feeling even more dissatisfied with her own. But now there was Tony.

'I'll let you know tomorrow night. I'll try to find out what Tony's plans are.'

Jemima looked sceptical but she said nothing. Privately, she hoped that for once the young man just might have the courage to stand up to his mother. She sighed. He was soon going to have to summon up another kind of bravery. She hoped he would be up to it.

During her lunch break the next day, Kathy went to the manager's office.

'Go straight in, Miss Burton.' Miss Foster smiled at her fondly.

Kathy entered and closed the door behind her,

leaning on it a moment to watch Tony working over a sheaf of papers. When he looked up, a smile lit up his face. He jumped up at once and came round the desk, his hands outstretched. They snatched a brief kiss, before Kathy launched into the reason for her visit to his office.

'I'm sorry if you're busy—'

'No, no, it's all right. It's just all this form filling one has to do these days. There's so many new regulations now, my head aches with it all.' But he was laughing as he said it.

'Am I going to be able to see you over Christmas?' she asked. 'Because, if not, I've been invited to go with Miss Robinson to her family.'

Tony ran his hand across his forehead, agonizing over the decision. 'I want nothing more than to spend Christmas with you, darling, especially if Miss Robinson's away and we'd have the house to ourselves.' He pretended to leer at her. But Kathy couldn't smile in return. She'd already guessed what was coming next. 'Darling, you know I'm likely to be called up soon. It – it might be the last Christmas I get to spend with Mother . . . and Father,' he added hurriedly.

Now Kathy smiled, surprised to find his decision didn't hurt as much as she'd thought it would. She wound her arms around him, not caring for once if anyone came in. 'It's all right. Really, but there's just one thing.'

'What?' Tony was anxious.

'You're spending New Year's Eve with me.'

His worried expression cleared. He kissed the tip of her nose. 'Darling, I do love you so.'

*

'I do hope you're not breaking any food rationing regulations, Edward,' Jemima said primly, as they all sat around the laden table watching Ted Robinson carve the goose. 'We've all received our ration cards, you know.' But there was a mischievous twinkle in her eyes, which was mirrored in her brother's glance.

'Aye well, didn't Betty tell you? This is going to cost you two coupons a slice.'

'Now, don't you listen to him, cariad,' Betty said, bustling in with dishes of steaming vegetables. 'Rationing doesn't start in earnest until January.'

'Maybe not – officially, but there are already shortages in the city,' Jemima said seriously now.

'Then you let us know what you need and we'll send it,' Betty said firmly. 'Living on a farm, we'll be luckier than most.'

'That's kind of you, dear,' Jemima murmured. 'But then, you've always been good to me, Betty, haven't you?'

The two women exchanged a look across the table and smiled at each other.

'More potatoes, Kathy?' Morry, sitting beside her, passed the dish.

'I thought you had an evacuee staying with you?' she asked as she helped herself.

'We did,' Morry answered. 'A comical little chap from London. A typical cockney. Half the folk round here couldn't understand him.'

'I could,' Amy declared. 'He's a little sweetheart, Kathy. He'll be back in January, but he went home for Christmas.' She glanced across at her father and smiled. 'Dad paid for his fare home.'

'Now, now, Amy lass, don't go giving all my secrets away.'

'You know me, Dad. I always say if you've anything to hide, don't tell me.'

'Is it safe for him to go back?' Kathy asked.

'I think they're hoping that there won't be any bombing over Christmas.'

'Like in the last lot, you mean, when the soldiers on both sides got out of their trenches and played football?'

Everyone laughed, but beneath his breath so that only Kathy could hear, Morry said, 'I wouldn't trust Hitler to do anything like that. I hope the little chap's going to be all right.'

'Eat up, everyone,' Betty said cheerfully as she sat down. 'There's plenty more.'

'Aye, we'd better make the most of it. Goodness knows what we might all be eating by next year.'

'Oh, it'll not last as long as that, Ted,' Betty said, ever the optimist. 'We'll all be back to normal before you know it. Now, let's forget all about the war and enjoy our meal. And don't forget, we've got a little surprise for Kathy after our dinner.'

'A surprise? For – for me? What is it?' Kathy looked across at Amy, who shrugged her shoulders and said, 'I don't know. They haven't told me.'

'Of course we haven't,' Morry laughed. 'Else it certainly wouldn't stay a surprise for more than two minutes, would it?'

Everyone, including Amy, laughed, but Kathy could wheedle nothing more out of anyone.

'Wait and see, cariad,' was all Betty would say.

While the women cleared away and washed up the mountain of pots after a superb Christmas dinner,

Morry disappeared. From the kitchen, they heard the engine of the old farm truck start up.

'Where's he going?' Amy asked.

'Wait and see,' Betty said again, her plump arms deep in the sink.

'It must be a big present for Kathy if he's got to fetch it in the truck.' Amy tried to prise something out of her mother, but Betty was tight-lipped.

Half an hour later, they heard the vehicle returning.

'Go and open the door for him, Kathy,' Betty said.

'I'll go,' Amy said, throwing down the tea towel and heading for the door, but Betty stopped her.

'No, Amy – let Kathy go,' her mother said, quite sharply for the easy-going Betty.

Kathy shrugged and went to the back door. Opening it, she saw her mother climbing out of the passenger seat.

'Mam, Oh, Mam.' Tears coursed down her face as she threw her arms wide and ran towards Edith.

'My darling girl,' Edith whispered, holding her close. 'I haven't long. Your father's asleep by the range. He doesn't know I've come and Maurice has promised to take me back in half an hour. Let's hope he doesn't wake up before then.'

Betty appeared near the back door. 'Come in, come in.'

'I didn't ought to,' Edith said, as arm in arm she and Kathy moved towards the house. 'I've had to come out in my wellingtons. When I go back, I'm going to make out I've been feeding the hens.'

She hugged Kathy's arm to her side and smiled up at her, almost enjoying the intrigue and, hopefully, getting the better of her husband for once.

'Oh, Mam,' Kathy whispered, her tears of joy

turning to sadness. How awful it was that her mother was like a prisoner in her own home, that she daren't even come out to see her daughter for a brief half hour.

'Come away in, cariad,' Betty insisted. 'Don't you think I'm used to wellingtons tramping in and out all day?'

'Well, just into the kitchen then.'

They were left alone together, just the two of them, sitting in Betty's warm kitchen over a cup of tea. They talked non-stop, Edith wanting to know everything that had happened to her daughter since she'd left home. She'd heard snippets from the Robinsons, but it meant so much more to hear it from Kathy herself.

Edith held her daughter's hands tightly. 'Are you happy, my darling? Truly happy?'

'I'm happy with Tony, Mam. You'd love him, I know you would. But – but it's his mother . . .' She went on, the words spilling out about Beatrice Kendall's possessiveness.

When, at last, Kathy fell silent, Edith smiled gently. 'I can understand it. A mother's love is something very special. Some say, the strongest love there is. But sometimes, it can become "smother" love and that can be dangerous. But I feel for her. She must be desperately anxious about him being called up.'

'Along with thousands of other mothers. Why can't she just let him live his own life? You did with me.'

Fresh tears welled in Edith's eyes. 'It wasn't easy, darling. In fact it was the hardest thing I've ever had to do in my life.'

'Then – then why did you let me go?'

'Because it was the best for you,' she said simply, and her unselfish love for her daughter was summed up in those few words.

There was a soft knock and Morry poked his head around the kitchen door. 'I hate to do this, but you've been here nearly an hour, Mrs Burton, and . . .'

'Oh my Lor',' Edith cried, jumping up at once, her eyes wide with fear. 'If he's woken up . . .'

Morry moved into the room and put his arm around her shoulders. 'I'll park in the lane and we'll walk up to the farm and then sneak into the henhouse . . .'

'No, no, I'd best go on my own. If he sees you there, he'll start asking questions. I'll be all right.' She hugged Kathy swiftly. 'Whatever happens, it was worth it just to see you, darling.'

'Oh, Mam,' Kathy said shakily and hugged her hard in return.

Later, Kathy kissed Morry on the cheek. 'That was the very best Christmas present you could have given me. Thank you.'

Morry didn't answer but the look in his eyes said it all. I'd do anything for you, Kathy. Anything at all.

Nineteen

'Mr Kendall, whatever are you doing here?'

The man stood awkwardly in the centre of the millinery department, twirling his cloth cap through his agitated fingers and looking decidedly uncomfortable. Kathy hurried towards him. 'Is something wrong?'

''Fraid so, lass. Can you tell me where I can find our Tony?'

'Of course. I'll take you straight to his office.' She put her hand on his arm and was about to lead him through the maze of departments and corridors when she saw Muriel coming towards them.

'Ah,' she murmured. 'I'd better ask permission to leave the floor. Miss Curtis, Mr Kendall needs to see his son on a matter of urgency. May I take him up?'

Muriel nodded towards Mr Kendall, who smiled thinly. 'Of course, but come straight back. Stella is on her lunch break and we're quite busy this morning.'

As they hurried up the stairs, Kathy asked, 'What's wrong? Is it Mrs Kendall?'

'Sort of, lass. She's had a nasty shock and fainted clean away. Good job I was at home. I've been on nights and I was in me bed. I heard this thump and went downstairs and there she was on the floor with a letter in her hand.'

'A letter? A letter had caused her to pass out?'

He nodded grimly. 'It's Tony's call-up papers, lass. He's got to go.'

As they reached the top of the stairs, Kathy stopped and turned to face him. 'But – but I thought your wife said she could arrange a deferment for him?'

Sadly, George shook his head. 'She'd like to think she could, love. But the truth is there'll be nothing she can do. Nothing anyone can do. He's not in the sort of job that could get deferment. Now she's clinging to the hope that he'll fail his medical.' He leaned closer and lowered his voice. 'She even asked our doc if he'd write a certificate saying Tony has a weak heart.'

Kathy gasped and her eyes widened. 'He can't do that, surely?'

'Of course he can't. Something like that could end his career.'

'Then – then Tony'll really have to go?'

''Fraid so, lass. Now, where's his office?'

'I don't care what he says, I'm going to their house.'

'I wouldn't,' Jemima warned. 'It's snowing like mad out there. There's a couple of inches fallen already and a lot more on the way by the look of the sky this afternoon. With the blackout too . . .' Seeing the determined look on the girl's face, Jemima stopped, sighed and shrugged.

'I've not even seen him. If his father hadn't come looking for him, I wouldn't even have known.' She was feeling hurt that Tony hadn't sought her out at once to tell her that his call-up papers had come.

'He left the store to go home to his mother,' Jemima said.

189

'Now why doesn't that surprise me?' Kathy said, unable for once to keep the bitterness from her tone.

For once, Jemima gave up. 'Be careful, dear. Wrap up warmly. It's bitterly cold. I'm just thankful it's Sunday tomorrow.' She stroked the cat on her knee. 'Taffy and I intend to stay snug and warm by the fire.'

Kathy trudged through the darkness, pulling her coat tightly around her and squinting against the driving snow that stung her cheeks and caught her breath. But her anger and resentment drove her on. She was ready to do battle, but when she arrived at the Kendalls' home Kathy found Beatrice Kendall in a state of collapse. She could see at once that this time the woman's distress was genuine. Beatrice lay back on the sofa, looking thin and white. Tony sat on a footstool beside her, chafing her hand as if trying to bring some warmth, some life almost, back into her.

He glanced up, a mixture of pleasure and apprehension on his face, as his father ushered Kathy into the stuffy, cluttered room.

'Look who's here,' George said cheerfully. 'Come to see if she can lend a hand. Isn't that kind of her?' Before giving anyone time to make a comment, George went on. 'Tell you the truth, lass, I'm glad to see you. I could really do with a hand in the kitchen. I've to go to work. I'm late for me shift already with all this to-do and I haven't had time to cook Tony a meal or try to tempt Beatty with a little something. Mind you, I've done the shopping, so there's everything you need. I could only get sausages at the butchers. The shortages are starting already, I reckon. There'll be enough for you, an' all. I shan't have time to stay to eat.'

'Can I make you some sandwiches to take with you?'

'Oh no, lass,' he smiled. 'Me pack-up's all done. I just haven't time to eat now. Still,' he laughed and patted his rotund stomach. 'Won't hurt me to miss a meal for once, will it? Now, I'll show you where everything is and if you could make a milky rice pudding for the Mrs, she might manage a bit of that.'

'I couldn't eat a thing,' came Beatrice's quavering voice from the couch. 'Whatever are we going to do? I can't bear it. This is going to kill me.'

'Now, Mother, don't take on so. Please. I'll be all right and I'll come home just as often as I can.'

'But I'll never see you,' the woman wailed. 'You'll want to be with – with *her*, won't you? She'll take you away from me.'

'Kathy can come here, then I can be with both of you.'

Beatrice raised her head from her pillow and pointed a trembling finger at Kathy. 'I won't have her here. I won't have her in my house. Get her out!' Her voice rose hysterically. '*Get her out!*'

'Now, now, Beatty. You know I've got to go, and this lass here has kindly offered to cook Tony's meal for him. You don't mind her doing that, surely?' Before his wife could answer, he took Kathy's arm. 'Tek no notice, lass,' he whispered as they left the room. 'She's overwrought with the news. She'll calm down in a bit. Let's leave Tony with her. It's him she wants with her when she has a bad turn.'

Don't I know it! Kathy thought, but she said nothing.

George left for work and Kathy busied herself in the unfamiliar kitchen. First, she made up a rice pudding, as it would take the longest to cook. She peeled potatoes and set them to steam and then found a frying pan for the sausages. 'Bangers and mash,' she murmured, and smiled, thinking that it was hardly what she would have wished for as a meal she was preparing for her future husband.

When everything was ready, she tapped on the door of the sitting room and entered carrying a tray set with a snowy white tray cloth and a bowl of the rice pudding with a dollop of jam in the centre.

'Mr Kendall thought you might be able to eat a little rice pudding. I hope you like it.'

Beatrice raised her head and glared up at her.

'Isn't that kind of Kathy, Mother? Now let me help you sit up.'

As Kathy leant forward to place the tray on Beatrice's lap, the woman suddenly lashed out, hitting the tray upwards. The rice pudding splashed down the front of Kathy's blouse and skirt, and the bowl and tray clattered to the floor.

'What on earth did you do that for?' For once, Tony was angry. 'Kathy was only trying to help.'

'Get – her – out – of – my – house,' Beatrice gasped. Then she clutched dramatically at her chest and moaned. 'Tony – my pills. Fetch my pills.'

As Tony hurried out of the room once more, Kathy stood looking down at Beatrice. 'You know, if you carry on like this, you will lose him. Sooner or later, he's going to see right through you and then – he'll go.'

Through gritted teeth, Beatrice spat, 'Get out.'

'Oh, I'm going – for now. But I'll be back. You won't get me to give up like poor Muriel Curtis did.' As they heard Tony returning, Kathy leant forward. Putting her face close to Beatrice's, she said, 'You won't get rid of me quite so easily. I promise you.'

'We'll see about that, won't we?' Beatrice hissed and

then flopped back against the pillows as Tony entered the room.

As he passed close to her, he faltered and looked into Kathy's face. 'I'm so sorry. I don't know what came over her. It must have been an accident. I'm sure she didn't mean to do it.'

Swiftly, Kathy made her decision. She smiled sweetly. 'Of course not, darling. I'll go and clean myself up and then I'll see to this.' She indicated the smashed bowl on the floor and the splashes of rice pudding on the carpet.

'Oh, I'll see to it . . .' Tony began, but Kathy interrupted firmly, 'No, your dinner's waiting for you in the kitchen. As soon as you've given your mother her pills, you go and get it. I'll keep an eye on her and fetch you if she needs you.'

'Well . . .' He was torn between the two of them, and to tell the truth he was very hungry. He hadn't eaten since breakfast.

Kathy went back to the kitchen and cleaned the front of her blouse and skirt as best she could, then, finding a dustpan and brush and a cloth to mop the carpet, she returned to the front room.

'Off you go,' she said gently to Tony.

'You'll fetch me if she needs me.'

'Of course I will.'

With that he left the room, but as the door closed behind him, Kathy moved towards the sofa and bent over Beatrice.

'Round one to me, I think,' she said softly.

Twenty

'I'm to join the RAF. I'm to report on Monday, the nineteenth of February.'

Kathy could see both excitement and apprehension in his eyes. She wound her arms around his neck and laid her cheek against his shoulder, as she whispered, 'You will be careful, won't you?'

His arms tightened around her. 'Of course I will,' he said gently. He smoothed the hair back and kissed her forehead. 'Do you really think I'd endanger our future together?'

She raised her head and looked up at him. 'You really think we have a future together?'

'Of course.' It was obvious he was shocked that she could doubt it. 'Oh darling, I know Mother's difficult and I'm so sorry for what happened the other day.'

Kathy smiled weakly but said nothing.

'I had a long talk with Dad last night. He – he told me a lot of things about the past that I hadn't either known or realized. It – well – I suppose it explains a lot of things.' He paused. Still Kathy said nothing. She'd never been one to pry into the secrets of others. If Tony wanted to confide in her then he would. If not, then it was really none of her business what had happened in his family's past. All that concerned her was – their future. Hers and Tony's.

'His advice to me was that I should take this opportunity to cut loose the apron strings, as he put it.' Tony smiled. 'And the very best piece of advice he gave me was to say that I should marry you and be quick about it before some other eligible chap snaps you up behind my back.'

Kathy gasped and stared up at him in surprise. Then she threw back her head and laughed aloud. 'Well, that's the best I've heard yet. That a young man is "under orders" from his father to get married.'

Tony laughed with her, though slightly sheepishly. 'So, what do you say? Will you marry me? Right away? Before I go? I mean, there's only just over three weeks.'

Kathy hugged him tightly. 'Oh yes, yes, *yes*!'

'Can you arrange everything for the Saturday before I go?'

'Just try and stop me.'

'We might need a special licence. I'll sort that out. Will you want to get married at home? In your local church?'

Kathy bit her lip and tears sprang to her eyes. Wordlessly, she shook her head. Her girlish dream had been to float down the aisle of the little village church on her father's arm to the sound of her friends in the choir singing for her. But it was not going to happen. Apart from anything else, her father would more than likely stay away from her wedding. But if that happened, she knew the very person she would ask to give her away. Ted Robinson. She didn't know quite how Morry would take the news, but Amy and her parents would be thrilled for her. And Amy of course would be her bridesmaid. That had never been in doubt.

But there was one cloud blighting her happiness. Would her mother be able to attend the ceremony?

Would she be brave enough to go against her husband and attend?

'I'll have to go home and tell them, but, no, we'll be married here, in Lincoln. It'll be easier, since we're both living here. And – and – well – things could be difficult back home.'

'Whatever you think best, darling. And now – ' he tapped her nose playfully – 'you'd better go and talk to Miss Robinson and see if she can sort out a wedding dress for you.'

'Oh, but I don't know if I can afford . . .'

'Now, now, it can all be put on account and you can pay a bit off each week. And I should be able to send you some of my pay as a married serviceman.'

It sounded very strange to hear Tony refer to himself as a 'serviceman' but even more so as 'married'.

'Come on,' he said, grabbing her hand. 'Let's go into the kitchen and tell Miss Robinson.'

A few moments later, passers-by might have heard a squeal of delight from the kitchen of the little terraced house as Jemima threw her hands in the air and then hugged both Kathy and Tony. She was not given to such displays of emotion, so it made the moment all the more special for the three of them. Only Taffy, ears flattened, rushed for the back door, his tail thrashing wildly in disgust at the commotion.

'You're doing the right thing, my dears. I know you are. You are so right to grab your happiness in these uncertain times. Never mind what anyone else says, just don't listen to them. You must do what is right for you.' She glanced at them, first one and then the other. 'And I can see by your faces that it is right for both of you.' She laid her hand on Tony's shoulder and added,

'And forgive me for saying so, young man, but this will be the making of you.'

Far from taking offence, Tony laughed. 'D'you know, that's just what my dad said.'

Jemima nodded and said softly, 'Well, he would. Your dad's a sensible chap – most of the time.' Then she shook herself and added, 'And now we'd better think about your wedding finery. We haven't much time. Despite the shortages, I think we can find you a gown in the wedding department and there should be a dress to fit Amy. Oh . . .' She clapped her hand over her mouth and her eyes brimmed with laughter. 'I'm rather taking things for granted, aren't I?'

'Don't worry,' Kathy reassured her. 'Who else would I have other than my very best friend as my bridesmaid?'

'Well, let's just hope she's not gone before then.'

'I hope so, but first – I'll have to go home.'

Jemima's face sobered. 'Yes, my dear, you will. After all, you're under twenty-one. I think you'll need your father's consent.'

Kathy's lips parted in a startled gasp and her eyes widened in horror as she stared at Jemima. 'Oh no!'

Kathy was trembling as she pushed open the gate into the farmyard of her childhood home the following Saturday afternoon. Jemima had given her the day off, and though Muriel had raised her eyebrows, she had said nothing, not daring to argue with her superior.

Kathy had brought a small overnight suitcase, but she wasn't sure of a welcome. But if necessary, she knew she could stay with the Robinsons. Despite her having hurt Morry, the Robinsons were big-hearted enough to welcome her any time. And her unexpected arrival would cause them no trouble. Betty always kept the spare room bed made up and aired.

Sounds of early evening milking came from the cowshed and Kathy breathed a sigh of relief. Perhaps she could find her mother first and put off the moment she would have to face her father for a little longer. She pushed open the back door and tiptoed through the washhouse and into the kitchen. She saw her mother standing at the kitchen sink washing up.

'Hello, Mam.'

Despite the softness of Kathy's voice, Edith jumped and turned with frightened eyes towards the door. Seeing her daughter, she gave a cry of delight and rushed across the space between them to throw soapy hands around her. Laughing, Kathy hugged her in return.

Edith drew back and, after the first joyful reaction, her eyes were suddenly anxious. 'Is something wrong? Have you come back home?' There was both hope and apprehension in her tone. While she would have loved to have her daughter back home, she knew that would not be the best for Kathy.

'No, Mam, I've come to tell you something and – and to ask your permission.'

Edith pulled in a sharp breath. 'Oh no! You – you're going to join up, aren't you? Oh, Kathy, are you sure?'

'No, Mam, I'm not volunteering. I – I'm getting married.'

'Married!'

If she had told her mother that she was flying to the moon, Edith could not have been more shocked.

'But – but who?' Then suddenly, her face cleared and her joy was complete. 'Oh it's Maurice, isn't it? Oh, do say it's Maurice!'

Kathy shook her head. 'No, I'm sorry. It isn't Morry. It's – it's Tony Kendall. I told you about him at Christmas. Remember? He's the manager of the store where I work. He's the great-nephew of the owner.'

'But you haven't known him long.'

'I love him, Mam, and he loves me. And he's been called up.'

'Ah.' Her mother sighed deeply and let her hands fall away. 'So you want to get married before he goes.'

'Yes.'

'And when do you plan to—?'

'Three weeks today, so there's not much time, and because I'm under twenty-one, I need your consent.'

'Your father's consent, you mean, and he'll never give it.'

'Wouldn't yours do, Mam? Surely it doesn't have to be both parents, does it?'

'I don't know.' Edith rubbed her hands nervously down the front of her apron. 'I don't think I dare . . .' She stopped and was suddenly very still for a long moment. Then she raised her head and met Kathy's eyes. With more firmness in her tone than Kathy had ever heard, Edith said, 'Yes, yes, I'll do it. If you're sure it's what you want, then I'll give my consent, whatever your father says.'

'Oh Mam . . .' Tears flooded down Kathy's face as she enveloped her mother in a bear-hug.

At last Edith patted her back. 'There, there, love. Now you'd better go and tell your father.'

'Mam, are you really sure? I don't want him to take it out on you later.'

Edith gave a wan smile. 'Oh, I don't mind. All I care about is your happiness. It's too late for me now. But you – you've got all your life in front of you.'

'Why don't you leave him, Mam?'

Edith shrugged. 'Where would I go?' she asked simply.

'To me. To us,' Kathy said impulsively. 'When we're settled in a home of our own, you can come and live with us.'

Edith smiled gently. 'We'll see, love, we'll see,' was all she would say.

'I suppose you're pregnant, a' ya?'

Shocked, Kathy stared at her father, her heart pounding in her chest. She felt a guilty flush creep up her face. The previous night, while Jemima had been at one of her WVS meetings, Tony had made love to Kathy in the big lumpy bed she occupied in the spare room. It had been her first time and she had been nervous at first. But Tony had been so gentle, so loving, that she had given herself to him willingly and, finally, with joyful abandon. Amid all the uncertainty everyone now faced, their few hours together had been an oasis of bliss. But now, facing her father, she felt the flush creep up her face. Hoping he would see it as indignation, she declared hotly, 'Of course I'm not!' Mentally she crossed her fingers, hoping that what she said was the truth.

'Then why the hurry? And who is this chap anyway?'

Kathy explained, but her reasons were lost on her

father. 'Now if it was Maurice you were marrying, well, that'd be different.'

'So you won't give your consent?'

'No.'

Kathy shrugged. 'Very well then.'

Her father glanced at her suspiciously. Suddenly, there was a gleam in his eyes. 'And don't think your mother can give her consent instead. It has to be me.' Kathy stared at him as he smiled with satisfaction. 'Aye, I thought so. Wheedled your way round her, have you? Got her to promise to give her consent 'cos you knew I wouldn't.'

Kathy wasn't sure of the law, but she would find out. For the moment, she turned away without another word and went back into the house.

Standing in the middle of the kitchen, she told her mother tearfully. 'He says you can't do it. I didn't tell him, Mam,' she added hastily, 'but he guessed.'

'He would,' Edith muttered bitterly. 'To be honest I'm not sure either, but there must be a way round it.' She laughed softly. It was the first time that Kathy could remember her mother laughing in years. 'If the worst comes to the worst, you'll have to run away to Gretna Green. But then, I suppose his parents would be upset if you did that.'

'His father would, but his mother . . .' Kathy hesitated. 'She's even more against our marriage than Dad is – if that's possible!'

'Doesn't she like you?'

'No, but then she has never liked any girl Tony has taken home. She's an invalid and she plays on it to keep him tied to her apron strings. Well, that's what it seems like, anyway,' Kathy added hastily, anxious not give her mother a false impression. She sighed. 'She has her husband and her son wrapped around her little finger, but to be honest, no one knows for sure just how ill she is. Not even they do.'

'Yes, I remember.' Edith sighed. 'It sounds as if you're taking on a lot, Kathy love. Are you sure?'

'Yes, Mum. Whatever the problems, I love Tony and I want to marry him.'

'I tell you what, go and talk to Mr Nightingale. He'll know.'

Kathy's face cleared. 'Of course.' She giggled. 'Only trouble is I might get roped in to sing with the choir tomorrow morning.'

Her mother smiled. 'Well, that'd be nice, wouldn't it?'

'Yes. Yes, actually it would be very nice.'

Kathy sang her heart out at morning service in the little village church where she had worshipped since childhood. Afterwards, as she walked home arm in arm with Amy, she felt more at peace than she could ever remember.

'That was a lovely sermon old Mr Nightingale gave. Evidently he was a padre in the last war, so he knows what's ahead.' Amy sighed. 'D'you know, Kathy, part of me's terrified about joining up and yet – I can't help it – I'm excited too.'

'I don't blame you. I would feel just the same.'

'Why don't you join up?'

'If I wasn't getting married, I would, but I want to be there for Tony whenever he can get leave. I shall volunteer to do some sort of war work in Lincoln instead.'

'Are you coming for dinner with us? Mam and Dad'd love to see you and there's always plenty – even with the rationing!'

'No, if you don't mind, I'll go home. I want to see as much of Mam as I can while I'm here.' She sighed. 'If I marry Tony, I doubt I'll be welcome at home any more.'

Amy squeezed her arm. 'Well, you're always welcome at our place, you know that.'

Kathy felt a lump in her throat. It was good to have such loyal friends.

They parted at the fork in the lane where one path led to Amy's home, the other way to Thorpe Farm.

As she pushed open the gate she looked up in surprise to see her father standing in the middle of the yard. It was obvious he was waiting for her. Without any kind of greeting, he said, 'I'll give my consent on one condition.'

Kathy drew in a deep breath of surprise. She said nothing, just stared at him, waiting for him to go on, knowing that she probably wasn't going to like what he had to say.

'I'll make a new will leaving everything to Maurice Robinson. If you marry this chap, you won't get a penny.'

Kathy tried hard to hide her delight, but failed. 'You mean it, you really mean it? You'll give your consent?'

He stared at her for a moment before saying harshly, 'Does this farm mean nothing to you? It's been in my family for years. Don't you care?'

Kathy shrugged. 'You've never made me feel as if I'd a right to care. Because I'm not a boy, you never once gave me any reason to think you'd pass it on to me. All you could ever think about was marrying me off to Morry and him having the farm. Well, as far as I'm concerned, he can have it and good luck to him.'

With that she marched into the house and slammed the back door behind her, leaving her father staring after her with a puzzled expression on his face.

Twenty-One

With her father's written consent secured, Kathy returned to Lincoln on the Sunday evening.

'You do surprise me,' Jemima said when Kathy told her the news. 'He's a vindictive old beggar, isn't he? Fancy any father cutting his only child out of his will like that. Mind you – ' her bright eyes twinkled mischievously – 'it's all the better for Maurice.'

Kathy laughed and hugged Jemima impulsively. 'And it couldn't happen to a nicer bloke. I mean it, I'm more than happy that it would be Morry to benefit.'

Jemima smiled sadly. 'I'm sure he'd rather have you than all the farms in Lincolnshire, though.'

Kathy sighed. 'I am sorry, truly I am. But I can't pretend to be in love with him. I've seen at first hand what a loveless marriage is like. I don't want that for myself – or for Morry. And a one-sided marriage would probably be even worse in a way.'

'I expect you're right, dear,' Jemima said briskly. 'Now, we'd better get this wedding planned. Who's going to give you away?'

'I'd like to ask your brother, but is it fair? I mean – because of Morry?'

'Don't worry about that. Ted will be tickled pink. You can phone him from work tomorrow.' The Robinsons had been the first in the village, apart from the

205

vicar and the local doctor, of course, to have a telephone installed.

'I can't wait to see Tony in the morning and tell him the good news.'

'Let's just hope . . .' Jemima began and then stopped.

'What?'

'Oh nothing, dear, nothing. Now, let's get to bed. We've got an exciting three weeks ahead of us.'

Later the following morning, during her dinner break, Kathy rushed upstairs to Tony's office. As she knocked and opened the door he sprang up from behind his desk and came towards her. He swept her off her feet and swung her round. 'I've organized the licence and James has agreed to be my best man.'

'Mr Hammond has? Oh how wonderful.'

'He is my mother's cousin.'

'I bet that's pleased her, hasn't it?'

The smile faded from Tony's face. 'Darling, nothing – but nothing – will please my mother. She's refusing to come to the wedding.'

'That makes both our parents. Mam would come but I don't know if she'll dare and as for Dad . . .' She took a deep breath and told him all that had happened over the weekend ending, 'You – you don't mind about the farm? I mean, I'm not bringing anything to the marriage.'

Tony hugged her to him and kissed her firmly on the mouth, murmuring, 'You silly goose. You're all I want. Besides, what would I do with a farm? I hardly know which end of a cow the milk comes out of.'

Kathy giggled. 'It comes out in the middle. Well, sort of.'

'There you are then? What do I know?'

'Miss Curtis, could I have a word with you, please?' It was the moment Kathy had been dreading all day, yet it was something she had decided that she must do herself. She should be the one to tell Muriel.

'Of course . . .' Muriel glanced at her watch. 'We close in five minutes. We'll talk then.' She smiled at Kathy's worried face. 'I do hope you're not going to leave us to join up. You've proved yourself to be an excellent sales assistant. I wouldn't want to lose you.'

Kathy smiled thinly but said nothing.

When all the other staff had left the floor, Muriel said, 'Now, what is it?'

Kathy took a deep breath. 'I wanted to tell you myself, I didn't want you to hear it from anyone else. Tony and I are getting married on the seventeenth. You probably know he's been called up and and we want to be married before he goes.'

For a moment Muriel stared at her, then tears welled in her eyes.

'I'm so sorry. I know it must hurt you.' Kathy was crying too.

Muriel shook her head. 'I'm being silly. It would never have worked for us. I know that. I – I just want him to be happy. That's all I've ever wanted. So, I wish you joy. Really I do, Kathy. But – please – make him happy. That's all I ask. Make him happy.'

Impulsively, Kathy hugged her. 'You're such a good,

generous person. You will come to the wedding, won't you?'

'No – don't be offended, but no, I won't come.' She smiled tremulously through her tears. 'That would be asking a bit much, don't you think?'

Kathy nodded. 'Yes, I suppose so.'

'But I wish you well – both of you. Truly I do. Now,' Muriel went on, gently easing herself from Kathy's arms. 'Have you got everything you need for the big day? If we can help you, we will.'

'Aunt Jemima – I mean, Miss Robinson – told me to wait for her here and she'd help me look out a wedding dress. She'll have spoken to the head of the department by now.'

Muriel brushed away the last of her tears and smiled bravely. 'May I help? I used to work in that department until they made me head of millinery. There are rumours that eventually we'll have clothes coupons too, so make the most of it and get everything you need. We can put it on account for you.'

Tactfully, Kathy didn't remark: That's what Tony said. Instead she said tentatively, 'If – if you're sure, then, yes, that would be lovely. I'd value your opinion.'

The three women spent the next two hours happily. Even Muriel buried her own thoughts and threw herself into helping Kathy choose her wedding finery, never tiring of carrying gown after gown for Kathy to try on.

'It's such a pity you haven't time to have one made, but the workroom is so busy just now. Now, try this one, Kathy. It's last year's model, but it really is pretty.'

Carefully she helped Kathy ease the gown over her head, while Jemima stood, her head on one side, appraising each one.

The silk gown had a fitted bodice, buttoning down the back, long sleeves and a full skirt and train with scalloped-edge pleats. A long veil, reaching to the ground, completed the ensemble.

'That's the one,' Jemima nodded, firmly. 'You look a picture, dear.'

By the time the three women left the store, Kathy had not only a wedding dress and veil, but shoes and silky white underwear too.

'I've had a letter from Auntie Betty. Uncle Ted's said he'd be delighted to give me away and they're all coming to the wedding. Even – even Morry.'

'I should hope so too,' Jemima answered with asperity. 'I should think a lot less of him if he stayed away out of pique.'

Kathy smiled. She guessed that wasn't strictly true, but she understood what Jemima meant. Her smile widened as she added, 'And guess what? They're bringing my mother.'

'My dear, I am so pleased for you.'

'I can hardly believe it. She's really dared to stand up to my father.' Kathy's eyes clouded. 'I – I just hope he won't take it out on her afterwards.'

'Don't you worry your pretty head about that. Ted and Betty will keep an eye on her. You just enjoy your big day. It's what she would want.'

'I know, and it'll mean the world to me to have her there. I just wish . . .' Kathy began and then stopped.

'That your father would come too,' Jemima said softly, but Kathy shook her head.

'No, actually, it was Tony's mother I was thinking about. I wish she would change her mind and come to the wedding. I know it would make Tony's day if she did.'

'His father will come though, won't he?'

Kathy grimaced and shrugged. 'I don't know. I expect she'll try to stop him. And she'll probably succeed.'

'Oh well,' Jemima said kindly, but without much real hope. 'Maybe George will manage to persuade her to come.'

'I do hope so,' Kathy said fervently.

Jemima glanced at her, but said nothing. It wouldn't do to say so, the older woman was thinking, but it might be a lot better if Beatrice Kendall did stay away from the wedding.

The following Sunday morning, Kathy walked across the city carrying two shopping bags containing everything she needed to cook a Sunday roast lunch for the Kendalls. She'd had to queue for all the things she needed and now, with the rumours that meat was going on ration at the beginning of March, that too was getting scarce. But she'd managed to get a piece of mutton.

She knew that George wasn't finishing his night shift until eight o'clock or even later, and she knew the poor man would be weary. The last thing he needed was to have to come home and start cooking. As she trudged up the slope of the hill on which their house stood, she saw him ahead of her, pushing his bicycle through the gate.

'Mr Kendall,' she called.

As he looked up and saw her, his face break into a

welcoming smile. Well, Kathy thought, there was no mistaking that he, at least, approved of her.

'Hello, lass, what are you doing here?' He chuckled. 'I'd've thought you'd be busy sorting out your trousseau.'

Kathy laughed. 'It's all sorted, Mr Kendall. Such as it is.'

'You'll look a smasher whatever you wear, love,' he said gallantly.

'Now I can see who your son takes after. Flattery will get you everywhere. At least, a Sunday dinner,' she teased.

'A Sunday dinner?' He eyed the bags she was carrying. 'You don't mean you've come all this way just to cook us a dinner, lass, do you?'

'I certainly have. I thought you could do with a little help, seeing as you're on nights. And Tony tells me the extent of his culinary skills is boiling an egg.'

George laughed. 'That's about the size of it, lass. Well, this is a nice surprise. You must have known it's my birthday. Did you?'

Kathy's eyes widened. 'No. Is it?'

'Actually, it was yesterday, but no one remembered 'cept me.'

Kathy was shocked. 'Not even Tony?'

George shrugged. 'He's a lot on his mind. Not only the wedding, of course, but his mother's taken the news very badly, lass, I'm sorry to say. She had a nasty turn yesterday. Tony was called home from work. Did you know?'

'I guessed as much when he sent a message that he couldn't see me last night. That's partly why I've come today. I thought – I thought if your wife realized I'm

211

not trying to take him away from her, that I – I'd like to be thought of as one of the family, then . . .' Her voice trailed away.

'You're already one of the family as far as I'm concerned.' He sighed. 'But I don't mind telling you, love, you've got a battle on your hands before Beatty will see it that way.'

'But while Tony's away, I thought – well – I thought I could be company for her. For both of you. I could help out – if you'd let me.'

'Oh, I'd let you, lass, no doubt about that. And you'd be a daughter to me. Always wanted a daughter, I did,' he murmured dreamily.

I wish you'd tell my dad that, Kathy thought.

He shook himself out of his reverie. 'Let's get inside and you can get cracking. My word, I'm looking forward to this. Tony'll be that pleased to see you.'

Will he? Kathy wondered, but she did not voice her doubts.

Tony was surprised to see her there and a little on edge. 'Look, it's good of you to come, but do you mind staying in the kitchen? That way Mother won't know you're here.'

'You mean if she knows I've cooked the dinner, she won't eat it?'

Tony shrugged. 'Probably not. We'll not tell her.'

'I'll do whatever you want me to do, darling. Besides, I'll need to be in the kitchen most of the time anyway. We'll eat in here, if you like.'

'We usually do,' George said as he washed his hands at the deep sink in the scullery. 'Now, lass, is there anything I can do?'

'No, you go upstairs and have a rest. Tony will call you when dinner's ready. You go back to your mother,

Tony, but if you don't want her to realize I'm here you'd better keep popping out to see when it's all ready.'

'Right you are and – thanks.'

'It's okay,' she said, deliberately keeping her tone light. But it wasn't really okay. It was anything but. It was a ridiculous situation and she couldn't see how it was ever going to be resolved.

Twenty-Two

As they were finishing dinner, the little bell that Beatrice kept close at hand tinkled and Tony went rushing through to see what she wanted. He came back carrying the tray with an empty plate on it. As he set it down on the table, he laughed. 'Mother says your cooking's improving, Dad.'

George chuckled and winked at Kathy. 'You've done it now, lass. You'll have to come again.'

'Any time. I've enjoyed doing it for you.'

'It was a real treat, I don't mind telling you. And now I insist you let me and Tony do the washing up.'

'No, no. Tony, you go back and sit with your mother. And you –' she wagged her finger at her future father-in-law – 'should go back upstairs and sleep.'

'I will when I've helped you. You wash, I'll dry,' he said, picking up a tea towel. 'And I won't take "no" for an answer.'

Kathy laughed and capitulated. As they worked together, Kathy asked tentatively, 'How long has Mrs Kendall been an invalid?'

George sighed. 'It's a long story, love. I don't know if you'd be interested.'

'Of course I'm interested. And not just about Tony either.' She had grown very fond of George Kendall. He was such a kind, gentle man, but she couldn't for

214

the life of her see how he had become entangled with someone like Beatrice, let alone married her!

He sighed, and his round, pleasant face fell into lines of weariness and disappointment as he chose his words carefully. 'It seems such a long time ago now,' he murmured. He forced a smile as he began, 'Once upon a time . . .'

Kathy smiled too, knowing that he was trying to lighten a story that perhaps had little happiness or joy in the telling.

'I belonged – ' now he sighed heavily again – 'to a reasonably wealthy family. My grandfather – my father's father, that is – was a farmer at Wellingore. We lived in a very nice house on the edge of the hill there overlooking all his lands. They were good days. I had an idyllic childhood. Although we never lost our broad dialect . . .' His smile widened and Kathy knew he was not apologizing. He was proud of his birthright.

'Quite right too,' she said stoutly. There were traces of it in her own speech, a trait she had no intention of trying to eradicate.

'I think you could say we were classed as "country gentlemen". My father held shooting parties on his land and mixed with the businessmen and dignitaries of the city.'

His eyes clouded with painful memories. 'And then came the depression. A lot of people went bankrupt. My father among them. He had to sell up, and on the day of the sale, when strangers where tramping through the house, poking and prodding into personal belongings, he took his twelve-bore shotgun and went into a little copse at the end of the meadow. It was where he and I had spent our happiest times. When I was little, he'd play hide and seek or cowboys and

Indians. My dad could be great fun. But that all ended in the little copse.'

'You mean – he – he—'

George nodded and said flatly, 'He shot himself. My mother never got over the shock. She died only six months later. And Beatty, of course, well, she's never got over the shame.'

'Poor man,' Kathy murmured. 'I know how hard it was then. I was only ten or so, but I've heard my father and Ted Robinson talk about those times.' She was pensive for a moment, realizing, perhaps for the first time, just how hard her father had worked to save his own family's farm. But surely, she reasoned, even if he'd been through some hard times, there was no reason why he'd become so embittered.

There was a long silence before Kathy asked tentatively, 'So – when you married Beatrice your folks were – ' she smiled – 'well breeched?'

George gave a wry laugh. 'You could say that. It was through her uncle I met her. Have you seen the old boy yet?'

'Only once. His son brought him through the store in a wheelchair.'

'Aye well, he'll be getting on a bit now. He must be nearly ninety.'

'He still looked bright as a button,' Kathy laughed. 'I overheard him finding fault with a display. "See to it, boy," he said. He called Mr James "boy".' She was giggling now at the memory.

Despite the gravity of their conversation, even George chuckled. 'Aye, he was always the success of that family, old Anthony.'

'I presume Tony's named after him?'

'Oh yes,' George smiled wryly. 'Beatty always had

her eye on the main chance, though where she got her social-climbing ideas from, goodness knows. Her parents were lovely folk. Oh dear – ' he grimaced comically – 'that sounds terribly disloyal to my wife, doesn't it?'

Kathy whispered, 'There's only you and me here and you can trust me.'

His dark eyes, so like Tony's, looked deeply into her. His voice was a little unsteady as he said, 'Aye, I know that, lass. I know that.' He paused and then went on with his story. 'Her uncle – the old boy – used to come shooting on our land. James too, when he was old enough. And because Anthony had no daughter of his own – James was his only child – he used to make a big fuss of Beatty. Perhaps that's how she got a taste for the luxurious life. Her own father, John Charlesworth, was just a good, honest working man but he wasn't a high flyer like his brother-in-law. It was always said Anthony had the Midas touch. He started as a market trader on Lincoln market, would you believe? And look at him now. Must be worth thousands. I wouldn't be surprised if he's not a millionaire.'

'And you fell in love with Beatrice?'

George sighed again. 'I suppose I must have done.' It seemed he was having difficulty in believing it himself. So much had happened since then to kill any love he'd had for the resentful, bitter woman that he could hardly remember the golden days of their youth. 'Oh, that sounds awful,' he groaned. 'But you wouldn't recognize the girl she was then in the woman you see now.'

'But what's made her like she is? Is it just because of what happened in your family?'

217

'I suppose so. Unless it's because I'm so – so boring and – and ordinary. I think she despises me.'

'She's no right to do that,' Kathy declared hotly. 'You're a lovely man.'

He smiled sadly. 'You're a dear girl to say so.'

'It's true. She should've supported you when your family hit such a terrible time. Not – not turned against you and blamed you.'

'She thought she was marrying into a well-to-do family. Folks with land and property and a prosperous future. She didn't know it was all going to disappear. Nor did any of us. I have to say her uncle's been good to us. Still is. He, and James too, have given Tony a marvellous opportunity. But even then Beatrice is still resentful, seeing it as a right rather than a privilege. I sometimes wonder, though, if he's really up to the job. If he's just there because of who his relatives are.'

Kathy tried to be objective. 'I don't think so. Everyone thinks very well of Tony, at least—' she hesitated.

'What? Tell me, lass.' He smiled wryly. 'Since we're being honest with each other.'

Kathy lifted her shoulders in a helpless gesture. 'It was just that he was known as rather a "ladies' man". He had a reputation for having several girlfriends and – and, well – not treating them very well.'

George nodded. 'I guessed as much.'

'You – you knew about the flat?'

'I guessed. When he didn't come home some nights, I guessed he must be staying somewhere. For some time I though it was at a friend's house or at a girl-friend's. But when he never brought any of them home, I guessed he must have a little place of his own some-where.'

'But he brought Muriel Curtis home, didn't he?'

'Yes. She was the first.' He was quiet for a moment before murmuring, 'In fact, the only serious one before you. Poor Muriel. She was a nice lass. I never really knew what happened and to be honest, I don't think Tony did either. He was quite cut up when she broke off their engagement without giving any real explanation.' He held Kathy's gaze steadily. 'I always thought Beatty had something to do with it, but I don't know what.'

Kathy couldn't prevent the colour rising in her face.

'But you know, don't you?' he added softly.

She couldn't lie to him. Slowly, she nodded. 'Yes, I do know, but I was told in confidence and I can't betray that person's trust.' Already she'd tested Jemima's belief in her, and she would never again lie to the woman who had befriended her or break her confidence. 'The only thing I will tell you is that, yes, you're right. Your wife did interfere.'

'Aye, well, lass, you're not breaking your promise to anyone by telling me that. I guessed as much and I'm sorry.'

George put his hand on her shoulder and gave it a gentle squeeze. His voice was husky as he added, 'Just mind you don't let her break you two up, eh?'

'No,' Kathy said firmly. 'I won't.'

'You're lucky with the weather, my dear. It's cold but fine – at the moment. Let's hope it holds,' Jemima said, as she entered Kathy's bedroom on the morning of the wedding carrying a tray of cereal, toast and a small pot of tea.

'Now, sit up,' she commanded. She set the tray across Kathy's knees and then moved across the room to open the curtains.

'Oh, Aunt Jemima, you shouldn't have!'

'Every bride should have breakfast in bed on her wedding day and since your mother isn't here to do it, I'm the next best thing.'

'You're very good to me,' Kathy said huskily, her eyes filling with tears.

'Now, now, none of that. This is a happy day, the happiest day of your life.'

Kathy smiled but said nothing. Though she didn't voice it, her tears were not for herself but for this woman who had shown her such brisk kindness. A woman whose own past was something of a mystery, but who, Kathy believed, had once known love herself. And yet, though something must have gone terribly wrong, Jemima, instead of wallowing in bitterness, had done everything she could to encourage Kathy's romance with Tony. 'Aunt Jemima,' Kathy said hesitantly.

'Yes, my dear. What is it?'

'Just – thank you. Thank you for everything.'

Jemima waved her hand and said, 'Oh, phooey, girl. I've enjoyed every minute of it. And here comes Taffy to wish you well today.'

The cat jumped on to the end of the bed, kneaded the eiderdown with his huge paws, turned round three times and then lay down, curling himself into a neat circle.

Kathy laughed. 'Are you sure, or does he just want a comfy bed to sleep on?'

Jemima's eyes twinkled. 'Probably the latter. Shall I take him away?'

'No, no, I like having him here. He'll be company while I get ready.'

'All right, but just don't let him get his claws in your wedding gown.'

Kathy finished the bowl of cereal and nibbled at the toast. She drank half the cup of tea and then lay back against the pillows and glanced through the open curtains.

Fluffy white clouds scudded across the sky, but the pale winter sun was shining and today she was going to marry the man she adored.

What more could a girl ask for?

She was almost ready when there was a flurry of activity downstairs and the sound of voices all talking at once. Footsteps sounded on the stairs and the bedroom door was flung open.

'There you are,' Amy began and then stopped, her mouth open in a gasp. 'Oh Kathy, you look beautiful.'

'I was just beginning to get a bit worried. You'll have to be quick getting ready.'

Amy waved her hand in the air nonchalantly. 'Don't worry. I'm all ready apart from putting my dress on. Are you okay? Need any help?'

'It's just my veil, but I was waiting deliberately. I – I was hoping Mam might help me put it on. I think she'd like that. She – she has come, hasn't she?'

'Well – er – yes. She's on her way,' Amy said, as she stepped into her dress and Kathy helped her with the tiny buttons.

'What do you mean "on her way"? Didn't she come with you?'

'No. There wasn't room for both of them in our car, not with the four of us.'

'Both of them?' Kathy was startled. 'You – you don't mean . . . ?'

Amy nodded. 'I do. Your father's come and he's insisting on giving you away. Says he doesn't want the neighbours gossiping about him for refusing to give his daughter away.'

'I see,' Kathy said grimly. 'It's not because he wants to do it either for me or for himself, but because of what others might say.'

'I – suppose so. I'm sorry, Kathy.'

'It's not your fault.'

There were soft footsteps on the stairs and the two girls said no more as Edith came into the room, her arms outstretched to envelop her daughter and tears of happiness in her eyes.

'Oh Mam, I'm so glad you're here.'

'Amy's told you? About your dad?'

Kathy forced a smile. 'Yes. Isn't it great?'

'Ted understands. He says he's pleased 'cos it's only right and proper.'

Kathy nodded. If truth be told, she would rather have had the kindly Ted Robinson leading her up the aisle than her own father. But that secret thought remained unspoken.

Edith drew back and looked at her daughter. 'Darling girl, you look beautiful.'

Jemima's voice drifted up the stairs. 'Edith, Amy – time you were going to the church.'

There was a flurry of activity downstairs and then the house was suddenly quiet. Taking a deep breath as she prepared to face her father, Kathy went carefully down the narrow stairs and into the kitchen.

Her father was standing with his back to the range. They stared at each other for several moments, before Kathy felt obliged to say, 'Thanks for coming, Dad.'

He frowned and muttered. 'I hope you're not going to expect me to pay for any of this. Hiring a car, for heaven's sake. A lot of fuss. And it won't last. You mark my words, it won't last. A man in his position marrying someone like you. Huh!'

'Mr Hammond has lent us his chauffeur for the day. It's not costing us anything.'

'Who's Mr Hammond when he's at home?'

'The owner of the store where I work and where Tony is the manager. Tony's related to him.'

For a moment, Jim Burton's eyes gleamed. 'Wealthy, is he? Is the lad in line to take over some day then? Maybe you've got a bit more sense that I gave you credit for.'

'Mr Hammond senior is Tony's mother's uncle and I think he will always see that Tony has a good job. But no, he's not in line to take over as you put it. Mr Hammond has a son of his own.'

Jim sniffed. 'Huh! I thought as much. I thought you hadn't the sense you were born with.'

There was the sound of the car drawing up outside. Relieved, Kathy said, 'Time to go, Dad.'

They paused in the porch and Amy, smiling from ear to ear, slipped in behind them as the organ music struck up and they began the slow procession up the aisle. The congregation was pathetically small, but Kathy felt a flood of happiness sweep through her. The only people who really mattered to her were all here. Even Morry. Though she knew she could never love him as he deserved to be loved, in the way that he wanted, she was extremely fond of him and the only cloud on her day was the thought that she was hurting him. As she drew level with the end of the pew where he was sitting, she risked a glance at his face.

Morry's eyes were full of tears but he was smiling and he gave a little nod of encouragement. He leant forward and whispered, 'You look wonderful, Kathy. Be happy.'

Those words from Morry meant more to her than anything anyone else could say to her on her wedding day.

A few more steps and she was standing beside Tony. She looked up at him to find him smiling down at her. He looked so handsome in his dark suit that her heart turned over with love for him. She glanced beyond him and saw that James Hammond was standing beside him as his best man. A movement in the pew just behind them caught her eye. Kathy's eyes widened as she saw Tony's father sitting there, and beside him, dressed in black from head to toe, was Beatrice Kendall.

Twenty-Three

Kathy smiled tremulously at Tony, who reached out and squeezed her hand. 'This is it, darling? You ready?'

'Oh, yes,' she breathed, as the vicar moved closer and opened his prayer book. He smiled benignly at the young couple, silently praying that their hopes and dreams would be fulfilled and that their future would not be torn asunder by this dreadful war. He was conducting so many marriages these days, hastily arranged, before the imminent departure of the groom into the armed forces. This, he knew, was another such one.

'Dearly beloved . . .' he began, and Kathy, delirious with happiness, tried to concentrate on what he was saying and on being sure she made the right responses in the right place.

The service went on, and then it came to that moment that all brides and grooms joke about and tease each other. 'Therefore if any man can show any just cause, why they may not lawfully be joined together . . .'

The vicar got no further. From the front pew came a gasp, a moan and then a thud. Everyone turned to see that Beatrice had slumped sideways onto the pew and had only been prevent from rolling on to the floor by George grabbing her. He knelt in front of her.

'Beatty – Beatty!' he hissed in a fierce whisper, but the woman only moaned and put her hand to her chest.

Her eyes closed, her face white, she whispered, 'Oh the pain, the pain. George – my pills.'

Tony turned away from Kathy and knelt beside his father, cradling his mother in his arms, while George scrabbled in her handbag for the box of pills.

A murmuring ran around the small congregation and necks craned to see what was happening. Kathy stood watching the scene. Her heart pounded. Her hands trembled until her bouquet shook and all the happiness slowly drained out of her. But no one was taking any notice of Kathy. All their attention was focused on Beatrice Kendall.

'Dad, we should call an ambulance,' Tony whispered worriedly. 'This is a bad one.'

'Let's see if her pills work first. Just hang on a moment, son.'

'Dad, I'll never forgive myself if . . .'

'Hold on, son, just hold on a minute.'

'Can I help?' the vicar enquired. 'A glass of water, perhaps?'

Tony glanced up, 'Yes, yes, please.'

The vicar laid down his book and hurried away towards the vestry. He returned in a moment with a glass of water, but by now Beatrice was limp in Tony's arms, her eyes closed, her mouth gagging open.

'Dad, she's unconscious. We must call an ambulance.'

George stood up, pausing only a brief moment to look down at his wife before he turned to James Hammond, who was standing close by looking on anxiously. 'James, would you find the nearest telephone box and ring for an ambulance, please?'

James hurried down the aisle and the murmuring amongst the guests grew louder.

'What's up with her?' Jim muttered in Kathy's ear.

Kathy ran her tongue around her dry lips. 'She – she has a bad heart.'

She heard her father's familiar sniff of disapproval. 'Huh! Very convenient, if you ask me.'

For once, Kathy was in full agreement with her father.

There was no way they could continue the service with the groom's mother apparently unconscious in the front pew and waiting for the arrival of an emergency vehicle.

Kathy felt the vicar's light touch on her shoulder. He cleared his throat, obviously embarrassed at what he had to say. 'My dear, I am sorry, but I have another wedding service in an hour. There are so many to fit in these days . . .' His voice trailed away apologetically.

Kathy tried to smile. 'If we could just wait for the ambulance, maybe . . .'

At that moment there was the sound of a clanging bell and a noisy motor drew up outside the church. Two ambulance men hurried in, carrying a stretcher between them.

'Here – down here.' Morry had stepped into the aisle and was pointing towards the front pew. He was directing them towards the sick woman, but his anxious glance was upon Kathy. There was no mistaking that his whole concern was really for her.

Kathy stood motionless, watching while the ambulance men gently lifted a limp and unresponsive Beatrice on to the stretcher. They picked it up and carried her down the aisle and out of the church.

George walked close behind and Tony, without even so much as a glance at his bride, followed him. Half-way down the aisle, George stopped and glanced back.

Kathy saw the surprise on his face as he realized his son was just behind him. He said something, though Kathy could not hear his words, but she saw him gesture towards her. And then she saw Tony shake his head. Anger crossed George's face and he pointed at Kathy and spoke again and this time his voice was raised high enough for Kathy to hear, loud enough for everyone in the church to hear. 'You go back to that lass and carry on.'

Tony hesitated and then turned and hurried back towards her. 'Kathy – darling,' he caught hold of her hands and gripped them tightly. 'I have to go with her. It looks bad. If anything happened, I . . . You do understand, don't you? Wait for me, darling, please. I will come back . . .'

Without even waiting for her answer, he turned and almost ran back down the aisle. He did not even look back at her. Not once.

'Well, this is a find how-do-ya-do, I must say,' Jim Burton growled. 'What happens now, might I ask?'

Kathy had not moved. She was motionless, still staring down the aisle, her eyes fixed on the point where Tony had disappeared from her sight. The truth came at her like a tidal wave, flooding through her, engulfing her, swamping her. It would always be like this. Even though Tony would have to go away, would have to serve his country, and it looked as if even his mother could not prevent that, Kathy could see that there was no future for her within his family. While George might welcome her, he was as helpless against Beatrice as his son.

Dimly, she was aware that two people were moving towards her, coming to stand one on either side of her.

Jemima took her arm and Morry put his arm around her waist.

'Come, my dear, let's go to the vestry and see what the vicar has to say.'

For a moment Kathy gave no sign that she had even heard, but then, slowly, she shook her head.

'No,' she whispered. 'It's no use. There's no future for us. How blind I've been.' With stiff, jerky movements, she began to walk down the aisle.

'Hey, what's going on?' Jim's voice blared, echoing round the church, but Kathy walked on, tears blinding her. Morry hurried after her and caught hold of her arm. 'Kathy . . .'

She pressed her lips together and shook her head, unable now even to speak.

As she emerged from the church door, Morry still at her side, the photographer with his box camera on a tripod called, 'Ah, the happy couple, hold it there. Let's get a nice picture of you.'

Kathy continued to walk towards him.

'I say, wait a minute—'

She paused beside him, stared at him for a moment and then flung her bouquet at him. 'There's been no wedding. Nor will there be. You'd better go home.'

'But – but – Mr Hammond—'

Kathy stalked towards the car that had brought her to the church.

'You'd better go into the church. They'll explain,' she heard Morry tell him as she climbed into the car. Then he hurried after her and climbed in beside her.

'Morry, please. I want to be on my own.'

'You probably do, but for once, Kathy, I'm taking no notice of you. I'm not leaving you on your own.'

'Oh Morry, I've been such a fool.' Tears were close now. She fought valiantly to stem the flow, but failed. Morry mopped her face with a clean, white handkerchief. 'No, you haven't. It's a difficult situation,' he said, with gentle reason. 'Jemima's told me what Mrs Kendall's like, but really, you can't blame Tony. If it was my mother, I'd be just the same. I know I would.'

Kathy tried to smile, but it was only a wry twist of her mouth. 'You're very understanding – and forgiving. I don't think I can be that generous. Not – not today.'

'I know. It's dreadful for you. It's your bad luck that the vicar is so hard pressed that he can't just give us an hour or two to see what happens. Perhaps, when they've got her settled in hospital, Tony will come back and the vicar can perform the ceremony later. I know your special day is in tatters and none of us can say whether Mrs Kendall's illness is real or – or induced at just the right moment to halt the ceremony.'

'It's that all right,' Kathy said bitterly. 'I know it is.'

'But can you really, in your heart of hearts, Kathy, blame Tony? Can you really expect any man with any decency to turn his back on his mother, to ignore her cries for help? You see, he can't be sure, can he? He can never be sure. If she's really ill – if she were to die even, he'd have to live with that for the rest of his life. He'd never be able to forgive himself. Or – you.'

'It'll always be like this, won't it?'

'Maybe not. Perhaps when he's been away from home in the forces – and that's nobody's fault – things might change. If she can't deal with that either, then that's not Tony's fault or yours. But maybe when the break with him has been forced upon her, there's just a chance that things might be different.'

Kathy lifted her tear-streaked face and looked into Morry's round, open and honest face. 'Oh Morry – ' she bent her head against his shoulder and wept bitterly – 'Oh Morry, why couldn't I have loved you?'

Morry whispered huskily, 'I only wish you could, Kathy.

The house was deathly still as Morry opened the back door with the key that Jemima had slipped to him. Kathy got stiffly out of the car and walked down the passageway towards the back gate, ignoring the curious glances of the neighbours. Time enough for the gossip to spread, she thought.

As they stepped inside, Kathy turned to him. 'Thank you for your kindness, Morry. I'll never be able to thank you enough, but now I'm going upstairs. I need to be alone.'

Understanding as ever, Morry nodded. 'Of course you do. I'll stop anyone coming up.'

'Thank you. Just one more thing, could you undo the buttons down the back of my dress.'

She turned away from him, her back towards him.

'Oh Kathy, I . . .'

'Please, Morry, just do it.'

She felt his fingers trembling as he struggled with the tiny buttons.

'That's fine,' she said, pulling away when she felt that he had undone enough for her to slip out of the garment. 'Thanks.' Without a backward glance, she headed for the stairs and the sanctuary of her bedroom.

A little later she heard voices downstairs and knew that the others had returned from the church. Then she heard her father's raised voice.

'Get out of my way, Maurice. I've a right to see my own daughter.'

There were sounds of a scuffle and then of heavy footsteps on the stairs. Kathy closed her eyes briefly and groaned. This was what she had dreaded most.

'Jim, please, leave her alone . . .' Edith's voice drifted up the stairs.

'Shut up, woman, and leave this to me.'

The door opened and he was in the room, slamming it behind him with such force that it bounced open again. But Jim was too intent upon shaking his fist at his daughter to notice.

'You want horsewhipping, girl. Bringing such shame on me like this. Well, I'll give you one last chance. You come home now with us and you settle down and wed Maurice and we'll say no more about it. Though there's plenty I could say. Plenty.'

And you will, Kathy thought bitterly. I shall have all this dragged up and thrown at me for the rest of my life – or rather for the rest of yours. She shook her head. Her voice was husky, but there was a note of resolution in her tone. 'No, Dad, I will not marry Morry. I wouldn't do that to him.'

'Huh!' Jim was scathing. 'So I was right. You are expecting that whippersnapper's bastard, are you? Well, Maurice will still marry you. He's besotted with you. God only knows why, but he is. I'll pay him, if I have to.'

Wearily, Kathy said, 'Dad, for the last time, I'm not pregnant.'

'So what's the problem?'

'I don't love Morry.'

'What's that got to do with anything? I've never loved your mother.'

Slowly Kathy raised her head to look at him. 'No,' she said quietly. 'And that's the tragedy of both your lives.'

They stared at each other until quick, light footsteps sounded on the stairs and the bedroom door was flung wide.

'Jim Burton,' Jemima said coldly, 'Leave my house this instant. We've heard every word of your conversation. *Every* word. Kathy stays with me. You're a stupid man, Jim. You don't realize what a fine girl you've got.'

'Fine? Fine, you say, when she's brought all this shame on me.'

'Shame? What shame?'

Jim's lips curled. 'Well, you wouldn't know anything about that, Jemima Robinson, would you? You're nowt but a dried-up old spinster 'cos none of us village lads were good enough for you, were we? Turned your nose up at us, didn't ya? Thought you could do better for yarsen in the city, but it dun't look to have got you far.'

'Get out!' Jemima, her eyes sparking with fiery anger, spat at him. 'Get out of my house.'

'I'm going.' He turned towards Kathy one last time and pointed his finger at her. 'But if I do, don't you ever, ever come knocking on my door again. From this day forward, you're no daughter of mine.'

It wasn't his threat, it wasn't the fact that she might never see him – or her mother – again, that was Kathy's undoing. It was his use of the words from the marriage ceremony that tore at her heart and caused her face to crumple and the tears to flow again.

'Aye, you can cry, girl. But you've brought all this on yourself. You've only yourself to blame.'

233

With that, he turned and stamped out of the room and down the stairs. The last words she heard were, 'Come along, Edith, we're going home, and if you ever have anything to do with that girl again, I'll throw you out an' all.'

The back door slammed and there was a stunned silence throughout the whole house.

Twenty-Four

'Well, I never did hear the like.' Kathy heard Betty's voice drift up the stairs. They were still all sitting down there in Jemima's front room, drinking tea and talking over the shattering events of the day. Kathy stayed alone in her room. She couldn't face the kindly faces of the Robinsons and their sympathy. Only Jemima's brisk attitude was bearable at the moment.

She was best left alone and they all seemed to sense this.

'What's going to happen, d'you think? Will they get married, quiet like, another day?' Ted's booming voice asked.

'I really don't know,' Jemima said in a matter-of-fact way. 'It's up to them. They're best left to sort it out between themselves.'

'I doubt very much whether that young man will ever be able to do that.' Ted sighed. 'It's a real shame. He seems like a nice young feller. A bit weak, mebbe, where his mother's concerned, but who are we to judge?'

'Precisely,' Jemima said. 'More tea, Betty?'

'No thank you, Jemima cariad. We'd best be on our way. We want to be home before dark. Before the blackout. Oh dear me, and to think that poor Tony will be gone on Monday. I don't think there's going to be much time for them to sort anything out, do you?'

'Sadly, no, I don't. His mother will do her best to keep him at her bedside until Monday morning. Still, don't you worry about Kathy. I'll look after her.'

'Shall we say goodbye to her?'

'Best not. I'll tell her later. And I'm sure she knows she has your support.'

'Give her our love and tell her there's always a home for her with us – whatever happens.' This last was from Ted, and Kathy's tears flowed afresh at the kindness in his tone.

Why, oh why, couldn't she have fallen in love with Morry? Life would have been so simple then. But she knew she could never marry him. He was a dear, dear friend but – for her – nothing more.

She could hear Amy's tearful voice. 'Tell her I'll write, because I don't know when I might have to – to go.'

'I will, dear. Now, chin up, you'll soon be a Wren. Wrens don't cry.'

'This one does.' Amy tried to laugh through her tears.

There was much hugging and kissing and calls of 'goodbyes' before Kathy heard them all clattering down the passage and out into the street. Car doors banged, the engine started and they were gone.

Kathy heard Jemima moving about below, heard the clatter of pots and cutlery, and knew she should go down and help. But she couldn't move. She remained sitting motionless on the edge of the bed, still in her wedding dress with the buttons undone down the back, her fingers knotted so tightly together that the knuckles were white.

Footsteps on the stairs and Jemima came in bearing

a cup of hot, strong tea. 'Now, my dear, dry your tears and drink this. Then we must think what to do.'

She sat down on a spindly-legged bedroom chair facing Kathy. 'Come along, drink it up.'

Kathy obeyed meekly and suddenly found she was very thirsty.

'Would you like me to trot along and see the vicar? Just to ask if there's a chance he can fit the ceremony in some time tomorrow?'

Kathy shook her head. 'It's no use unless we hear from Tony.'

'I take your point.' She was silent a moment before adding, 'Perhaps we'll hear something from him this evening.'

Kathy raised her head and looked directly into Jemima's honest eyes. 'Do – do you think her attack was genuine?'

'No – I don't. It was too contrived. Oh, I don't say she couldn't have suffered some sort of attack during the service with the stress of it all, but to happen just at that very moment, just when he was asking the congregation that all important question. It was straight out of *Jane Eyre*, now wasn't it? So melodramatic as to be unbelievable.'

'I know,' Kathy agreed sadly. 'But we can't prove it. No one can. And Mr Kendall and Tony just – just daren't take the risk of calling her bluff.'

'Well, if the worst comes to the worst, we'll just have to arrange a very quiet ceremony when Tony gets his first leave.'

Kathy set her cup down carefully on the bedside table. 'But the same thing will happen. It'll go on happening. She said – she told me that she'd see to it that he never married me. I didn't believe she could do it, but she has. She's managed it.'

'You might find that this enforced separation – Tony having to go into the armed forces – will be the making of him. I've never said a word against him. He's a nice young man but, between you and me, maybe that's his main fault. He's *too* nice. He's not strong enough to stand up to his mother, but now he's going to be forced to make the break. It's being done for him and it might turn out to be a blessing in disguise. You might well find that when he comes home on leave he'll be a very different person.'

'I – I don't really want him to be any different. I love him as he is . . .' She smiled sadly as she added wryly, 'Despite his mother.'

'Well, in that case, my dear, you'll never be free of her and you can take it from me that she'll never stop trying to prevent your marriage. And, even if you succeed in that, she'll never stop interfering in your lives. If Tony survives the war—'

Kathy covered her face with her hands and cried out, 'Oh no, don't say that, Aunt Jemima. Please, don't even think it.'

'It's a possibility that has to be faced, my dear,' she said quietly, and added in a whisper, 'And I should know.'

Guiltily, Kathy raised her face. Here she was selfishly taking all the generous support Jemima had to give when the poor woman had spent a lifetime of loneliness. Somehow, she had lost the love of her life. Kathy was sure of it.

'I'm being very selfish and self-centred, Aunt Jemima. I'm sorry.'

'Oh, phooey.' Jemima flapped her hand. 'We've just got to think what's best to be done now.'

There was nothing to be done. Tony didn't come to Jemima's house that evening or the next morning. After breakfast, of which Kathy ate hardly anything and even Jemima ate only a little cereal instead of her usual bowlful followed by toast and marmalade, they washed up the pots together and then sat in the kitchen, waiting. As the clock crawled to half past eleven, Jemima jumped up from her chair.

'I can't abide all this sitting about. Shall we walk up to the hospital and make enquiries? At least we might find out if there's any chance he . . .'

Kathy shook her head. 'He'll come when he can. It – it must have been more serious than we thought. I feel so guilty now for having thought badly of her.'

'Huh!' Jemima was not yet ready to be so understanding. 'Either that or she's keeping up a very good act. She should have been on the stage, that one.' She paused and paced up and down the small space for a moment. As if she could not bear to sit, she muttered, 'Then I'll walk along to the church and see if . . .'

'It's no good,' Kathy said, sounding far more reasonable than she was actually feeling inside.

'Come on, girl, don't give up. Not now. At least if we could get you married today . . .'

Again, Kathy shook her head. 'That's not how I want it to be. Not all rushed and – and underhand as if – as if . . .'

'As if you've *got* to get married?'

Kathy lowered her gaze and said nothing. Jemima

sank into her chair and leant her head back, closing her eyes. 'Yes,' she said flatly, 'you're right. I'm pushing you too hard. It's just – it's just . . . Oh, I'd so like to have seen you married before he has to go away. It'd give you both something to hang on to. It's not going to be easy for either of you. He's going to have to face God only knows what and it's going to be hard for you, trying to carry on as normal when nothing's ever going to be "normal" again. Oh why, why, can't those in power see the futility, the stupid, stupid waste of it all?'

The clock ticked steadily on as the two women fell silent again and waited once more.

He came just after five o'clock, looking white and dishevelled. He was still wearing his wedding suit; dark shadows ringed his eyes and anxiety clouded their brightness.

'They're keeping her in for observation.'

'Where is she?'

'At the moment, she's in the County but we're trying to get her moved to the Bromhead Nursing Home.'

Jemima sniffed. 'I should leave her where she is. It's a good hospital.'

'Well, yes, I know, but she likes her own room. She likes her privacy.' He turned to Kathy and took her hands. 'Darling, I am so sorry about what happened. I couldn't help it. You do believe that, don't you?'

Before Kathy could answer, Jemima said, 'Well, now you're here, I – er – have to go out. I must see Mabel Spencer. WVS business, you know. We've – um – a lot to discuss.'

They both knew she was deliberately leaving them alone together. Within minutes she had donned her hat and coat. 'Just feed Taffy for me at six o'clock. You know how he likes his routine.' And then she was gone.

'Let's go into the front room. Jemima insisted on lighting a fire in there – in case you came.'

'In *case* I came? Darling, surely you knew I would come as soon as I could?'

'Well, yes, of course I did,' Kathy said, trying to sound as if she meant it. 'But I didn't know when that would be, did I? And – and you have to catch the early train tomorrow morning, don't you?'

'Yes, I do. And there's nothing I can do about that. I could be on a charge if I'm late reporting.'

They sat, huddled together, on the sofa. 'We should be on our honeymoon now. You should have been Mrs Kendall for a whole twenty-eight hours. Darling, I am so, so sorry.'

'I know,' Kathy said simply. She twisted in his arms to look up at him. 'But – but we could still have our honeymoon. At least, a bit of it. We—' She blushed as she said shyly, 'We could go upstairs. Aunt Jemima won't be back for ages . . .'

Their lovemaking was bitter sweet, each of them knowing deep in their hearts that this night together might be all they ever had, and afterwards they lay in each other's arms. While Tony slept, Kathy wept silently against his shoulder.

Only when Taffy's meowing outside the bedroom door reminded her that she had forgotten to feed him did they rouse, dress and go downstairs.

'I don't suppose she'd mind if you stayed. I – I think she'd understand.'

Tony shook his head sadly. 'I have to go back to the hospital before visiting ends. And then – then I have to pack.'

'Of course,' Kathy said huskily. She was about to offer to help him but she bit back the words, realizing that his father, too, deserved a little time with his son before . . . She closed her eyes and dared not think about what was to happen in the morning.

Just before he left, Tony handed her a long, thin box. 'I was going to give you this on our wedding night. I still want you to have it.'

Kathy opened the box and gasped when she saw the single string of pearls nestling against the dark blue velvet lining. 'Oh darling, it's beautiful. Thank you.'

As she kissed him, he murmured, 'Wear them always for me, Kathy. And remember, whatever happens I really do love you.'

Twenty-Five

'How did it all go then?'

Stella was excited the next morning. She had so wanted to attend the wedding, but with Kathy, Miss Robinson, Tony and even Mr James Hammond all off for the day, the store had been severely understaffed.

'It didn't,' Kathy said shortly. Out of the corner of her eye, she saw Muriel Curtis moving closer.

Stella gasped. 'What do you mean "it didn't"? Do – do you mean he jilted you? Left you standing at the altar?'

'Not exactly.'

'What then?'

Kathy raised her eyes and glanced around. There were no customers yet, so she moved towards Muriel with Stella following in her wake. 'I might as well tell you together. The wedding didn't happen,' she said bluntly.

Kathy watched Muriel's face closely, half expecting to see relief, perhaps even triumph, on the other woman's face. But to Muriel's credit, there was neither. Instead, she frowned and asked in a concerned tone, 'Why? What happened? Oh . . .' She sighed heavily and closed her eyes briefly, saying flatly, 'Don't tell me. His mother was taken ill.'

'How . . . ?' Kathy began and then stopped. She'd been about to say: How did you know? But of course she realized exactly how Muriel knew. Instead, she said flatly, 'Yes. During the service. Just at the moment when the vicar asks the congregation about "just cause" and all that.'

'Huh! I call that perfect timing,' Muriel said sarcastically. 'I'm so sorry, Kathy, truly I am. I – just want to see him happy. You know that. And if you were the one to do it, then I wished you well.' She gave a wry smile. 'I tried as hard as I knew how to hate you when you first started going out with Tony. But I couldn't. And I'd have liked nothing better – now – than to see the two of you happy together.'

'You're very generous,' Kathy said huskily. 'But it doesn't look as if it's going to happen now. He – he left this morning on the early train. And goodness knows when he'll get leave.'

'He should get a few days when he's completed his basic training and been posted,' Stella said. 'My cousin did. Mind you, that was the Army. Mr Kendall's joined the RAF, hasn't he?'

Kathy nodded, not trusting herself to speak for the huge lump that felt as if it was growing in her throat.

'Work, that's the best thing for you,' Muriel said, almost adopting Jemima's brisk manner. 'And here's the first customer of the day. Forward, Miss Burton, if you please,' she added with a smile. As Kathy moved towards the lady entering the department, Muriel whispered to Stella, 'As we don't work on commission here, Stella, perhaps you'd let Kathy take most of the customers today. Keep her busy.'

'Of course, Miss Curtis. Poor thing. What a dreadful thing to happen.'

'Yes,' Muriel murmured. 'Isn't it?'

*

With the help of her colleagues' thoughtful actions, Kathy was kept busy all day and the time passed quickly. About mid-morning, Jemima walked through the department. It was not unusual, so Kathy thought nothing of it. It was also quite normal for the supervisor to stop and speak to the head of department, so seeing Jemima and Muriel with their heads together in conversation caused Kathy no discomfort. Though, perhaps, if she had thought for a moment, she might have guessed that this morning their exchange was not wholly about stock and displays.

'I expect she's told you,' Jemima began, and Muriel nodded.

'I'm so sorry.'

'That's generous of you, in the circumstances.'

'What happened to me was nothing to do with Kathy and I'm sorry to see nothing has changed. That woman . . .'

'Precisely, but sadly there's nothing any of us can do. If I had thought for a moment that interference from me would have helped, I'd have been up at their house in a trice. But I knew such an action would only make matters worse.' Jemima pulled a wry grimace. 'If they could get much worse. He's gone this morning, you know.'

'Yes.' Now Muriel's voice was husky. She still loved him and, even though now she was seeing him with someone else, she was trying to move on with her own life. And there would always be a place in her heart for her lost love. A part of her that would be devastated if he should be hurt or – God forbid – killed. 'I'm trying to keep her busy. Trying to keep her mind off things.'

'Good. Thank you, Muriel.' Jemima moved on, and

without even a glance towards Kathy, who was serving a customer, she left the department.

Evenings were going to be the most difficult. The long hours that stretched into an even longer night. Hours of darkness when Kathy lay staring into nothingness, wondering what might have been and what, if anything, could be done. Once more, Jemima attempted to come to the rescue.

Kathy arrived home before her that first evening and was feeding Taffy, still apologetic that she had neglected him the previous night, though, as he arched his back under her gentle stroke, she believed herself forgiven. He wound himself around her legs as she prepared his dinner and miaowed and purred in ecstatic anticipation.

As she placed his dish on the floor, she heard Jemima's quick tripping steps down the passageway.

'I've just been talking to Ron Spencer,' Jemima began, almost before she'd stepped inside and closed the door. 'He wants to know if you're going to the choral society on Thursday evening. Evidently they're trying to get a special concert together for the war effort. In fact, he'll probably ask you if you can spare any more time. I told him I'd ask you.'

Kathy hid her smile. She wondered just which of them it really had been who had suggested trying to fill Kathy's empty evenings. Touched by their kindness, Kathy said at once, 'Yes, of course I'd be glad to help. I'd been thinking of offering to help you at the WVS too, but I do want to go and see Mr Kendall. Just—just to see if I can help him at all. He'll miss Tony's help with – with . . .'

'He certainly will and I'm sure he'll welcome you with open arms. But what *she* will do is another matter.'

Kathy climbed the hill to the Kendalls' house the very next evening, but no one answered her knock. She tried to squint through the blackout curtains to see if anyone was in, but the whole house appeared empty.

Perhaps Mrs Kendall was still in hospital and George was visiting her or was still at work on the evening shift. Kathy turned away and retraced her steps. As she turned into the side street, she saw Ron wheeling his bicycle up the slope towards her.

'Hello, love. I'm just on my way to the school now. Are you going to join us?' His eyes showed his concern for her, but he made no mention of her disastrous wedding day. For that, she was grateful.

Kathy took a deep breath and forced a smile. 'Why? Is there a practice tonight? It's only Tuesday.'

'Not exactly. A few of us are meeting to discuss how we can help the war effort. Some chap in London has set up an entertainments' unit of civilian artistes who are willing to travel anywhere to entertain not only troops but factory workers, shipyards, hospitals – in fact, any group of workers involved in the war. Some of us in the society would like to get involved.'

'I see. But – but you said travelling. I mean – I have a job, and – and I want to be here whenever Tony comes home on leave.'

Ron patted her shoulder understandingly. He had heard all about Saturday's fiasco and his heart went out to this girl. 'Of course you do, my dear. But – tell you what – come along with me now and at least hear what's involved. We're none of us too sure ourselves yet, but we've got some bod coming from London to talk to us tonight. We might all know a bit more by the end of the evening about exactly what they're looking for a group like us to do. A lot of our members have day jobs, but they'd be able to travel reasonable distances in the evenings and at weekends. Besides, some employers can be surprisingly helpful if they know it's for the war effort.'

Kathy shrugged. 'Well, I've nothing else to do. Why not?'

'That's the ticket.'

The evening was a merry one. The 'bod' from London was something of an entertainer himself, and his talk to the company was littered with jokes and anecdotes that had the members of the normally rather staid choral society rocking with laughter. There was also a young man there, a stalwart of the Lincoln Operatic & Dramatic Society, Martin Montgomery. He was tall and broad with fair hair. His chin was firm and square and he had the cheekiest grin and the most mischievous blue eyes that Kathy had ever seen.

He doubled as a stage manager for the local society, he told them, but his real love was being on stage. He then proceeded to demonstrate with monologues and a comedy routine that had the audience in stitches. Between them, the two visitors gave the choral society much to think about.

As they walked home together through the blackout, Ron Spencer pushing his bicycle so that he could walk alongside her, they were both still chuckling.

'I was rather impressed with his idea of forming a

concert party that was more than just singing,' Ron remarked.

'Yes. The man from London – what was his name again?'

'Sid Warren, I think. Yes, that's it, because it made me think of rabbits.' Ron chuckled. 'I wonder if he includes producing a rabbit out of a top hat in his act.'

'He said the show should include a comedian, a juggler and a speciality act. What's that, exactly?'

'It's an act that's a bit out of the ordinary. Like a hypnotist. That sort of thing. And, of course, there should be pretty dancing girls. Are you any good at dancing, Kathy, because you're certainly pretty enough?'

Kathy laughed. 'I've got two left feet. No, I'll stick to singing, if you don't mind.'

'Fair enough. The dancing world's loss is the singing world's gain. But I'll keep in touch, Kathy. I still think you might be able to help, even if you can't travel far. Goodnight, love,' he said as they reached the passageway leading to his back gate.

''Night, Mr Spencer.'

'So, how did it go?' Jemima asked as soon as Kathy was in the house.

'It didn't,' she said, referring to her attempt to visit Mr and Mrs Kendall, but then she went on to tell Jemima about the choral society's meeting. 'They're disbanding the usual meetings and putting all their efforts into entertaining war workers and such.'

'That sounds wonderful. D'you know, I've never even heard you sing, dear. Solo, that is, only beside me in church. I really should have come along to one of the society's concerts. How remiss of me.'

Kathy laughed. 'You wouldn't have heard me among

249

all the rest there either. Mind you, I did do a bit of a solo one evening.'

'Well, if you decide to join their entertainment party I'll certainly come and hear you if you're performing locally. Be sure to tell me.'

'I will,' Kathy promised, but now her mind was drifting back to Tony, wondering where he was and what he was doing. And if he was thinking of her.

The days dragged on. Ten dates later, a letter arrived from Tony, reassuring Kathy of his love and promising her that they would be married during his leave.

Basic training's going well, he wrote, *and I'm thrilled because I've been selected to train as a fighter pilot. I'll likely be posted down south though, as that's where all the fighter action is likely to be . . .*

His letter was like one from an excited schoolboy who has been sent away to boarding school for the first time and finds, to his astonishment, that he loves it. To Kathy's surprise, Tony didn't even mention his mother. She couldn't help wondering what his letters home were like.

The next Sunday, she went again to the Kendalls' house and this time George opened the back door to her knock.

'Hello, lass. You're a sight for sore eyes and no mistake. Come away in.'

'How's Mrs Kendall?' Kathy asked as she stepped over the threshold. 'Is she home from the hospital?'

'Oh yes. They only kept her in three days. Just until after Tony had gone.'

So, Kathy thought, the woman had been in when she had called the previous week.

George's face fell into lines of sadness. 'I told them what had happened, like, and how he had been called up and was leaving early on the Monday morning. They said they'd keep her and see how she coped with him leaving.'

'And did she?'

'What?'

'Cope?'

George shrugged. 'Case of having to, love, isn't it? But she's very down. Tony's very good, though. He writes to her every other day or so.' He pulled a wry expression. 'Mind you, I'm not sure if it helps or not. She gets so upset when a letter comes, yet I know she'd fret if he didn't write at all.'

Kathy swallowed her resentment. Tony had only written to her once in the two weeks since he'd been gone. But instead she smiled brightly at George Kendall and asked, 'Is there anything I can do to help you?'

He gazed at her for a moment and then shook his head as if he couldn't believe what he was hearing. 'You are a remarkable lass, you know. Not many'd come here and offer to help after what happened last week. I just wish . . .' His voice broke and he stopped, as if unable to go on.

Kathy touched his arm. 'I know,' she said gently. 'I know you wish the marriage had taken place.' She took a deep breath and smiled tremulously. 'But it can't be helped now. Maybe when Tony gets leave, well, we'll have to see.'

'Just do it, lass. Next time, don't tell anyone except p'raps Miss Robinson. Just slip away, the two of you, and do it.'

Kathy smiled sadly. 'Yes, I think you're right.' Then she took a deep breath and said, with new determination, 'Now, what can I do?'

For the next two hours, Kathy helped George cook a meal. Then she cleaned the kitchen, ending up by washing the red tiled floor. Just as she was finishing, she glanced up to see a pair of feet standing just in front of her. Feet encased in women's shoes. Kathy held her breath as, slowly, her gaze travelled up and up, stopping eventually when she met the hostile eyes of Beatrice Kendall.

'And what, may I ask, are *you* doing here?'

Kathy scrambled to her feet and dropped the floorcloth into the bucket of soapy hot water. 'Helping out.' She smiled brightly. 'I thought Mr Kendall could do with a hand now Tony's not here to help.'

Beatrice put her hand to her chest and staggered to one side, slumping against the table. 'Oh, you cruel, heartless girl,' she gasped. 'How could you say such a thing to me?'

Kathy spread her hands helplessly. 'What have I said wrong? I'm only stating the obvious.'

Tears trickled down Beatrice's face. 'But to remind me so callously.'

Kathy said quietly, 'I wouldn't have thought you needed reminding. I certainly don't. Look, Mrs Kendall, why can't we be friends? I'd like to help you. Help your husband care for you . . .'

'Friends?' the woman shrieked. 'Friends, you say, when you're trying to steal my son away from me. My only child, who's everything in the world to me. If I lose him, I don't want to live any more.'

'But don't you see – can't you see – you'd be gaining

a daughter? I don't want to take him away from you. I'd never dream of doing any such thing.'

'You already have. I've hardly seen him these last few weeks. These precious last few weeks. What if he never comes back? What if he gets killed . . . ?' Her voice rose hysterically.

Kathy felt the colour drain from her face. 'Don't say that! Don't even think it!'

George came hurrying into the room. 'Oh, Beatty, what are you doing in here?' Beatrice leant against her husband. 'Send her away, George. I don't want her here. She reminds me . . .'

'Come along, dear, let's get you settled back on the couch and then we'll talk about it.'

While George half carried his wife back to the front room, Kathy emptied the bucket of dirty water down the drain in the back yard and replaced it in the wash-house. Returning to the kitchen, she washed her hands at the now sparkling white sink and took down her coat from the peg. She stood, listening a moment and then, when there was no sound of George returning, she let herself quietly out of the back door.

The formation of the concert party was going well, and by the end of March Ron Spencer had rounded up enough people to make up a variety show.

'I'm just short of a soprano,' Mr Spencer said, sitting down in Jemima's kitchen and picking up the cup of tea she had offered him. He looked across at Kathy. 'Won't you reconsider, Kathy? You're perfect.'

'But you're going to be travelling all round the country, aren't you?'

'Well, I have to admit, that's the idea now. We've found enough folk who are free for one reason or another. One or two are even prepared to leave their jobs. They're trying to make their way into the entertainment world and they see this as an ideal opportunity to get themselves known. And we've got official backing from ENSA and we're even going to be paid for our efforts. There's no stopping us now. We can go anywhere we're wanted.'

'I could see if Mr James would keep your job open for you, dear,' Jemima put in. 'He's anxious to do whatever he can to help with the war effort and, to tell you the truth, we don't need so many staff nowadays. Sales are dropping alarmingly.' There was silence between the three of them. They all knew that many of the items that the store sold could be classed as luxury items. 'It's a case of "make do and mend" now. Mr James is seriously looking at what else they can stock. Things that people really need and want.'

'Yes, I'm afraid a lot of things are going to change.' Ron glanced again at Kathy. 'So, what d'you say?'

Kathy ran her tongue around dry lips. 'I – I'll think about it,' she murmured, avoiding his gaze. She would have loved nothing better than to have said 'yes' there and then. But there was another worry niggling at her mind now. A worry that gripped her afresh each morning as she leant over the bowl in her bedroom and retched.

Twenty-Six

'You're pregnant, aren't you?' Jemima said bluntly as, for the fourth morning in a row, Kathy pushed aside the untouched bowl of cereal.

Kathy hung her head, unable to meet Jemima's eyes. Miserably, she whispered, 'I think I must be.' She'd managed to hide the morning sickness for a month. At first she'd believed it was just because she was so devastated by her ruined wedding day. Then, as the days went on and there was only one letter from Tony, her misery had deepened. But now, she had to admit, the sickness was happening far too regularly to be just that. The truth had to be faced. How gleeful her father would be, she thought bitterly, that what he had accused her of was now a fact.

Jemima sighed heavily and lowered herself into the chair on the opposite side of the table. It was Sunday morning, so there was no need to rush. 'So, what are you going to do about it?'

Kathy's head snapped up. 'I'm not going to get rid of it, if that's what you're thinking.'

Jemima shook her head sadly. 'Kathy, how can you even think that I could suggest such a thing?'

Kathy hung her head again. 'I'm sorry,' she muttered. 'I – I'm not thinking straight.'

'I know, I know,' Jemima whispered. There was a

pause before she added, 'So, what are we going to do about it?'

'We?' Kathy's voice was high-pitched. 'Don't you mean me? What am I going to do about it? This is my problem. I don't want to bring shame on you. I'll – I'll think of something.' Her voice trailed away, because she had no idea at this moment what that 'something' might be.

There was a long silence in the room before Jemima said softly. 'Kathy, my dear, I'm going to tell you something now that will probably shock you. I'm sure most people – including you – view me as a dried-up old spinster who has never known a man, who has never – ' her lower lip trembled for an instant – 'has never known love and passion. But you'd be wrong. Quite wrong. You see, during the last war – rather like you – I wanted to get away from the farm. I wanted to do my bit, so I joined up to be a nurse. A VAD nurse. I even went to France.' Now her eyes took on a dreamy expression, but there was sadness there too. 'I saw some terrible sights, Kathy. Sights no young girl should ever see, and death and suffering that no young man should ever know. That's why I was so upset when this war started. You see, the very people who should know better have let it all happen again.'

She paused and was pensive for a few moments. 'I met someone out there, Kathy. An officer. And we fell in love.'

Kathy was silent. She didn't want to break the spell. Besides, she didn't really know what to say.

'Of course, such – such liaisons were frowned upon. He could have been in serious trouble and so could I, but we didn't care. We were in love and we lived for the moment. We had to, because we didn't know if we had a future. Either of us.'

Now Kathy could guess what had happened. At least, part of it. 'Was he – was he killed?'

Jemima nodded. Her voice was flat and emotionless as she went on. 'I came home. I – had to. I was pregnant.'

Kathy gasped. She had not expected this. 'But – I mean – what . . . ?' She fell silent. Now she really was lost for words.

Jemima looked up with a half smile. 'Can't you guess?'

Kathy stared at her. Conflicting thoughts were whirling around her head. What was she supposed to guess? That the baby had died? That it had been adopted? What? Slowly she shook her head.

'I had a baby boy,' Jemima whispered, as if trying to give her a clue.

Kathy was still puzzled.

'When I came home my father was so angry I thought for a moment he was actually going to kill me.'

Suddenly, Kathy remembered the exchange of glances, the strange conversation between Jemima and her sister-in-law, Betty Robinson. She had thought it odd at the time but had never dreamed it could have such significance.

Jemima paused only briefly and then continued. 'Ted never went to the war. His work was on the land, and just about the time I came home he and Betty were about to get married. They took my baby and brought him up as their own.'

Kathy's mouth dropped open. 'Morry?' she breathed. 'Morry is your son?'

Jemima's smile flickered briefly as she said, 'Yes, he is. And I don't regret his birth for one minute. Not one minute, Kathy. He's all I have left of Charlie.' Then her smile faded, to be replaced by a haunted look of anticipated anguish. 'But now? Who knows? Maybe I'm going to lose him too.'

Kathy moved forward and took her hands. 'Oh no. Morry won't have to go. He's a farmer. He won't *have* to go.' She paused and, as if the doubt had pervaded her own mind, added, 'Will he?'

Jemima sighed. 'Who knows? Who can guess what regulations they'll bring in? But, of course, he may – feel it's his duty to go. He may volunteer.'

'Does – does Morry know? I mean – that he's your—?'

'Oh yes. And Amy too.'

'*Amy* knew?' Kathy burst out before she could stop herself. Chatterbox Amy, who couldn't keep a secret for love nor money, had never breathed a word, never even hinted at such a family skeleton.

Jemima smiled fondly. 'Yes, even Amy has kept my secret. And I'm asking you to do the same now. There was no point in hiding such a thing – at least not from the members of my family. And we all agreed that Maurice should always be told the truth, though I'm not sure about the neighbours.' She cast a comical look at Kathy. 'I'm sure the gossip was that Ted and Betty had had a shotgun wedding.' She laughed wryly. 'I don't expect your father would have been so keen to marry you off to Maurice if he'd known he was my bastard son.'

Kathy flinched. 'Don't call Morry that. It sounds awful.'

'It's what he is, but thanks to Ted and Betty he's

never had to suffer because of it. But remember, Kathy, I have trusted my secret with you. Not a word to a soul.'

Kathy shook her head and said huskily, 'Of course not.'

'And so you see now why I say, "What are *we* going to do about it?"'

Now Kathy raised her head slowly, tears in her eyes. She had fully expected to be thrown out of the house, to be cast out in disgrace with no home, no family and nowhere to go. She had, like all the girls at work she was sure, viewed Jemima Robinson as a strait-laced spinster who had perhaps never known romance, let alone borne a child. The news came as a shock to Kathy, yet now she understood why Jemima was not turning her back on her and why she was offering, so generously, to stand by her and help her.

But there was one difference between their plights. A huge difference. Jemima's lover had been killed before he even knew about the child. There was nothing he could have done even if he had wanted to. But the father of Kathy's child was still alive.

As if reading her thoughts, Jemima said, 'Can we get in touch with Tony? Perhaps he can get compassionate leave and you can be married.'

'No!' The word came out like the crack of a whiplash. Then more quietly, Kathy said, 'I – I don't want him to know.'

'Don't want him to know?' Jemima repeated. 'Why ever not?'

'Because I don't want anyone saying he married me because he *had* to.'

'But – but, that's not the case.' Jemima was mystified. 'You were going to be married.' She gave a snort

259

of disgust as she remembered Beatrice's antics. 'You almost were.'

'I know,' Kathy said flatly, 'but it's different now.'

'Why is it different? Tony loves you. He'll probably be thrilled about the baby anyway.'

'He – he's only written to me once.'

'Oh, phooey! The poor man's probably exhausted. Basic training must be pretty tough.'

Kathy met Jemima's open gaze. 'But he's written every other day to his mother.'

Jemima raised her eyebrows. 'How do you know?'

'Because his dad told me.'

'I see,' Jemima said thoughtfully, then added, 'Well, I expect he's trying to keep her happy.'

'Mm.' Kathy was not convinced.

There was a silence. 'Let's get ready and go to St Mary's. Aren't you singing there today with the choral society before they disband?'

Kathy sighed. 'Yes. And I'm supposed to be singing a solo. But I don't know if I'll manage it.'

Jemima forced a smile. She'd looked forward to hearing the girl sing, but the occasion would be spoilt by the dark cloud hanging over their heads.

'Courage, my dear. Now's the time to show your mettle. Put a brave face on. Hold your head up high. Now, you go and get ready while I clear away.'

Kathy began to protest, but Jemima waved her away. 'I'll do it.'

Upstairs, Kathy sat on her bed and stared vacantly into space. She had to face the awful truth. She was pregnant. And she couldn't help but think how gleeful her father would be that he'd been proved right.

She heard the back door open and close and Jemima's footsteps trot along the passage. She glanced at her alarm clock, wondering if she had lost track of time and Jemima was already setting off to church. But no, she had only been sitting there for ten minutes or so.

With a sigh, Kathy got up. Perhaps Jemima was going to see Ron Spencer, was going to tell him the news, tell him that there was no way that Kathy could become a member of his concert party now.

She felt a little cross that Jemima might be spreading the news so quickly, but then she sighed. He would have to know sooner or later, though, and at least Jemima was saving her, Kathy, the embarrassment of having to tell him herself.

When she went downstairs a little later, Jemima was waiting for her. 'Come along, we'll have to hurry.'

There was no chance for conversation as they walked quickly along side by side. This morning they were attending the church where Kathy and Tony should have been married. When they reached the church porch, Ron was waiting for them. 'I was getting a bit anxious. I thought you weren't coming.'

Kathy smiled weakly. Why should he think that? she wondered. Surely Jemima had told him they would be attending service when she'd spoken to him earlier?

Ron fussed around her, leading her to her place in the choir and ensuring that she had everything she needed for her solo.

'Don't be nervous,' he said patting her hand. 'You'll be fine.'

Reading far more into his words than just encouragement for her performance, tears sprang to her eyes.

The service went well and when Kathy stood up to sing, she closed her eyes and blanked her mind of everything except the words and the music. Her clear voice echoed through the church and, emotional as she was feeling, she put such feeling into the words of the hymn that there was scarcely a dry eye in the congregation when she had finished.

As the worshippers filed out, Kathy found herself being shaken by the hand or patted on the back. People she hardly knew smiled and congratulated her.

'Does everyone know?'

'Of course they don't,' Jemima retorted. 'They're praising you for your singing, my dear. Nothing else. I hardly think,' she added dryly, 'that many here would consider your – er – news as something for congratulation.'

'But did you . . .?' she began, but at that moment, Ron Spencer came towards them, rubbing his hands with glee. 'Beautiful, my dear girl, just beautiful. Now, have you made up your mind about joining the concert party? I do hope it's going to be a yes.'

Kathy stared at him. She'd been wrong. He knew nothing about her condition. She bit her lip and shook her head. 'I'm so sorry, Mr Spencer, but it – it has to be no.'

His face fell. 'Well, I'm disappointed. Very disappointed. Perhaps you'll change your mind once your young man's been home and you've got him hooked, eh?' He laughed at his own joke.

Kathy flinched. Even if Tony came home and they were married, she could imagine some of the gossip when word got out that she was expecting his child.

'Couldn't escape a second time, could he?'

'Made sure she got him this time, eh?'

And so on.

There and then on the steps of the church where six

weeks ago she should have been married, Kathy made her decision.

She would not marry Tony at all. By the time he came home on leave, she would be gone. She would disappear and no one would know where she had gone. Only perhaps one person. She would confide in Jemima.

When they turned into the street, Kathy saw the Robinsons' car parked outside the front of Jemima's house.

'Oh no!' she breathed and stopped. 'Did you know they were coming today? I can't face them. Please . . .'

Jemima took hold of her arm with a firm grip. 'Kathy, my dear, listen to me. I rang them from the telephone box at the end of the street.'

Kathy wrenched herself free and turned to face Jemima. 'You did what?'

'I telephoned Betty,' Jemima repeated calmly, quite unapologetic. 'You should go home.'

'Home?' Kathy's laugh had a note of hysteria. 'Are you mad?'

'Well, if not to your parents, then to Betty and Ted's. They'll look after you.'

'No.' Kathy shook her head. She was adamant. 'No. I will go away, but not back to Abbeytoft. Never back there.'

'At least come in and talk about it. Please.'

'You – you've told them?'

'I had to. We need their help.'

'No, I don't. I'll—'

'Stop being so melodramatic, Kathy. You're not the first and you're certainly not going to be the last.' Again she took hold of Kathy's arm, and this time there was no wriggling free.

Kathy's heart plummeted even further as she stepped into the kitchen and saw that there was only one member of the Robinson family there.

'Hello, Morry,' she said flatly, avoiding his eyes.

'Kathy.'

'Go into the front room,' Jemima said briskly, peeling off her gloves and removing her hat, 'while I make some tea.'

Woodenly, Kathy led the way through and sat stiffly on a chair beside the empty grate, while Morry sat awkwardly on the sofa. The same sofa where she had spent so many happy hours with Tony . . .

She averted her gaze.

'Does he know? Have you told him?'

'No, and I'm not going to. He's been gone six weeks and I've only had one letter, right at the beginning, yet he's written to his mother every other day. Just shows where his thoughts are, doesn't it?' she added bitterly. She pulled in a deep breath. 'I've made up my mind. I'm not going to marry him. I'm not even going to tell him. It's over.'

'Everyone wants you to come home with me,' Morry blurted out. 'We'll take care of you.'

'Oh, Morry, don't be kind to me. I don't deserve it.'

'I could never be unkind to you, Kathy.' His hand tightened on hers. 'You know how I feel about you.'

'Stop it! You'll make me cry.' But already it was too late. Tears were coursing down her face.

Morry knelt beside her chair. 'I'd do anything for you, Kathy. Marry me and I'll take care of you and your baby. I swear I'd treat it as my own. You'd never hear a word of reproach from me. I promise you.'

For a moment she closed her eyes and rested her head against his shoulder. How very easy it would be to give in. To take this wonderful man's offer. To let him care for her for the rest of their lives. And she knew he would. She would be safe and secure and, yes, loved by a good man . . .

'I can't,' she whispered. 'I can't do that to you.'

'I don't expect you to love me.' Morry was still not ready to give up. 'Well, not in the way I love you. But we're friends, aren't we? Maybe in time . . .'

Kathy raised her head and shook it slowly. 'You deserve so much more, Morry.'

'What if I don't want any more, Kathy? What if all I really want is you?'

'Morry, don't,' she moaned. 'You make me feel so – so ashamed.'

'You've nothing to be ashamed about, Kathy. You – you loved him and you thought you were going to be married. Don't blame yourself.'

'I should have known,' she said flatly. 'I should have known that somehow his mother would stop it. She told she would. She told me she'd never let him marry me. And now it looks as if she's got her wish.'

'Come home with me. We'll look after you anyway, even if – even if you really don't want to marry me.'

She closed her eyes, trying to hold back the tears, trying to remain firm in her resolve. 'I can't. It's – it's too near home. You know what my father's like. He – he'd make my life a misery. And probably yours and all your family's too.'

Morry gave a wry laugh. 'Do you really think Jim Burton's ranting bothers my dad? Or any of us for that matter?'

'It wouldn't be fair,' Kathy was adamant, her mind made up. 'I'm going away, Morry. Right away.'

'Where, Kathy? How will you manage?'

'I – I don't know yet. But I've got to handle this on my own. As my father would say, I've made my bed so now I've got to lie on it.'

Morry knew he was beaten, but even yet, he couldn't quite let go. 'You'll write to me, Kathy? Just to let me – us – know that you're all right? At least do that. Please?'

'All right. Just so long as you promise not to try to find me.'

He sighed, defeated at last. 'All right. I promise.'

She didn't know if she believed him, but it was all she could do.

They begged, they pleaded, they reasoned, but Kathy was adamant. She was going away. Somewhere where no one knew her. She would find some sort of work until she couldn't work any more and then she would go into a mother and baby home until the child was born.

'And then?' Jemima asked bluntly. 'What then?'

'I – I don't know.'

'You mean you'll give it up for adoption?'

Kathy's head snapped up. 'No. Never. I'll never do that.'

'But how will you manage? Society doesn't look kindly on unmarried mothers.'

Kathy flinched at Jemima's bluntness, but she was only speaking the truth, painful though it was to hear it.

'I – I don't know. But I'll manage somehow.'

There was a long silence before Morry rose. 'I must be getting back.' He stood looking down at Kathy for a long moment. Then he put his hand on her shoulder and squeezed it gently. 'I know you don't want me to come looking for you, but promise me one thing, please, Kathy.'

She looked up at him.

'Promise me that if ever you need a friend you will come to me.'

Slowly, Kathy nodded.

Twenty-Seven

Kathy stood on the sea front looking out across the cold grey water.

She had been living in Saltershaven for five months now. The day after Morry's visit she had packed her suitcase, accepted the money that Jemima pressed upon her and gone to Lincoln bus station. She hadn't even looked where the bus was heading, and after a journey that had seemed to last for ever but was in fact only about two and a half hours, she had found herself in the seaside town. As she'd stepped down from the bus, she'd allowed herself a wry smile. How different she felt this time. The day she'd spent here the previous Easter with Amy and Aunt Jemima had been filled with happiness. The only cloud in her sky then had been because Tony had not been there too. And now – only a year later – she was running away from them all.

For the first two nights, Kathy was obliged to spend some of the precious money Jemima had given her at a bed and breakfast. But when the local newspaper came out on the Wednesday, she found lodgings among the advertisements. '*Furnished rooms. Season or longer. Full board if required.*' There was a box number to answer. She went into the paper's office and left a short note. The next day she was contacted and went to view the rooms.

'How long will you be here?'

'I'm not sure, but it will be for at least four months. Perhaps a little longer.'

'Mm . . .' The woman owner of the house divided into bed-sitting rooms seemed doubtful as she looked Kathy up and down. Slyly, Kathy said, 'I can pay you a month's rent in advance instead of the week you're asking for, if you like.'

That clinched it, as the woman held out her greedy hand. 'No pets, no children and no followers,' she said tartly.

Kathy did not answer.

From the same newspaper, Kathy listed two or three jobs from the 'Wanted' column and the following day tramped the streets looking for work. She found it as a waitress in one of the seafront cafés for the season.

'You'll probably only be needed until September, if we get any kind of a season at all with the wretched war on,' Mr Bates, the proprietor – a doleful man in his fifties – informed her.

'That's fine. That's all I want anyway.'

'And the work'll be quite hard. You'll be on your feet all day.' He too looked her up and down, just like the landlady had done. But he seemed to like what he saw, for he smiled and said, 'But you look strong.'

Now Kathy could raise a smile. 'Oh, I am. I worked on my father's farm,' she told him, but did not add about her months working in the fancy department store in the city.

The weeks and months had passed quickly and already it was September. And today, the young girl who was the kitchen maid in the café had said, 'By heck, Kathy, I reckon you're putting on weight but I don't know how you're managing it with all this rationing. Poor Mr Bates is doing 'is nut 'cos he can't get the stuff he wants.'

Kathy had been able to conceal her condition with the loose overall she wore when working. But now the growing bulge could no longer be hidden.

She sighed as she watched the waves rolling in towards the shore and breaking on the smooth sand. It was a lovely beach and she longed to walk on it, but ugly rolls of barbed wire barred the way and danger signs forbade entry.

Hands deep in the pockets of her coat, Kathy walked along the seafront as far as she could. She was trying to come to a decision. Jemima's final words to her had been, 'Wherever you're going, my dear, you must see a doctor, and don't forget to sort out your ration books.'

Kathy had handed her ration book to her landlady, who provided her meals, but she had not been able to bring herself to visit a doctor. However, she'd found out that there was a home for unmarried mothers and their babies on the outskirts of the town. And today she must visit it and seek admittance. She was putting off the moment for as long as possible, but by lunchtime she forced herself to walk along the road leading southwards out of the town towards the square house that sat in its own grounds.

She walked through the gateway, noticing that, though there were posts and hinges, the gates had been removed. For the war effort, she supposed. She crunched up the gravel driveway and pulled on the bell rope. After what seemed an age, in which she almost lost her nerve and ran back down the drive, footsteps approached and the door was pulled open.

A young girl, obviously far advanced in pregnancy,

stood there. Kathy and the girl exchanged a solemn glance of mutual sympathy and understanding before the girl smiled and invited Kathy inside.

'I . . .' Kathy faltered, not knowing how to begin, but the girl filled the moment of awkwardness by saying, 'My name's Lizzie Marsh. We call each other by our Christian names but the staff here call us by our surnames.' She grimaced and laughed wryly. 'It's supposed to make us feel even more degraded than we do already.' She put her arm through Kathy's. 'Don't look so terrified. It's not so bad. If you behave yourself and do exactly as they tell you, you'll be fine.' She laughed again and this time there was a brief hint of a mischievous sparkle in her eyes. 'I don't, so I'm always in trouble.'

Kathy warmed at once to the girl. 'I'm – I'm Kathy Burton.' So nearly had she become Mrs Kathy Kendall. Another few minutes and she would not be having to seek sanctuary in such a place.

'I'll take you to see Matron.' Lizzie leaned closer and whispered. 'That's what we all have to call her – "Matron". But I won't tell you what we call her behind her back. You'll hear soon enough.'

The girl led the way and knocked on a door on the left-hand side of the wide hallway. In a moment, Kathy found herself standing in front of a broad desk behind which was sitting a large, sour-faced woman in a navy blue dress with a white cap perched on top of her short, straight grey hair. The bright light from the window behind the woman shone in Kathy's eyes.

'Thank you, Marsh,' the matron snapped and Lizzie turned to leave. Unseen by the matron she gave Kathy a broad wink.

Once the girl had gone the matron appraised Kathy from head to toe, but she did not invite her to sit down.

'How far gone are you?'

'Nearly seven months.'

'Have you seen a doctor?'

'No.'

'Is this your first pregnancy?'

Kathy felt the colour creep up her face. Embarrassment, shame – a tumult of emotions – swept through her. But she tilted her chin a little higher and met the woman's cold stare. Deliberately deciding to take Lizzie's advice – at least for the moment – she said, with feigned humility, 'Yes, Matron.'

The woman pulled a notepad towards her and picked up her pen. 'I'd better take some details. Name . . .'

The questions went on, endlessly it seemed to Kathy, until her feet were aching.

'I shall need a referral from a doctor. Are you registered with anyone locally?'

Kathy shook her head.

'I'll see that you are put on Dr Williamson's list. It was he who started this place and he attends the confinements of all our inmates.'

Kathy flinched at the word. It sounded like the workhouse and she was suddenly very much afraid that it would be little better.

The matron laid down her pen at last, rested her elbows on the desk and steepled her fingers. 'This place is run on charity. Women of standing in the community raise funds and support our efforts. And the girls are expected to contribute by working. We employ no staff other than myself and two more part-time qualified

nurses who come in when required. All other work –
cooking, cleaning and laundry – is done by the
inmates.'

That dreadful word again, Kathy thought, and now
it sounds even more like a workhouse.

'I understand, Matron.'

'We also keep chickens, pigs and a small herd of
cows. We grow our own vegetables. Even more so,
since the war started.' She glanced down at her notes.
'I see you were brought up on a farm, so no doubt you
would be most suited to the outside work.'

Kathy felt hysterical laughter bubbling up inside her.
She had left home to escape a life of drudgery and
now, just because she had made the mistake of falling
in love with Tony Kendall, she was back at the start. It
was like a game of snakes and ladders and she had just
slid down a very long snake.

She quelled her laughter and composed her face,
saying meekly, 'Yes, Matron.'

'Now, if you'll sign these papers of consent, then I'll
be able to admit you.'

In a blur of misery and shame, Kathy scribbled her
name at the foot of several typewritten sheets of paper,
which the matron laid before her. Then she returned
to her lodgings to pack her few belongings and collect
her ration book. Carrying her suitcase, she gave in her
notice at the café and trudged back to the isolated
house that was to be her home for the next few months.

Kathy couldn't remember ever feeling so lonely in
the whole of her life.

The days passed with monotonous routine. The work
was hard, though no worse than Kathy had been used

to on her father's farm. But the months of comparatively soft living in the city made feeding pigs, milking
cows and cleaning out the chicken huts seem doubly
hard. Kathy was lucky. She was physically strong, and
after a week or so slipped back into the routine as if
she had never left it. She even helped some of the girls
who found it exhausting, though this earned her a reprimand from the matron.

'They're here to work,' Miss Delamere reminded
her.

'To be punished, you mean,' Kathy muttered.

'What did you say?'

'Yes, Matron,' Kathy said, staring boldly into the
woman's steely eyes.

'Get on with your work,' she snapped, turned and
marched away. Behind her back, Kathy pulled a face
and one of the other girls laughed. The matron glanced
back, glared at Kathy for a moment and then walked
on. But Kathy knew she had made an enemy.

Despite the harsh routine and the unhappy circumstances that brought them together, friendships grew
among the girls. There were one or two spats, as was
inevitable amongst a group of lonely, frightened young
woman forced to live day and night in each other's
company. But the others quickly resolved any argu-
ments. From feeling desolate when she entered the
house, Kathy soon felt among friends. Only the matron
and nurses held themselves aloof and disapproving.
Even Dr Williamson seemed to be a benign benefactor.
He was middle-aged, round-faced and balding, and
smiled over his steel-rimmed spectacles at Kathy when
she entered his consulting room.

When he had finished his examination of her he

pronounced her fit and healthy. 'You'll have a fine baby, my dear, that some lucky couple will be delighted to adopt.'

Kathy stared at him. 'Adopt? What – what do you mean?'

The doctor smiled at her. 'Well, you are not in a position to keep the baby, are you, my dear?'

Kathy gasped. 'Not – not keep my baby?'

'Oh no. That's out of the question. We cannot allow it. You came in here of your own free will, didn't you? Nobody forced you to, now did they?'

'Well, no, but I didn't realize—'

'So, you thought you could come in here . . .' Suddenly, the blue eyes behind the spectacles were no longer friendly. They were sharp and greedy. 'Be cared for and cosseted. And then what did you expect? After the birth? That you'd be found a home and supported? I think not, my dear. I don't know your background or your circumstances, but obviously you don't have a family prepared to forgive you and support you, else you wouldn't be here.'

Kathy leapt to her feet. 'Then I won't stay here. I had no idea that I'd be expected to allow my baby to be adopted.'

The once benign face suddenly creased into an angry frown. 'You signed the papers when you came in.'

Kathy gasped and stared at him in horror. 'I – I thought they were just something to do with my admittance here. I was never told that it was anything to do with – adoption.'

Dr Williamson shrugged. 'You were told—'

'I was not told anything of the sort,' Kathy shouted. 'Don't raise your voice to me, young lady.' All pretence at benevolence was gone. 'You've signed the papers. Your child will be adopted. Look,' he said, his tone softening. 'Sit down and let me explain.'

Slowly, Kathy sank back down into her chair. Not so much because she wished to sit, but because she felt as if her trembling legs would no longer keep her standing upright.

'Look, my dear . . .' The cajoling tone was back, but now Kathy knew it was insincere. 'If your baby is taken by a couple who are unable to have children of their own and are desperate to adopt, isn't it going to have a much better life than with you? All its life it will bear the stigma of being a bastard.' Kathy flinched and Dr Williamson nodded sagely. 'Yes, you may well wince, but that, my dear girl, is exactly what your child will suffer the whole of its life. It will have that dreadful name called after it in the playground, in the street. It will never be able to hold its head up. It will be an outcast from society. It will never get a decent job, or marry well. The stigma will follow it all its days,' he ended pompously.

Kathy closed her eyes and groaned inwardly. Had she been wrong to run away from those who would have helped her? Jemima and all the Robinson family? And Morry? Especially Morry? She even wondered if she should have given Tony another chance. Perhaps she should have waited until he'd come home on leave instead of rushing away in pique.

But no. If nothing else, she was an honest girl. She could no more force Tony into marriage than she could accept Morry's proposal. And yet . . . Now she was being forced to give up her baby. She'd never even thought of such a thing. Yet now she had to face it.

Calmer now, she stood up. 'I'll think about it.'

The doctor was all smiles again, though now Kathy saw them as sinister. She gave him a brief nod and marched out of the room. She would talk to Lizzie and the other girls. Surely, she thought, there are others here who don't want to give up their babies?

'Of course we don't *want* to,' Lizzie said as three of the girls huddled together in the dormitory after lights out. 'But what other choice do we have?'

'How can we work and look after our babies?' Pamela put in. She was near her time and every day her eyes became sadder and more haunted with the thought of what she must do. 'I would if I could, believe me. I don't want to give my baby away.' Tears filled her eyes and Lizzie put her arm about her. 'But your baby will go to a good home.'

'You make it sound like a litter of puppies that goes to "a good home",' Kathy snapped.

Lizzie shrugged philosophically.

'Why can't we get a place together? Three or four of us and help each other.' Kathy was clutching at preposterous ideas. 'We could get work and one of us could look after the babies.'

'I thought of that, but it's been done,' Pamela sighed, wiping her eyes.

'And?'

'It didn't work. The locals accused the girls of keeping a brothel.'

Kathy stared at her, open-mouthed, to think that people could be so cruel. 'You'd think in nineteen forty and in the middle of a war, folks would be a bit more understanding, wouldn't you?'

'You would,' Lizzie said quietly. 'But they're not. We're still "fallen women" in most folk's eyes.'

'So – is everyone here giving their babies up for adoption?'

No one spoke. No one denied it.

'Lizzie?'

'It's the best for the child,' Lizzie said, though her voice trembled.

'But what about your baby's father. Won't he . . . ?'

Lizzie pursed her lips, trying to hold back the tears. She shook her head. 'No. He didn't want to know. He – he even said he didn't know if the baby was his.' Now her tears fell. 'How could he say such a thing to me? He was my first boyfriend and he knew that.'

'I was an absolute fool,' Pamela murmured. 'My baby's father was married, but I was so head over heels in love with him . . .' She needed to say no more. Each one of them knew what it was to fall in love, to be so sure that their lover felt the same. That nothing would ever come between them . . . Oh they'd heard it all before but they believed it would be so different for them. But it wasn't. And now they found themselves here, brought together by a common bond, their only fault having loved too much.

'And – and I take it your parents . . . ?' Kathy began, but she got no further. There was wry laughter.

'You must be joking,' Pamela said. 'My parents arranged for me to come here. I can only go home again when it's all over and then only so long as it's without the baby.'

'But it's their grandchild. How can they . . . ?'

'Oh they can. Very easily, it seems,' Pamela said.

'My parents just turned me out,' Lizzie said dolefully. 'I'd nowhere else to go except a place like this. A

278

friend of mine whose sister had a baby out of wedlock told me about Willow House.'

Two other girls told their similar, sorry, tales and then all eyes turned to Kathy.

'I was almost married,' she said bitterly. 'Five minutes more and I would have been.' And she went on to tell them the details of that chaotic day.

'That's awful, but couldn't you have waited till he came on leave again? It doesn't sound as if he's deserted you. Just – just circumstances,' Lizzie said logically.

'I know,' Kathy sighed. 'Maybe I've been a bit hasty. I see that now. But I still don't think there's much hope. He's a mother's boy and that's never going to change.'

'Does he know? About the baby?'

'No,' Kathy said firmly. 'And he's not going to. Not from me and no one knows where I am. I – wanted to handle it myself, but – but I didn't realize it involved giving up my baby.' She turned to Lizzie and said softly, 'And I'm not going to. Once I've had it, I'm out of here and taking my baby with me. At least I do have a place to go back to. Someone I lived with in – in the city. She'll stand by me. I know she will.'

The girls all glanced at each other. 'You're lucky then,' Pamela said. 'Good luck to you.'

They crept back to their beds and Kathy lay staring into the darkness and planning how she could escape from this place that was like a prison.

Twenty-Eight

Pamela gave birth to a baby girl. She refused to look at it or hold it and the child was handed over to eager parents at a week old. The next day, Pamela said her goodbyes and returned home. Several other girls gave birth and stayed for about six weeks, caring for their child, feeding it, dressing it and bathing it.

When the day came that they too had to part with their babies, they were heartbroken.

'I'll never see her again,' a young girl called Rachel sobbed on Kathy's shoulder. 'I'll never see her smile or nurse her when she's teething. I won't be there when she starts to walk. And it won't be me she learns to call "Mummy".'

Kathy held her close and stroked her hair, but she could think of nothing to say to comfort the girl. There was nothing she could say.

And then it was Lizzie's turn.

'Stay with me,' she begged Kathy. 'Don't leave me. I'm so frightened.'

'There's nothing to be frightened of,' Kathy tried to reassure her as the girl writhed on her bed in agony.

But there was plenty for Lizzie to be afraid of. She endured three days in labour to be delivered in the end of a stillborn child. A week later, distraught and weakened, Lizzie succumbed to an infection and followed her child to the pauper's grave in the nearest churchyard.

On the morning of the funeral, Kathy sat by the window looking down the road towards the church. She had begged and pleaded to be allowed to attend her friend's funeral but Matron was adamant in her refusal. 'You cannot appear in public in your condition,' she was told harshly, making her feel even more ashamed.

Now Kathy had no one left to whisper with. No new girls had come into the home since she had arrived, and with all those that had gone recently, there were only a handful left. She tried to make friends with one or two but they were withdrawn and uncommunicative, lost in their own private world of sadness and shame.

Once more, Kathy felt completely alone.

Kathy felt the first pangs of labour one cold, blustery November morning. She was put in the labour room and left.

'I'll be back soon. You've a long way to go yet.'

There was no one to sit with her, no one to comfort her. When the pains grew stronger and closer together and Kathy cried out, the nurse put her head round the door and said, 'You can stop making all that noise. It'll get worse yet.' And she disappeared.

Kathy sobbed and cried out again, but no one came. There was no one who cared. Anger flooded through her, and the next time the pain came in a huge, crescendo, she bit hard down and refused to cry out. Over the next twenty minutes she made no sound, and her silence brought the nurse in faster than had her cries.

The birth was long and exhausting. As the pain

became unbearable and Kathy could no longer quell her cries, she was aware that Matron had entered the room.

With experienced, but ungentle, hands the two women positioned her to give birth and then barked orders at her. 'Push down hard. Now pant – now push . . .' until with one valiant effort that took the last ounce of her strength, Kathy felt a strange emptying feeling and heard a baby's cry.

'Oh – oh. What is it?'

No one answered. She tried to raise herself up to see, but weariness overwhelmed her and she fell back. She was aware of movement in the room and the cries of her child grew fainter.

'Please . . .' she begged, but then she remembered no more.

When she came round, she was back in her own bed in the ward. She felt battered and bruised. She tried to sit up, but pain seared through her and she gave a cry.

One of the young girls, Peggy, who had come in the week before, came to her bedside.

'Can I get you anything? Would you like a drink of water?'

'Please,' Kathy croaked through parched lips.

Peggy raised her up and held a glass to her parched lips. Kathy drank gratefully.

As she lay back again, she asked, 'My baby? Where's my baby?'

The girl shrugged. 'They've taken him away.'

'A boy? It was a boy?'

'Yes.'

'Where've they taken him?'

The girl shrugged. 'He'll have gone to his new parents, I suppose.'

'What? Already? They can't do that. I haven't even seen him. I haven't given my permission. I haven't even – even held him.' Tears coursed down her face. 'They should have let me hold him. I should have him with me for a few weeks. Why – why have they taken him?'

Peggy leant closer. 'I heard Matron talking to one of the nurses, telling her not to let you have him. "She's trouble, that one," she said. "Doctor said she wants to keep him, but he's got an ideal couple waiting. Keep her sedated for two days. When she comes round, he'll be gone. And she won't be able to find out where." That's what she said.'

'Have I been asleep for two days?'

Peggy nodded. 'They kept rousing you and giving you more pills or they stuck a needle in you.'

'But how can they do that? I thought the rules were that mothers nursed the babies for five or six weeks.' Kathy passed her hand over her clammy forehead. She was still feeling dizzy and sick. It must be all the sedatives they'd given her.

'What rules?' Peggy laughed wryly. 'They make their own rules here, believe me. Matron – and the doctor. They can do whatever they like because they own this place between them. Didn't you know? They're brother and sister.'

No, she hadn't known. And now she was beginning to doubt the integrity of this place. But she was too weak to do anything about it. Too exhausted even to get out of bed. Her strength had drained from her and even her spirit was defeated and broken.

Kathy turned her face to the wall and wept bitter, scalding tears.

*

When Kathy was strong enough, she dressed and walked down to the matron's office.

She faced the woman across the desk. 'I didn't know that those papers you had me sign when I came in here were adoption papers. You never told me what they were.'

The matron smiled. 'Now, sit down, my dear. You've been through a very difficult birth and you're not feeling strong yet. We can let you stay another week but then you'll have to leave.'

'But my baby,' Kathy felt tears of weakness flow down her face. 'What have you done with my baby?'

'He's gone to a loving couple. He will have a wonderful home, my dear. Everything that you could never give him. Isn't that the very best thing for him?'

'Where's he gone? Who's taken him?'

'I can't possibly tell you that. It wouldn't do.'

'But what are they like, these people? Surely you can tell me something?'

'It's our rules that neither side know the names or anything about each other. Secrecy is best for all concerned. All we can do is assure you that the adoptive parents are respectable people and suitable to bring up your child as if he was their own. Now, dry your tears and concentrate on getting yourself fit and well. Then you can leave and get on with your life. But if you'll take my advice, you won't be so foolish enough to find yourself in here again.'

Kathy rose and left the room without another word. As she reached for the door handle, she caught sight of three wooden filing cabinets, each with four drawers, placed against the wall just inside the door of the matron's office. On each drawer there were letters A–B, C–D and so on through the alphabet. Kathy didn't pause in her movement towards the door and out of the room, but as she left, her heart was beating a little faster.

In those drawers were the details of the people who had taken her baby. She was sure of it.

Kathy told no one of her plan. If only Lizzie were still here, or even Pamela, she might have confided in one of them, but she didn't feel as if she knew the girls that were left well enough to trust them. They all seemed downtrodden, with no spirit left in them. She waited impatiently for another two nights, until she felt stronger. Luckily, she was now in a room on her own, so when she thought the household would be asleep, she crept out of her room and down the stairs, stopping in alarm every time a tread creaked. It sounded so loud in the silence of the night.

She reached the door to the matron's office and tried the door handle. To her relief, it wasn't locked. Quietly, she slipped into the darkened room. She didn't want to turn on a light, so she opened the curtains to let the bright moonlight shine in. Then she went to the cabinets. They were locked. She bit her lip and looked about her. Then she tiptoed to the desk and quietly opened the middle drawer. A bunch of various-sized keys lay there. She lifted it up, wincing as the keys jangled together. She paused and listened, holding her breath, but there was no sound of anyone coming to investigate.

She tried various keys in the topmost drawer, A–B. She was beginning to lose hope and her heart was beating faster, fearing that at any moment she would be discovered. But then, she argued, what more could they do to her? They had already robbed her of her baby. She worked on, trying every key in the bunch. The last key but one fitted and turned the lock. She pulled open the drawer, wincing as it squeaked loudly.

The files were in alphabetical order and she pulled out the one marked B. She turned to the back of the file, knowing 'Burton' would be one of the last. And there were the notes in the matron's own handwriting made on the day Kathy had first visited the place. If only she had turned tail and run then. She scanned through the pages until she came to the place where she had signed. Reading now, for the first time, she saw that she had indeed signed a paragraph that gave permission for her baby to be adopted. Kathy groaned and then read on. As she did so, her pulse quickened with excitement. The names of the couple who had adopted her baby boy were Mr and Mrs Henry Wainwright and the address was right here, in Saltershaven.

Carefully, Kathy replaced the file, closed the drawer and locked it, returned the keys to the drawer in the desk and then closed the curtains. She tiptoed from the room and quietly shut the door of the matron's room. She had no need to write down the name and address. It was seared in her mind.

She gained her room without discovery and, once back in bed, began to breathe more easily. She couldn't believe that she had not been caught, that it had been so easy. If the matron had locked the office, or taken the keys to the filing cabinet with her at night, there would have been nothing she could have done. She wondered if other mothers ever did what she'd done or if they, unlike her, were relieved to part with their child.

'But not this mother,' Kathy whispered into the

night. 'Not this one. I'll find my baby and I'll snatch him back if I have to.'

By the end of two weeks since the birth of her child, though she wasn't really fully recovered, Matron deemed her fit enough to leave Willow House.

Kathy had the feeling that the woman wanted to be rid of her, so she packed her suitcase and left without a backward glance, glad to be free of the place. She walked back to where she had rented a bed-sitting room, on the top floor of a row of three-storey, terraced town houses.

'Oh, it's you. Been away, 'ave ya?' The woman who owned the house and lived on the ground floor greeted her.

'Yes, but I'm back now. Any chance of a room again?'

'Yes, as a matter of fact your old room's just come vacant again. Young feller who worked at the bank moved out. Bin called up, 'ee 'as.'

'May I take it then? Straight away?'

'What, now?' Mrs Benson looked her up and down.

'Yes, I – I've just arrived back and I've nowhere else to stay.'

'You look a bit peaky. You look thinner. Not sickening for summat, a' ya? Don't want no illness in the place.'

'No – no, I'm fine.'

Mrs Benson pulled open the door with a sniff. 'Ya'd better come in then. Same terms as afore. No children, no pets an' no followers.'

'That's fine,' Kathy said. She still had some thinking to do about how she could find her child and what she would do when she did. Obviously, where they would live together would be something else she would have to think about. And what they would live on was another worry. Her money was fast running out and she was too proud to ask Jemima for more.

She settled quickly back into her old room and in some ways it was as if she'd never been away from it. Sleep didn't come easily as she lay awake staring into the darkness and laying her plans.

The following morning, Kathy asked Mrs Benson if she knew the road where the Wainwrights lived, but she didn't mention their name.

'Oh aye, it's near the golf course on the way to the Point. Right on the seafront. Them's posh houses up there. Why a' ya asking? Hoping to get a job there, a' ya?'

Kathy stared at her, her mind working quickly. That hadn't occurred to her.

'I – er – saw an advert for a housekeeper,' she lied. 'I thought I might go and have a look.'

'If I'd known you were planning on leaving so soon, I wouldn't have let you have ya room back.' She sniffed. 'Messing me about. Them's usually live-in jobs.'

'I'm not messing you about, Mrs Benson. I'll be here at least the month I've paid you for.'

'Aye, well, mind you are. All this coming and going and changing ya mind. I can't be doin' with it.'

Kathy had walked at least a mile along the road Mrs Benson had indicated she should take. She stopped to rest on a low wall in front of one of the houses. Perhaps she'd been foolish to try to walk so far, so soon. But she was anxious to see where her baby son was.

A delivery boy, with a huge basket on the front of his bicycle, came riding past, whistling loudly.

'Excuse me . . . ?' Kathy put out her hand to attract his attention.

'Yes, miss,' he grinned as he applied his brakes and the bicycle slithered to a halt. 'Can I 'elp ya?'

Kathy explained and the boy said, 'A bit further along, you'll see the golf course, turn left up the road leading towards the sea just before it. Then at the end of the road turn right and that's the road you want. Looking for anyone in particular?'

'The Wainwrights.'

'Oh aye, that's the big house right at the end. Big white one.'

Thanking him, Kathy walked on again wrapping her coat tightly around her as the cool breeze whipped in off the beach. At last she stood before the huge wrought-iron gates, peering through them at the elegant house at the end of the steep driveway. It was a magnificent house, painted white with gleaming windows overlooking the sandhills and the beach, right to the sea.

As Kathy stood there uncertainly, she saw a woman emerge from a side door, turn and pull a perambulator into view. Kathy's heart skipped a beat. Her son was in that pram. Her little boy. The woman, whom Kathy presumed to be Mrs Wainwright, pushed the pram down the drive towards the gate. She was smiling and talking all the while to the child in the pram. Kathy shrank back and began to walk away. Her heart was thumping in her chest. She had to see the baby, but she knew she must seem like a passer-by, merely making a polite enquiry. She mustn't appear too interested. She mustn't alarm the woman. She strolled along as if out taking a walk, but in truth was waiting for Mrs Wainwright to catch up with her. As she heard the wheels of the pram behind her, Kathy stepped off the pavement and stopped, turning to look back as if to let the woman and her baby pass by. She smiled and nodded casually, but Kathy was actually taking in every detail of her appearance. She was a little older than Kathy would have imagined, but dressed in a smart, well-cut navy blue coat. Her smooth complexion was expertly made up and her black hair peeped out from beneath a small hat that matched her coat.

'Hello,' Kathy said in a friendly manner. The woman's smile widened and she stopped.

'May – may I see your baby?'

'Of course. I'm so proud of him. He's beautiful and so good. He's only two weeks old and this is his first time out. You have to be so careful with November weather, don't you?'

Mrs Wainwright leaned forward and pushed back the hood and Kathy looked down on her son for the first time. He was asleep, but she could see his smooth skin, the silky black hair and his round little face. Tears welled in her eyes as she searched the tiny face for any hint of likeness to herself or to Tony.

'He's lovely. Perfectly lovely,' she said, trying to keep her voice steady.

'Oh, he is. We're so lucky.'

Kathy straightened up and turned to face the woman. 'You look very well. Should you be out walking so soon after the birth?'

The woman smiled a little sadly. 'We've adopted him. My husband and I couldn't have children of our own. We've had our names down with various adoption societies for ages and then last week, out of the blue, we got word from Willow House that there was a baby suitable for us. And he is, Oh, he is. He could be our very own. We shall spoil him, I know, but he will have everything that we can give him. And Oh, how he will be loved.' She shook her head in wonderment, as if she still could not believe their luck. 'We feel very blessed.' She looked straight at Kathy with clear, earnest blue eyes. 'To have been given such a gift and entrusted with his care. He will want for nothing.'

'I – I can – can see that,' Kathy whispered. 'May I ask what – what his name is?'

'James,' the woman said. 'After my husband's father. And I shall insist on him always being called James, not Jim or Jimmy.'

Kathy nodded unable to speak. How ironic, she thought, that Tony's child should be given a family name. She wondered what Beatrice Kendall would say if she knew that she had a grandson named James. And what, indeed, would James Hammond think if he knew?

Mrs Wainwright was speaking again and moving on. 'I must go. I'm just going to the end of the road and then back home again. It's far enough for his first outing.'

As they walked along, Mrs Wainwright chattered. 'Do you live nearby?'

'No – I – er – I've only just arrived. I've found lodgings and tomorrow I'll look for work.' Her answers came automatically, she was hardly thinking clearly. Her thoughts were in turmoil. She couldn't do it. Her plans lay in tatters. She couldn't snatch her baby away from this happy, loving woman who would give little James everything. What could she, an unmarried girl, with no proper home, no job, scarcely any money left, give him in comparison? She faced the awful, heart-wrenching truth. The answer was 'nothing'. She could give her son nothing, except love. But love alone could not feed him, clothe him and keep him warm.

They reached the end of the road and Mrs Wainwright turned the pram around. 'There, my little precious, time to go home.'

The baby whimpered and she leant forward, pulling down the coverlet. 'Are you hungry, my little one? Soon be home.'

Kathy felt a tingling in her breasts as if, hearing her baby's cry, her body responded naturally. Kathy tore her gaze away from the baby to meet the woman's eyes.

'I must go,' Mrs Wainwright said pleasantly. 'I think he wants feeding. Goodbye. It's nice to have met you. I hope you find a job.'

Kathy nodded, unable to speak as Mrs Wainwright walked away, every step taking Kathy's son further and further away from her. She stood watching them walk the length of the road, saw the gate open and them disappear through it. Not until then did Kathy turn away and begin her long, lonely walk home.

She didn't cry. She couldn't. She felt as if there was a leaden weight in her chest, a sadness too deep even for tears.

Twenty-Nine

It was the wrong time of the year to seek work back at the café, but Kathy was lucky. She found work at one of the local cinemas, the Grand, which had a stage that could be used for live theatre. There were two different programmes of films during the week, each one lasting three days. Sometimes on Sunday evenings there was a live show, usually with a wartime theme. Artistes from units of the forces stationed in the district put together a programme of music and orchestras, and bands from the Royal Marines played.

During the day Kathy worked in the box office, at night she was an usherette.

'I'm so glad I took you on,' Larry Johnson, the cinema's manager told her. 'You're so willing to do anything we ask you.' He was young, fresh-faced and eager and Kathy wondered why he had not been called up. It wasn't long before he was confiding, 'I wanted to join the RAF, but I have a weak heart, so – ' he spread his hands, almost apologetically – 'I thought I'd try to do something to keep everyone's spirits up.'

Kathy smiled sympathetically, 'I'm sure you're doing a wonderful job and I'm only too glad to help out.'

She wanted to fill every waking moment. Nights were the worst, when she lay lonely and sleepless, aching to hold the warm little body in her arms. Then she would turn and sob into her pillow until exhaustion overtook her. She grew thinner and paler, but still she pushed herself on, no longer caring what became of her.

Any time she had free during the day she took the long walk out of the town towards the south, just on the offchance of meeting Mrs Wainwright wheeling James out in his perambulator. In the evenings, the darkness of the cinema hid her tears.

Five girls, smartly dressed in WRNS uniform, came up the steps and into the cinema a little after the start of the evening's programme. Mrs Riley, the elderly, grey-haired lady who manned the box office in the evening, gave them their tickets and directed them to the door leading into the stalls. 'The film's only just started, you've not missed much.'

Kathy forced a smile on to her face as the girls entered the auditorium, stumbling and giggling in the darkness.

'Sh,' someone from a nearby seat hissed. 'Can't you be quiet?'

'Sorry we're late,' Kathy heard a familiar voice say. 'We've only just got off duty.'

The complaining voice was mollified. 'Oh, Wrens, are you? Well, we'll let you off then. There are seats here.' The man stood up, inviting them to sit beside him.

'Sorry, I think my friends want to be nearer the front,' the girl said cheerfully and turned to follow the wavering light of Kathy's torch leading them down the aisle.

As she stood, pointing the beam of her torch

towards the empty row of seats about half way down the aisle, she felt someone touch her arm and the voice she knew say softly, 'Kathy!' Then boisterous arms were flung around her and she was hugged tightly. 'Oh, darling Kathy, it is you.'

A chorus of 'sh' came out of the darkness.

'Amy – sit down,' Kathy whispered. 'I'll see you later.'

'You won't disappear? You promise?'

'I promise, but please – sit down now, or else you'll get me the sack.'

Amy squeezed her hand but sat down without another word, while Kathy walked back to her seat near the door, ready for any more latecomers.

Kathy sat in the darkness staring at the brightly lit screen, yet she saw and heard nothing. Her mind was in a turmoil. She was tempted to break her promise, plead sickness to the cinema manager and leave before the interval, when she knew Amy would seek her out. But something held her in her seat. Was it an over-whelming desire to see her dearest friend again? To feel, just for an hour or so, that someone cared for her? She longed to know how the Robinson family were. All of them, Ted and Betty, Morry and, of course, Aunt Jemima. And she wanted to hear any news that Amy might have of her mother. She won-dered if Edith knew that she had a grandchild. Would the Robinsons have told her parents that she had been – as her father rightly predicted – pregnant? She didn't think they would betray her secret, yet Betty might have succumbed to an overwhelming desire to tell Edith. Part of Kathy hoped she had done so.

The first film ended and the Pathé News came on.

As the house lights went up, Amy was out of her seat and running up the aisle towards her before anyone else had moved.

'Kathy, Oh Kathy, I'm so glad I've found you. Why didn't you write, you naughty girl? We've been so worried – all of us. Can we go somewhere to talk?'

'Not until after the last film,' Kathy said. 'I'm still on duty.'

'Of course. All right.'

'You coming to the bar across the road, Amy?'

'Yes – yes, you go on. Port and lemon for me, please. I'll be there in a mo. I've just met an old friend.'

'We gathered,' the other girl smiled and another quipped, 'That's her way of getting out of paying for the drinks.' She winked at Kathy. 'I bet she doesn't know you from Adam – or rather Eve – does she?'

'Oh, yes,' Kathy said huskily. 'She – she's my best friend.'

Another hug and Amy followed her friends, saying again, 'Don't you dare disappear again. I'll see you afterwards in the bar. Okay? And the drinks will be on me.'

Kathy looked forward to, and yet at the same time dreaded, the end of the show.

When all the cinema-goers had finally gone, Kathy took a deep breath and made her way across the road.

'Here she is.' Amy jumped up at once and beckoned her to the corner where the five girls were seated. She made the introductions. 'This is Dorothy, Millie, Janet and Vicky.'

'What are you doing here?'

'We're just up the road at a holiday camp that's been turned into a training camp for the Navy,' Amy explained. 'It's my first posting. But none of us know how long we're here for.' She hugged Kathy again enthusiastically. 'Oh, it's so good to see you. Tell me everything.'

'Well . . .' she hesitated, not wanting to talk freely in front of the others.

'Look,' Dorothy said, perceptive to Kathy's hesitation. 'You two go off on your own. We're fine here. We'll give you a shout when we're ready to leave. The Liberty Bus leaves in fifty minutes and we mustn't miss it.'

'The Liberty Bus?' Kathy smiled as they rose and, carrying their drinks, moved to a table in a quiet corner where, above the hubbub, their conversation would not be heard. 'Whatever's that?'

'It's the bus that brings us from camp into town,' Amy giggled. 'Brings us to liberty, I suppose.'

There was a pause before Kathy asked haltingly, 'How – how's everyone? Your mum and dad and – and Morry?'

'They're all fine, but we've all been so worried about you. Tell me everything, Kathy. How've you been and – ' she lowered her voice – 'what about the baby?'

Suddenly it all came pouring out, like the floodgates opening. She told Amy everything that had happened to her since she had left Lincoln, ending with, 'He – he's been adopted by a nice woman, I have to admit. She looks smart and lives in a big house on the outskirts of the town. And there's no doubt she – she loves him.'

'You – you know who she is? I thought they didn't let you know anything about the adoptive parents, just in case . . .' Amy faltered and stopped.

'Just in case I tried to snatch him back or made a nuisance of myself, you mean?'

'Well – yes.'

Kathy sighed, and explained how she had found out the Wainwrights' address.

'You rogue,' Amy said with admiration. 'I wouldn't have dared.'

'I think that's what the matron depends on. Why she's not more careful to secure her records. She doesn't think anyone would dare to go into her office. Mind you, I'm surprised no one has.'

'Perhaps they have. They're not going to tell anyone, are they? Any more than you've done.'

'No,' Kathy smiled. 'I suppose not.'

'So, what are you going to do? Try to get him back somehow?'

Kathy was silent for a long moment while she searched her heart and her mind. Her heart told her to run to the house this very minute, bang on their door and demand her child. But her head told her that the Wainwrights could give her son everything that she could not. And, most important of all, Kathy had seen for herself the love that Mrs Wainwright had for the baby boy. He would be cared for and cosseted and loved. He would have a legitimate name, not some vile insult called after him in the playground. Her head won. Slowly she said, 'No, I can't. I can't do that to him. He deserves better than I can give him. And besides, it's too late. That woman loves him, really loves him. How can I do that to her now?'

'But he's your child. You're his mother. He should be with you,' Amy persisted.

Kathy closed her eyes and groaned. 'I know, I know. But he'd carry the stigma of illegitimacy all his life.

This way he has a good home with people who love him and can give him everything.'

Softly Amy said, 'But you love him, don't you?'

'Of course I do,' Kathy cried out so loudly that one or two nearby glanced round at her. She turned her face away to hide her tears. 'Of course I do,' she whispered again. 'And that's why I know it's the right thing that he should stay where he is. Oh, it wasn't done in the right way. Those people at the home – there should be a law against what they're doing – but in the end, what choice do I really have?'

'You could come home and marry Morry,' Amy said simply.

Kathy went with them to the bus. Amy hugged her as they parted. 'If you change your mind, you know where we still live and Morry won't ever change his.'

Amy's words did nothing to ease Kathy's conscience over Morry, yet she knew she was right not to give in. A one-sided marriage was no marriage at all. And she was too fond of Morry to do that to him, even if, at the moment, he might think otherwise.

'Won't you at least come home for Christmas? I've been really lucky; I've got a seventy-two. We could go together.'

'I—' For a moment Kathy was very tempted. She yearned to be enveloped in the loving Robinson family. 'I can't,' she said at last and her tone was full of regret. 'I have to work.'

Amy pulled a face, hugged her swiftly one last time and climbed aboard the bus. She was still waving from the back seat as it drew away.

Kathy walked back to her lodgings feeling a turmoil

of emotion. Seeing Amy had been wonderful and yet it left her with a strange feeling of unrest.

'I must move on,' she murmured aloud as she walked home through the blacked-out streets, with only a thin pencil line of a torchlight to guide her. 'Go somewhere else. Now Amy has found me, I'll have the whole Robinson clan down on me.' And yet she couldn't drag herself away from the place where her son lived. Though she couldn't see him, couldn't hold him, she did feel close to him. She could stand outside the gate and look up at the windows and imagine him in his cot or lying on a rug in front of the fire, while Mrs Wainwright knelt beside him, playing with him, caressing him with adoring eyes.

But the days passed and no one came. She saw Amy briefly now and again, until on one meeting in the pub in late March after Kathy had finished her duty, Amy said, 'I've been posted down south. I've a week's leave before I go, so I'm going home. Do – do you still want me to keep quiet about where you are?'

Kathy raised her eyebrows, surprised that her loquacious friend had kept her secret thus far. But then she remembered. Despite giving the opposite impression, Amy was really very good at keeping secrets. Kathy nodded. 'I don't expect you to lie for me if anyone asks you straight out, but unless they do, yes, I'd prefer that no one knows.'

'Okay,' Amy nodded. 'I don't suppose they'll think to ask me anyway. But . . .' she bit her lip and looked awkwardly at Kathy.

'What? What is it?'

'Well, there is some news. Not good, I'm afraid.'

'Is it – is it my mam?'

'No, no, not that. They're fine, at least – ' Amy pulled a face – 'as fine as they'll ever be.'

Kathy smiled weakly. But she could see from Amy's worried expression that the news had something to do with her.

'Tell me.'

'Aunt Jemima told us. She only heard quite recently and Mum's written to tell me. But, of course, she didn't realize that I often see you.' Amy took a deep breath and took hold of both Kathy's hands, gripping them tightly. 'You know that Tony went to train to be a fighter pilot?'

Kathy nodded, her heart beating painfully. She almost knew what was coming before Amy said the words. 'It seems he was involved in the Battle of Britain. You know, all that fighting that went on in the south and over the Channel last autumn?'

'I – I've heard about it, though at the time . . .' Kathy's voice faded away and she shuddered as she remembered being shut up behind the grim walls of Willow House, cut off in shame from the world outside and everything that was happening. She began to tremble. She couldn't speak, could hardly breathe.

'He – he was shot down and – he was posted missing, presumed killed.'

The room seemed to spin. Kathy clutched at the table, her hands pulling free of Amy's grasp as she felt herself falling sideways. She knew no more until she opened her eyes to see Amy's face bending over her, chafing her hand.

'She's coming round,' a strange voice said. 'Don't let her get up too quickly though. There, steadily does it.'

'Can we help?' said a man's voice and Kathy found herself lifted bodily from the floor by two sailors and placed gently on the chair where she'd been sitting.

'Can I get you anything?' one asked.

'Thank you, she'll be fine now. I – I just had to give her some bad news.'

The fresh-faced young man grimaced. 'Tell me about it. Well, if you're sure you're all right . . .'

'We're fine, but thanks for your help.'

'Don't mention it.' He laid his hand gently on Kathy's shoulder. 'Hope you'll be all right, miss.'

Kathy murmured her thanks. Her head was still woolly as the landlord of the pub arrived at the table. 'Here, miss, drink this brandy. It'll help. On the house, love,' he said to Amy as she offered to pay.

Kathy sipped the liquid and colour came back into her cheeks.

'Are you going to be all right?' Amy said anxiously. 'Because I daren't miss the bus.'

'I'll be fine in a minute. It was – it was just the shock.'

They sat a few moments longer in silence, neither knowing what to say now, until Amy was obliged to say, 'I'll have to go.'

'Yes, yes. I know. I'll be all right. Honestly.'

Amy kissed her. 'This is "au revoir" for the moment then. Take care of yourself, and I'm so sorry I had to break such news to you, but – but I thought you should know.'

'Of course,' Kathy said flatly.

All hope was gone now. Any dreams she might have had that one day she would meet Tony again were blown away by those few words. 'Missing, presumed killed.'

But even amid her own sorrow, Kathy spared a thought for Beatrice Kendall.

It was the first time she'd felt any sympathy for the woman. Now that she had given birth to her own son, and lost him, she understood the devastation Tony's mother would be feeling.

Thirty

After she knew Amy had gone, Kathy felt even more bereft than ever. And to be left with such heartbreaking news, too, was almost too much to bear. The days now passed in a blur. Kathy was hardly aware of what she was doing. She did her job but she couldn't even force the cheery smile she always plastered on her face. Before she knew it, it was spring and Saltershaven was flooded with personnel from the RAF training centre that had been set up in the town.

One Sunday evening towards the end of April, when there was a live show on the stage of the cinema instead of a film, several airmen came to the cinema, laughing and joking and flirting with any girl in sight.

Kathy looked at them with bitterness. Why should they be alive when Tony was dead? Immediately she felt guilty.

'Cheer up, love, it'll never happen,' said one cheery young man. He looked no more than a boy, Kathy thought. He looked as if he shouldn't be out of short trousers yet, never mind flying off to face the enemy.

Now, for the first time since Amy had told her the awful news, Kathy's smile was genuine as she said huskily, 'Not with you brave boys defending us, it won't. Good luck to you.'

The young man's face sobered for a moment and then he nodded and said, 'Thanks, but tonight, we've got a night off. We're looking forward to this. Have you seen the show before?'

Kathy shook her head. 'No. It's the first time this particular concert party's been here.'

'I hear they're from Lincoln?'

'Really?' Kathy glanced down at the programme she held in her hand. So lost had she been in her own private grief that she hadn't really taken in the name of the concert party appearing tonight. But now she saw the name on the programme she gave a gasp of delight. 'The Lindum Lovelies' bring you *Sing As We Go*, a musical extravaganza of laughter and song,' she murmured aloud. 'Of course! I should have known.'

The lights began to dim as she showed the young man into his seat. Then, taking her own seat at the back, Kathy looked eagerly towards the stage, wondering if there would be anyone among the artistes whom she might recognize. And there was. The very first person to come on to the stage as compère for the evening was none other than Ron Spencer.

He stepped up to the microphone and spread his arms wide. 'Ladies and gentlemen, welcome one and all . . .'

Kathy smiled in the darkness and sat back to enjoy the show, pushing aside, just for a couple of hours, the sadness in her heart. But it was not quite what she had expected. Knowing Ron, she had anticipated a programme of choral works, but instead it was more like a music-hall revue. Then she remembered the plans that they'd had just before she'd left so hurriedly. This is exactly what they'd planned. She smiled in the darkness, thrilled that it had all come about just as they'd hoped.

The young comedian, with a pencil-line moustache

and a garish suit, shamelessly impersonated the great Max Miller, while the girl vocalist sang a medley of favourite songs of the thirties from 'Roll out the Barrel' to 'Smoke Gets in Your Eyes'. But throughout her performance, Kathy couldn't help wincing. The girl, Melody Miles, though pretty and vivacious and attracting whistles and catcalls from the young men in the audience, could hardly sing in tune. The three dancers, with long shapely legs, were a definite hit with the audience and were seen in various guises in the comedy sketches, as too was Melody. And in two of the sketches, Kathy spotted Martin Montgomery. What a good actor he was, she thought in admiration. They all were, and Melody was a much better actress than she was a vocalist. Her comic timing was perfect and the audience's laughter threatened to damage the roof far more than any bomb!

The finale brought a medley of sentimental ballads and the whole show ended with a rousing rendition of 'Land of Hope and Glory' followed by the National Anthem, led, Kathy was thankful to see, by the male vocalist, who could sing in tune!

As the curtain fell, Kathy stood up. As soon as the audience had filed out, she went backstage. There was a lot of chatter and laughter coming from the dressing rooms.

'Do you know where Mr Spencer is?' she asked a woman carrying an armful of dresses.

'Star dressing room, love. Just 'cos he formed the party, he reckons he's top billing. If you ask me that should go to the female vocalist – if we had a proper one, that is. Melody's a lovely girl, but she can't sing for toffee.' She leant forward. 'But don't tell 'er I said so. Mind you, she's a good little actress. I'll give her that. Funny, too. What's the word? Coquettish. That's it. And sparkle! That girl sparkles more than all the sequins on these dresses.'

Kathy smiled weakly. She said nothing, but she couldn't help agreeing with the woman she presumed was the wardrobe mistress. The cameo parts the girl had played in the sketches had been brilliant, but like the woman said she couldn't sing for toffee.

Kathy knocked on the door and heard Ron's familiar voice. 'Come in.'

He was sitting at the dressing table, removing his stage make-up. When he saw in the mirror who was standing behind him in the doorway, he sprang to his feet and turned with his arms outstretched all in one movement. 'Kathy! My dear girl. How wonderful to see you? Whatever are you doing here?'

'I work here. In this cinema.'

'Oh, are you the resident singer?'

'No – no, I'm an usherette and—'

'An usherette! My dear girl, with your talent. An usherette! Oh dear me, we can't have that! Here, sit down.' He moved some clothes from a chair and dusted it. 'We must talk about this.'

His tone brooked no argument and, smiling self-consciously, Kathy did as he bade her.

'It was a lovely show, Mr Spencer.'

Ron chuckled. 'Oh, it's Ron now, to one and all. No standing on ceremony these days, love.'

'So – it all worked then? All the plans you were making when I – I left.'

Ron regarded her solemnly for a moment. He seemed about to question her, but then he changed his mind, smiled and nodded. 'Yes, and we're all having a great time.' His smile faded briefly as he added, 'Of course, we see some dreadful sights, when we go to hospitals especially. And it's heartbreaking seeing all the bomb damage in the cities. And then, of course, when we go to the docks when the army lads are going abroad, that's hard, Kathy, that's really hard.'

'You go all round the country then?'

Ron nodded. 'We were in Coventry in February.' He sighed and shook his head. 'My, that's a dreadful sight, Kathy. And London's had it very bad, haven't they? And even poor old Lincoln got a bit of a pasting last month.'

'Yes, we had a couple of raids here too. What about our street? Is it okay?'

'So far, love. Mabel writes regularly. I always let her know where we're going to be. She keeps me up to date with all the news.'

'I presume you're here because of all the forces personnel in the area?'

'That's right. We have a list of all the theatres near to army camps, airfields and training centres. Lincolnshire's becoming known for its airfields and, of course, there's the naval training centre up the road and so – here we are.' He spread his hands as if that explained everything. And in a way, it did. 'Of course,' he went on, 'we have to travel a lot and it means staying away from home, sometimes for weeks at a time, but Mabel's all for it. She says she's lucky I haven't got to go into the forces and she's busy with her war work in the WVS. She and Miss Robinson do a lot of work together.'

Suddenly, Kathy was overwhelmed by a wave of homesickness. Not for the farm and her parents, but for the tiny terraced house in Lincoln, Aunt Jemima and her cat.

'How – how is Miss Robinson?'

Ron eyed her keenly. 'Missing you,' he said as bluntly as Jemima herself would have answered. He leaned forward and patted her hand. 'We were all sorry about what happened on your wedding day, but we've all missed you, Kathy. Don't hide yourself away here forever, will you? Unless, of course, there's someone here . . . ?'

Kathy took a deep breath. Oh yes, there was someone here all right, and for a brief moment she was very tempted to tell Ron everything. What a relief it would be to spill it all out. Yet, still something held her back. Instead, she shook her head, not trusting herself to speak the lie aloud.

'Then would you consider joining us?' He smiled ruefully. 'I expect you heard poor little Melody tonight. She's a great little actress, but she's not a singer. Now you . . .' Again he spread his hands and then went on. 'They're a good crowd, very friendly and most of them are a similar age to you. You'd fit in very well. Kathy, dear girl . . .' He grasped her hands and held them tightly. 'Please say you'll think about it.'

Kathy smiled and said impulsively, 'I don't need time to think. The answer's yes. I'd love to join you all.'

Now he put his arms around her and held her close. 'I'm so pleased. We're in the area until next Saturday night. Can you leave with us first thing on Sunday morning? I'll see the cinema manager if you have any problems leaving your job.'

'I'll talk to him. I'm sure he'll be all right about it.'

'That's wonderful. Wonderful! I can't wait to tell the others. They'll be thrilled. We've really missed having a decent female vocalist with us.'

'But what about Melody? Won't she be hurt?'

Ron laughed. 'Heavens, no! The poor girl will be relieved. She's been begging me to find someone to take her place. Oh, she'll not leave us. Like I say, she's brilliant in the sketches and she helps Martin write some of them too. No, no, you don't need to worry about Melody. She's very talented in all sorts of ways, but sadly not in singing.'

For the first time since her disastrous wedding day, Kathy walked home feeling she had some hope for the future.

The cinema manager was most understanding and released her from her job at once. He made up her pay packet until the end of the week and even gave her another week's wages on top.

'Just in case you need a few things,' Larry said kindly. 'But I do feel a little put out.'

'I know – and I'm sorry if I'm letting you down . . .' she began, but he interrupted.

'No, it's not that. I just wish I'd known you could sing. I'd've had you on that stage myself before you could say "Jack Flash", especially when we had one or two acts we'd booked for our Sunday shows let us down. We were booked to have an RAF band last night, you know, but there was some sort of flap on and they cancelled. This concert party was the only replacement I could get at short notice, but I wasn't sure if we were doing the right thing having a variety show on a Sunday,' Larry added worriedly. 'Some people might think it a bit out of place.'

'I think people are relaxing their attitude a bit these days,' Kathy tried to reassure him. 'I wouldn't worry.'

'I'm sure you're right. It's a difficult time for all of us, but "The show must go on" is a very good adage to cling to just now. There are a lot of people with cause for tears but they put a smile on their face and carry on, and if concert parties like the one you're about to join can help folks to do that, then good luck to you.'

Kathy nodded. She could not speak for the tears that welled in her throat, but she took the kindly man's words to heart. Though her own heart felt as if it was breaking, she would put on a brave smile and sing to bring a little joy into the lives of others. Maybe it would help ease her own heartache, even if only for a little while.

Kathy's landlady was not so understanding. 'I need a week's notice. That's what you agreed to, so if you're leaving on Sunday, you'll 'ave to pay me for next week, an' all.'

'That's all right,' Kathy said, silently blessing the manager's generosity.

'Oh, flush are we?' the woman said sarcastically. 'I've a good mind to demand another week.'

'Well, you won't get it. Here, this is what I owe you and that's all you're getting.'

Kathy pushed the money into the greedy woman's hand and headed for the stairs, thankful she'd some packing to do. With a bit of luck, she'd never be back here again.

But once in her room, as she closed the door behind her and leant against it for a moment, she realized that of course she would come back. Perhaps not to this dingy room, if she could avoid it, but she would come back to the town. Oh yes, she'd be back, if only to try to catch a fleeting glimpse of her son.

311

Thirty-One

On the Saturday afternoon Kathy walked along the road running parallel to the beach to the white house at the end. As she neared the entrance she could see that the wrought-iron gates had disappeared, taken, no doubt, for the war effort. Hungrily she gazed at the house, wondering which of the windows was her son's nursery. She ached to see him. He'd be five months old by now. Was he trying to sit up yet? Was he smiling and laughing? Oh, how she wished she could hear his baby laughter.

She saw a face at one of the upstairs windows and saw that the woman was standing there with a child in her arms. Her heart skipped a beat and she held her breath, gazing up at the window, squinting to see the child more clearly. Mrs Wainwright stared down at her for a few moments and then moved away. Kathy waited but she did not come back to the window. With a sigh, Kathy was about to turn away when she saw the front door open and Mrs Wainwright hurried down the steps and came towards her.

Kathy made to turn away, but the woman called out, 'Wait!'

Kathy bit her lip and her heart beat a little faster. She didn't want to cause any trouble. She just wanted to . . .

'Hello again,' Mrs Wainwright greeted her pleasantly. 'I thought it was you. In fact I think I've see you once or twice.'

'Yes, yes, I just walk along to the end here and – and back again. It – it makes a pleasant walk along here. With the sea just over the sandhills. In fact, I think I'll go back along the beach.'

Mrs Wainwright smiled and nodded. 'If you go down that little path there through the bushes, you'll come to the beach.'

'Thanks,' Kathy smiled. 'Nice to see you again. I – I'm leaving tomorrow. I've joined a concert party touring round to entertain troops and war workers.'

'How wonderful. I would've liked to have done something like that, but now I have the baby . . .' She smiled, not in the least unhappy that she could no longer do any such thing.

'Of course. How – how is he?'

'He's fine. Growing fast. Would you like to see him?'

'I – I'd love to, if you don't mind.'

'Of course I don't. I'm such a doting mother, I must be boring all my friends with my constant baby chatter. Come along in. Perhaps you'd like a cup of tea before you walk back into town.'

'Thank you. That would be nice,' Kathy said mechanically, but her heart was skipping madly. She was going to see her son.

She followed the woman into the house, through the vast high hall and into a room on the right-hand side.

Mrs Wainwright opened the door quietly, 'Here he is, my little darling,' she said as she approached the sofa where the child was lying, surrounded by cushions.

Mrs Wainwright laughed. 'I have to put these here when I leave him for a few moments. He can nearly roll over now and I'm so frightened he might fall off the settee.' She picked him up and rocked him for a moment, looking down into the little face with such love that Kathy felt a lump in her throat. The child reached out and touched the woman's face with his tiny fingers. And then he smiled and Kathy's heart melted.

'I'll just make some tea,' Mrs Wainwright said. 'Would you like to hold him while I fetch it?'

Kathy sat down on the sofa and held out her arms. Trembling a little, she took the warm little body into her arms and looked down at him with eyes that were blurred with tears. 'He's beautiful,' she said huskily. Then she whispered, 'Hello, James. Hello, my darling boy.'

The tea forgotten, Mrs Wainwright sat down in the armchair. 'You're – you're his real mother, aren't you?' she said.

Kathy looked up and met her steady gaze. She couldn't read the expression in the woman's eyes, but she was relieved to see there was no fear or panic.

She looked down again at the little boy in her arms as, trying to keep her voice calm and level, she said, 'I believe I am his natural mother, yes. But you are the one he is going to know as his mother. And please, don't think I'm going to cause trouble for you, because I'm not. I – we're not supposed to know who the adoptive parents are, but I found out.'

'I see. Yes, we were assured that you would not be given our name and certainly not our address.' Still Mrs Wainwright spoke calmly.

'But you see, I signed the papers when I went into Willow House thinking they were just admission papers. I never dreamed I was signing away all rights to my baby even then. And after he was born – I had a difficult time – they took him away. They never even showed him to me, never let me hold him. I didn't even know it was a boy until one of the other girls told me.'

Now Mrs Wainwright gasped. 'That's dreadful. We were told that his mother had been given every chance to keep him herself but that she was adamant that she wanted him adopted.'

'That's certainly not the case,' Kathy said, 'More than anything I wanted him. But since then I've realized that you can give him a far better life than ever I can now.' She took a deep breath. 'James's father and I were to be married. Five minutes more and we would have been.'

'Five minutes?' Mrs Wainwright's smooth brow puckered. 'Whatever do you mean?'

'Tony's mother was taken ill during the service, just before – just before we were to make our vows.' She smiled with wry sadness. 'You know the part in the service where they vicar asks the congregation whether they know of any just cause . . . ?' Wordlessly, Mrs Wainwright nodded. 'That's when Mrs Kendall – very conveniently – had a heart attack.'

There was a pause before Mrs Wainwright asked hesitantly, 'Do you – do you mean his mother was against the marriage?'

'Yes,' Kathy said bitterly. 'She told me to my face that she'd never let it happen. And she kept her word.'

'But – but what happened later? I mean – didn't your fiancé arrange another date?'

Kathy shook her head. All the time they had been talking, Katy's gaze had been on her baby. She was drinking in the sight of him, not knowing when she would see him again. If ever. 'Tony had been called up.

The wedding was on the Saturday and then he was at the hospital until the Sunday evening and then – and then he had to report on the Monday morning. That's why the wedding had been arranged so hastily. Not because I was pregnant – because I wasn't. Not then.' She blushed at the memory of their lovemaking, but not for one moment did she regret it. The result of it lay in her arms. How could she regret bringing such a perfect little being into the world, even though it was breaking her heart to part with him?

'But couldn't you have been married later? When he came on leave? I'm sure if the authorities had known they would have granted your fiancé – Tony, is it? – ' Kathy nodded – 'compassionate leave.'

'He – he doesn't know about the baby.'

'Doesn't know?' Now Mrs Wainwright was shocked. 'But – but why?'

'He went away. He wrote to me once. But he wrote to his mother every other day.' She spoke flatly, without emotion, but the pain and disappointment – the betrayal almost – was plain to see on her face. 'It was never going to stop, was it? She was always going to be there between us. He would always put her first. And then . . .' Her eyes softened as she gazed at the child. 'I didn't want anyone to think he'd been forced to marry me.'

'If you don't mind me saying so, my dear, I think you should have fought a bit harder. My goodness!' She clapped her hand over her mouth, her eyes wide. 'What am I saying? If you had, I wouldn't have my adorable boy.' Now there was fear in her eyes as she added, 'You – you won't take him away from me, will you?'

Kathy shook her head. 'No – I won't. I promise.'

'But when your fiancé comes home on leave . . . ?'

Kathy pressed her lips together, trying to stem the tears that were never very far away. Huskily she said, 'He's never coming back. He was a fighter pilot and I've heard that he was shot down. Missing, presumed killed.'

'Oh my dear – I'm so very sorry. I don't know what to say.'

'Could I just ask you one thing?'

Mrs Wainwright nodded warily.

'I know I haven't any right to ask, but may I write to you? Would you write back to me and let me know how he is? Perhaps you could send me a photograph now and again if I give you my address in Lincoln.'

The woman relaxed and smiled. 'Of course. It's the least I can do.'

And that was all Kathy could ask, but it was more than she'd ever dared to hope for.

The train journey from Saltershaven on the east coast to Yorkshire, where their next performance was to take place, was long enough for Kathy to meet the other members of the concert party. Ron Spencer made the introductions, reminding her, 'And from now on call me "Ron". No more of this Mr Spencer lark. We're a friendly crowd and we're going to be spending a lot of time together. Now, this is Martin. He's an actor, but he also doubles as our stage manager.'

'Yes, we met before.' Kathy smiled and held out her hand. He was still as fit and healthy-looking as he had been and she couldn't help wondering immediately why he had not been called up already. Ron's next words explained. 'And we'll have to make the most of him because he'll likely be called up next year. I shall apply for a deferment for him, of course, but whether I'll get it is another matter.'

Martin took her hand in his huge paw and shook it with a strong grasp. His smile crinkled his swarthy face.

Kathy smiled back. 'You look as if you're used to working out of doors. Have you worked on a farm?'

Martin gave a deep, rumbling laugh. 'No. I worked for a brewery.' He flexed his huge arms. 'Heaving barrels about all day. Now I heave stage props and scenery about, as well as a bit of acting now and again. And writing the odd sketch too.'

Kathy laughed. 'Is there anything you *don't* do?' Then she glanced from one to the other, puzzled. 'But don't the theatres we visit have their own stage managers? The cinema at Saltershaven did.'

'Yes, some of them,' Ron agreed. 'But you see we're not always in theatres or even cinemas with a stage. We go to factory canteens, shipyards, as well as to airfields and barracks – anywhere we can entertain. Even docks, if we hear of troops about to embark.'

'And we have to improvise with scenery,' Martin put in, 'build a stage sometimes. I'm the chap who begs, borrows and steals whatever we need.'

'Folks are very good. Martin asks around the locals and he always comes up with the goods.'

Kathy smiled up at the good-looking young man. 'With a smile like that, I bet he has them eating out of his hand.'

'Now, who's next?' Ron went on. 'Ah yes . . .'

The introductions continued until Kathy's head was dizzy with all the names. The only one she really remembered was Rosie, with whom she would be sharing a room in whatever digs could be found in the various places. She was a member of 'The Cinderellas', a group of three girl dancers. Like Melody, they all took part in the comedy sketches. Most of the men were Ron's age and too old to be called up, with the exception of Martin and one other. Lionel was pale and thin, with light brown hair and pale, hazel eyes. He was very serious and hardly ever smiled.

'He's failed his medical,' Ron whispered. 'And he's a bit cut up about it. Evidently he has a heart problem, but he's determined not to be an invalid.'

Kathy said nothing, but already she admired the young man, who was still determined to 'do his bit'. What a contrast to Tony's mother, she thought. 'What does Lionel do?'

'He's the comedian.'

'Really?' Kathy couldn't hide her surprise.

'Doesn't look like one,' Ron chuckled, 'but you wait till you see him on stage. He has the audience – and us – in stitches. He writes his own material and some of the sketches too, along with Martin and Melody. We're always wanting new material because we sometimes visit places more than once and they don't want to see the same old thing again. He's really very clever.'

As Ron brought them together, Lionel held her hand and gazed earnestly into her eyes. 'Can you act?'

'I – I don't know.'

'We'll try you out. You've a very pretty face. I could write some good parts for you.'

With that he turned away. Evidently, Kathy thought, Lionel was not one to engage in small talk.

But Rosie was, and so were the other two Cinderellas, Maureen and Joan. For the rest of the journey Kathy sat beside Rosie and the other two girls sat facing them. The carriage resounded with their chatter, now and again punctuated with shrieks of laughter.

In their merry company, Kathy felt her spirits lift. She would never get over the sadness buried deep in her heart, but from now on she would keep a smile on her face and hide her heartache. She would give herself over to entertaining others, trying to lighten the drudgery and hardship of wartime conditions. Many in the audiences, she knew, would have just as much grief as she did. If she could make people forget, even for a few moments, their heartache, then maybe she could forget her own for a little while.

The first show in which Kathy took part was in a factory canteen in Leeds.

'What do they make here?' Kathy asked innocently, as she pulled on the strapless evening gown and asked Rosie to fasten the single string of pearls that Tony had given her around her neck.

'Ooh, don't ask,' Rosie said. 'We never ask questions, wherever we go. Ron says it doesn't do. It might sound as if we're spies. Besides – ' she shrugged – 'I'd rather not know. If it's munitions or something dangerous I'd rather not be thinking we're all going to get blown to kingdom come any minute.'

Kathy laughed. To her surprise it was a genuine laugh that had come spontaneously. It was a long time since she'd laughed so readily. Impulsively, she turned and hugged Rosie.

'Whatever's that for? I only fastened your necklace.'

'Just – Oh, I can't explain, Rosie. It's just – just that I've been through a bit of a tough time since the war started and – and – well, you've all been so friendly and – and kind.'

'We're a nice bunch, I'll grant you that. Specially that Martin.' There was a sudden sparkle in Rosie's blue eyes.

Kathy found herself laughing again. 'I think you'll find that he's just a little friendlier towards you than to the rest of us. Not that he isn't, I mean,' she added swiftly.

Rosie grinned and her cheeks were pink. 'He's nice. I do like him, Kath. Do you think he likes me?'

'Ask a silly question, Rosie. 'Course he does. Now, come on, we'd better get down to the side of the stage.'

'The wings, you mean,' Rosie giggled.

'I'll never get used to all the names. Upstage, downstage – I still haven't got the hang of it.'

'Don't worry,' Rosie said, linking her arm through Kathy's as they left the draughty little room, no bigger than a cupboard, that served as their dressing room. 'When you go the wrong way, it all adds to the fun.'

Kathy took a deep breath as they neared the side of the stage and peeped through the curtains. 'Oh heck! There's hundreds out there. I was hoping for a small audience for my first time.'

Rosie looked out too. 'How many million times have I told you not to exaggerate? There's fifty at the most.'

'It looks like hundreds to me,' Kathy said nervously.

'You'll be fine. Everyone said what a lovely voice you've got when they heard you in rehearsal. Melody's quite envious.'

Kathy turned. 'Oh, Rosie, she's – she's not upset that I've come, is she?'

'Lord, no. It's given her the chance to do what she's really good at. Be a comic actress. And she's quite a good impressionist. I think Ron is thinking of giving her her own spot if she can come up with enough impersonations. Have you heard her do that woman off the wireless, the one that's in ITMA that says, "Can I do you now, sir?" '

'Mrs Mopp, you mean?'

'That's the one. Melody sounds just like her. Brilliant she is.' Rosie giggled. 'Funny thing is, when she impersonates Vera Lynn, she sings just like her. In tune and everything. Yet, when she tries to sing as herself, it's awful. Funny that, isn't it?'

'Mm,' Kathy murmured, her mind once again on the audience filing into the canteen. 'I do hope I remember all the words when I start to sing. At this moment, everything's just flown out of my head.'

Rosie squeezed her arm. 'You will.'

Ron, as compère, introduced all the acts, and when it came to Kathy's spot, he said, 'Now, today we have a young lady making her very first appearance with us. Please give a warm welcome to our very own nightingale, Kathy Burton.'

Taking a deep breath, she stepped out on to the makeshift stage that Martin had set up at one end of the canteen. She forced a smile as she neared the microphone. Still she couldn't remember the words, nor even what song she was supposed to be singing.

This is awful, she thought, as the butterflies in her stomach turned into vultures. I can't remember a word. I'm going to make a complete fool of myself and let Ron and all the others down . . .

The clapping died away and the pianist struck the first chord and played the introduction. Kathy opened her mouth and from somewhere the words came: 'I'm Gonna Sit Right Down and Write Myself a Letter . . . '

The applause at the end of the first song gave her a little confidence and as she finished her second song someone from the back of the room shouted in a cockney accent, 'Sing us "The Lambeth Walk".'

'Nah sing us, "On Ilkley Moor . . ." '

'But we're miles from home, mate. Let's 'ave "Lambeth Walk"?'

While the argument went on, with others joining in, Kathy turned to the pianist. 'Do you know either of them?'

Terry nodded. 'I think so, but I'll have to improvise a bit. Do you know the words?'

She laughed. 'Not all of them but I think I'm going to get some help, don't you?'

Terry grinned at her and struck the opening chord, and Kathy began to sing the opening line of 'The Lambeth Walk'. At once the group of workers sitting at the back of the room were singing loudly and swaying to the music. One or two of the women got up and began to dance, linking arms and kicking up their legs.

As the song ended with a resounding 'Oi', the pianist went straight into the second of the requests and now the rest of the audience joined in. Kathy only knew one or two verses of the song, so was left conducting the singing from the stage.

At last even the born and bred Yorkshire folk ran out of verses and tumultuous applause broke out. Some even stood up, whistling and cat-calling, as Kathy curtsied and left the stage to be met by a beaming Ron and an excited Rosie.

'That was terrific. You're a real trouper, Kathy. Go

on,' Ron added, giving her a little push. 'Go and take another bow.'

As she stepped back onto the stage the applause was thunderous, and when she finally returned to the wings, there were tears in her eyes.

For the ten minutes she had been on stage she had not thought about Tony or even little James.

At last she had found a way to bury her heartache, even if only for a few moments each day.

It was a start.

Thirty-Two

For the next four months, they toured the north of England playing in army camps, airfields, shipyards and factories.

At one factory Ron warned, 'You can't wear any jewellery, not even hair-clips or watches today.'

'Not hair-clips,' Rosie wailed. 'Why ever not?'

'They make high explosives here. Anything that might cause the slightest spark has got to be left behind.'

'Don't blame me if my hair's flying all over the place when we dance then,' Rosie said tartly, tossing back her thick mane of auburn hair.

'Don't worry, Rosie, the fellers'll love it.'

'Can't I – can't I wear my pearl necklace?' Kathy asked, her voice trembling a little.

Ron's eyes softened. He'd guessed how much the piece of jewellery meant to her. She was never without it.

'Sorry, love, but I'll keep it safe for you, if you like.'

The minor irritations of the unusual regulations were all forgotten when the performers heard the clapping and cheering and stamping feet of the enthusiastic audience.

'We don't often get concert parties coming to us,' the manager of the factory told them, 'so we really appreciate you coming here. You've really lifted all our spirits.'

The members of the company felt a warm glow on hearing his words. It made all the travelling on draughty trains and sleeping in hard, lumpy beds worthwhile.

'So, where are we off to now, Ron?' Rosie asked as they all boarded a train out of Manchester.

'Liverpool. We're to play to the lads awaiting embarkation. There's a ship leaving on the twenty-eighth.' He glanced round the carriage to make sure that there were no servicemen overhearing what he was about to say. 'It'll not be easy. They're just going to war. Young lads, most of them. Probably away from their homes and families for the first time. And a lot of them . . .' he paused before adding softly, 'might never come back.'

'Liverpool was blitzed earlier in the year. May, I think it was, when London got it so bad.'

There was silence now in the carriage, each member of the party lost in their own thoughts and quietly vowing to give the boys as good a send-off as they possibly could, despite the dangers. Nothing was going to stop them. Not even Adolf and his bombs.

Kathy chose her programme of songs very carefully. 'Should I keep it all bright and cheerful?' she asked Ron.

To her surprise, he shook his head. 'No, love. It might bring a tear or two to their eyes, but they like the odd sentimental ballad, you know. One or two that were popular in the last war might be appropriate. 'Pack up Your Troubles' . . . and 'Tipperary' . . . but also songs like 'Keep the Home Fires Burning' – that sort of thing.'

Ron was quite right. As Kathy stood on the draughty dockside, the soldiers gathered around her, lifting her bodily onto the makeshift stage that Martin had built. Within minutes, they were joining in the rousing songs, but the ballads were just as warmly received, sung softly and with feeling.

The cheers for Kathy were always the loudest, but no one in the company seemed to begrudge her the affection from the 'boys'.

'You're our "sweetheart",' one shouted from the front row as she began her final song. For a moment she thought she wasn't going to be able to sing for the lump in her throat. But she had to; this time 'Wish Me Luck' held a very special meaning for each and every one of them.

Kathy rested her aching head against the cool glass of the carriage window. It had been a late night, and maybe the hospitality of the NAAFI on the army camp where they'd played to an enthusiastic audience who'd whistled and stamped their feet had been just a little bit too much. But she could sleep on the train, she'd promised herself as she'd dragged herself out of bed to finish her packing before it was even light. She'd glanced at the other bed, which had not been slept in. Rosie was missing again. Kathy had sighed. She'd seen the romance blossoming between the young girl and Martin and now it seemed it had taken a more serious turn. She just hoped Rosie wasn't going to get herself into trouble like she had. It wouldn't be many weeks now before Martin received his call-up papers, and despite Ron's belief that he would be able to get deferment for the young man, Kathy very much doubted it. She would have liked to warn the young girl, but Rose was a chatterbox. Even if she confided in her, Kathy didn't believe she was capable of keeping a secret. And although Ron Spencer knew what had happened on her wedding day, he knew nothing about her baby. All he thought was that she had gone away to get over her broken romance with Tony Kendall.

She felt someone ease themselves into the empty seat beside her. To her surprise it was not Rosie, but Ron, who said, 'Do you know where we're going now, Kathy?'

'Mm,' she murmured sleepily. 'Not really. I just get up in a morning, catch the train, sing, act a little, and then go to bed. Next day, I do it all again. I've lost track of where we are or even what day it is.'

She'd been with the concert party for over five months and already the weather had a definite autumnal feel about it. Though her heart was still in Saltershaven, she had not regretted her decision to join Ron's troupe for a moment. The travelling and the performing and then more travelling were very tiring, but it kept her busy and her mind occupied.

Ron chuckled. 'Well, I'll tell you. We're going home.'

Kathy's head shot up. She was wide awake now. 'To Lincoln? You mean we're going to Lincoln?'

'That's right. We'll be there by mid-afternoon. We've got four days off and we all meet up again on Wednesday. Now, how about that?'

Kathy wasn't sure. She fingered the key she always carried in her coat pocket. The key that Jemima had pressed on her when she'd left.

'This is your home, Kathy. You're welcome back any time you want to come. You hear me. I'll keep the spare room bed aired and you're to regard it as your room.'

A sudden longing to see the brisk, no-nonsense woman again was overwhelming.

After all this time away, she hoped Jemima Robinson's promise still held good.

Ron suggested taking a taxi from the station. 'We'll treat ourselves. We're not dragging these heavy cases another inch. Let's arrive home in style.'

Kathy insisted on paying half the fare and, when the vehicle drew up in the street, the driver carried her case right to the front door of Jemima's house.

'Don't I get a hand?' Ron asked in a mock plaintive tone.

'You're not as pretty as her, sir.'

Ron laughed. 'Well, I have to agree with you there.'

Ron and Kathy waved to each other. 'See you Wednesday morning, lass. Don't be late. Train goes at eight thirty.'

'Want picking up?' the cheeky taxi driver asked.

'Good idea,' Ron said. 'Eight fifteen all right?'

'I'll get you there in time for the train, sir.'

With a saucy wink at Kathy, he walked back to his taxi. 'Though I wouldn't mind makin' that 'un miss the train.' He jerked his thumb back over his shoulder towards Kathy. 'I'd like to tek her home wi' me. Mind you,' he sniffed. 'I don't know what the missis'd say if I did.'

The three of them laughed and then, as the taxi was driven away, Ron and Kathy went into their homes.

As Kathy inserted the key into the lock and pushed open the back door, the familiar warm furry body wound itself around her legs and miaowed a welcome.

'Darling Taffy,' Kathy murmured as she bent to stroke him. He rubbed his face against her hand and purred ecstatically.

She carried her suitcase upstairs, the cat bounding ahead of her as if showing her the way. As soon as she opened the bedroom door, Taffy pushed his way into the room and took a flying leap into the middle of the bed, where he turned round three times, kneading the cover.

'Not on Aunt Jemima's second best eiderdown,' Kathy laughed, picking up the cat. She flung back the satin eiderdown and set the cat on the blanket underneath. 'You shouldn't really be on the bed at all,' she scolded him lovingly. 'But I'm so pleased to see you, you can stay while I unpack my clothes.'

The cat closed his eyes to satisfied slits and purred even louder.

A little later, Kathy scooped Taffy up from the bed and carried him down the stairs, stroking him and talking to him as she went.

'Now, let's see what's for your tea and then I'll find something to cook for your mistress when she comes home. Won't that be a nice surprise?'

The meal was cooked and sitting in a warm oven by the time Jemima was due. The cat was fed and sitting sleepily on Kathy's knee as she sat in the chair in the corner in the darkness, with only the light of the fire she had lit in the grate for company. She dozed, waiting for Jemima to come home, the warm weight of the cat on her knee a familiar comfort she had so missed since she had been away.

She didn't hear the back door open and so Jemima's

cry of surprise as she turned on the light woke both her and Taffy. The cat dug his claws into her leg in fright and then jumped down and fled towards the door and out into the night.

'Oh my, you gave me such a fright,' Jemima said, recovering a little and laughing. Kathy jumped up and the two women moved towards each other, arms outstretched. 'But how lovely to see you, my dear.' Jemima hugged her and then stood back, still holding Kathy by her shoulders. 'Let me look at you.' She paused and then added, 'You look tired. I expect Ron's been working you far too hard.'

Of course, Jemima knew all about her touring with the concert party. Kathy had written to tell her and, besides, Ron's wife would be keeping her well informed too.

'It's okay,' Kathy smiled tremulously. She was surprised how emotional she felt at seeing Jemima. She had told her nothing in her letters about her traumatic time at Willow House, the birth of her little boy and all that had happened since.

Time enough for that in the evening when they had eaten and were sitting together in the firelight.

Then she would tell Jemima everything that had happened to her.

'So,' Kathy began when they had washed up the pots together and were sitting close to the fire, Jemima in her chair, Kathy on the rug at her feet. The late September evening was surprising chilly and Jemima had insisted on lighting a fire in the front room. 'How is everyone? Uncle Ted and Auntie Betty and Morry? And have you heard from Amy?'

'Yes. I get a letter from her most weeks.' Jemima regarded Kathy over her spectacles. 'She's a better letter writer than you, Katherine Burton. You disappointed me. I had hoped you would keep in touch right from the time you left.' She reached out and patted Kathy's hand. 'I do care about you, you know. I wanted to know that you were all right.'

'I'm sorry,' Kathy said at once. 'It – it was difficult.' Her face was haunted as she was forced to remember her time at Willow House.

And then, like the flood gates opening, it all came tumbling out. She told Jemima about the harsh regime at the home for unmarried women and the almost inhumane treatment meted out to her when she had been in labour. And then, worst of all, how she had been tricked into signing away her baby.

'I never held him, never even saw him,' she said huskily.

Jemima's face twisted in sympathy. Her own plight all those years ago seemed as nothing compared to what Kathy had suffered.

'But you knew it was a boy?'

'I wouldn't have done, but one of the other girls told me.'

'I see. But you've never seen him.'

'Well, yes, I have. Now.' Kathy went on to explain how she had found the address of her little boy's adoptive parents and how she had even got to know Mrs Wainwright.

'Do you think that was wise, dear?' Jemima said, and then added swiftly, 'Oh I don't blame you. I don't blame you one bit and maybe I'm not the best judge. I've been lucky all these years; able to see my son and even have Maurice know who I am. But – but won't you always be drawn back to go and see him? And I'm so worried that while his mo— Mrs Wainwright might seem friendly enough now, there might come a time when she'd rather you didn't see him. When he becomes old enough to ask awkward questions . . .' Jemima's voice trailed away.

Kathy was not hurt or offended by the older woman's words. She knew the outspoken Jemima well enough by now to know that whatever she said was spoken with good intention, even if the words were not always what one wanted to hear.

'I know,' Kathy said quietly, 'and I'm ready for that happening. I'm trying to build a life without him, but, Oh, Aunt Jemima, it's so hard.' Suddenly, unable to hold back the tears any more, she buried her face in Jemima's lap. The older woman stroked her hair tenderly and gazed into the fire's flickering flames, for once quite lost for words.

A little later, when she was calmer, Kathy asked, 'Have you heard how my mother is?'

'She's fine. Betty keeps an eye on her. Of course, her life is hard, we all know that and short of leaving your father, it always will be, but Betty keeps her posted about you and . . .'

Kathy drew in a sharp breath. 'You mean – you mean she knows?'

Jemima shook her head. 'No, not about that. We wouldn't divulge such a thing unless you told us we could.'

'I suppose,' Kathy said pensively, 'I wouldn't mind my mother knowing, but then it puts her in a very difficult position having to keep it from my father, so it's – it's best she doesn't know. Not yet, anyway. Maybe one day, I'll be able to tell her.'

There was such a wistful longing in the girl's tone that Jemima's heart went out to her. Instead, she said briskly, 'It's best not. And she'd only worry more about you. Kinder that she doesn't know for the time being.'

'Have you heard how Mr and Mrs Kendall are?'

'Not good,' Jemima sighed. 'Poor George is heart-broken, though he still trudges to work and looks after Beatrice.'

'And Mrs Kendall?'

'Much the same.'

'I'd've thought it might – well – have made her worse. Much worse.'

'Killed her, you mean?' Jemima was as blunt as ever.

'To be honest – yes.'

'Mm,' Jemima was thoughtful. 'We've always thought her illness was put on, haven't we? Now I'm sure of it. If she really had a weak heart, news of the death of her only beloved son would surely have made her very ill or worse. Instead, it was poor George who had to take a fortnight off work when they got the telegram, but it was Beatrice who just lay there on the couch as always, weeping and wailing and playing the part of the bereaved mother to perfection.'

'How do you know all this?'

'Because I went to see them.'

'You did?'

Now Jemima looked embarrassed. 'To tell you the truth, Kathy, I was about to commit an unforgivable sin. I went with the intention of telling them that you had had Tony's baby . . .'

Kathy gasped and her eyes widened in surprise. She

was appalled that Jemima could even think of doing such a thing.

'But I didn't do it,' Jemima went on hastily. 'When I got there, I just couldn't betray you in such a way. And besides, I'm not sure it wouldn't have made matters worse. Poor George was shattered and struggling to keep going. I arranged for Beatrice to go into a nursing home for a week. Mr James paid for it, just to give poor George a rest.'

'Is he all right now?'

Jemima sighed sadly. 'He went away for a few days while Beatrice was in the nursing home. He looked much better when he came back. Though there was still that awful haunted look in his eyes. I don't suppose he will ever get over losing his only son. His only child.'

'And her?'

'Oh, she's all right,' Jemima said, with not a scrap of sympathy for the hypochondriac. 'Beatrice and her like will be all right, because, my dear Kathy, despite what she'd like the world to think, there's only one person she's ever cared about and that's not, as she would have you believe, her beloved son, but herself. Beatrice Kendall is the epitome of the very worst kind of selfishness.'

There was silence between them for a while until Kathy murmured. 'I'd like to go and see his dad.'

'I wouldn't, my dear, not this time anyway. Perhaps when you come home again.'

Kathy smiled up at her, tears in her eyes. It wasn't just the woman's kindness and understanding, it was the inference that Jemima's house was Kathy's home that brought a lump to the girl's throat and an over-whelming gratitude.

Thirty-Three

'Now I know the members of this concert party of Ron's do get paid a little, but it can't be much . . .' Jemima began on the Wednesday morning as they breakfasted together before Kathy had to leave.

'Aunt Jemima, it's very kind of you, but I couldn't possible take any more. You've already been more than generous.'

'Oh, phooey.' Jemima dismissed her protests with a wave of her hand, then her green eyes twinkled mischievously. 'So, I'm to take it you're rolling in it, am I?'

Kathy laughed wryly. 'Not exactly, but—'

'No more "buts". Take it.'

'You're too good to me,' Kathy said, her voice trembling.

'More than likely,' Jemima said crisply, but she was smiling as she said it.

Moments later, as she drove away with Ron Spencer in the taxi, Kathy looked back to see Jemima standing outside her front door with Taffy in her arms waving goodbye.

When they arrived at the railway station, Ron rounded up all the party and stood on a nearby seat to say, 'We're not going on the train. I've got a surprise for you all. Follow me.' He jumped down and led them all out of the station.

'What's going on?' Rosie asked.

'Search me,' Kathy said. 'He didn't say anything in the taxi.'

'Ooh, 'ark at her. Taxi, is it? Come into money, have we?'

Kathy grinned. 'Actually, we treated ourselves to a taxi home last week – Ron and me live in the same street. Well, this lovely driver took us home and promised to pick us up today. And do you know what . . . ?'

'He wouldn't let you pay this morning.'

Kathy's eyes widened. 'How did you know?'

'Because it's what a lot of them do when they know who we are and what we're doing.'

'Oh.' Kathy felt deflated and Rosie pinched her arm, laughing. 'I was only teasing you, you know. I don't care if you're a millionaire – I'd still be your friend.'

'If I was, we wouldn't be travelling about on draughty trains any more— Oh my!' She stopped short as the whole party came to a halt.

'It doesn't look as if we're going to anyway,' Rosie said, as they all saw Ron pointing proudly towards a single-decker bus with the words 'The Lindum Players' painted on the side. 'The local bus company have donated one of their old buses for our permanent use and, better still, one of their drivers who's just reached retirement age has volunteered to come with us. This, ladies and gentlemen, is Keith.'

The whole party cheered the man, who gave them a cheery wave. 'Hello, there. We'll get to know each other, but for now let's get you all stowed aboard and we'll be off.'

*

The concert party grew even closer now that they travelled together all the time, so every time someone was called up, the gap they left was even harder to fill. New members joined and were welcomed into the group, but those that had gone were still missed.

Ron's face wore a perpetually worried frown, and at the beginning of December 1941, even he began to lose heart.

'They're going to call up all single women between twenty and thirty,' he told the company dolefully. 'How are we ever to keep going if we lose all the young singers and dancers?'

Rosie put her arms around Ron, 'Then we'll all just have to get married,' she joked.

Ron smiled thinly but the anxious frown never left his forehead. 'I'm serious. How are we to hold the party together?'

'Can't you apply for deferment for us like you did for Martin? We're doing our bit for the war effort, when all's done and said.'

Ron's face lightened a little. 'I could try, I suppose. But whether they'll let you all stay . . .'

'It's worth a try, Ron,' Rosie and her fellow dancers chorused.

Ron's application was successful – at least for the time being. More and more the work of ENSA was being recognized as being a valuable part of the war effort. Entertainment of any kind, especially live shows, helped cheer troops and war workers alike, especially at Christmas for those who could not get home. And when America entered the war after the attack on Pearl Harbor, it was likely that there would soon be servicemen stationed in Britain who were thousands of miles from home. Keeping up morale was going to be more important than ever.

She knew she was part of something special, but Kathy still felt restless. She longed to go back to Salters-haven to see James. Despite her promise to write, Kathy had received no letter or photograph of her little boy from Mrs Wainwright and the passage of time only seemed to make her longing greater, not less. He would be a year old now. Was he walking yet? Had he said his first words? She so longed to know, but she was very afraid that Mrs Wainwright had changed her mind. Perhaps she'd told her husband and they'd decided that they should cut off all contact with their son's natural mother.

'We'll write a pantomime.' Ron interrupted her thoughts, knowing nothing of her inner torment. Kathy sighed and forced a smile. 'I want you to play principal boy,' he went on. 'You've lovely long legs and Melody can play principal girl. Yes, I know, I know, she can't sing, so that's why we've got to rewrite it. We'll make her part more comic and she can do some of her impressions. It'll be different and you can sing all the serious ballads. All right? Now, when can you help Lionel and Martin get to work on the script?'

'As soon as you like,' Kathy said summoning up enthusiasm. A new challenge would help take her mind off her son.

'That's the ticket.'

The party's rewrite of *Jack and the Beanstalk* was a roaring success and enjoyed by the concert party as well as by all their audiences. They kept it running for two months, over the Christmas period, altering the topical jokes to fit in with what was happening in the news, lampooning Hitler and his cohorts mercilessly. Early in the New Year they played to audiences of children when the camps invited the locals to the show. By February, they were back to their usual show, travelling by bus from city to city, airfield to army camp, from factory canteen to hospital wards. The routine continued through the spring. In the summer they made another fleeting visit to Lincoln and Kathy was appalled to hear from Jemima, and to see for herself, the damage that bombing had inflicted on the city. But she was pleased to see that, despite the shortages and the constant fear of the bombing, Jemima was coping well. And she was relieved to hear that all was fine at Sandy Furze Farm.

'Your mother's keeping well too, dear,' Jemima greeted her. 'Betty's roped her in to help out with war work in the village.' Jemima smiled impishly. 'Your father grumbled, but as it was Betty asking, there was nothing he could say. He doesn't want to fall out with Edward and Maurice. They're helping him out a lot on his farm because he flatly refuses to have land army girls. And evidently it's doing poor Edith the world of good getting out and meeting other folk. Like I always say, it's an ill wind that blows nobody any good. Oh, and there's a letter for you, dear. It arrived two weeks ago, but I didn't know where to send it on to and I didn't want it to get lost. Mabel said you were due back here this week, so I hung on to it. Maybe it's from your mother.'

Kathy took the letter eagerly, but the handwriting was not that of her mother. It was not one she recognized and the envelope felt stiff, as if there was something else in it besides folded pages of writing paper. Her heart leapt as she opened the envelope carefully and eased out the contents. There was a short letter on one sheet of notepaper, but it was the other item that captured her attention. It was a photograph of a dark-haired little boy, taken at about eighteen months old. He was beaming at the camera and raising one chubby little hand in a friendly wave.

Her legs gave way beneath her and she sank into a chair. 'Oh look,' she breathed, not taking her gaze from the snapshot she held in her trembling hand. 'Aunt Jemima – do look. It's him. It's James. Mrs Wainwright has sent me a letter.'

Jemima held out her hand for the photo and, almost with a reluctance that was quite unnecessary, Kathy handed it to her. While Jemima looked at it, Kathy read the letter aloud.

'*Dear Kathy, I hope this reaches you eventually, as I know you are travelling a lot. I hope you like the picture of James. He is such a sweet little boy and so good. He is walking, of course, and talking too. He is getting quite a chatterbox and is adorable. I know you'd like a photograph of him. The enclosed was taken about a month ago . . .*'

'He's a handsome little chap,' Jemima said truthfully. 'And there's no mistaking who his father is, Kathy.'

She took the photo from Jemima and gazed at it again. 'No,' she whispered. 'I wonder if I should—'

'No, you shouldn't,' Jemima said, reading her mind. 'It could be disastrous to reveal to Beatrice Kendall that she has a grandson. Goodness only knows what she might try to do.'

'You're right,' Kathy admitted. 'But I would so like Mr Kendall to know.'

'Perhaps in time,' Jemima said.

The letter and the photograph brought Kathy some comfort. Now she had an image of her son that she carried everywhere with her, yet she still yearned to hold him.

The door slammed behind Kathy as she sat at the dressing table applying her stage make-up. The sound made her jump and smudge her lipstick. 'I do wish you wouldn't do that, Rosie.'

'I hate him. I don't ever want to see him again.'

'*Now* what? Can't you and Martin go five minutes without a blazing row? Really! For a couple supposed to be madly in love, you take the biscuit.'

'I'm not madly in love with *him*. I wouldn't marry him if he was the last man on earth.'

'You wouldn't get the chance. You'd be killed in the rush.' Calmly, Kathy rubbed away the smudged lipstick and started again. 'What – is it – this time?' she asked, stretching her lips as she applied fresh lipstick.

'He's going to join up even though Ron got him a deferment for six months. He says he doesn't want folks thinking he's a coward.'

'They won't think that,' Kathy said.

'*I* know that, but try telling him.'

The door opened with a dramatic flourish.

'You don't know what it's like to be a fit young man and have people staring at you wondering why you're not in uniform,' Martin shouted.

'You just want to be a hero,' Rosie screamed. 'You're

342

doing a good job here else you wouldn't have been given a deferment.'

'There's no talking to you.' Martin turned and left, slamming the door behind him. But Rosie dragged it open and followed him across the corridor into his dressing room.

'Well, I don't want to talk to you if all you want to do is go and get yourself killed.'

She came back into Kathy's room and slammed the door again.

'That door is going to fall off its hinges if we're here much longer,' Kathy remarked mildly.

Rosie collapsed into the rickety armchair in one corner of the dressing room and dissolved into noisy weeping.

'Oh, Rosie,' Kathy sighed, getting up. 'I'm on your side. I don't want Martin to go either . . .' She paused, wondering whether to confide in the girl of her own loss, but decided it might only make things worse. Martin was the one she should tell that to, if anyone. As far as she knew, only Ron knew about the loss of her fiancé. Theoretically, he had still been her fiancé when he'd been killed.

'But you have to let the men do what they feel they need to do.'

'What would you know about it?' Rosie sniffed sulkily. 'You haven't even got a boyfriend.'

Softly, with a catch in her voice, Kathy said, 'I know more than you might think.'

Rose stared at her for a moment and then jumped up. 'Did you – have you – lost someone?'

She hadn't meant for it to come out, but now there was no point in lying about it. Biting her lip, Kathy nodded.

Rosie stood up and put her arms about her. 'Kathy, I'm so sorry. I didn't mean to upset you. But – but you must know how I feel, then.'

'I know exactly how you feel. But it's no use, Rosie love. If they want to go, there's nothing we can do to stop them.'

'I can have a jolly good try though. I'll go down fighting,' Rosie declared. The two girls stared at each other and then collapsed against each other laughing.

'Come on,' Kathy said at last. 'We'd better finish getting ready. The show'll be starting in ten minutes and you're on in the opening number. Just one more piece of advice: don't spend your last few days before he goes – if he does go – fighting. If . . . if anything did happen to him – and God forbid that it does – but if it did, you'd regret it.'

Rosie gazed at her. 'Is – is that what happened to you?'

'Not exactly, but – but I have a lot of regrets. Things I didn't do – things I . . . I didn't tell him that . . . that I should have done. And now I never can.'

Rosie's tears ran afresh, but now for a different reason, as she hugged Kathy again.

'Now, come along. Go and make up with Martin before the show starts or you'll both be looking as black as thunder all the way through and you know Ron— he'll pick up on it.'

Rosie smiled, rushed out of the door, across the corridor and into the dressing room opposite. Kathy saw Martin with his arms outstretched and Rosie flying into them. She turned away, the familiar lump rising in her throat and a physical ache in her arms at their emptiness.

The show began to tumultuous applause and Ron

smiled and nodded in delight. 'That's what I like to hear. A good audience from the off.'

At the end of every number there was rapturous applause, whistling and stamping feet. The audience was a mixture of servicemen and women from a nearby camp, factory workers after a long day's shift and munitions workers letting their hair down, released for a few hours from their dangerous work.

There was such a lot of noise that no one heard the sirens begin to wail until an ARP warden came rushing into the theatre, down the centre aisle towards the stage, shouting and waving his arms. The music petered out and the audience shuffled to their feet. Now, everyone could hear the sirens. The warden climbed on to the stage and grabbed the microphone.

'There's an underground shelter down the street,' he began, but Ron tapped him on the shoulder.

'Is it big enough to take all of us?' He swept his arm in a wide arc to encompass all the cast of the show and the audience too.

'Er – well – no, probably not, but . . .'

'Then we're staying here. The show goes on. We'll give those who want to go time to leave, but we're going on.'

His announcement, heard over the mike, was greeted with a huge cheer, and many of the audience who had stood up sat down again, settled themselves comfortably back in their seats and looked expectantly towards the stage.

'Get on with it then,' shouted a voice from the middle of the auditorium. 'Let's show old 'itler 'ee can't stop us having a bit of fun.'

Laughter rippled through the theatre and more people sat down again. In the end only a handful left, either to go home or to hurry to the shelter. The warden shrugged his shoulders and left the way he had come in, muttering darkly, 'On your own head be it then. And it probably will be. We'll likely be digging you all out in the morning.' He was greeted with catcalls and pelted with crumpled-up cigarette packets by those nearby who heard his words. But he ducked out of the door with a good-natured grin on his face. He was worried that his words would be prophetic, but, deep down, he admired the spirit of the players and those who stayed to watch. They were cocking a snook at the enemy and he liked that. It was what he did every night on duty.

The show went on; the quintet who served as the concert party's orchestra played Kathy's opening music and she went on stage to tumultuous applause. She sang her usual songs to end the first half of the show, but during the interval she sought out Ron and the pianist, Terry.

'Do you think it'd be a good idea to change the finale to our wartime songs? I'll lead the singing with the whole cast behind me?'

Ron glanced at Terry and they nodded together. 'Good idea, Kathy, and we'll keep going until the "All Clear" sounds, even if it takes all night.'

The word went round the cast of the change in their programme. The first half began again, sooner than normal. Without the music and the clapping and cheering, the occasional "crump" of a falling bomb was unnerving some of the audience. Though no one else left the theatre, everyone was relieved when the show began again to drown out the noise of the air raid.

As they began the finale, there was a loud thud close

346

by and the whole theatre seemed to shake, but Kathy stood in front of the microphone and belted out the words to 'It's a Long Way to Tipperary' without so much as a tremor. The audience clapped and cheered. Kathy waved her arms, inviting the audience to join in. By now the show was over-running by half an hour, but no one left. They stayed in their seats clapping and cheering and singing and ignoring the bangs and thuds outside. With perfect timing Kathy was singing 'When They Sound the Last All Clear' as the noise of the sirens began again and everyone heard the "All Clear" in reality.

As the song ended, a cheer rippled through the audience and Ron approached the microphone.

'Ladies and gentlemen, I'd just like to say thank you for your support . . .'

'No, mate, thank you,' a voice came out of the darkness, and the whole auditorium erupted in applause yet again.

When Ron could make himself heard again, he said, 'We'd like to end our show with 'Land of Hope and Glory', led by our very own soloist, Miss Kathy Burton.'

By the end of the song, there wasn't a dry eye in the house. As they always did at the end of the show, the cast went to the foyer of the theatre to stand in line and bid the audience good night as they filed out.

There were handshakes and hugs and kisses.

'Brilliant.' 'So brave to carry on.' 'Thank you.' 'God bless you.' 'You're doing a grand job.' The whole cast basked in the praise. Kathy, standing next to Rosie and Martin, seemed to receive the most plaudits, but it was pretty, blonde Rosie who got the admiring glances.

347

'You're a doll.' One airman in his smart blue uniform kissed her soundly on both cheeks. 'When are you going to let me take you out?'

Before Rosie could utter a gentle refusal, Martin butted in, 'Sorry, old boy, she's taken.'

The airman turned slowly to look Martin up and down. What he saw was a tall, fit young man old enough to be in uniform. He said nothing, but his scathing glance spoke volumes. He turned back to Rosie and shrugged. 'If that's what you prefer, honey, good luck to you.'

The young airman turned away to follow his mates, leaving Martin staring after him, his expression thunderous.

'That does it. I'm volunteering tomorrow.'

Thirty-Four

There was nothing anyone could say now to dissuade him. Within a week Martin had left the party to go home, pack his case and wait for his papers to arrive.

Rosie walked about in a trance, her eyes permanently swollen with weeping. But like the trouper she was, she insisted on carrying on with the show.

'I just need thicker make-up,' she remarked drily.

'That's the ticket, love,' Ron commended her as he patted her on the shoulder and winked at Kathy, who knew what he was hinting. She gave him a little nod that said a silent Yes, I'll keep my eye on her.

But who, she thought sadly, is keeping their eye on me? Ron knew about her loss, but not the whole of it. No one else here knew about her yearning to hold her tiny son again.

'What on earth are we going to do without Martin?' Ron moaned. 'It'll take about three people to do the work he used to do.'

'I thought you'd found a new stage manager,' Kathy said.

'I have, but he doesn't help write the scripts like Martin did, nor does he want to take part in the sketches.'

'There's still Lionel and Melody to write, and maybe

you'll find someone else to join us. Have you been in touch with ENSA? They might know of someone looking to join a concert party.'

Ron's face brightened. 'Now that's an idea, Kathy. Why didn't I think of that?'

'Because you've got a lot of other things on your mind, that's why.'

His sighed and his face fell into worried lines again. 'But I don't think we'll be able to write a pantomime for this year. It's a huge task. Have you any ideas?'

'Not for a pantomime, no. I presume you don't want to revive *Jack* . . .'

Ron shook his head. 'We'll be visiting some of the same places we did last year. They won't want to see the same old stuff again.'

'True.' Kathy was thoughtful before she said, 'Then why don't we put together a Christmas show? You know – seasonal songs with one or two sketches with a festive flavour. I'm sure Lionel and Melody could come up with one or two brand new scripts. They're used to producing new material all the time.'

Ron put his hand on her shoulder and at last he was really smiling. 'Now that *is* a good idea.'

'Well, there's nothing like rubbing it in, is there?' Rosie said bitterly, slamming the door of the bedroom she and Kathy were sharing in their current digs.

The Christmas-themed shows instead of a pantomime had worked well and the party had worked all over the festive season, not even getting home to see their families.

'All the lads and lasses in the forces have to be

away, so we can too,' had been Ron's suggestion. He wasn't surprised when everyone had agreed with him. Christmas was a tough time for those forced to be away from their loved ones. The least they could do was to bring a little laughter into their dull routine. Now they were into the new year of 1943. Kathy could hardly believe that another whole year had gone past. James would be two by now. She still only had the one photograph of him. She looked at it each morning when she woke and at night before she fell asleep.

Kathy's eyes widened. 'Why? What's happened?' Her heart began thumping painfully. Oh, surely nothing had happened to Martin?

'We're going to a hospital, would you believe, to entertain the patients?'

Kathy breathed a sigh of relief, but now she was puzzled. 'But – we've been to hospitals before. Why – why are you so upset about this one?'

Rosie bit her lip. 'We've always just played to an audience that could come to us in a big room in the hospital or a nearby hall. *This* time Ron wants us to go into the wards. There are some very – very sick lads there. Badly injured and – and – ' Tears filled her eyes. 'We might even see someone – someone *die*. And all the time I'll be thinking – it could be Martin.'

Kathy stood up and put her arms around her. 'Try not to think like that. Try to think that he'll be one of the lucky ones. That – that he'll come back.' Kathy's voice quavered and at once Rosie returned her hug. They held each other close. 'I'm so sorry. I was forgetting. I'm being selfish, aren't I, when there's countless other girls feeling just the same? You're right and we have a job to do. Martin – ' now her voice too was unsteady – 'Martin would be the first to say "the show must go on", wouldn't he?'

Next day, the whole party clambered into the bus to travel to the north of England, to a hospital in a town just south of Newcastle. Travelling was much more fun now with everyone together. There was laughter and banter and even singing throughout the journey. It left Kathy – and now Rosie too – less time to brood.

As they neared the town where the hospital was situated, Ron stood up at the front of the bus. 'Now listen, you lot. I understand that the hospital has kindly found accommodation for all of us. The girls are to go to the nurses' home and the boys are in a hotel nearby. It's where a lot of the parents, wives and so on stay if they come to visit the lads in the hospital. They do special rates for them and they'll do the same for us. The hospital administration says that visits like ours help keep up the staff's morale as well as the patients'.'

An appreciative murmuring at the compliment rippled through the bus and when, a few moments later, they turned into the driveway leading up to the hospital and drew to a halt at the front steps, they saw two nurses standing at the top. At once they came running down, smiling and waving. When Ron stepped down, Kathy heard a merry voice greet him.

'You must be Mr Spencer. I'm Brenda and this is Elsie. I'm to take the ladies to the nurses' home and Elsie will take you gentlemen to the hotel. It's only just there.' She waved her hand to the right of the hospital. 'Nice and handy. And you can park the bus round the back of the hospital.'

Ron shook their hands. 'Thank you. You're very kind.'

'It should be us thanking you,' Brenda laughed. 'We've all been looking forward to you coming so much. There was a raid in Newcastle last night and some of the bombs got a bit close. It's unsettled some of the patients, so you've come at just the right time.' She glanced up at the windows of the bus and saw Rosie's and Melody's young faces. Her own face sobered and she leant a little closer to Ron to say, 'We do have some very sick boys here. I – I hope all your party are – prepared.'

'I'll have a little word before we come into the wards,' Ron said quietly. 'Thank you for warning me.'

Brenda chattered all the way as she led the girls in the party to the nurses' home, situated to one side of the huge hospital. 'You'll have to sleep in a dormitory. I hope you don't mind. One or two have moved out temporarily so you can all be together. I hope we've prepared enough beds . . .' She did a quick head count. 'Oh yes, that's right. Five of you. That's what we were told. What do you all do? Sing? Dance? What?'

'I'm the female vocalist,' Kathy volunteered. 'Rosie, Maureen and Joan are dancers and Melody here, well, she's a very talented actress.'

'And she does some wicked impersonations too,' Rosie put in, while Melody blushed prettily.

'Sounds like a great show,' Brenda said, leading them up two flights of stairs and flinging open the door to a long, airy room with beds and lockers down each side, each one separated by a green curtain. 'Here we are. I hope you're going to be comfortable. I'll see you settled in and unpacked and then I'll take you down to the canteen. They've got a meal waiting for you.'

'Thank goodness for that,' Maureen spoke for the first time. 'I'm starving.'

The men of the party joined them in the canteen.

'Now,' Ron began when everyone had finished. 'We're going to build a bit of a stage at the end of the room there, but not all the patients can get here. Some are too ill, so, as you may know, Matron has asked that we take one or two of the acts into the wards. Our two vocalists – ' he nodded towards Kathy and Roly – 'and Lionel, of course, but it's not really possible for the dancers to do their routines in the wards. Sorry, girls, and we won't be doing the sketches in the wards either, but we thought perhaps Melody could do some of her impressions. All right, love?'

Melody nodded, though, glancing at her, Kathy thought she looked a little apprehensive.

The show in the canteen went well. Only the 'walking wounded' were there, with arms in slings and legs in plaster. 'They mostly have GSWs,' Brenda explained.

'What's that when it's at home?' Kathy asked as she brushed her hair. It had grown longer over the last few weeks and fell in shining waves and curls to her shoulders.

Brenda laughed. 'Oh sorry. Gun shot wound, but they're not serious. One or two have broken legs or arms but mostly—' She stopped when she saw Rosie's face turn pale. Concerned, Brenda touched the girl's arm. 'Are you sure you're up to this? I mean, one or two in the wards are much worse than this.'

Rosie pressed her lips together. 'Oh, yes. If you can look after them and face all – all that you have to, then I can certainly do a bit of high-kicking for them. That's nothing compared to what you must have to do day after day. Besides, I'm a dancer. If I want, I can chicken out of going into the wards.' Bravely, she forced a smile to her lips. 'But I don't want to. I'd like to go and talk to one or two, if we're allowed.'

'So would I,' Kathy put in at once, before she could change her mind.

'*Allowed!* That'd be fantastic. Some of the lads don't get any visitors. Their families live too far away. They'd be so glad to have someone to talk to other than us for a change.'

'Right you are then. Now – ' Rosie turned her back towards Brenda – 'make yourself useful. Fasten me up, will you? Goldilocks here's too busy fussing with her tresses.'

As they trooped into one of the wards a little later, Kathy took a deep breath and steeled herself for what she might see. Was this what had happened to Tony? Had he died in a hospital just like this one, far from home? Or had he been shot down and killed immediately? She shuddered inwardly, but determined to keep the smile on her face and her voice pure and steady when she sang.

'Right,' Ron said. 'Roly, you open this little mini show and then we'll have Lionel telling a few jokes, and close your ears, girls, because with an all-male audience he tends to get a little risqué. After that we'll have Kathy bring a little decorum back to the proceedings and then finish off with Melody's impressions.'

Roly sang some rousing songs in his rich baritone voice and Lionel was a great hit with his saucy banter, but it was Kathy's sentimental ballads that brought a tear to one or two eyes. And it wasn't just among the patients. The nurses too, sitting or standing by the beds, reached for their handkerchiefs. But despite the tears, the cheering and clapping told her that she had touched their hearts.

'Your turn, Melody,' she said, as she left the ward and returned to the corridor just outside where the young girl was waiting. Melody got up and pushed open the door into the ward. Something in the girl's face made Kathy turn and watch her through the glass panel in the door. She saw her walk to the centre of the room without glancing to left or right. Melody reached the spot that Kathy had just left. Then she raised her head but no sound came. Kathy held her breath.

'What is it?' Ron said, coming up behind Kathy.

'I'm not sure,' she murmured, 'but I think . . . Oh Lord!' She pushed open the door and walked towards Melody. She spread her arms wide and began to sing the famous Gracie Fields song that Melody always used to open her spot. It was always instantly recognized and the girl did a magnificent impression of the much-loved singer. But not tonight. Poor Melody stood transfixed by the sight of the wounded soldiers.

Kathy reached her and put her arm around her shoulder, trying to give the girl the strength to go on. But the younger girl gave a little sob, put her hand over her mouth and turned and fled out of the ward, crashing the door back against the wall in her desperate bid to escape. Without faltering, Kathy sang on, swiftly going into the second of Gracie's songs that Melody

356

used. 'It's the Biggest Aspidistra in the World.' Though she couldn't emulate Gracie's distinctive voice, she managed to inject the singer's sense of humour, and soon she had the patients smiling and joining in the chorus. She ended with the song that Melody ended her act with, 'Sing As We Go'.

The clapping continued as Roly and Lionel joined her for a curtain call, even though this time there was no actual curtain.

'Is she all right?' Kathy muttered to Rosie as they came out of the double doors.

'Don't know. Ron's gone after her. He's asked us to stay and talk to the patients. You all right?'

'I'm fine,' Kathy said. 'Right. Let's do it.'

The four of them spent the next hour sitting by the bedside of those too ill or incapacitated to get to the canteen to see the full show.

'And this is Charlie,' Brenda said, trying hard to keep the laughter from her tone. The young man was lying face down. ' "Tail-end Charlie", we call him. He – er – caught it in the posterior, hence his prone position.'

'You can laugh,' he muttered morosely. 'How'd you like to be laid here like this all day long with nowt to look at but the bloody pillow.' Charlie twisted his head and looked up at Kathy. ''Scuse me not getting up.'

'That's quite all right,' Kathy said, sitting down near the head of the bed so that he could glance up and see her.

'My – you're pretty. Pity I couldn't see you when you were singing. You are the singer, I take it?'

'Yes.'

'Nice voice too. I say, there was a bit of a kerfuffle, wasn't there? I couldn't see. What went on?'

'It was nothing, really,' Kathy said airily. 'One of the young girls got a bit of stage fright, that's all.'

He looked up at her knowingly. 'Chap in the next bed told me the lass took one look at us lot and scarpered. Can't say I blame her.' He looked – and sounded – depressed.

Kathy bent down to him. 'Well, *we're* here, aren't we? You can't be that frightening.'

'How long are you staying?'

'I'm not sure. Three nights, I think. We do a full show in the canteen and then come to the wards.' She forbore to add: to entertain the bedridden.

'Right,' the young man said, with a new determination in his tone. 'Tomorrow I'll see if I can get on my feet and come to the show. I might have to stand at the back, but it'd be worth it to get a proper look at you.'

Kathy chatted a little longer, and as she was leaving, Brenda caught hold of her arm. 'What did Charlie say?'

'Oh, nothing much really. He didn't seem to want to talk about his family.'

Brenda's mouth tightened. 'Not surprising, poor love.'

Kathy was intrigued. 'Why?'

'No one's been to visit him, yet they only live in York. They could get here if they wanted. Rumour has it he's got a fiancée, but she's sent him a "Dear John" letter. You see,' Brenda bit her lip, 'we try to jolly him along and tease him about getting hit in his behind, but it's a bit more serious that that. He got it in the you-know-what's an' all, and I don't think he's much future as a husband, if you know what I mean.'

'Oh,' Kathy breathed. 'Poor chap. Oh, how awful. And how cruel of his fiancée.' Silently, she thought, I'd've cared for Tony for the rest of our lives no matter what injuries he had, if only he were still alive. Aloud she asked, 'But what about the rest of his family? His parents?'

'Seems they can't cope with the news either. Can't bring themselves to come and see him.'

Kathy stared at her. She was quite lost for words now. Whatever had happened to their son, she couldn't imagine any parents not wanting to rush to his bedside.

'There's some folk don't deserve to have children,' she muttered bitterly. 'While others . . .'

'You can say that again,' Brenda said with feeling.

Thirty-Five

On their last night at the hospital, after the show, Ron came to the small room near the canteen allocated to the girls as a dressing room. Kathy was alone there and one look at his face told her that something was dreadfully wrong.

'Oh no, Ron. Don't tell me it's Martin?'

Ron shook his head, seeming unable to speak. He pulled up a chair, sat down and took her hand in his.

'What is it? What's wrong,' Kathy demanded, her heart thumping, her mouth dry.

'My dear, there – there's been a bomb fall in our street.'

Kathy let out a squeak of alarm and her free hand flew to her mouth. Her eyes were wide with fear as she asked, 'Is – is anyone hurt or – or . . .' She couldn't bring herself to voice her greatest fear. Aunt Jemima. Was she badly hurt or killed? And Ron's wife? What of her?

'Mabel's safe. It was her rang here to the hospital. She always knows where we are,' Ron said quietly. 'She was out at the time, thank God, but . . .' he chewed at his lip for a brief moment before adding, 'But Miss Robinson's house took a direct hit and – and no one can find her. They're still digging but . . .'

'But there's not much hope?' Kathy said flatly.

Ron shook his head. 'They found her cat. He was

on top of the washhouse roof, howling pitifully. Mabel tried to take him home with her – at least, to where she's staying with some friends. Our house was badly damaged too, but old Taffy keeps escaping and going back home. He just sits on top of the rubble, she says, miaowing.'

'When did it happen?'

'Yesterday, some time. I don't know exactly when.'

'Friday,' Kathy mused. 'Well, in the daytime, she should have been at work and if it was evening, Friday's one of her WVS nights. Are they absolutely sure she's not gone to a friend's, maybe even to her brother's in the country?'

Ron was shaking his head sadly. 'Mabel's been asking all round but no one seems to know anything. And besides,' he added, 'she wouldn't have left old Taffy, would she?'

The hope in Kathy's eyes died. 'No,' she whispered hoarsely. 'No, she wouldn't. But they are still digging? They're still looking?'

Ron nodded but there was no hope left in his eyes. 'I'm so sorry, love.' There was a pause before he asked, 'Do you want to go home? We can manage for a night or two, though it won't be the same without you,' he added hurriedly. 'The audiences love your songs.'

'I – I don't know. I mean, do her family know yet?'

Ron lifted his shoulders. 'I've no idea. I expect the authorities will inform them as soon as – as soon as they have some definite news.'

'When they've found her – her body, you mean?'

He nodded.

'Poor Ted and Betty. And Morry – oh, poor Morry,' she added, though she didn't confide in Ron just why her heart went out to Morry.

'Fond of his aunt, was he?' Ron asked kindly, but Kathy could only nod, her throat too full of tears to speak.

'I didn't tell you before the show. There's nothing you could have done. You do understand, Kathy, don't you?'

Briefly, a sarcastic retort sprang to her lips, castigating him for having kept the news to himself until the show was over. Oh, nothing must get in the way of 'the show going on', must it? she almost said. Instead, she bit back the words. She had seen for herself how their concert party helped others, how it brought a little brightness into the dull lives of those trapped in the daily drudgery of wartime Britain. It even had the power to keep people in their seats all the way through an air raid.

'You were right,' she said huskily. 'I wouldn't have been able to go on if I'd just had that news and it's what Aunt Jemima —' she smiled fondly at the thought of her — 'would have expected me to do.'

Kathy spent a restless night, and both she and Rosie got up the following morning tired and bleary-eyed. They breakfasted, packed their belongings and stripped the beds they had occupied in the nurses' dormitory.

'Are you gong home?' Rosie asked as, lugging their suitcases, they walked towards the bus parked at the rear of the hospital's main building.

'Yes, I'm going to ask Ron if I can catch a train to Lincoln this morning instead of coming to Leeds with you all. He did say he didn't mind.'

They reached the bus and stood with some of the party until everyone else arrived.

'I can't imagine life without Miss Robinson,' Kathy murmured. 'My home was with her and now it's gone.'

'Have you lost much? Possessions, I mean?'

Kathy shrugged. 'Not really. I didn't have much.' She didn't care about material things, but sadly she realized that the people she cared about most in the world, apart from her mother, were being taken away from her one by one. Even though she was surrounded by her friends in the concert party, Kathy still felt very lonely.

Ron and the rest of the party arrived. 'Everyone here? Right then, we'd better be off . . .'

'I say, wait a minute. Wait!'

They all turned to see Brenda running across the car park towards them. 'Anybody here by the name of "Burton"?'

'Y – yes. Me,' Kathy stammered.

'Phone call for you,' the nurse panted. 'Long distance. In the matron's office. Come on, I'll take you.'

Kathy's heart leapt in her chest. She dropped her suitcase and ran after Brenda. Inside the matron's office, she picked up the receiver with shaking hands. Ron had followed her and was standing uncertainly just inside the doorway.

'H – hello?'

'Kathy, my dear, it's me. I though you might be worried—'

Tears flooded down Kathy's face as she spluttered, 'Oh Aunt Jemima, Aunt Jemima – you're safe. Thank God!' She turned to see Ron beaming from ear to ear. 'She's safe,' Kathy cried. 'She's safe.' Ron smiled and lifted his hand in acknowledgement, then disappeared to tell the others of Kathy's good news.

'Where were you? Are you hurt? Where are you now?'

'I was in the cupboard under the stairs. I'd just got home when the raid started and I could already hear bombs dropping. It was too late to go out again to the nearest communal shelter, so I dived for the cupboard.'

'How long were you there?' Kathy shouted into the instrument. The line was crackling.

'Oh, hours, all night and half the next day,' Jemima said cheerfully. 'And it's only thanks to dear old Taffy that they found me. I could hear him miaowing and one of the rescue party told me afterwards that it was because of him they'd kept digging. They were sure he knew I was under there.'

'Are you all right?'

'A few cuts and bruises, but we're both safe and we're at Edward and Betty's now. I couldn't ring you before, dear girl. I couldn't find out where Mabel was to get the telephone number from her. Are you there tonight?'

'No, we're about to leave to go to Leeds, but I was coming straight home from there.'

'Shouldn't bother, dear. There's no home to come to at the moment. Of course you can come here if you like, but there's no need to if you want to stay with the party.'

'Are you sure you're all right?'

'We're fine. Truly. You carry on. You're all doing such a fine job.'

'All right, I will then, if you're really sure?'

'I am,' were Jemima's final words as the line went dead. Kathy replaced the receiver and sighed with relief. Ron had come back and was standing just outside the office, waiting for her. 'Well, are you going or staying now she's safe?'

'I'm staying,' Kathy told him with a grin.

'That's the ticket.'

There was one piece of news that caught up with Kathy about a week later. They were due to stay in Leeds for a full week. Mabel had given Jemima the address of the theatre so that she could write to Kathy and re-assure her that both she and Taffy were now safely at Sandy Furze Farm and that she was not to worry.

> *There is one piece of sad news, which I ought to tell you though, my dear. In the same air raid in which you and I lost our home, poor Stella was killed. Although she lived in a village outside the city one or two stray bombs dropped there and their house took a direct hit. Her parents were killed too . . .*

Kathy sat on the edge of the bed staring into space, remembering the young girl with whom she'd worked for a few months.

'We never did get that trip to the cinema I promised you. And you were so looking forward to it,' Kathy whispered aloud to the empty room. 'I'm so sorry, Stella.'

At the end of that week, Ron called the members of the company together.

'There's been a slight change of plan. The canteen of the factory where we were due to play next has been bombed, and as the theatre there is closed for the duration, we've been asked to go back to Saltershaven. We're going to play for the RAF boys billeted in the town. We'll be there a week.' He looked around and caught Kathy's gaze. 'You'll be singing in the cinema where you were usherette, lass. That be all right?'

Kathy felt her heart leap. It'd be more than 'all right'. At last, she might have a chance to see James. She'd certainly try. She could hardly wait.

As the bus drew into the town, it was like coming home, except that her memories of the place were very mixed. The dreadful nightmare of her time at Willow House, the heartbreak of having her baby snatched from her, but then the joy of holding him in her arms at last. And the kindness of the woman who was now her son's mother. She would never forget that. But now she was back here, she was apprehensive. Seeds of doubt had been sown in her mind. Perhaps Mrs Wainwright would not be so welcoming this time. She'd had time to think about things and perhaps she'd come to the conclusion that it would be better if Kathy had nothing to do with the boy. In the two years since she had last seen her son, there had only ever been that one letter from his adoptive mother. Kathy had written regularly, but no further word had come back to her. Kathy had made all sorts of excuses in her mind. Perhaps the woman's letters had been lost in the post or had arrived after the concert party had moved on. Perhaps she hadn't managed to get any photographs taken. Perhaps ... Kathy dreamed up all sorts of reasons to comfort herself, but now she was back here in the town, she was scared about what she would find.

There was no opportunity for her to go to Sea Bank Road that first day. The party had to settle in at their digs and then meet in the cinema for a rehearsal before the concert started at seven thirty.

But the following morning, Kathy was up early, unable to sleep for excitement. Today she might be able to see her darling boy. With gentle fingers she wrapped the toy rabbit she had knitted so lovingly during her idle hours sitting in dressing rooms and digs.

'Who's that for?' Rosie had asked.

Kathy had felt a blush creeping up her neck as she was forced to lie. 'It's – it's for a friend of mine.' But was it really a lie? she'd asked herself later, because James was Mrs Wainwright's child now. Not hers. The thought broke her heart all over again.

But today she might see him. For a few brief moments perhaps she could hold him and play with him and pretend he was still hers. Clutching the knitted toy, she set off on the long walk to the Wainwrights' house.

There was a cold wind off the sea as she walked the long road to the outskirts of the town, turned left past the golf course and then turned right into the road that ran parallel with the sandhills. She glanced briefly to her right at the houses, but her gaze came back time and again to the house standing at the end of the row. As she drew nearer, she frowned. There was something not quite right about the house. It looked different. As she walked closer, her hands felt clammy and her legs were weak. As last she stood in the gateway, staring at the house in horror. Half of it was gone, reduced to a mound of rubble and leaving rooms, still with furniture in, gaping open to the elements. Wallpaper was half torn from the walls and fluttered pathetically in the breeze.

For a moment Kathy thought she would faint as she staggered and leant against the rough brickwork of the gatepost. Wildly, she looked about her, but the place seemed deserted. The shattered house was empty and forlorn, the once neat garden neglected and overgrown. James, her baby boy! What had happened to him? She glanced at the neighbouring house and saw a movement through the window.

Galvanized into action, Kathy ran up the drive, her heart beating erratically. She banged on the side door, shouting, 'Please, please help me. What happened?'

The door opened and a woman stood there, frowning slightly at the noise. 'Whatever's the matter?'

'I'm sorry,' Kathy panted. 'But please tell me, what happened to the people next door? To Mrs Wainwright and – and her little boy?'

'Who are you?'

'I – I'm a friend. Of Mrs Wainwright. I've been away. On tour. With a concert party. I didn't know . . . Please . . .' She was begging now.

'Then I'm very sorry to have to tell you that your friend was killed.'

Kathy gasped and felt the colour drain from her face. Her knees began to buckle and she clutched at the doorframe. 'Oh no.'

'You'd better come inside and sit down a moment,' the woman said briskly. 'I don't want you fainting on my doorstep.'

She took Kathy's arm and almost pulled her into her kitchen and pushed her into a chair near the table. 'I'll make you a cup of tea.'

'The child?' Kathy burst out. 'What about James?'

'He wasn't hurt, thank God. He was in the nursery upstairs on the far side of the house, but Beryl was downstairs in the kitchen on this side and, as you can see, she didn't have a chance.'

Now Kathy felt faint with relief, but she took a few

short panting breaths and her head stopped spinning. 'Where is James now?'

'I've no idea. With Mr Wainwright, I suppose.' She smiled. 'Funny, I always called him that. I knew Beryl well, but not him so much. He was always "Mr Wainwright".'

'Do you know where he is? I – I'd like to see him.' Whether the 'him' Kathy referred to was Mr Wainwright or James, the neighbour was not to know.

'I've no idea where they're living now, but I expect they're still in the town somewhere. Mr Wainwright wouldn't leave his job. Very important work he does.' She smiled again. 'At least he seems to think so. But you'll know all about that.'

Kathy bit her lip. If she wasn't careful, she was going to let slip that she didn't know the Wainwrights as well as she was trying to make out. Surely a friend of the family would know what he did. But Kathy had no idea. Mr Wainwright had hardly been mentioned in her conversations with his wife. She chewed her lip and asked. 'Was there other damage in the town?'

The woman shrugged. 'Not much. They say it was a lone raider who offloaded his bombs as he flew back out to sea. The swimming pool and several houses in the town were damaged. There were one or two more killed besides Beryl. Poor Beryl,' she mused. 'I've never seen her so happy as she's been these last two years since she got that baby. And poor little mite. What'll happen to him now, I don't know.'

Kathy's heart missed a beat. She had to take a risk. She had to push the woman to tell her more. 'What do you mean? Won't – won't Mr Wainwright look after him?'

The woman glanced at her, a question on her face, but Kathy smiled and, mentally crossing her fingers, said, 'I'm a bit like you, I didn't know him awfully well. It was Beryl I was friendly with.'

The neighbour nodded, 'Mm, yes, well, I know what you mean. All I know is that his job was everything to him. He thought this town would fall to pieces if he didn't put in an appearance in his office at the Town Hall all day and every day.' Her tone was a little scathing. 'That's why I say "poor little mite". Goodness knows who he's been palmed off with to look after him.'

Kathy's heart leapt. The Town Hall, the woman had said. Mr Wainwright was 'something important' in the town and he worked at the local council offices.

The woman set the cup of tea down in front of her and Kathy sipped it gratefully. She was feeling a little better now. James was obviously safe, though where he was she would have to find out. But now she knew where Mr Wainwright worked, she could see him there. Make an appointment, do it properly. With a restraint she didn't know she possessed, she continued to sit in the kitchen and listen to the woman relating the details of the bombing. 'We were lucky not to get more damage than we did. All our windows were broken and part of the roof damaged. We were both out at the time, but when we got back, oh the mess. There was soot everywhere that had been blown down the chimneys . . .' On and on the woman went and Kathy sat there, hiding her impatience to be gone. At last she felt she could stand up, thank the woman for her kindness and the tea and make her escape.

She walked back down the drive, stood a moment longer to look at the Wainwrights' home and then turned and walked back towards the town. There was nothing more she could do today, and tomorrow was Sunday, but on Monday morning she'd be outside the Town Hall waiting for the offices to open.

Thirty-Six

'Do you have an appointment?' the severe-looking receptionist asked. 'Mr Wainwright can't just see anyone who turns up unannounced, you know. The town clerk is a very busy man. What is it about?'

'It's a personal matter.'

'Personal? To whom? You – or Mr Wainwright?'

Kathy was about to say 'both', but then realized the implication. She took a deep breath and said, 'He might not know me, but I was friendly with his wife. And I just . . .'

'Can't you write him a letter of condolence?' the woman snapped. 'I'm sure he doesn't want to keep being reminded. Especially when he's at work.'

'I realize that, but – but I just wanted to ask him about his son. How he's coping and – and if I could be of any help.'

The receptionist's eyes narrowed as she regarded Kathy with a steady, calculating stare. 'Mm,' she said noncommittally, but then seemed to come to a decision. She picked up the receiver of a telephone on her right and dialled a number.

'I have a woman here in reception asking if she might see Mr Wainwright. She says she was a friend of his wife's and that she's anxious to see if she can be of any help with the baby. You know what the situation is, I just wondered . . .' There was a pause while Kathy felt herself scrutinized again. The woman lowered her voice to say into the mouthpiece, 'Well, she looks all right. Very presentable, in fact. I mean, we both know he's looking for . . .' She broke off and then added, 'Oh, has he? I didn't know that. Anyway, do you think he'd see her? She's brought a little gift for the child.' There was quite a long pause until she said, 'Right,' and then replaced the receiver.

'Mr Wainwright's secretary will be down in a moment.'

Kathy beamed at her. 'Thank you. Thank you very much.'

Kathy sat on the edge of a chair to wait. People walked through the reception area, their feet clattering on the tiled floor. After what seemed an eternity but was in fact only a few minutes, a young woman appeared out of one of the doors. She came towards Kathy. 'Miss – er . . .'

Kathy jumped up. 'Miss Burton.'

'If you'd come this way, Miss Burton, Mr Wainwright will spare you a moment. It won't be long, though, I'm afraid. He has a meeting at ten.'

The secretary led the way up polished oak stairs, along corridors, until they came to her office. She bade Kathy sit down a moment and then went to another door, which led into an inner office. The layout reminded Kathy poignantly of Tony's office, with Miss Foster sitting guard in the outer office, deftly fielding all unwelcome calls upon her boss's valuable time. After a moment the young woman returned and, with a smile, ushered Kathy into the office of the town clerk of Saltershaven.

The man who rose from behind his desk was older than Kathy had anticipated. He was thin, but not very tall. The word 'dapper' sprang to her mind as she shook the hand he held out to her. He was immaculately dressed in a pinstriped suit with a white shirt and sober tie. His hair was thinning and his eyes, behind the round, steel-framed spectacles, were as cold as the grey waters of the North Sea.

'I'm so sorry to hear about your wife. She was a lovely lady.'

'Thank you. Please sit down. What can I do for you?'

'I just – I just wanted to give you this for – for James.' She held out the carefully wrapped parcel. 'It's nothing much, but I made it myself and I – I so wanted him to have it.'

'That's very kind of you.' He placed the gift meticulously on the corner of his desk. 'I'll certainly make sure he receives it.'

'How – I mean – where is he? Is he with relatives?'

Mr Wainwright shook his head. 'No. Sadly, my wife and I have few relatives and certainly no one living close.'

'Then – then you have a nanny for him?'

'No. He's gone back to Willow House!' Kathy gasped, but he didn't seem to notice and went on. 'I'm putting him back up for adoption. I really can't cope with a young baby.'

'Adopted? You're going to have him adopted?' Kathy was desperate. At least at the moment she knew where her baby was. If he were to be adopted again, then she would certainly lose touch with him. She couldn't bear it. 'But – but couldn't you employ a nanny to look after him? A live-in nanny?'

'I suppose I could. But it was my wife who wanted a child. Not me. I only agreed to it to keep her happy.

And I'd need a bigger place. I'm living in a one-roomed flat at the moment. It's totally unsuitable for a young child and my house is uninhabitable.'

'I know. I've seen it.'

He spread his hands helplessly, though to Kathy he was far from being a helpless man. 'Then you see my position.'

'But you'll get another house?'

He nodded, 'Oh yes. I'm in negotiations now with one of the estate agents in the town, but it might be a while . . .'

'But you haven't actually signed any adoption papers yet?'

'Well, no, I haven't, but . . .'

'Oh please don't, Mr Wainwright. It's not what your wife – what Beryl – would have wanted, is it?'

It seemed as if, at last, she had touched a nerve. His face crumpled briefly and he passed his hand across his brow. But in moments he was in control of himself again. He doesn't love James, Kathy thought shrewdly, but he did love his wife. He leant his arms on his desk and sighed heavily. 'I've felt guilty enough about my decision, but I didn't know what else to do.' He stared at her. 'Just who are you and how did you know my wife?'

Kathy licked her lips. She could tell the truth, but not all of it. 'I was walking one day along the road where you live and Beryl was out pushing the pram. We got talking and then I met her again and she invited me in to see the baby. We – we became friends.' Kathy made it sound as if the friendship had gone on over a period of time and was deeper than it had been. 'She – she didn't mention me to you?' Kathy held her breath, fearing that if his wife had told him that she'd met the girl who was James's natural mother, Mr Wainwright might very well now put two and two together very quickly and realize exactly who she was.

'I don't think so,' he murmured, wrinkling his brow. 'What's your name again?'

'Burton. Kathy Burton.' Now Kathy felt a little easier. She couldn't remember ever giving Beryl Wainwright her name.

'No – no, I don't recall hearing her mention you, but then,' he gave a wry, rather sad smile, 'I'm afraid I was guilty of not always listening to my wife's chatter about domestic affairs.' He looked up and seemed to be appraising her again.

'You live here? In Saltershaven?'

Kathy avoided answering directly. 'I've been away touring with a concert party. We're affiliated to ENSA and we entertain servicemen and women, factory workers, hospitals.'

'Really?' Mr Wainwright's eyebrows rose fractionally. 'That sounds very commendable. And what do you do?'

'I'm a singer. A soloist.'

There was another pause before Kathy asked tentatively, 'Won't you consider employing a nanny? He's your son. Surely . . . ?'

He smiled a little wearily and said flippantly, 'Are you applying for the job?'

Kathy gasped in surprise. It was more than she'd dared to hope for. 'Yes. I am. I'd like nothing better than to care for Beryl's baby as she would have wanted.' She felt no guilt in ruthlessly exploiting the man's one and only weakness, if it meant she could be close to James.

He nodded slowly. 'I'll think about it. I promise I will give it serious thought. You're right about one thing. Beryl wouldn't have wanted me to give him back for adoption. She loved the little chap.' It was almost an admission that he did not. 'I presume you're still with the concert party at the moment?'

Kathy nodded. 'Yes, we're here for the whole week. At the theatre. But I could stay. I needn't go with them. The cast aren't under any kind of contract. It's all voluntary.'

'I see.' He was thoughtful again. 'Of course, I'll have to find out what the position is regarding your eligibility for call-up. At the moment, I presume you're classed as doing valuable war work. I'm not sure that becoming a nanny for one child would be viewed as such. However, I'll make some enquiries. Come and see me at the end of the week some time on Friday. Check with my secretary for a suitable time and I promise I will have an answer for you by then.'

He rose and Kathy knew herself dismissed. She shook hands with him again and left his office, not quite sure if her trembling legs were going to carry her safely down the stairs and outside the building before she could give way to the tears that welled up inside her.

She was close, oh so close, to being with her baby. To holding him, feeding him, dressing him, loving him – to being able to spend every moment with him. But then common sense intervened and she tried to calm herself and not get too hopeful. After all, if Mr Wainwright felt very little affection for the child, why would he want to keep him at all? At the moment, he felt an obligation to the wife he had loved and lost. It would have been her wish, but as time went on and his grief lessened he might view bringing up a child that wasn't even his as a burden he could well do without. Kathy decided she would tell no one within the company until she knew Mr Wainwright's decision.

Thirty-Seven

How she got through the rest of the week, Kathy didn't know. The time seemed to crawl and she passed the days in a trance. She could sleep, yet she didn't feel tired. She was buoyed up with hope and excitement. She was bursting to confide in someone, yet she dared not. She felt that if she voiced her hopes aloud, her dream would be shattered.

Friday came at last and she was once more waiting outside the council offices for her early appointment with Mr Wainwright. The moment she stepped into his office she knew the news was good. He rose from behind his desk and came towards her with his hand outstretched to shake hers.

'Good morning, Miss Burton,' he smiled. 'Please sit down. Now, let me tell you straight away that I have decided to give you a month's trial in the post as James's nanny. In fact, to give us both a month's trial.' He sat down at his desk again, rested his arms on its surface and linked his fingers together. 'I went to Willow House to see James. He's being well cared for, but it's a grim place. I – Beryl wouldn't have been happy to think he was back there.' He paused, remembering his wife. 'Anyway, we'll give it a try, but please understand, I am not making a long-term commitment at this stage. I – I really don't know if I can. And like I said before, you may be called up. But for the moment,' he went on briskly, adopting his business-like manner once again, 'let's discuss practicalities. I have agreed a price on a house, and though they're hurrying things up as much as possible, I can't move in for two weeks. You won't be expected to do very much in the way of heavy housework, though perhaps you wouldn't mind cooking the occasional meal? I have a daily help, Mrs Talbot, where I'm living now. She's good in her way,' he added wryly, 'but she is burdened with an idle, good-for-nothing husband who resorts to illness as a means of having a few days off work. But domestics aren't easy to come by these days so I shall be keeping her on when I move.'

'Of course I wouldn't mind helping out.'

'Good. Now, in the meantime, perhaps you could give me the name of two people. I like to take up references; it's the way we do things here. But I'm sure it's only a formality, so, if you'd like to make arrangements with the concert party to leave in two weeks' time and return here then?'

Kathy nodded, her eyes shining. No matter what the future held, at least she would be able to spend a month with her little boy. It wasn't much, but it was better than nothing.

'I'll be here,' she promised.

'A nanny? Whatever do you want to become a nanny for? Have you any experience with children?' Ron was aghast. 'Of course I'll give him a reference . . .' Ron was one of the two names she had given Mr Wainwright, the other being Mr James Hammond, which had seemed to impress him. 'But I can't understand why you want to leave us to look after someone else's child. My dear,' he took her hand and patted it gently. 'It won't be a substitute for your own, you know. I know you had a dreadful time but one day you will meet a nice young man and . . .'

Tears filled Kathy's eyes as she shook her head. 'You don't understand. This is something I have to do. Something I want to do – more than anything else in the world.'

Ron stared at her. 'Why, Kathy?' he said softly. 'Just tell me why? We're going to miss you so much in the party and you bring such pleasure to the audience. A pretty girl – a very pretty girl – with a beautiful voice and you want to bury yourself away here to devote yourself to just one child. Oh my dear, don't cry. I'm sorry. It's none of my business, but I just can't understand it. I thought you enjoyed being with us. You get on with all the other members in the party, don't you?'

Kathy nodded wordlessly.

'Then . . .'

Kathy sighed. This man had been so good to her, so kind. He deserved to hear the truth, even if it cost her a good reference. But she knew instinctively that she could trust him. He was a devout man who would not betray her confidence.

'If – if I tell you the real reason, will you promise me that it'll remain just between us?'

'Of course, but . . .'

'Then please sit down, Ron. This is going to take a while . . .'

She told him it all, starting right back at the beginning with her life of drudgery at home and how she had longed to escape. 'If my father hadn't hit me that day, I'd probably still have been there.' She smiled wryly. 'Dreaming of the bright lights, no doubt, but still there milking cows at the crack of dawn.'

Ron smiled. 'I always wondered how come you were so good at getting up in a morning to catch the early train. I almost have to drag some of the others out of bed, but there you were, bright and early and with a smile on your face . . .'

Her story went on. How the Robinson family had taken her in and how Jemima had found her a job.

'That was how I met Tony. And then – and then . . .'

'And then the wedding that didn't happen.'

She nodded and went on huskily, 'But there's something you don't know. After – after Tony had gone away, I – I found I was pregnant.'

'Oh, my dear girl.' There was no censure in his tone, just sympathy and understanding.

'I came here to a home for unmarried mothers and babies. I – I wanted to keep him but I was tricked into signing adoption papers and they took him away from me. They never even let me see him or hold him . . .'

She went on with the whole story, right up until the previous day when Mr Wainwright had offered her the post of nanny.

'It's my little boy. James is my little boy, Ron. Do you see now why? I just have to grab this chance to be with him. Even if it's only for a little while.'

'Of course I do. But, Kathy love, are you sure you're not just building up further heartache for yourself? What if, at the end of the month, this Mr Wainwright decides he doesn't want to keep the child? What if he decides to put him up for adoption again?'

'I don't know,' Kathy said bleakly. But then she lifted her chin with a new determination. 'But I'm not

going to live on "what ifs". I'm just going to take each
day as it comes.' She paused and then, putting her head
on one side, added wistfully, 'I don't suppose you feel
like giving me a reference now, do you?'

'My dear, dear girl,' Ron said, surprising her by
pulling her to him and hugging her. Though a kindly
man, he was not given to displays of affection. 'Of
course I'll give you a reference. A glowing one. What
better "nanny" could that little boy have than his own
mother?' He pulled away and looked into her eyes.
'And you need have no worries. Your secret is safe
with me.'

'Thank you, Ron,' she said simply.

The two weeks passed surprisingly quickly. There were
four engagements for the party. They played in and
around Nottingham: in a factory canteen, the NAAFI
of an RAF station near Newark and two hospitals.
This time, with help and encouragement, Melody took
part in the show in a hall attached to the hospital, but
she did not visit the wards. After Kathy's final performance, Ron organized a leaving party for her. She was
touched by the gifts she was given. Perfume, handkerchiefs, a pretty scarf, and from the comedian in the
party, a pair of earplugs. 'That's for when he cries too
much.'

They all laughed and Rosie pressed her gift into
Kathy's hands. 'That's from me and Martin. I know
he's not here, but he'd want to join in. I know he
would.' It was a children's picture book. 'I don't know
whether I envy you or think you're mad.' She laughed.
'I want children of my own one day, but I don't think
I could ever look after someone else's.'

Kathy smiled and deliberately avoided meeting Ron's glance. 'Thank you, Rosie. It's lovely,' was all she said, neatly avoiding commenting on the girl's statement.

And then she was on her way to Saltershaven. Soon now, she would see her little boy again.

'Can you go to Willow House to pick him up?'

Kathy's heart missed a beat. How could she? They might recognize her!

'I – yes, of course,' she said boldly. 'But – but do you think they'd hand him over to me? I mean – I could be anybody.'

'Mm. I hadn't thought of that. I'll write a note. Better still, I'll get my secretary to type it on headed paper. That way they'll know it comes from me.'

'Wouldn't you – like to fetch him yourself?' Kathy ventured, trying to make it sound as if it was an occasion he ought not to miss.

'I really haven't the time,' he said and pressed the buzzer on his desk that brought his secretary into the room.

He dictated the letter he wanted written and then scribbled on a piece of paper the address of the house he had just moved into and which was to be Kathy's new home. 'Get yourself settled in first,' he said. 'Make sure you have everything you need for the boy and then you can fetch him tomorrow.'

Kathy took the piece of paper from him and waited in the outer office until his secretary had typed the letter. As she left the Town Hall, she was still wondering how on earth she was going to take James out of Willow House without being recognized. And if she

384

was, she was sure the matron would lose no time in telling Mr Wainwright just who his new nanny was.

The new house Mr Wainwright had bought was situated on a road at the opposite end of the town to the one where he'd lived with his wife. It was a grand house, set high on a ridge of land that ran parallel with the shore and overlooking the sea. She was surprised that he had chosen one that had such a similar setting and view to his old home. But perhaps, she thought, he wanted to live with his memories and wanted to be reminded of his wife. She let herself in with the key he had given her and wandered through all the rooms until she came to the one that had been decorated and furnished as a nursery. The workmen he had employed must have worked very hard to have everything completed so quickly. She crossed the room to the connecting door and found herself in the neighbouring room, which was obviously to be hers. Fresh flowers had been placed on the dressing table, by the daily help, Kathy presumed. She couldn't imagine the career-minded Mr Wainwright taking the time to get the flowers himself, much less arrange them in a vase and place them in her room.

Mrs Talbot, the "daily", turned out to be a jolly round little woman who lived two streets away. She arrived later in the afternoon to prepare Mr Wainwright's dinner and to see that the new nanny had everything she needed.

'Ee's told me you're going to fetch the little one.'

'Yes, I'm going tomorrow morning.'

'Like me to go with you?'

Kathy hesitated. She had formed a plan. A daring one, certainly, but she hoped that with her new-found acting skills, learned while taking part in the numerous sketches which were part of the concert party's show, she could pull it off. But Mrs Talbot would undoubtedly think it strange and would more than likely mention it to her employer.

Kathy smiled widely at her. 'That's awfully kind of you, but if you wouldn't mind being here and having something ready for him to eat.'

'Oh aye, that's mebbe for the best. Let's see, how old is he now?'

Kathy knew to the minute, but she pretended uncertainty. 'Er – I think he's about two years old.'

'I'll make him one of my special egg custards. Little ones love my egg custards.' She winked and tapped the side of her nose. 'And made with fresh eggs, let me tell you. But don't ask me how, 'cos I aren't telling.'

Kathy laughed. It seemed they both had secrets they were not about to share, though she liked Mrs Talbot. In some ways she reminded Kathy a little of Auntie Betty.

'The mester said you was to take a taxi tomorrow morning. It's a long way out to Willow House. D'you know where it is?'

'I think so,' Kathy made the pretence of sounding doubtful.

'Well, the taxi driver'll know anyway.'

But Kathy had already made up her mind that she would walk there, because first there was somewhere else she had to call.

Thirty-Eight

'Well, well, fancy seeing you here again. Come for your old job back, Kathy? We've got a vacancy for an usherette. You can start tomorrow and I don't need references.'

'Thank you, Mr Johnson, but I have a job.'

'Shame. You were a good lass. I haven't had one since who's prepared to do all the jobs you didn't mind turning your hand to, I must say. Anyway, what can I do for you?'

'I've come to ask a favour. I – I've been invited to a fancy dress party and – and I wondered if I could borrow some props.'

Larry Johnson waved his arm in the direction of the room where the props were kept. 'Help yourself. Mrs Jervis isn't here at the moment, but I'll square it with her. Mind you let us have whatever you borrow back though. Costumes are hard to come by.' He adopted a comic sarcasm. 'There is a war on, you know.'

'I had noticed.' Kathy giggled.

Kathy found what she wanted and, alone in the dressing room she had shared with Rosie, donned the black wig and the spectacles. The false hair hung to her shoulders, and she covered it with a wide-brimmed felt hat, which she pulled down low over her forehead. She decided to wear her own clothes, but now she was wearing a smart, tailored suit and looked nothing like the waif in a cheap cotton dress who had presented herself at the door of Willow House seeking admittance. She found some gloves that almost matched her suit and regarded herself in the mirror. Well, she looked the part. Could she now play it?

She picked up her handbag and the copious shopping bag she had brought with her. She walked out of the dressing room and along the passageway towards the stage door that led to the street behind the theatre. Luckily, there was no one about backstage and, once in the street, she let out her breath and began to walk briskly away.

She took a taxi from the town out to Willow House. She didn't want any delay in her getaway. At the gate of the home, she hesitated for just a moment to look up at the forbidding building. The next few minutes would certainly decide her fate one way or the other. Taking a deep breath, she walked up the driveway and knocked boldly on the door. It was answered a few moments later by a heavily pregnant girl. Kathy's heart went out to her and she longed to smile warmly and talk to her, but she had a part to play. The most important part she would ever undertake in her life.

Feeling like a traitor to her own kind, Kathy looked the young girl up and down disdainfully and saw her cringe. Her courage almost failed her, but instead she took a deep breath and said in an affected, upper-class tone. 'I have come to collect the child, James Wainwright. Whom do I have to see?'

'Come in, please, ma'am,' the girl said and pulled open the door. 'If you'd just wait here in the hall, I'll tell Matron.'

The girl walked away with that peculiar rolling gait

reserved for the heavily pregnant towards the door of the matron's office.

Kathy remained in the shadowy hall, praying that she would not be invited into the woman's office, where she knew she would be obliged to stand facing the bright light from the windows.

But the matron came bustling out of her room. 'Oh good morning, Miss – er . . .'

Kathy felt panic twist her stomach. She hadn't thought of a false name. But then, she thought, I have to use my own. Mr Wainwright will have used my real name in the letter. Oh, how foolish she'd been. She was about to be discovered and all because she hadn't thought soon enough to use a pseudonym.

Deciding that the best form of defence was attack, she said in imperious tones that implied that giving her name to such a woman was beneath her, 'You have the boy ready?'

'Oh, yes.' The matron seemed quite flustered and so unlike the woman Kathy remembered that she almost laughed out loud. 'Mr Wainwright telephoned this morning. Everything is in order.'

Kathy made no attempt to hand over her letter of authority from Mr Wainwright and, silently, she blessed him for having taken the trouble to contact the home in person.

'You, girl—' The matron now spoke in the manner that Kathy remembered so well. She shuddered inwardly, but managed to keep her authoritative composure. 'Go and bring the child here. Mind you bring his belongings with him. Get one of the other girls to help you.'

The girl hurried away as fast as her bulk would allow her.

'Would you care to wait in my room?' the matron asked with an obsequious smile once more.

'No, thank you,' Kathy replied stiffly, avoiding meeting the woman's eyes. She gazed at the staircase, willing the girls to hurry, but she knew the poor creatures would be unable to do so in their advanced condition.

'You're to be Mr Wainwright's nanny, I understand?'

'That is correct.'

'He's a lovely boy. You do know he's adopted?'

'So I understand.'

'He came from here. His natural mother was a lovely girl, but you know how it is. The best of them can make mistakes.'

Kathy almost laughed aloud to hear the kindly understanding in the matron's tone, when she knew how very different the reality was. Oh, how she'd love to wipe that false smile off her face.

'Such a tragedy, Mrs Wainwright being killed like that, but I'm so pleased to hear that Mr Wainwright has decided to keep the child. Ah, here they come . . .'

Kathy held her breath as two girls now descended the stairs, the first one leading the little boy by the hand as he carefully negotiated each step, the second carrying a bag of his belongings.

'There we are . . .' The matron took hold of the child's hand from the girl and passed him to Kathy. Deliberately, she avoided meeting the matron's glance and kept her gaze fixed on her child. At last, she had him back where he rightly belonged. No matter that no one knew he was hers, just so long as she could be with him.

'Do you need any help? The bag's quite heavy.'

'I have a taxi waiting . . .' Kathy snapped and turned towards the door, anxious to make her escape. The matron herself opened the door. 'Bowen, carry the child's bag out to the taxi for Miss – er . . . for the lady.'

Kathy was out of the door and down the steps and willing herself to walk sedately down the drive to the waiting vehicle as she matched her step to the child's. But all the time she felt a prickling sensation down her back as she felt the matron's gaze still upon her. Any moment she expected to hear a shout, ordering her to stop. But she walked on and with every step she breathed a little more easily.

The taxi driver leapt out of the vehicle and, taking the bag from the girl, opened the door for Kathy to lift the child in and then climb in beside him. As the girl lumbered back up the drive, the driver started the engine with a twirl of the starting handle and then climbed into the driver's seat.

'Eh, it's grand to see another little chap leaving that place. He's not yours, I suppose, is he? He's older than the ones I usually have in my taxi. Not meaning to pry, like, but I just wondered if he was actually yours and you'd come back for him.'

Kathy decided that it was better to keep up the pretence a little longer. The fewer people who knew the truth, the better. You never knew, she thought, in a small town like this just who knew who. If she were to confide in the taxi driver, he might well turn out to be Mrs Talbot's second cousin twice removed. You just never knew.

Although she wanted to shout it from the rooftops. Yes, he's mine. Of course he's mine. Instead she said, 'His mother was killed in the air raid . . .'

'Oh, poor little chap.'

'But from now on, yes, he's mine.'

'Then his luck's changed, madam, if you don't mind me saying so.'

'Thank you.'

In the back of the taxi, Kathy removed her black wig and the glasses. She pulled the hat back on and tucked her own blonde hair beneath it, hoping, at the last ditch, that the taxi driver wouldn't notice the sudden dramatic change in his passenger's appearance.

He didn't. When the vehicle pulled to a halt outside the house, James started to whimper and the driver quickly helped her out and carried her bag up the drive to Mrs Talbot waiting at the door. He hardly gave Kathy a second glance as she handed the child to the daily help and then paid her fare.

At last, the door closed on the outside world and they were safely home.

'Isn't he a little love?' Mrs Talbot cooed. The child's tears dried instantly and he smiled, his whole face lighting up as he beamed and chuckled. 'I bet you're hungry, aren't you? I bet they've not fed you right at that horrid place. Now, you come with me and we'll see what we can find for you in my kitchen.'

Kathy smiled. She had her son back. She could be with him all day and all night too. For the moment, she was quite content to let Mrs Talbot fuss over him. Time enough for her to cuddle him and get to know him when they were alone.

He had Tony's eyes and his dark hair too. Even his nose had the makings of being the same shape. As she bathed him that night, Kathy examined every inch of him, touching him with gentle, loving fingers, revelling in the smooth skin, the rounded arms and legs. She kissed his forehead, his feet and his hands.

'Oh, my darling boy,' she murmured. 'I'll never let you go again. Somehow, I'll find a way to stay with you.'

And James smiled his beatific smile.

Mr Wainwright had certainly not misled Kathy in his attitude towards his adopted son. He hardly saw the child. Though he made sure that Kathy had everything she needed for him and for herself, he wanted nothing to do with little James. That first evening, Kathy brought him down to the dining room where Mr Wainwright was eating his meal alone at one end of the polished mahogany table.

'We've come to say "Goodnight",' Kathy said.

Mr Wainwright looked up, a startled expression on his face. 'Oh – er – yes – right.' He made no move to get up but just gave a curt nod and said, 'Goodnight then.'

Kathy stared at him for a moment and then looked down at the child standing quietly beside her. He was gazing at the man with a blank look, as if he was a complete stranger.

'That's your daddy,' Kathy said.

Mr Wainwright set his spoon down in the empty dish. 'Er – I've never liked the term "Daddy". I always called my father by his proper title. "Father". And I'd be obliged if you would teach James to use that name for me.'

Again Kathy stared at him. What a cold, unfeeling man he was. But she smiled dutifully and said, 'Of course. Is there anything else I should know? I mean, when would you like to spend some time with him?'

'I wouldn't,' Mr Wainwright said bluntly. 'He's your responsibility – entirely. Please ask me for anything you need and I'll see you get it – if possible, of course, in these difficult times. But – I don't want to have anything to do with him. I – I'm not good with babies or toddlers. Perhaps when he gets a little older. School age, perhaps, then I might find him a little more interesting.'

'I see.' Kathy tried very hard to keep any note of disapproval out of her tone. She didn't want to do anything that might endanger her position here. But she couldn't resist the urge to say, 'Don't you even want to see him in the evening, just – just to say "Goodnight"?'

For a moment Mr Wainwright regarded the child thoughtfully. James beamed and waved his chubby hand at him. ''Night, 'night,' he said, endearingly. Kathy saw the man's expression soften a little.

'Very well, then,' Mr Wainwright said at last. 'Just at night, when I've finished my dinner, you may bring him to my study.'

'Thank you, Mr Wainwright.' As she turned to go, he said, 'Oh, Miss Burton, please feel free to use the sitting room whenever you wish. I shall be spending very little time in there. More often than not I shall be working in my study in the evenings. And please use the radio whenever you wish, though I'd be glad if you'd keep the volume turned low so that it does not disturb me.'

Kathy was tempted to say that it was unlikely she'd have the radio playing so loudly that she would not be able to hear James. Instead she thanked him politely and carried the little boy up to his cot in the nursery. Clutching the knitted rabbit, he settled down at once and his eyelids closed as soon as she had tucked the covers around him.

She set the nightlight and tiptoed into her own room and glanced around it. It had been furnished as a bed-sitting room. The bed was in one corner, with a bedside table and lamp on it. Nearby was a dressing table and wardrobe, but near the window that looked out over the back garden of the house, an easy chair and low coffee table had been placed. There was even a book-case to one side, filled with a variety of books. Kathy ran her finger along the titles and smiled. There was a battered copy of *Pride and Prejudice*. She took it from the shelf, sat down in the chair and opened the book. On the flyleaf, in scrawling handwriting was written, 'To dear Beryl on her fifteenth birthday from her loving Aunt Mary'.

Kathy smiled. By the appearance of the book, it had been a treasured and much-read possession. Something else she had in common with Beryl Wainwright.

Thirty-Nine

The Wainwright household settled happily into a routine. Mrs Talbot did most of the housework and cooked evening meals during the week for the master of the house. Kathy had usually eaten by the time Mr Wainwright came home, for it coincided with James's bedtime ritual. On the days Mrs Talbot did not come – at the weekends – Kathy cooked for both Mr Wainwright and herself and they both ate a little earlier, at six o'clock instead of seven. For the first two weeks Kathy ate in the kitchen with James while Mr Wainwright took his meal alone in the dining room.

On the Sunday evening of the third weekend, Mr Wainwright came into the kitchen. Kathy jumped to her feet at once. 'Is there something—?'

He put his hand out, 'No, no, please, don't get up. I was just thinking—' He paused and eyed James sitting quietly in his chair, his brown eyes regarding Mr Wainwright solemnly. 'Is he a good boy? I mean, at mealtimes? At the table?'

Carefully Kathy said, 'Usually, yes. I'm trying to teach him the way to behave. I – I don't think one can start too young.'

Mr Wainwright looked pleased and nodded. 'Quite right. To be honest, Beryl was a little lax with him at times.' A pause and then he went on. 'What I was thinking was that it seems a little silly for you to be sitting in here and me in there – on my own. In the week, of course,' he added hastily, as if not wanting to give away too much of his privacy, 'it's better to keep to James's routine, but at weekends when you do the cooking – for which I'm very grateful incidentally, as that was not part of our original agreement.'

'I don't mind. I enjoy it. And James sits in his chair watching.'

'I was thinking we might all eat together in the dining room at weekends.'

'That would be very nice. Thank you, sir.'

'Of course, if I have guests . . .' He never entertained, so Kathy couldn't understand him even mentioning it, but dutifully she said swiftly, 'Of course. A proper dinner party is no place for a child.'

He nodded. 'Right, that's settled then. And – er – please call me "Henry".'

So a slightly altered routine was established. During the week, Mr Wainwright – or rather Henry as Kathy now must think of him – ate alone, and the only time he encountered his son was when Kathy took him downstairs, bathed and dressed in his pyjamas. At weekends, the three of them ate in the dining room together, Henry at the head of the table, Kathy at one side with James's chair beside her. For the first three weeks things passed calmly enough, but on the Saturday night of the fourth weekend, James was fractious. He was whimpering as Kathy sat him in his chair, and as she tried to feed him with a spoon his cries increased and he turned his head away.

'Is something the matter with him?'

'Perhaps he's getting another tooth.' It pained her to admit it even to herself that she wasn't sure at what age children cut their various teeth. 'See how red his cheek is?'

'Are you sure that's all it is? He hasn't got a temperature, has he? He looks awfully hot.'

'That's because – if it is a tooth coming through – his gums are hurting and he's cross.'

She tried James with another spoonful but he screwed up his face and pushed her hand away, spilling the food from the spoon on to the carpet. Kathy mopped it up at once with her napkin, but it left a dark, wet stain on the floor.

Henry's face was thunderous. 'Perhaps this wasn't such a good idea after all.'

Kathy rose, leaving her own meal untouched. 'I'll take him upstairs.'

'But what about your own meal?'

'I'll just put him in his cot and come back.'

'Very well.' Henry carried on with his own meal and didn't even speak to or look at the child as Kathy carried him out.

She laid him in his cot. 'Poor little man,' she murmured. 'Is that nasty old tushypeg hurting, then? I'll be back in a jiffy. I must just go down and clear our plates away. I'll be right back.'

She ran lightly down the stairs and went back into the dining room. 'I'm so sorry about that,' she said. 'I'll mind not to bring him to eat in here if he's fractious.'

She began to pick up her plate and James's dish.

'Aren't you going to sit down and eat your dinner?'

'He's crying. I must get back to him.'

A look of annoyance passed over Henry's face. 'Let him cry. It won't hurt him for once.'

'No,' Kathy said quietly, hoping that defying her

employer would not bring about her instant dismissal. 'It's not naughtiness. If it was I'd be the first to let him cry out his paddy, but he's got toothache.'

'As you wish,' Henry said stiffly. 'I see now that you're as soft as Beryl when it comes down to it.'

'Not when it's naughtiness, I assure you. Only when he's so obviously in pain.'

With that, she gathered the dishes and left the room, returning only to move James's chair back into the kitchen.

Henry Wainwright continued his meal in stony silence, a churlish look on his face. Kathy was smiling as she ran back up the stairs. If that same look had been on James's face, she would have classed it as mardy.

They continued to dine with Mr Wainwright when James was sunny-natured and well-behaved. If he showed the slightest sign of 'playing up', as Mrs Talbot fondly called it, they ate in the kitchen. Kathy still waited on her employer, serving him his dinner and then clearing away and washing up after James was in bed and asleep.

One evening about ten o'clock, when she was putting away the last cup and saucer in the cupboard, Henry wandered into the kitchen carrying two brandy glasses. He held out one towards her. 'A nightcap.'

She smiled and took it. 'Thank you.'

'Is the child asleep?'

'Yes.'

'Let's go into the sitting room.' He turned to lead the way, but Kathy hesitated. She didn't want to anger

Henry – he seemed in a particularly mellow mood – but she couldn't be sure of hearing James if he cried.

As if reading her thoughts, Henry said over his shoulder, 'You can leave the door ajar. You'll be able to hear him then.'

Breathing a sigh of relief, she followed him into the room and sat, a little self-consciously, on the sofa while he took his usual armchair by the fire. He swirled the brandy around in the glass and looked across at her through narrowed eyes. 'Tell me about yourself.'

Kathy's heart missed a beat. It was the sort of question she'd dreaded him asking. She'd begun to feel safe here. Henry Wainwright seemed so wrapped up in his work, with little interest in his adopted son and even less in her, that she had been lulled into feeling secure.

'I – there's not much to tell, really. I was brought up on a farm but I wanted to see a bit more of life, so I went to work in Lincoln.'

'So how did you come to join the concert party and end up visiting this town?'

Unwittingly, he had made it so easy for her. Put another way, the question could have been impossible to answer truthfully. As it was, she could say honestly. 'Mr Spencer, who formed the concert party, used to be the conductor in a choral society I belonged to in Lincoln. He asked me to join him.' It was the truth, if not the whole truth.

'And are you quite happy here? I mean, it doesn't seem much of a future for a pretty young girl like you just to be looking after one child.' He paused and eyed her keenly. 'I mean, what about marriage? Wouldn't you like to get married one day? I thought that was the ambition of every young woman.'

'Perhaps one day,' Kathy said carefully, but her heart was hammering painfully. The questions were getting a little too personal and any moment she expected him to ask something that would trap her.

'Have you never had a young man?'

'I . . . there was someone, but – but he went into the RAF. He – he was a fighter pilot.' She knew her face looked bleak, her eyes haunted.

'So,' he said softly, 'you've lost the one you loved too, have you?'

Wordlessly, she nodded.

'I'm sorry to hear it, Kathy. Very sorry.'

Life might have continued in much the same way in the Wainwright household if the concert party had not returned to Saltershaven in June. Kathy saw the advertisement in the local paper, and on the afternoon of their first concert she wheeled James in his pushchair to the cinema knowing the cast would be rehearsing for the evening performance.

'Kathy, my dear girl.' Ron greeted her with open arms as she walked down the aisle towards the stage carrying James in her arms. 'Hello, young man.' He beamed at the child, and tickled him under the chin to be rewarded with a wide smile from James. 'He's a handsome little chap, isn't he?' He lowered his voice and winked at her. 'But then, of course, he would be, wouldn't he? How's it all going? Are you happy?'

'Yes, Ron, I am. I get to be with him all the time. Mr Wainwright isn't very interested in him. It seems it was his wife who really wanted children. I think Mr Wainwright is married to his job, if you know what I mean.'

Ron laughed. 'I do. I've met a few like that in my time. Oh well, my dear, as long as you're happy.'

'Have you seen anything of Miss Robinson?'

'Mabel gets a letter now and again. But I expect you do, don't you?'

'Yes, we write to each other regularly, but I miss *seeing* her. Do you think she'll ever go back to Lincoln?'

Ron shrugged. 'I doubt it. They've laid a few off at Hammonds. Business for them just isn't the same as it was before the war. You can't expect it to be. Folks haven't got the money – or the coupons! I don't think she'll even try to go back there. She's still with Ted and Betty. She seems happy enough.'

And why shouldn't she be? Kathy thought. She's with her son too.

Forty

'Kathy, I have something to ask you.'

Ron was standing in the kitchen of Henry Wainwright's house, twirling his hat nervously in his hands. On the day she had been to the theatre to see him, he'd promised to come and see her before the party left town and now here he was. But she hadn't expected this.

'What is it?'

'I wondered if you'd come back to the party . . .' As she opened her mouth to refuse, he put up his hand. 'Don't answer straight away. Hear me out – please.'

'Sit down, Ron. I'll make a cup of tea.'

'If you're sure. It's a long walk here.' He sat down gratefully but then added, 'What about the little feller?'

'Mrs Talbot's gone into the town shopping and she's taken him in his pushchair.'

'Ah, that's all right then.'

When they were both sitting at the table with a cup of tea in front of them, Ron cleared his throat. 'Now, I'll quite understand if you say "no", my dear, but I would just like you to think about this very carefully. We've been asked to give a series of very special concerts and I'd really like you to come with us. It'd only be for a couple of weeks, I promise.'

'I thought Melody had taken my place with her impressions?'

'That's right,' Ron said carefully. 'But she's very young and – and – well, I don't think she'd cope with the circumstances very well, seeing as what happened at that hospital near Newcastle. You remember?'

'Oh, I see. It's another hospital, is it?'

'Yes, but a very specialized one. Have you heard of Archibald McIndoe?'

Kathy stared at him. 'Yes,' she said slowly. 'I read an article in the paper only the other day. He's the plastic surgeon who's helping solders and airman with – with facial disfigurements, isn't he?'

Ron nodded. 'Especially – fighter pilots.'

'Oh Ron . . .' Kathy didn't know whether to laugh or cry. 'That's a low blow. You – of all people – resorting to emotional blackmail.'

'Sorry, my dear. But I so want you to come. We've been asked to go to the Queen Victoria Hospital in East Grinstead and also to the convalescent home where the airmen go between their many operations. You could cope – you've already proved as much – with whatever we're going to see. It won't be easy, but I know you could hide any – any embarrassment you might feel. We all need to go in there and take absolutely no notice of their terrible injuries and the operations they're undergoing. There are some weird and wonderful methods being used, so I'm told, but the marvel of it is they're working. These poor fellows have a future, thanks to a very clever and dedicated man.'

'I'd like to but – but I don't see how I can leave James. I mean, you know how very much this job means to me.'

'I know. I've been thinking about that. You told me that Mr Wainwright isn't all that interested in your – I mean – his son?'

Kathy nodded. 'He wouldn't want to be left with him. That I do know. He'd get someone else and I – I couldn't bear that, Ron.'

Ron patted her hand. 'I know that. But if you explained the situation to Mr Wainwright, said what it was all about, would he let you take young James out to the Robinsons' farm? They'd look after him for you, wouldn't they? Just for two weeks?'

Kathy thought of Betty and couldn't help smiling. 'Of course they would. Betty would love it.'

'So – do you think Mr Wainwright would agree to let the boy go there?'

Kathy shrugged. 'I can only ask.'

'I don't see why not.' Henry seemed unconcerned. 'I presume you know these people well?'

'I've known the family all my life. They lived on the neighbouring farm.'

'And they really wouldn't mind having a young boy in the house?' His tone sounded as if he could hardly believe there were such people.

'No, they wouldn't. They've already got an evacuee. So, do I have your permission to write and ask them?'

He shrugged. 'Yes, if that's what you want. How long would it be for?'

'About two weeks.'

'It's all right by me, if you're sure they wouldn't be put about.' He sounded as if he couldn't imagine anything worse than having a young child – and a stranger at that – foisted on him for two whole weeks. 'Now, if you'll excuse me, I have some work to do . . .'

*

As she had known they would, the Robinsons replied by return that they'd be delighted to have James. Kathy decided to take him there and then return to pack her own suitcase and travel down south by train to meet up with the concert party. She would stay at Sandy Furze Farm overnight and see James settled in.

'Oh, isn't he a lamb?' Betty cried, opening her arms wide to pick him up. Beaming, James held out his chubby arms and went happily to her.

'They always know when someone loves them,' Betty said. 'Now, my little man, what has your Auntie Betty got in her kitchen for you?'

'Pudding?' James said, smiling hopefully as Betty bore him away.

'My dear girl.' Jemima appeared and hugged Kathy. 'How good it is to see you. And look, here's Taffy to greet you. Just look at him. He's getting quite fat. He's spoiled rotten here. As, indeed, am I.'

Kathy had been concerned that the shock of losing her home and all of her possessions might have made Jemima thin and ill. But far from it, she looked fitter and happier than ever she had in the city. 'Now let me help you with your things. You must have had a tiring journey. It's not easy travelling with a little one.'

'The train was full of troops, but James had a great time being made a fuss of by all the soldiers. Have you heard from Amy? How is she?'

'She's fine. She's found herself a young man. A petty officer in the Royal Navy. He's been here with her once. He's a very nice young man, but . . .' Here Jemima glanced quickly at Kathy and bit her lip.

Kathy smiled sadly and murmured, 'I know, I know. But she's got to grab what chance she's got of a little happiness. I – I don't regret any of it. Not any more.'

'No,' Jemima said with her usual spirit that Kathy remembered so well. She leaned closer as she whispered, 'And neither do I, my dear. Neither do I. Now, let's get you settled in upstairs. And you must meet little Susan. She'll be home from the village school soon.'

'Susan? I thought it was a boy evacuee they had?'

'He went home. And now we've got Susan.'

Kathy smiled. Was there no end to the Robinsons' kindness?

It was a merry gathering that sat down to supper than evening with James the centre of attention sitting in an old battered child's chair that Betty had dug out of the loft the moment she had heard of the little chap's imminent arrival. Susan was a merry child of ten or so with blonde, unruly curls and bright blue eyes. She sat at the table close to James and talked non-stop to him in her cockney accent. The little boy watched her with wide eyes, beaming and reaching out to tug her curls. Later, when both children were sound asleep after a tiring day, Morry sought out Kathy.

'Are you happy, Kathy, because from what you say about this bloke, he might not object to the little feller being adopted? What I mean is, if – if you wanted, we could . . .'

'Oh Morry, dearest Morry, don't. Please don't. I know what you're going to say and I love you for it, but it wouldn't be right.'

Morry looked crestfallen once again, but he smiled. 'Oh well, it was worth a try. But I hope you know I'm always there for you if you ever want – well – anything.'

'I know,' Kathy said huskily. 'And I don't deserve you, Morry. I really don't.'

Now Morry really did blush.

Kathy arrived back in Saltershaven late on the Thursday evening. She was to travel south on the Friday and meet up with the concert party for their first show on the Saturday evening.

'Mr Wainwright's asked that you wait for him to get home tonight and have dinner with him, seeing as how you haven't got the little boy to look after,' Mrs Talbot greeted her.

'Oh, right – thank you. Then I'd better get my packing done before he gets in.'

By the time Mrs Talbot called up the stairs, 'Right, I'm off now, love. Your dinners are in the oven. I'll see you in a couple of weeks, then, shall I?'

Kathy hurried to the top of the stairs. 'Yes. Goodbye, Mrs Talbot. Thank you.'

By the time she heard the front door open and close and knew that Henry was home, Kathy was all packed and ready for her early start in the morning.

'I've brought some wine. I hope you like red. Mrs Talbot said it was beef tonight, though I hope it's not as stringy as the last lot we had. I'll open it. Let it breathe a little . . .'

Kathy served the main course and they sat down at the table, Henry in his usual place at one end of the table, Kathy on his left-hand side. But tonight there was no James on her left.

They ate in silence for a while until Henry opened the conversation. 'You do know what you're letting yourself in for, don't you?'

Kathy nodded. 'We played a lot of hospitals when I was with the concert party. Some of the injuries we saw then were pretty horrific.'

'I suppose so,' he murmured. There was a long silence before he burst out, 'You will come back, won't you? I mean, it really is only for two weeks?'

She stared at him in surprise. 'Yes, of course I'll come back. I love my job and – and I – I've grown to love James.' She was treading on dangerous ground, but she wanted him to know that there was no way she was leaving for good. Then another thought struck her. A terrible thought that made her heart pound anxiously.

'You – you do want me to come back?'

'Of course I do.' The swiftness of his answer surprised her. 'In fact . . .' He hesitated then added, 'Look, let's go into the sitting room. There's something I want to ask you.'

'I'll clear away . . .' she began, getting up.

'No, leave it.'

She sat on the edge of the sofa in the sitting room, feeling strangely apprehensive. Was he going to tell her that he'd decided to have James adopted again after all? It seemed to take him an age to pour out two brandies and to hand one to her. Then he sat down.

'Kathy, I've been thinking about this for some time. I have a sort of proposition to put to you. I've got used to having you around the house. You're quiet and seem to understand my need to work in the evening. Something Beryl didn't always seem to understand.

That's why I gave in to her overwhelming desire to adopt a child when we found we couldn't have any of our own.'

Kathy waited, becoming more alarmed at the way this conversation was going. He'd never wanted James and now he was going to say that he'd thought it through and decided he didn't want a lifetime of responsibility, however much his late wife might have expected it of him. She felt the lump begin to grow in her throat. Was she, once again, going to have her happiness snatched away from her?

'For myself,' he went on and her heart plummeted even more. 'For myself, I would give the child up for adoption again. He should have two parents, not one, but I know that's not what Beryl would have expected of me. I – I feel duty bound to honour what I know her wishes would have been. Kathy, what I'm trying to say in a very roundabout and clumsy way is – will you marry me and be a mother to James?'

Kathy stared at him and knew her mouth dropped open. She was in such a state of shock that she scarcely heard his next words.

'It would be a marriage of convenience. I do realize that you were very much in love with the young man you lost and I – well – I still feel Beryl's loss very keenly. I mean, if you wanted it that way, it would be a marriage in name only, though I would hope that perhaps in time . . .' He broke off, leaving the implication hanging in the air.

She couldn't understand it. Oh, she knew well enough what he was suggesting, but why? That's the part she couldn't understand. He was saying quite bluntly that he didn't have feelings for her, that he knew she hadn't for him. If he'd loved the boy and had

410

been suggesting their marriage to safeguard the continuity of the same two people in his life, safeguarding against a procession of nannies, then she could have understood it. But he didn't love the boy. He'd made that very clear. So, why . . . ?

'I need a woman about the place. I miss Beryl running the home. Oh, Mrs Talbot's all very well but she's not always reliable. I mean, that idle husband of hers has only got to stop off work a day and she sends a message that she can't come. I do so like everything to be just so. I like my life ordered in a strict routine. I do *not* like disruption.'

So, thought Kathy, that was his reason. He wanted a built-in housekeeper and nanny for James.

'And I thought it might help you too. I managed to get a temporary deferment for you, but I doubt I can for much longer. But if you were to be a married woman with our child to care for, then it would be a different matter. So, while you're away, will you promise to think about it?'

Kathy opened her mouth to retort that she would never entertain such a preposterous idea. It was almost immoral. In her eyes anyway. But then she closed her mouth. If she refused, what about James? Henry might well decide to have him adopted and look around for a suitable woman to be his housekeeper so that his well-ordered life could continue without the encumbrance of a child. A child who wasn't even his and who he'd never wanted in the first place. He'd only ever agreed to the adoption to keep his wife – the perfect housekeeper – happy.

'I – will think about it,' she said and stood up. 'But now, if you'll excuse me, I have an early start in the morning.' As she reached the door, he said, 'Oh, do you think you could cook my breakfast in the morning before you go? Mrs Talbot's husband has one of his famous stomach upsets.'

Keeping her face straight, Kathy inclined her head and said, 'Of course.'

Surprisingly, Kathy slept well and it wasn't until she was sitting on the train heading south that she had time to think once again about Henry's strange suggestion.

Well, if that's not about the most unromantic proposal a girl's ever had, she thought. But it had caused her a dilemma. If she accepted, she could be with her son always. True. But there'd be a price to pay. She'd be an unpaid housekeeper and, possibly, something of a concubine – though a married one – in the future. Men, she knew, even cold-hearted ones like Henry Wainwright, had their needs. And it seemed that eventually he would expect her to behave in every way like a wife should. He'd hinted as much.

On the other hand, if she refused him, she suspected that he would at once put James up for adoption and dismiss her. She would be parted again from her son and this time, there would be no way of finding out who his new parents were.

Of course, there was another solution.

As the train sped on the clattering wheels seemed to say, 'Marry Morry, marry Morry.'

Forty-One

Ron was waiting on the platform for her when the train drew in.

'How did you know what time I'd be arriving?'

'I didn't. We're staying not a hundred yards from the station, so I've been meeting all the trains since midday.'

'Oh, Ron!' She was touched by his patient thoughtfulness. 'How is everyone? How's Rosie?'

'She's fine – apart from fretting about Martin. Now he's flying on bombers she's worried sick, poor girl.'

'Bombers? As a pilot?'

'No – no. He's a tail-end Charlie – a rear-gunner – I'm afraid. Very dangerous. I'm just hoping she'll be able to cope with seeing these poor injured fellows.'

Kathy smiled sadly. 'I – I often wonder how poor Tony died. Whether he – he—'

Ron's face fell. 'Perhaps I shouldn't have asked you, lass. I'm sorry.'

But Kathy put on a brave smile. 'No, Ron. I'm glad you did. I'll feel I'm doing my bit for Tony.'

'Sure?'

'Absolutely.'

'That's the ticket,' Ron said, picking up her suitcase. 'Right, then, let's get you settled in. I want a bit of rehearsal tonight. The hotel's got a function room they'll let us use and we've got our first concert at the hospital tomorrow night.'

As they walked out of the station and along the road towards the guesthouse where most of the concert party were staying, Kathy linked her arm with Ron's. 'Oh, it's good to see you again.'

'How's that little boy of yours?' he asked softly.

Now Kathy smiled widely. 'He's wonderful, Ron.'

'And – and it's working out? You looking after him?'

'Yes – yes, it is.' She wrinkled her forehead. 'Of course, I've been worrying constantly that Mr Wainwright is going to change his mind and put him up for adoption but then, last night – he – he –' She paused, still unable to believe it had happened and wondering for a brief moment if she had dreamt the whole thing.

'He what?' Ron's tone was concerned. He'd heard about young nannies being seduced by their employers. Had the man made advances to her?

'He asked me to marry him.'

Ron breathed a sigh of relief. But guardedly, he asked, 'And did you accept?'

'Not – not yet. You see, it was a business proposition.' She laughed wryly. 'It certainly wasn't a romantic proposal, that's for sure.'

'So – he didn't profess to be in love with you?'

'No. Not at all.'

'What about your feelings for him?'

'I'm certainly not in love with him,' she said bluntly. 'I – I don't think I'll ever love anyone but Tony. He was the love of my life, like poor . . .' She stopped and bit her tongue. She had been about to say 'like poor Aunt Jemima', then she realized just in time that Ron Spencer knew nothing of Jemima Robinson's secret.

They'd reached the guesthouse, but paused outside before going up the steps. Ron turned to face her. 'So why exactly is he asking you to marry him?'

'He – he needs a wife to run his home and look after James.'

'But why,' Ron persisted, 'if – as you say – he has little interest in the boy, that they only adopted him because his wife wanted a child, why is he keeping him? Why doesn't he let him be adopted by another childless couple?'

Kathy's face was bleak at the thought. 'Because – because he believes it's what Beryl – that was his wife – would have wanted him to do. To keep James as his son and bring him up.'

'Mm.' Ron was thoughtful. 'So . . . he's marrying to get a built-in housekeeper and mother for the boy and you – well, if you do agree to it – you're marrying him just to be with your son?'

Kathy bit her lip and nodded. 'Put like that it does sound a bit – a bit calculating.'

'Oh it is, Kathy. It is. All I would say to you, my dear, is think very carefully about it before you give him your answer. Just think, what's going to happen when James grows up and leave home? What then, eh? Do think about it, Kathy.'

'I will, Ron. I promise. I've got these two weeks and by then I'll know what I should do.'

Everyone in the concert party welcomed Kathy with open arms, and Rosie was ecstatic.

'I've missed you so much. There's no one else I can talk to like I can talk to you. Have you heard? Martin's on bombers now and I'm so terrified . . .'

'I know, love. I know,' Kathy comforted her, but she couldn't in all honesty voice the words that the young girl wanted to hear. She couldn't reassure her that he would be all right, that he would come through. The life expectancy of anyone flying in bombers wasn't good, and for a rear-gunner it was even worse.

'How've you been? How's that little boy you've been looking after? Are you enjoying it? I really can't imagine why you'd want to look after someone else's child.'

Kathy smiled. If only you knew, she thought.

The rehearsal went well, and Kathy slipped back into the routines as if she'd never been away. 'I just daren't risk taking Melody,' Ron said. 'These boys need to be treated just as though there's absolutely nothing wrong. They'll be ultra-sensitive to people's expressions when they first meet them. Do you think you can manage it, Kathy? I mean, I'd rather you said now if you feel you can't.'

'I'll be fine, Ron. Really. I'm prepared for it.'

'Well, you're a good actress. You've been brilliant in some of the sketches in the past. But I'll warn you now – you're going to need all your acting skills when you walk into that place.'

The following night the members of the concert party were all subdued when they set off in the rattling bus to take them to the hospital. They were all thinking about how they were going to react and hoping that they would be able to greet the terribly injured men with respect and sympathy that was not overly gushing.

However much they'd thought about it and steeled themselves, not one of them was prepared for the sight of the ghastly injuries the airmen had suffered. And the skin grafts they were undergoing were just as strange and frightening. But Kathy walked on to the make-shift stage with a broad smile and looked out over the sea of disfigured faces with a calmness she had not expected to feel.

In the interval the cast congregated in a room that the hospital had set aside for their use. There were cups of tea and biscuits on a side table. As Kathy took a cup and poured milk and tea into it, Ron came to stand beside her.

'All right?'

She nodded. 'I'm fine. I'm coping better than I thought I would. I knew I wouldn't show revulsion, but I thought I wouldn't be able to hide my sympathy for them. I guess that's almost as bad.'

'You did wonderfully well. I was watching. In fact, everyone's been marvellous and we've got the worst over now. I don't think even meeting them later will be so bad. You do know we've promised to mingle after the show, don't you?'

Kathy nodded. That part had worried her the most, but now she felt she could do it.

'Some of the operations and treatments they're receiving look almost as bad as the original injuries,' Ron remarked.

'But isn't there a wonderful atmosphere? They laugh and tease each other,' Kathy marvelled. 'And they make jokes against themselves. I heard someone shout out something when we were doing that second sketch and he was poking fun at himself.'

'I know, but you know what, this chap McIndoe, he doesn't profess to be able to do the impossible and give them back their former looks, but to the lads here he's already working miracles. He's giving them hope for the future and that means everything to them. Everything, Kathy. They have such faith in him, it's humbling to see it.'

'They're so brave. They must be in terrible pain sometimes.'

'Of course they're brave. That's why they're here, because they were brave enough to go out and fight a war for us. You'd be amazed at the number of DSOs and DFCs that are in this room right now. See that tall chap standing near the window with his back to us? He's a DFC. They say his plane was shot down and on fire and instead of baling out as he could have done, he stayed with it until he was clear of a village and over open fields before he jumped. By then, of course, he'd been badly burned himself. That's what I call bravery, Kathy.'

Kathy set down her cup and saucer and smiled at Ron. 'And now it's up to us to show our appreciation. Do you think my usual finale is okay? All those patriotic wartime songs? Do you think they'll like them?'

'They'll love them.'

They did. The audience, which was mostly men with just a few female nurses standing at the back, clapped and cheered and catcalled for encores, and Kathy had to sing 'We'll Meet Again' twice and 'Land of Hope and Glory' three times before they would let her leave the stage.

As she walked back to the room where they'd all changed she was smiling, though her smile was tinged with sadness. This war had changed her life, and part of her wished she was still touring with the concert party, feeling she was doing her bit for the war effort and lifting the spirits of servicemen and women and war workers. But she couldn't leave James; she couldn't bear to be parted from him again. She might lose him forever. She might never see him again. A cold shudder of fear ran through her at the mere thought.

She sighed. In two weeks' time she must return to Saltershaven. And then she must give Henry Wainwright his answer.

During the fortnight, the concert party played other venues as well as the hospital, but they returned there several times, on each occasion playing to a slightly different audience. Each time they mingled with the patients afterwards, drinking tea and talking.

Kathy moved among them, laughing and chatting, each time looking straight into the patients' eyes whenever she could. She ignored their facial wounds, their scarred and misshapen hands, and their slurred speech when it was their mouth that was affected. As she moved away from a young man from Liverpool who had been shot down over the Channel during the Battle of Britain, she glanced around the room and saw a tall young man standing alone by the window. It was the same man Ron had pointed out to her a few days earlier. The airman was watching her, but as soon as she caught his eye he turned away and looked out of the window.

Kathy's heart skipped a beat. There was something about the tilt of his head and the way he moved that reminded her so heartbreakingly of Tony. He was even the same height. Drawn irresistibly to him, she threaded her way through the throng until she stood just behind him.

'Hello,' she said softly. 'Did you enjoy the concert?'

He remained standing perfectly still, looking out of the window. He didn't move, didn't turn round and didn't even speak.

She could only see a little of the left-hand side of his face. It was badly damaged and his left ear was gone. Perhaps he can't hear me, she thought. Gently she touched his arm. He started and spilt tea from the cup he was holding.

'Oh, I'm so sorry.' Kathy was contrite, gently taking the cup and saucer from his hand and setting it down. 'I didn't mean to startle you.' She moved to the side and leant around him so that he could see her face. Perhaps he could lip-read. Perhaps . . .

The man turned his back on her again.

'Can you hear me?' she asked softly. She saw him stiffen and knew that he could. He just didn't want to face her.

'My name's Kathy. What's yours?'

Again, an uncomfortable silence.

Kathy sighed. 'I'm so sorry. I didn't mean to intrude. I just wondered if you'd enjoyed our performance?'

'Yes,' he mumbled. 'It was – wonderful.'

Now it was Kathy who caught her breath, staring at the back of his head, at the broad set of his shoulders. His voice! Though it was muffled through swollen lips, the timbre of it was the same.

'Tony,' she whispered. 'Oh, Tony. It *is* you. Oh, dear Lord, please say it's you.'

Forty-Two

lowly, oh so slowly, while Kathy held her breath, he
turned towards her.

The left-hand side of his face was cruelly injured,
but now that she could see the right-hand side, she
knew it was him.

'Tony,' she breathed, drinking in the sight of him.
Tears filled her eyes. 'Oh, Tony, why?'

She only needed to say that one word for him to
understand exactly what she meant.

He stared at her for a moment. His left eye was half
hidden by a drooping, scarred eyelid. His cheek was
disfigured and raw. His mouth, that had kissed her so
gently, so passionately, was twisted out of shape. But,
strangely, the flames that had engulfed him had hardly
touched the right side of his face. His right hand was
whole, while his left was misshapen and clenched into
an unusable fist.

'Isn't it obvious?' he asked harshly. 'I wish you
hadn't come. If I'd only known, I wouldn't have come
to the concert that first night, but I never dreamed for
one minute—' He sighed and swept his good hand
through the wispy hair on the right side of his head.
'And then – when I knew the party was coming again,
I – I couldn't resist just one more sight of you. Please,
Kathy, just go. Leave me . . .'

She stepped towards him, so close that she could

feel his uneven breath on her face. 'I'm going nowhere.' She touched his face with tender fingertips. 'Darling, why didn't you tell me you were alive?'

'Looking like this?'

'Looking like *anything*! I've been heartbroken believing you dead.'

'But – but you went away. You left Lincoln. Mother said . . .'

'Ah yes, your mother,' Kathy said bitterly. 'But for your mother, we'd have been married.'

'I know.'

'And you didn't write . . .'

'I know.'

'Is that all you can say, Tony?'

'I don't know what else to say. If I could turn back the clock, believe me, I'd do it all so very differently, but it's too late now.'

'What – what do you mean? Too late now?'

When he didn't answer, her heart felt like stone. 'You – you mean you've met someone else?' She tried hard, but now, she couldn't help her voice from breaking. The last few days, seeing all these poor boys, had been emotional enough, but now finding that Tony was alive, was just too much. Her head dropped and the tears flowed. She buried her face against his shoulder and wept.

'Oh, my darling, don't cry. Please don't cry.' With his good hand he stroked her hair. 'Just go, Kathy, and forget all about me. Please. For the sake of the love we once had for each other, please just go.'

She pulled away and stood in front of him, dabbing self-consciously at her eyes, aware that others in the room were watching her. Ron pushed his way toward her and took her arm.

'Kathy, we should go now.' His voice was stern. He thought that she had let him down, that she had not been able to hide her pity for the injured airmen.

'You don't understand, Ron. This is Tony. My Tony. I thought he was dead, but he isn't. He's here. He's alive.'

Ron stared at the young man.

'I'm sorry, young feller,' Ron said, smiling and putting out his hand to shake Tony's. 'I didn't – ' he stopped, cleared his throat and changed what he had been going to say – 'realize.'

Tony smiled a little lopsidedly and murmured ruefully, 'You didn't recognize me, you mean.'

Ron looked embarrassed for a moment, but Tony laughed and said, 'It's all right. You couldn't be expected to. Besides, I've been trying to stay out of the way all evening. I – I didn't want Kathy to see me.'

Before he could bite back the words, Ron echoed Kathy's feelings. 'Why ever not?'

Tony groaned with mock irritation. 'Not you as well, Mr Spencer. Isn't it obvious?'

'Not to me, young feller. This lass here's never stopped loving you, despite what happened and then there's—'

'No, Ron. Don't . . .' Kathy butted in, afraid that he was about to divulge her secret.

Ron glanced at her and looked shamefaced. 'Sorry, lass,' he muttered and turned away. 'I'll leave you to sort it all out, but the bus'll be here in half an hour. We'll have to go then.'

He moved away, and despite the crowded room, the two young people felt as if they were alone.

Kathy had recovered a little and was able to say more calmly now, 'You've got someone else?'

'Of course I haven't,' he said impatiently, as if talking to a stupid child. 'How could you think that? There's never been anyone else but you . . .'

With a sudden lift in her heart, Kathy was even able to tease him gently and say, 'You mean, *since* you met me? There were a few before, if I remember rightly.'

He groaned and closed his eyes. 'Oh, don't remind me.'

Then her face sobered again and she shook her head. 'But you still don't want to marry me?'

'How can I? How can I expect you to live with – this?' He gestured angrily towards his damaged face.

For a moment, she wasn't quite sure how to handle the situation, how to answer his question. Deliberately, she put her head on one side and appraised him. 'You always did have an over-inflated opinion about your own good looks,' she said bluntly. It was not the truth and he knew it, and he realized too what she was trying to do. '*I* don't see so very much difference.' Then she softened her tone and touched his arm. 'You're – you're still my Tony. Still the man I love, and I'll tell you something, Tony Kendall. You won't escape so easily this time. This time, you're going to marry me whether you like it or not.'

'Did you tell him?' Ron asked quietly without preamble as he sat down next to her in the bus. Above the noisy engine, the rattling of the windows and the chatter of the rest of the party, no one could hear what they were saying. 'About James?'

Kathy shook her head and said huskily. 'I couldn't. I didn't want him to think I wanted to marry him because of James.'

'I know what you're thinking,' Ron said mildly. 'If you go back to Wainwright and tell him the truth that he'll be only too happy to hand the boy over to you.'

Kathy stared at him. 'How did you know?'

Ron smiled. 'Because it's what I was thinking. From what you've told me, it's a possibility. But no more than that. It's not a certainty by any means. And I don't want to see you getting your hopes up for a perfect ending to all the unhappiness when, my dear, it might not happen. I don't want to see you getting hurt all over again.'

'But – but I can't marry Mr Wainwright.' She paused and smiled at herself. The very fact that she still referred to the man who had proposed to her as 'Mr Wainwright' said it all. 'Not now. Not when Tony's still alive. Oh, he's still saying he doesn't want to tie me to him, but I know I can persuade him. Given time.'

Ron sighed. 'Are you sure? When he leaves here, won't his mother want him back to look after him?'

'I . . .' Kathy began and then stopped. Carried along in a fervour of happiness because Tony was alive, imagining them being married and living with their son, she had not stopped to think of all the things – or rather people – who still stood in the way of their happiness.

She groaned, closed her eyes and leaned her forehead on the cool glass of the bus window. Why, Oh why, was she so impulsive? Why did she never stop to think things out?

Then she raised her head and turned to look straight into Ron's worried eyes. 'I do know one thing, Ron. No matter what, I'm going to marry Tony and I will fight for my child. Our child.'

Ron nodded. 'I wouldn't have expected anything

less, my dear. Not from you, but I really think you should tell Tony the truth before you marry him. He deserves that at the very least.'

It was three days before the company were due to appear again at the hospital and Kathy felt unable to break her commitment with the party. She sang and acted, but now her heart wasn't in it. She wanted to rush back to the hospital to see Tony.

On the day the of next concert, Kathy sought out Ron. 'We're not rehearsing today, are we?'

'No. I thought we all need a bit of a break before the show tonight.'

'Good, then you won't mind if I go over there to see Tony and meet you there tonight?'

'No, of course not, dear. Break a leg.'

Kathy giggled. 'Thanks.' Then she winked. 'It might be one way of getting into bed beside him.'

'You little minx!' Ron chuckled. 'Get away with you.'

As Kathy walked up the driveway to the hospital, her heart was hammering and her knees were trembling. She couldn't remember when she had felt so nervous, except perhaps the time she had been waiting for Henry Wainwright to make his decision over whether to employ her or not.

She'd been so sure that Tony would want to marry her, but now she realized she'd bulldozed him into it. She hadn't given him the chance to tell her how he really felt. She'd taken it for granted that he'd been thinking of her, that he hadn't wanted to saddle her with marriage to an invalid. Goodness knows, he knew enough about invalids and what it could do to a marriage! And now, today, she was going to tell him the whole truth and perhaps *he* wouldn't want to marry *her* then. Perhaps he would think she was pushing him into marrying her so that they could adopt James . . .

He was waiting for her in the garden, sitting on the fallen trunk of a tree.

'It's shady here,' he explained after they had greeted each other. 'Sorry, but I can't stand the sun on my face.'

'Of course.'

There was a silence and then they both began to speak at once.

They smiled and then Tony said, 'After you.'

'There's something I have to tell you, Tony.'

'Ahhh.' He let out a long sigh. 'I thought so. You've changed your mind. I don't blame you, Kathy . . .'

'Will you let me finish? No, I haven't changed my mind at all. I want to marry you more than anything in the world, but, in fairness, there's something you should know first and when you've heard it – well, it might be you who wants to change your mind.' She grinned ruefully. 'I did act rather like a Churchill tank the other day. I'm sorry.'

He laughed. 'Maybe it's what I need. But go on. What is it? Is there someone else in your life?'

'Yes, but not the way you think. At least . . . Look, let me tell you everything from the beginning.' She took a deep breath. 'After the wedding and you went away, you only wrote the once.'

'I know,' Tony said, shamefaced. 'I tried so often and then screwed them up. I just didn't know what to say. How could I ever get you to forgive me for what had happened? And then, when I came home after training, I was coming to see you to sort it all out face to face, but Mother said you'd left.'

Kathy shook her head at the depths of deceit to which the woman was prepared to stoop to keep her son bound to her. She sighed. No doubt Beatrice Kendall would be even more of a formidable foe now that her precious son was so hurt. She would want to take him home and care for him herself. Perhaps it would even make her get up from her own sickbed, thinking that now she had him to herself forever.

Only she was reckoning without Kathy. Kathy was no longer the innocent country girl. She had been through a lot in the last few years and she was stronger. Oh, so much stronger. Now she would fight all the way for what she wanted.

'I left on the first of April—' She pulled a wry face. 'I thought it very appropriate at the time. So – when did you come home?'

'The beginning of April, I think.'

Kathy nodded. 'I probably would've been gone by then, but I doubt if your mother knew that. Not many people did at first. Didn't you go to Aunt Jemima's to make sure?'

Tony stared at her. 'You mean – you mean Mother *lied* to me?'

Still not wanting to hurt him, Kathy said gently, 'Truthfully, I don't know. It's all a matter of timescale.'

He nodded slowly, a bleak look in his eyes. 'She must have done. Like you say, she couldn't have known you'd gone. I was home for three days and then I went to fighter pilot training. I – I never got home again, because this – ' he pointed to his face – 'happened.'

She looked straight at him, examining the extent of his injury. 'Is Mr McIndoe helping you?'

'Oh, yes. He's marvellous.' Suddenly there was a light in his eyes, hope in his voice. 'It'll never look perfect, of course, but I'll feel able to face the world.' He gave a grin that was lopsided because of his disfigurement. 'As long as the world is able to face me.'

'You're not the only one, and as time goes on, most people will know about what's happened to you and all the others. They'll understand then.'

'I hope so. There are some poor chaps in here far worse than I am. Mr McIndoe is having to rebuild faces completely in some cases.'

'I know,' Kathy said quietly. 'I saw.'

There was silence between them for a moment, then Tony said softly, 'Go on.'

She met his steady gaze and held it, wanting to see his immediate reaction to what she had to say next. She pulled in a deep breath. 'The reason I left Lincoln was because I found I was pregnant.'

He stared at her and then burst out, 'Oh, Kathy! Oh, my darling! If only I'd known. Why – why didn't you write and tell me?' His reaction was genuine. Loving, concerned – hurt, almost. It was Kathy who felt embarrassed and a little foolish. She should have trusted him more.

'I – I didn't want you to marry me just because of the child. After what had happened . . .' Her voice trailed away in apology.

'It was all such a dreadful misunderstanding, wasn't it?' He paused briefly and then, to her surprise, there was a bitter note in his voice. 'And all because of my selfish, possessive mother.'

She stared at him but said nothing.

'I see it all now. How everyone – including you – must have been able to see her for what she was. Everyone but me and my poor old dad.'

With gentle fingers, she took hold of his hand, deliberately choosing the damaged one. 'It must have been difficult for both of you. Being so close to her. I do understand.'

'And the baby?' There was eagerness in his voice, but Kathy's eyes clouded. As she continued with her story, Tony's eyes too mirrored her sadness, suffered with her the trauma of her baby being snatched away. When she had told him everything, even up to Henry Wainwright's strange proposal, he let out a long, deep sigh.

'What can we do? Do you think – if you told him everything now, told him the truth – he'd agree to us adopting him?'

'He might, but – oh Tony, do you mean it? Do you still want to marry me?'

'There's never been any doubt about that,' he told her solemnly. 'Where I went wrong was being so soft over my mother.'

'But what about your mother now? I expect she can't wait to get you home and look after you herself.'

Tony stared at her. 'Of course, you won't know, will you?'

'Know? Know what?' She stared at him and then breathed, 'Has – has something happened to her?'

'No.' His tone was suddenly hard. 'No, she's fine.'

'Your dad? Oh, not your dad?'

He shook his head. 'No, he's fine. I do hear from

him and he's been down here a couple of times, but it's difficult for him to come all this way. I understand that.' He paused and then went on haltingly, as if even he couldn't believe the words he was saying himself. 'My mother doesn't want to see me like this. She can't bear it. She – she's cut me out of her life as if . . . as if I was dead. She even tells everyone I was shot down – which is true, of course, but she implies I was killed.'

'Well, you were posted missing presumed killed, weren't you?'

'Briefly, at first, yes. But it wasn't very long before they were informed that I had survived. If you can call it that,' he added bitterly.

Kathy raised his injured hand to her lips and kissed it gently. 'Don't you ever dare talk like that again in my hearing. Not ever.'

He leant against her. 'Oh Kathy, darling, it's so good to have you back. You'll never know how much I've missed you.'

'About the same as I've missed you, I expect.'

They gazed at each other and she leaned forward and kissed him tenderly on the mouth. 'That – that doesn't hurt you, does it?'

'No, not a bit.' He smiled as he added, 'And even if it did, it'd be worth it.'

They sat close together for a long time, not saying much, just holding hands and revelling in having found each other again.

'So,' Tony said at last. 'When am I going to see my son?'

'I'll go back and tell Mr Wainwright everything. We – we'll just have to hope and pray that he'll let us adopt James.'

Forty-Three

Kathy felt torn in two. She didn't want to leave Tony but she had to get back to Saltershaven, and yet she feared what awaited her when she did.

There were two more concert dates and then she could leave. The time dragged, and it seemed much longer than three days until Ron was loading her suitcase onto the train and thanking her profusely for joining the party for the very special concerts.

'It's me who should be thanking you, Ron,' she said, kissing his cheek. 'If I hadn't come, I wouldn't have found Tony again. I'd probably have spent the rest of my life thinking he was dead.'

'Kathy,' Ron said seriously, taking both her hands in his, 'can I ask you something?'

'Of course you can.'

'If you hadn't found Tony again, would you have married this Mr Wainwright?'

'You want me to be truthful?'

He nodded.

'It sounds awful . . .'

'Go on, my dear. This is just between you and me.'

'Then – truthfully – I don't know. I'm just so grateful that now I don't have to make that decision. I'm going to marry Tony.'

'Even if it means losing your child? You have thought that Wainwright might turn awkward?'

'Yes,' she said hoarsely. 'It's my worst nightmare, but I have to face it.'

'Then – break a leg, my dear, in fact, break two.'

She went straight back to Saltershaven, arriving at the house just before Henry was due home from work. Mrs Talbot was just putting on her hat and coat to leave as Kathy opened the door.

'How lovely to have you back. I thought it was today you were coming home, so there are two dinners keeping warm in the oven. Have you had a good time?'

'Oh yes, Mrs Talbot. Very good, thank you.'

'Well, you look as if you have, love. There's a light in your eyes I haven't seen before.' She put her head on one side and regarded Kathy with knowing eyes. 'Might it have something to do with coming home to a certain gentleman?'

'If you mean, James, then yes,' Kathy replied impishly, knowing exactly who Mrs Talbot meant.

The woman shrugged. 'Oh well, I can only try. I'd like to see the master settled again with a good woman. I just thought . . . But maybe it's a bit too soon yet. The poor man's got to have time to grieve.'

Kathy said nothing, but silently she thought that to her mind, Henry, despite his protestations about how much he had loved his wife, wasn't exactly the typical grieving widower.

'I'll get off, love,' Mrs Talbot said, realizing that her attempt at matchmaking was falling on deaf ears. 'My Dan will be wanting his tea.'

Left alone, Kathy was jittery, anxious for Henry to arrive home so that she could say what she had to say. Waiting was making her even more nervous. She kept glancing at the clock, but the hands seemed to be crawling round. At last, she heard his key in the door and ran lightly down the stairs to meet him in the hallway.

He smiled as he closed the door and held out his arms to her. 'Does this mean what I think it means? What I hope it means?'

Kathy froze. How could she have been so stupid? Rushing to meet him like that had given him the wrong impression entirely. She had been so full of her own hopes, she hadn't stopped to think of his.

'I'm sorry,' she blurted out. 'No, it doesn't. Oh dear, I didn't mean to say it like that.'

His smile had vanished and his arms dropped to his sides. 'I see.'

'No, you don't. Look, let's have our dinner and I'll tell you everything. You go up and change.' She knew he liked to change out of his pinstriped suit when he arrived home. 'And I'll have it all ready when you come down.'

Henry sighed. 'Very well, then.'

They ate in silence, though Kathy was only picking at the food on her plate. Though she hadn't eaten since early morning, her appetite had completely deserted her. But it wasn't until he had eaten both his main course and pudding that Henry laid down his spoon and looked across the table at her.

'So – what is it you have to tell me?'

'I'll make the coffee and bring it into the sitting room. It – it might take some time.'

Henry raised his eyebrows but did not demur. He rose, dropped his napkin on the table and left the room. For a moment, Kathy stared at the crumpled napkin that he had discarded so carelessly. That would have been my life, she thought. Just acting as his slave.

Clearing up after him, pandering to his every whim. Having to do everything just the way he demanded. She shuddered, thinking what a narrow escape she had had. Now it was a decision she didn't have to make any longer.

But there was still James. What was to happen to her darling boy? Was Henry, as both Tony and Ron had feared, going to turn awkward because she was refusing to marry him?

As she handed Henry the cup of coffee, he said, 'You're trembling. My dear girl, there is no need to be frightened of me. Whatever it is you have to say to me, I'm sure we can talk it through like sensible adults.' He gave a dry, humourless laugh. 'It isn't as if our emotions are engaged, now is it? And no one else knows about this. At least, I hope they don't.'

Kathy smiled weakly and sat down on the sofa. She set her own coffee on the nearby small table and then clasped her hands in front of her. 'There's something I have to tell you. I – I haven't been entirely honest with you.'

'Oh dear,' he said, with a slightly mocking air. He too set his coffee down beside him and got to his feet. 'I think I'd better pour us both a brandy.'

Another few minutes of waiting, while Kathy grew more agitated by the minute. When he handed her the bulbous glass, she took a grateful sip. He sat down again and leaned back in the soft armchair, swirling the liquid around the glass cupped in his hand.

'Now, off you go. What is on your mind?'

'I did meet your wife and I hope she counted me as a friend, but I – I wasn't as close to her as perhaps I made out.'

435

'Go on.'

'You see, I sought her ought deliberately. I found out your address from the files at – at Willow House.'

Henry was listening intently and Kathy could see that his mind was working swiftly. No doubt he was already way ahead of her. But he said nothing. He just sat watching her and swirling the brandy round and round.

'James is my son. It was a difficult birth and they took him away from me without even letting me see him or hold him or . . .' Her voice cracked, but she cleared her throat and pressed on. 'They'd tricked me into signing adoption papers when I was admitted. Of course, we're not supposed to know who adopts our babies, but I found out and I walked along your road so many times in the hope of just catching a glimpse of him.' She turned pleading eyes towards him. 'I want you to believe me that I meant no trouble. Though I never wanted to part with my baby, once I'd met your wife, seen how she adored him and how she was looking after him, then – then I had to admit he was in the best place, even though it broke my heart.'

'Did you tell Beryl who you were?'

'Not at first. And I never would have done. I swear I meant no trouble . . .'

He nodded and said quietly, 'I believe you. Go on.' But she couldn't tell from his expression or from his tone how he was reacting to her revelations.

'I was standing outside the house one day – after we'd already met, I mean – and she came out and invited me in to see the baby. It – it was when I was holding him that she guessed. She suddenly said, "You're his mother, aren't you?" I admitted I was, but I begged her not to say anything. I told her what had happened, that I just wanted to hold him – even if it was only once. She understood and she – she was very kind to me. Obviously, she never told you. She sent me a letter and a photograph of him when he was about eighteen months old.'

Henry sighed. 'Well, she wouldn't. Obviously, she'd taken a liking to you and didn't see you as a threat.'

'I wasn't.'

'And she probably thought that if she told me, I'd have reported you.'

Kathy looked down at her hands. Her heart was thudding painfully. There was a long silence before he asked, 'Why exactly are you telling me this? I had assumed, from what you said when I arrived home, that you are refusing my proposal.'

'I'm sorry, but yes, I am.'

'But you don't want to be parted from the boy?'

Kathy bit back the angry retort that sprang to her lips. *His name is James. Call him by his name.* But she said nothing, realizing that she must do nothing to antagonize him. Instead, she said quietly. 'No, I don't. But there's more to it now than just that.' The words came out in a rush. 'I've found him again. I've found Tony – the man I was engaged to. James's father. He's not dead after all. He was badly burned when his fighter plane was shot down. He's at Mr McIndoe's hospital receiving treatment.'

'And you're going to marry him?'

Kathy nodded.

Now he understood. 'I see. And you want to take your boy back?'

Again, all she could do was nod and watch his face.

'Mm.' Again the liquid twirled in the glass. There was a long silence before he said, 'So, after persuading me to keep him so that you could take the post as his nanny, you're now asking me to hand him back to you?'

Her voice was a hoarse whisper. 'Yes.'

Another long silence.

'Well,' he said at last, 'You've been very honest with me—' He smiled wryly. 'At least, now. And in turn I will be very honest with you. I've no interest in the child. It was Beryl who yearned for children, not me. And now she's gone, there's really no reason for me to keep him. You might think me a cold fish, Kathy, but I'm not completely heartless. I loved my wife dearly. She was the perfect wife for me and I indulged her in her desire for a family. And I thought you were right when you said she would've wanted me to keep the boy and bring him up, but what I *now* think is that she would want you to have him. You and his real father. She wouldn't want me to stand in your way.'

Tears were coursing down her face. 'Oh thank you, thank you . . .'

Henry swallowed his brandy in one gulp and got up. 'Please – don't cry,' he said coldly. 'I can't abide women's tears.'

Kathy scrubbed at her face with the back of her hand and sniffed. 'I'm sorry, but I can't thank you enough.'

'There's no need. If I'm honest you're relieving me of an encumbrance I never really wanted in the first place.'

Kathy stood up. Mindful of his position in the community, she said, 'You – you'll want it done properly though, won't you? Legally?'

He nodded. 'Of course. I'll instruct my solicitors in the morning.'

'There's no need for Willow House to be involved, is there? I don't want him to go back there. Please – don't send him back there.'

'I wouldn't think so for a moment. Besides, if what you've told me about that place is true – ' he held up his hand as she opened her mouth – 'and I've no reason to disbelieve you, then I think I might ask my solicitor – who is a good friend of mine – to look into the place. It sounds to me as if it's not being run properly. Whether they're doing anything against the law, I'm not sure, but it ought to be looked into. I can't have something like that going on in my area.'

Kathy almost laughed aloud. It was his reputation he cared about, not the welfare of the unmarried mothers and their children. But she said nothing. At least if it got the authorities to look at Willow House, it didn't matter how it came about – just that it happened.

'So – so what about James?'

He shrugged. 'You keep him. Just let me know your address so that I can send the papers through for you to sign. I expect it would be better if you and your fiancé were married first. Is that possible? I mean he's not too ill?'

'No, no. We can be married straight away, and I'm sure the people who've looked after James while I've been away won't mind keeping him a little longer. That's if you're sure . . . ?'

'Oh, I'm sure.' Henry laughed and there was an undoubted look of relief on his face as he added, 'And you're welcome to take all his belongings too. All the nursery furniture too, if it's of use to you.'

'That's most generous of you.'

He shrugged and added, 'It's of no use to me.'

He turned and left the room, heading across the hall towards his study. Kathy watched him go, feeling a fleeting stab of pity for the man. It probably wasn't needed. Henry Wainwright would be happy enough in his career and maybe, some day, he'd meet someone else who'd fit his exacting requirements in a wife. But now . . .

Kathy's legs suddenly gave way beneath her. She sank down on to the sofa and gave way to tears of thankfulness.

Forty-Four

Kathy spent the following morning packing up all James's clothes to take with her. She would arrange for the nursery furniture to be collected when she knew where she was going to be. Then she called a taxi, thankful that Mrs Talbot was not due to come that morning. She didn't want to get involved in lengthy explanations to the woman, yet, if she'd been there, Kathy couldn't have left without a word. The woman had been kind to her. Silently promising herself that she would write to the housekeeper, Kathy carried her cases out to the taxi when it drew up at the gate.

The driver helped her to load them and Kathy climbed in. She took one last look at the house where she had spent the last few months. As the taxi drove away, she did not look back.

'Is James all right?' was her very first question. 'Oh, I can't wait to see him.'

'He's fine, my dear. He's asleep just now, but let me have a look at you first.' After their first greeting, Jemima held her at arm's length and scrutinized her face. 'You look wonderful, Kathy,' Jemima greeted her, kissing her cheek. 'The change has done you the world of good.'

'Oh, Aunt Jemima, more than you could begin to

guess. I've so much to tell you, but – ' she hesitated and the light in her eyes was suddenly overshadowed – 'if you don't mind, I ought to tell Morry first. I owe him that much.'

There was an unspoken question in Jemima's eyes, but she nodded. 'Of course, my dear. You'll find him in the cowshed. It's almost time for evening milking.'

Morry was herding the cows into the byre for milking when Kathy pulled on the spare pair of wellingtons that always sat by the back door and crossed the yard towards him.

'Kathy!' The delight showed plainly on his round, beaming face.

'Morry,' she said softly and submitted to his bear-hug and a kiss on her cheek. Impulsively, she kissed him back and then wondered if, yet again, her impetuosity was giving out the wrong signals.

'Morry – dear Morry. I want you to be the first to know, Tony's alive. I've found him.'

'Alive? Oh Kathy, that's marvellous. Wonderful news.' He gripped her hands and his smile was even wider, if that were possible. Kathy searched his face anxiously but there was not a trace of disappointment or resentment, either in his eyes or in his voice. He was genuinely happy for her, and so glad to hear that the young man was not dead after all.

'Oh, Morry,' Kathy whispered again as tears filled her eyes and she leant her face against his shoulder. 'You're so good.'

'There, there.' He patted her back. 'You know I only want you to be happy, Kathy love. That's all I've ever wanted.' Unbidden, the image of Muriel's face came into her mind. She and Morry were so alike in their unselfishness.

And her tears flowed even faster.

'Now, come along, this won't do. I want to hear all about it, but you'll have to come into the milking shed with me. Some of these poor creatures will burst their udders if I don't get to them.'

Kathy drew back and dried her tears. 'I'll help you. I don't think I've forgotten how to do it.'

Morry laughed. 'I'm sure you haven't. It's like riding a bike.'

They followed the beasts into the long shed and herded them into the stalls. Then they sat back to back to milk a cow each so that they could talk. The cowshed was warm and cosy, the only sounds the contented chewing of the animals, the occasional swish of an impatient tail and the staccato sound of the milk spraying into the buckets.

She told him everything and when, at last, she fell silent, Morry didn't speak for a few moments.

'I can't understand why Tony's mother doesn't want to see him. Like you, I'd've thought she'd have wanted nothing more than to take him home and care for him.'

Kathy shook her head. 'I don't understand it either, and I think poor Tony's bewildered and hurt by it too. His father writes regularly and he's been to see him, but his mother doesn't want to know.'

Morry gave a wry laugh. 'Well, like Aunt Jemima always says, "It's an ill wind that blows nobody any good." Mrs Kendall's not going to ruin your next wedding, is she?'

Kathy turned on her stool to stare at him for a moment and then she burst out laughing.

*

Jemima and the rest of the Robinson family were just as genuinely thrilled as Morry had been. She went through the whole story again while she cuddled her son on her knee. She could hardly drag her gaze away from him, and she couldn't believe the incredible turn in her fortunes. She had found the man she loved, they were to be married and they had been given their son back.

'We'll get married down south,' Kathy told them. 'Tony has another operation coming up so he won't be able to leave hospital for several weeks. Maybe even months. I shall take James and get lodgings near the hospital and we'll be together.'

'What a lovely ending, cariad,' Betty said, wiping tears from her eyes. 'Well, almost. I still can't help feeling sorry for his poor mother. I know she's been spiteful and possessive, but she must be in shreds. And as for his poor father, he must be torn in two. Wanting to be loyal to his wife, yet desperate to see his son. Poor, poor man.'

Three days later, Kathy walked up the drive to the hospital.

'My, but you're heavy,' she chuckled to the child in her arms.

It was a bright, warm day and she knew most of the mobile patients would be out in the grounds. And she knew just where to look for Tony. In his favourite spot, sitting on the fallen tree trunk in the shade. She had almost reached him before he heard the soft sound of her footsteps on the grass. He turned, the right side of his face towards her, and for a fleeting moment it was the old Tony, the handsome unblemished face of the

444

man she loved, turning to her, standing up and holding out his arms. And now she saw his whole face, saw the ravaged left-hand side and knew she loved him even more if that were possible.

She stood before him and, with a catch in her voice, said, 'This is your son. This is James.'

The look of incredulous joy and wonder on his face swept away any lingering doubts Kathy might have had. All the misunderstandings, all the heartache was forgotten. They were together at last and whatever the future held for them, they would face it – together.

Forty-Five

Over the weeks that followed their poignant reunion, Kathy was carried along on a tide of ecstasy. She scarcely knew what was happening in the war, she was so totally wrapped in her own little world of happiness – a happiness she had never expected to find. But somewhere in the back of her mind lurked a feeling that all was still not quite right. That her happiness was not as complete as she had expected it to be.

They were married quietly in the local church, the congregation made up, almost entirely, of patients from the hospital. To crown their happiness, Tony's final operation was a success and the great man declared that there was really nothing more he could do for him. His face would always be scarred and he would never regain the full use of his left hand, but, as Tony himself said, he was better than a great many.

'We can go home,' he told Kathy. 'Back to Lincoln.'

Suddenly, Kathy realized what had been niggling at her. Tony's parents. Betty's words had stayed with her. The generous woman could still find it in her huge heart to feel pity for the lonely, twisted woman. But why? Why didn't Beatrice want to see her son any more? He had come back and yet she was still acting as if he was dead, as if she *wanted* him dead.

Understanding came to her as she was bathing James on the last evening before they were due to travel north back to Lincoln. Gently, as she soaped his smooth skin, she revelled in its perfection. She watched him splash in the warm water, listening to his happy chuckles. He was growing to be just like his father. He was going to be so handsome, so good-looking . . .

The realization came slowly, seeping into her mind. Now she understood. Beatrice had so loved her perfect boy that she couldn't bear to see him injured, couldn't cope with the tragedy of his marred good looks. All her life she'd wanted perfection. She'd been born into the wrong branch of the Hammond family. Though spoiled by her wealthy uncle, she'd still been the poor relation. In her eyes, her husband had disappointed her and now her son, on whom she'd pinned all her hopes, had failed her too. Beatrice was a bitter and twisted woman, but gazing now on her own son, feeling her love for him overflow, at last Kathy began to understand.

As she lifted the slippery, wriggling child out of the water and wrapped him in a warm, fluffy towel, she whispered, 'We're going home tomorrow, my precious boy. And do you know what? You're going to meet your grannie and granddad.' Her smile broadened as another thought entered her mind and she murmured, 'And what your other grandparents will say, I daren't think.'

But in her heart she already knew. Her father would grumble and grouse for a while, but then the realization would dawn on him. He had a grandson. A boy! At last, he had an heir for his family's farm. Kathy's smile was tinged with sadness. Perhaps, for once in her life, she had done something that would please her father. And as for her mother? Well, the moment James was placed in her arms she would feel a happiness she

hadn't known existed. No, the problem – as always –
was Beatrice Kendall.

Their long journey took them to Sandy Furze Farm,
where Tony was welcomed into the warm and loving
Robinson family. Even Morry shook his hand warmly,
slapped him on the back and joked, 'Just look after
our Kathy, else you'll have the whole of the Robinson
family after you.'

They stayed for a week, during which time Tony
and Kathy travelled backwards and forwards to Lincoln to find somewhere to live. 'And if you think I'm
going to live in a flat on Mill Road, you can think
again,' Kathy teased him.

They found a small terraced house on one of the
streets leading off Monks Road, not far from where
she had lived with Jemima, and signed the contract to
rent it for a year. Then they went into Hammonds'
store and sought out Mr James. He was in the office
that had once been Tony's.

The shock and then the delight that spread across
the older man's face touched Kathy. 'Anthony! You're
alive! My God! This is wonderful. Come in, come in,
sit down. How are you?'

He ushered them into his office, sat them down and
sent his secretary scurrying to unearth a bottle of
champagne. 'This calls for a celebration. And if I'm not
mistaken, there's another reason, isn't there? You're
married?'

Shyly, Kathy nodded. She glanced at Tony and gave
a slight nod, silently giving her permission for the rest
to be told.

Tony cleared his throat and said with a mixture of

embarrassment and pride in his voice. 'We – er – we have a son. His – his name is James.'

The man stared at them for a moment and then threw back his head and laughed aloud. 'You've named him after me?'

'Well – to be honest, not exactly,' Kathy said. 'It's a long story.'

'Let's hear it then.' Mr James stood up as his secretary returned with a dusty bottle and three glasses. As he popped the cork and poured it out, Kathy explained.

'I'm so glad it's ended happily for you both – for the three of you, I should say. But there's only one thing that disappoints me,' he added, looking directly at Kathy. 'That you didn't come to me. I would have helped you, my dear. But perhaps, then, you didn't know me well enough. I expect I was just Mr James, owner of Hammonds, and rather aloof?'

Kathy blushed and nodded.

'Then I'm sorry because, truly, I would have stood by you.' Now he looked sternly at Tony. 'And as for you, young feller, well, you're damned lucky to get a second chance to put the fiasco of that wedding right.'

'I know,' Tony said simply.

Mr James was smiling again. 'Just one thing,' he said wagging his finger at the pair of them. 'I insist on being the boy's godfather. Oh, and by the way,' he added with deliberate casualness, 'when can you start back to work?'

Tony and Kathy gaped at him.

'You mean – you mean you'll employ me? Looking like this?'

'Why ever not?'

*

They had been living in Lincoln for a month. Tony had settled back into his position at the store and James Hammond had given him more responsibility than ever, happy to return to his privileged life of golf and fishing.

'I think most people are getting used to me now. One or two customers still stare a bit. I suppose I shall always have to put up with that.' He smiled lopsidedly. 'The kids are the best though. They're so open and unafraid. They just come up to me and say, "What's the matter with your face, mister?" It's the parents who are embarrassed and try to shush them.'

He sat in silence, lost in his own thoughts. Kathy took a deep breath. 'Talking of parents, we should go and see yours. We should take James to meet his grandparents.'

The bleak look in Tony's eyes as he glanced at her twisted Kathy's heart, but she was resolute.

'They – they don't want to see me.'

'That's not quite true, is it? I'm sure your father does.'

'But Mother doesn't.'

Kathy sat on his knee and put her arm round his neck. Gently, she said, 'No, but she'd like to see James, now wouldn't she?'

He rested his cheek against her breast. 'You really mean you'd risk taking him to see her?'

'What do you mean, "risk"?'

'She'll want to take him over. Replace me with him. He's very like me. Like I used to be,' he added wistfully.

Kathy slid off his knee and knelt in front of him. With gentle hands she cupped his face and looked straight into his eyes. 'Tony Kendall, after all I've been through, do you really think I'm going to let anyone – *anyone* – take away my son from me again?'

Tony grinned sheepishly. 'No, I don't.' He was thoughtful for a moment before he nodded slowly, 'All right. We'll go. But on your own head be it.'

The following Sunday was a fine, bright day as they walked up the hill to the Kendalls' home, Tony carrying James in his arms. Kathy rang the front door bell and they waited, glancing at each other a little nervously until they heard George's slow and heavy tread approaching on the opposite side. The door opened and the man standing there stared at them, his glance going from one to another and then coming to rest, finally, on the child in Tony's arms. His expression softened and tears welled in his eyes.

'Hello, Dad,' Tony said at last. 'Aren't you going to invite your grandson in?'

Wordlessly, as if for the moment he had quite lost the power of speech, George pulled open the door and gestured to them to step inside.

'Is Mrs Kendall in the front room?' Kathy asked, taking the lead.

George nodded.

'Then I'll go and see her on my own first. You take James into the kitchen and introduce him to his grandfather properly.'

Without waiting for a reply, Kathy opened the door to the left of the hall and went into the room.

Beatrice Kendall was lying on the sofa, looking for all the world as if she hadn't moved a muscle since the last time Kathy had seen her. Except, Kathy recalled, the very last time she had seen the woman had been in the church, feigning a heart attack.

At the sound of the door opening and closing, Beatrice opened her eyes and lifted her head. She squinted against the light from the window to see who had entered.

'You! What on earth do you want?'

Kathy sat down in the armchair. 'I've come to see you. *We've* come to see you.'

Beatrice caught her breath. 'Anthony? Anthony's here?'

Kathy nodded.

The woman put her hand over her eyes in a dramatic gesture. 'I don't want to see him,' she wailed. 'I can't.'

'All right. You don't have to. But wouldn't you like to meet your grandson?'

There was a stillness in the room, the only sound the ticking of the bracket clock, the crackling of the logs on the fire.

Slowly, her hand dropped away from her eyes and she stared at Kathy. 'My – my grandson?'

'Yes, he's called James and he'll be three in November.'

'You mean – you mean he's illegitimate?'

'No. Because we're married and as I understand it, even if a child is born out of wedlock, when the parents marry the child is legitimized.'

'You're married?' Beatrice almost spat out the question.

'Oh, yes,' Kathy said airily. 'We're married.'

Beatrice pulled herself up and thrust her face towards Kathy.

'When?' she demanded.

'Six weeks ago.'

'Six weeks?' Beatrice's mouth twisted. 'Then how

do I know it's really Tony's child? It could be anybody's.'

Anger surged in Kathy's breast. Resentment and bitterness towards this woman welled up inside her. Beatrice hadn't changed. Not one bit, but Kathy bit back the sharp retort and with a serenity that surprised her, she said, 'Oh, I can assure you that he's Tony's son. You'll soon see for yourself.'

There were conflicting emotions flitting across the woman's face as she struggled to come to a decision.

'Bring him in,' she muttered at last. 'Just the child. Not – not Tony.'

'Oh no,' Kathy said firmly. 'James won't come without his daddy. It's both – or nothing.'

The two women stared at each other in a battle of wills. It was Beatrice who was the first to lower her eyes and submit with a brief nod.

Kathy rose and left the room, returning a few moments later. Tony followed her into the room, carrying the little boy. George hovered nervously in the doorway.

Beatrice's gaze was fixed on the child. Deliberately, it seemed, she avoided looking into her son's face. She didn't even greet him. Her whole focus was on the little boy. Tony bent forward and set the little chap in her lap. James looked up into her eyes and reached out to touch her face.

'Hello, Grannie,' he said, just as Kathy had taught him.

Tony stepped back to stand beside Kathy. She sought his hand and held it and together they watched. George too, from the doorway, watched. Before their amazed eyes, a change came over Beatrice. They saw it. All of them saw it for themselves, though had they not, not one of them would have believed it if it had been told to them.

The woman's face softened, seemed to grow younger even. She smiled, and her eyes were alight with a tenderness they had not shown in years.

'Anthony,' she breathed. 'My little Anthony. You've come back to me.' But it was not the grown man standing nearby to whom she spoke. It was the child.

Kathy moved then and knelt beside her. 'Mrs Kendall, it's not Anthony, but it is his son. This is your grandchild, but that – ' she gestured towards Tony – 'is your son.'

Slowly, with what seemed like a great effort, Beatrice raised her eyes and looked at Tony for the first time. He didn't flinch, didn't even turn the injured side of his face away, but met her gaze steadily.

'Oh – Oh – my – darling – boy,' she gasped at last and the tears flooded down her face. She held out her arms and, for a moment, the child on her knee was forgotten.

Kathy picked James up and carried him from the room, whispering to George as she passed close to him, 'I think we'll leave them together for a while, don't you?'

George followed her out. In the kitchen he took his grandson into his arms for the first time and held the boy close. In an unsteady voice, he murmured, 'You really have the most remarkable mother.' His gaze rested upon Kathy. 'Thank you,' he said simply. 'Thank you for your generosity of heart, lass.'

Kathy smiled and touched her baby's cheek as she said softly, 'I can understand her so much better. Now that I know what it's like to be a mother.'

Visit **www.panmacmillan.com** to read more about all our books and to buy them. You will also find features, author interviews and news of any author events, and you can sign up for e-newsletters so that you're always first to hear about our new releases.